LIFEFO
CLEO MAKES CONTACT

WRITTEN BY
MATT MAIR LOWERY

ART AND LETTERING BY
CASSIE ANDERSON

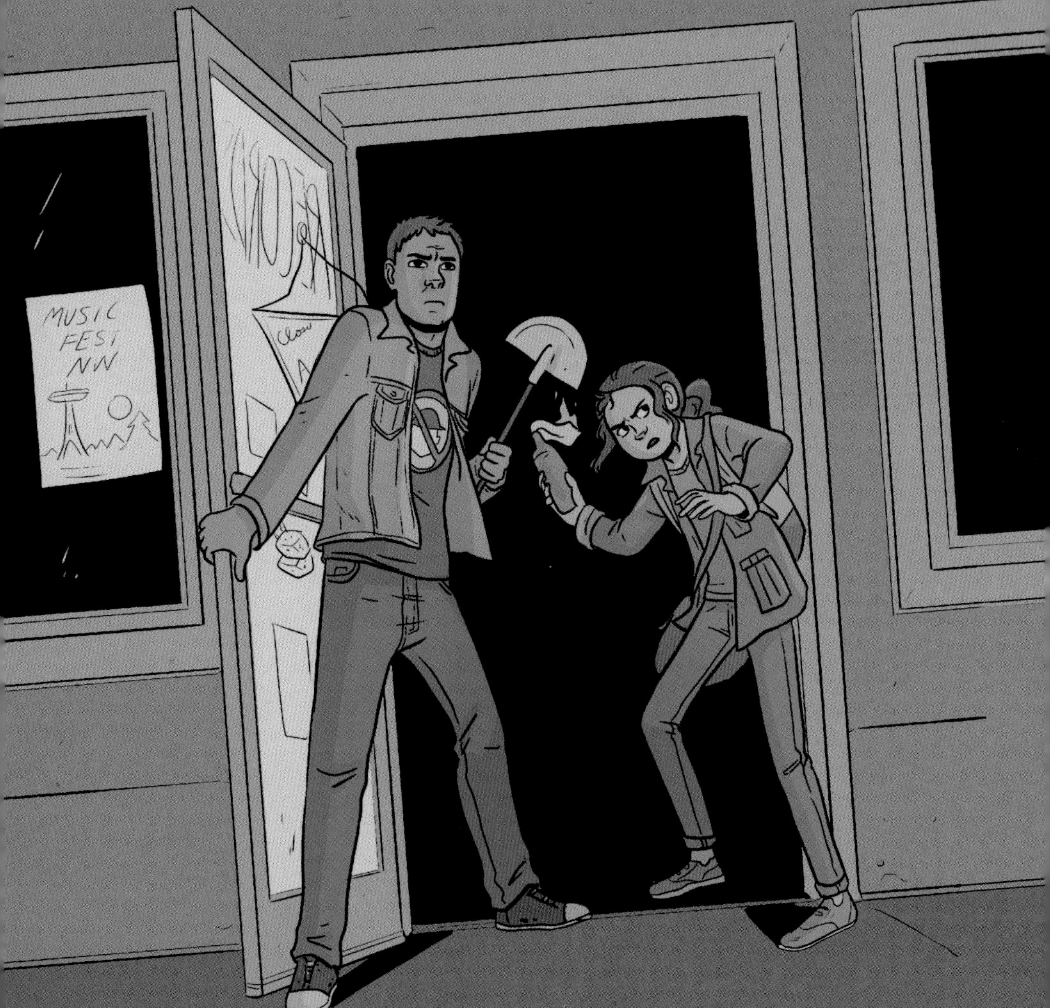

MUSIC FEST NW

DARK HORSE BOOKS

For Dad. I hope you like my spaceships. –CASSIE

For Katherine, my Hero's Journey study buddy.
You are missed. –MATT

PRESIDENT AND PUBLISHER **MIKE RICHARDSON**

EDITORS **AARON WALKER** AND **RACHEL ROBERTS**   CONSULTING EDITOR **DAVE MARSHALL**

DESIGNER **ETHAN KIMBERLING**   DIGITAL ART TECHNICIAN **MELISSA MARTIN**

Neil Hankerson, Executive Vice President · Tom Weddle, Chief Financial Officer · Randy Stradley, Vice President of Publishing · Matt Parkinson, Vice President of Marketing · David Scroggy, Vice President of Product Development · Dale LaFountain, Vice President of Information Technology · Cara Niece, Vice President of Production and Scheduling · Nick McWhorter, Vice President of Media Licensing · Mark Bernardi, Vice President of Book Trade and Digital Sales · Ken Lizzi, General Counsel · Dave Marshall, Editor in Chief · Davey Estrada, Editorial Director · Scott Allie, Executive Senior Editor · Chris Warner, Senior Books Editor · Cary Grazzini, Director of Specialty Projects · Lia Ribacchi, Art Director · Vanessa Todd, Director of Print Purchasing · Matt Dryer, Director of Digital Art and Prepress · Sarah Robertson, Director of Product Sales · Michael Gombos, Director of International Publishing and Licensing

Published by Dark Horse Books
A division of Dark Horse Comics, Inc.
10956 SE Main Street
Milwaukie, OR 97222

First edition: September 2017
ISBN 978-1-50670-177-6

10 9 8 7 6 5 4 3 2 1
Printed in China

International Licensing (503) 905-2377
Comic Shop Locator Service (888) 266-4226

Library of Congress Cataloging-in-Publication Data

Names: Lowery, Matt Mair, author. | Anderson, Cassie, artist, letterer.
Title: Lifeformed : Cleo makes contact / written by Matt Mair Lowery ; art and lettering by Cassie Anderson.
Description: First edition. | Milwaukie, OR : Dark Horse Books, 2017. | Summary: "In the wake of an alien invasion--and her father's death--a young girl must leave behind the life she knows to fight for the future of Earth"-- Provided by publisher.
Identifiers: LCCN 2017022532 (print) | LCCN 2017022965 (ebook) | ISBN 9781630085698 | ISBN 9781506701776 (paperback)
Subjects: LCSH: Graphic novels. | CYAC: Graphic novels. | Extraterrestrial beings--Fiction. | Survival--Fiction.
Classification: LCC PZ7.7.L687 (ebook) | LCC PZ7.7.L687 Li 2017 (print) | DDC 741.5/973--dc23
LC record available at https://lccn.loc.gov/2017022532

ONE

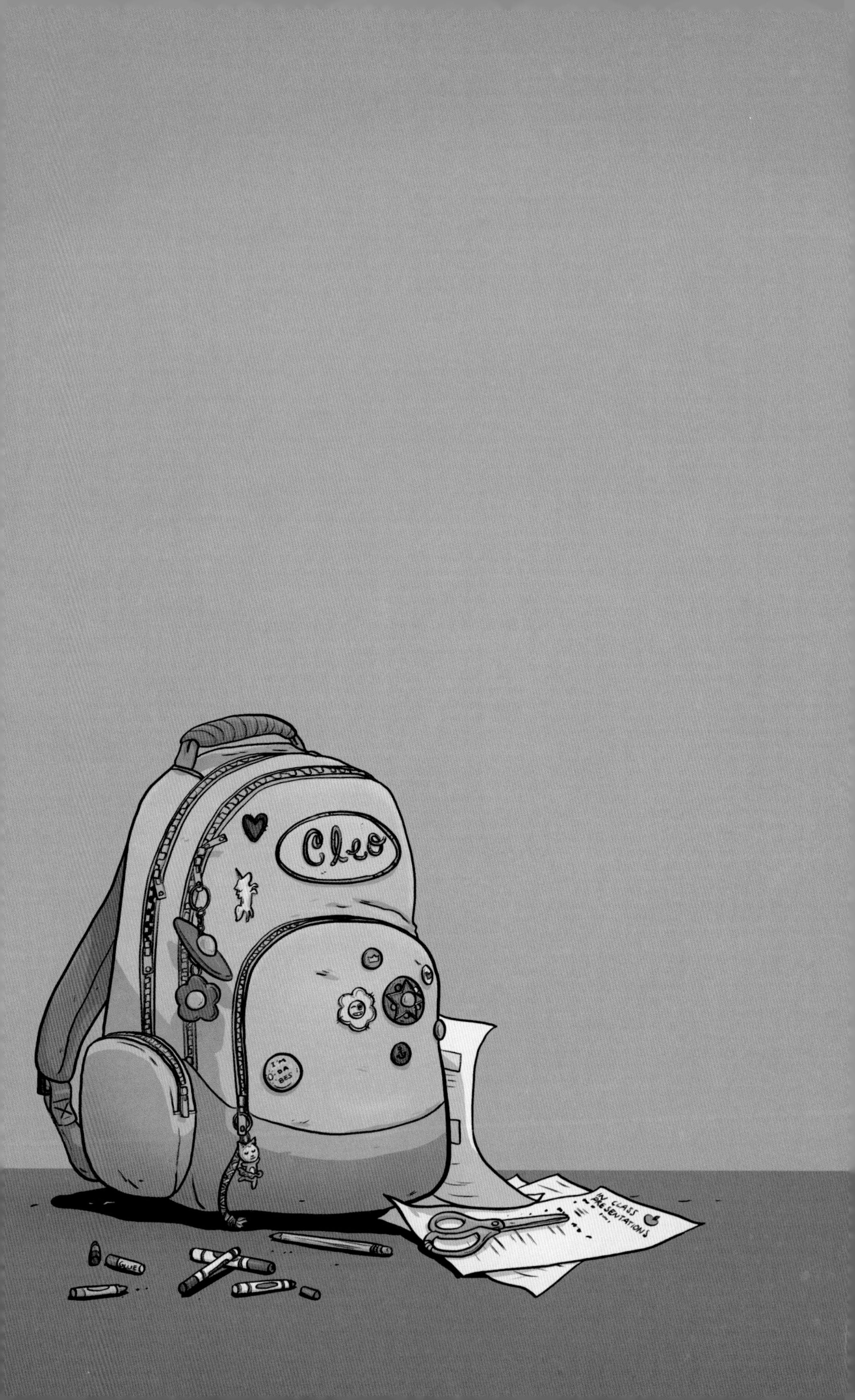
Cleo
I'M DA BES
GLUE
IN CLASS PRESENTATIONS

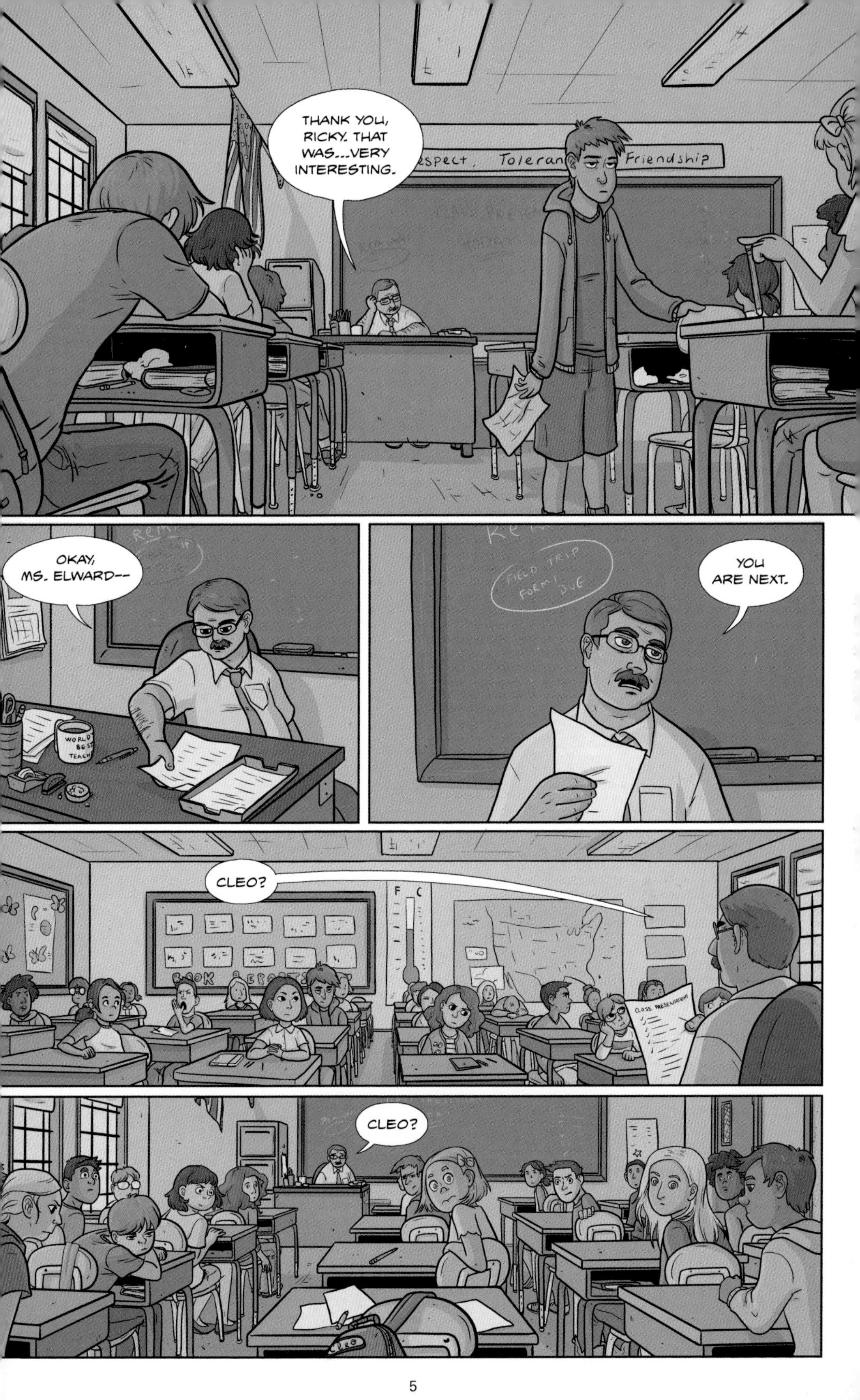
THANK YOU, RICKY. THAT WAS...VERY INTERESTING.
Respect, Toleran Friendship
OKAY, MS. ELWARD--
FIELD TRIP FORM DUE
YOU ARE NEXT.
CLEO?
F C
BOOK REPORTS
CLASS PRESENTATIONS
CLEO?

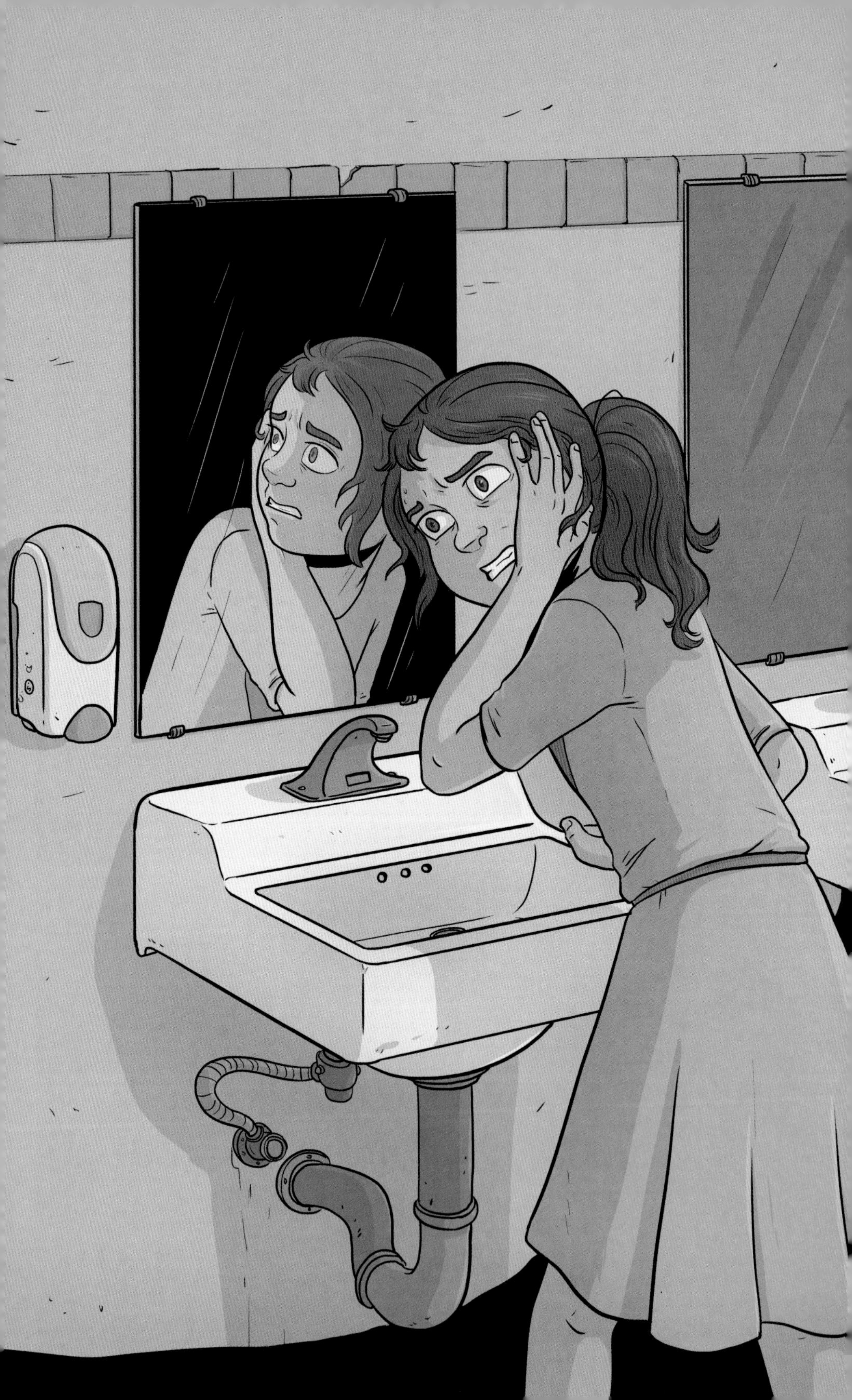

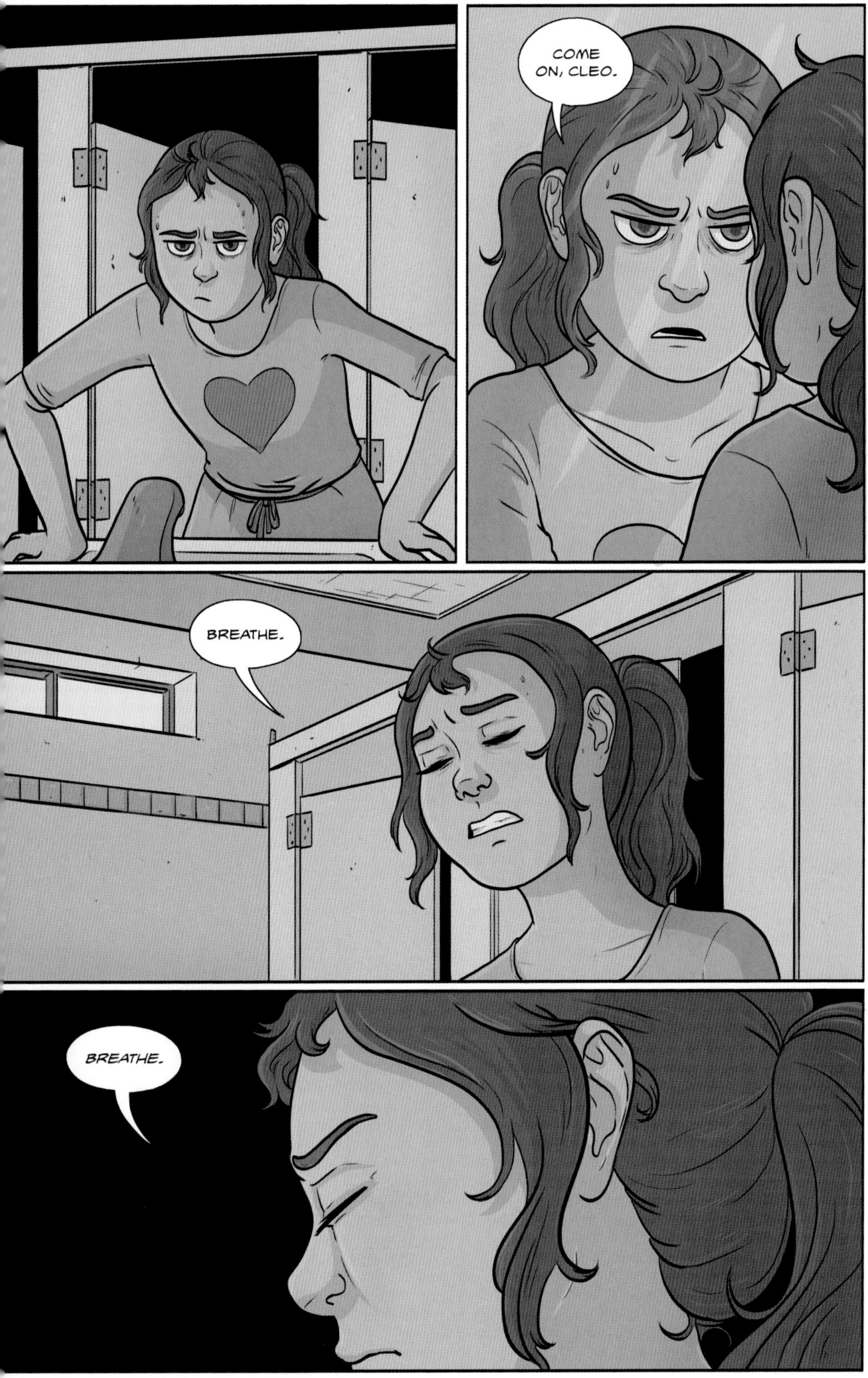
COME ON, CLEO.
BREATHE.
BREATHE.

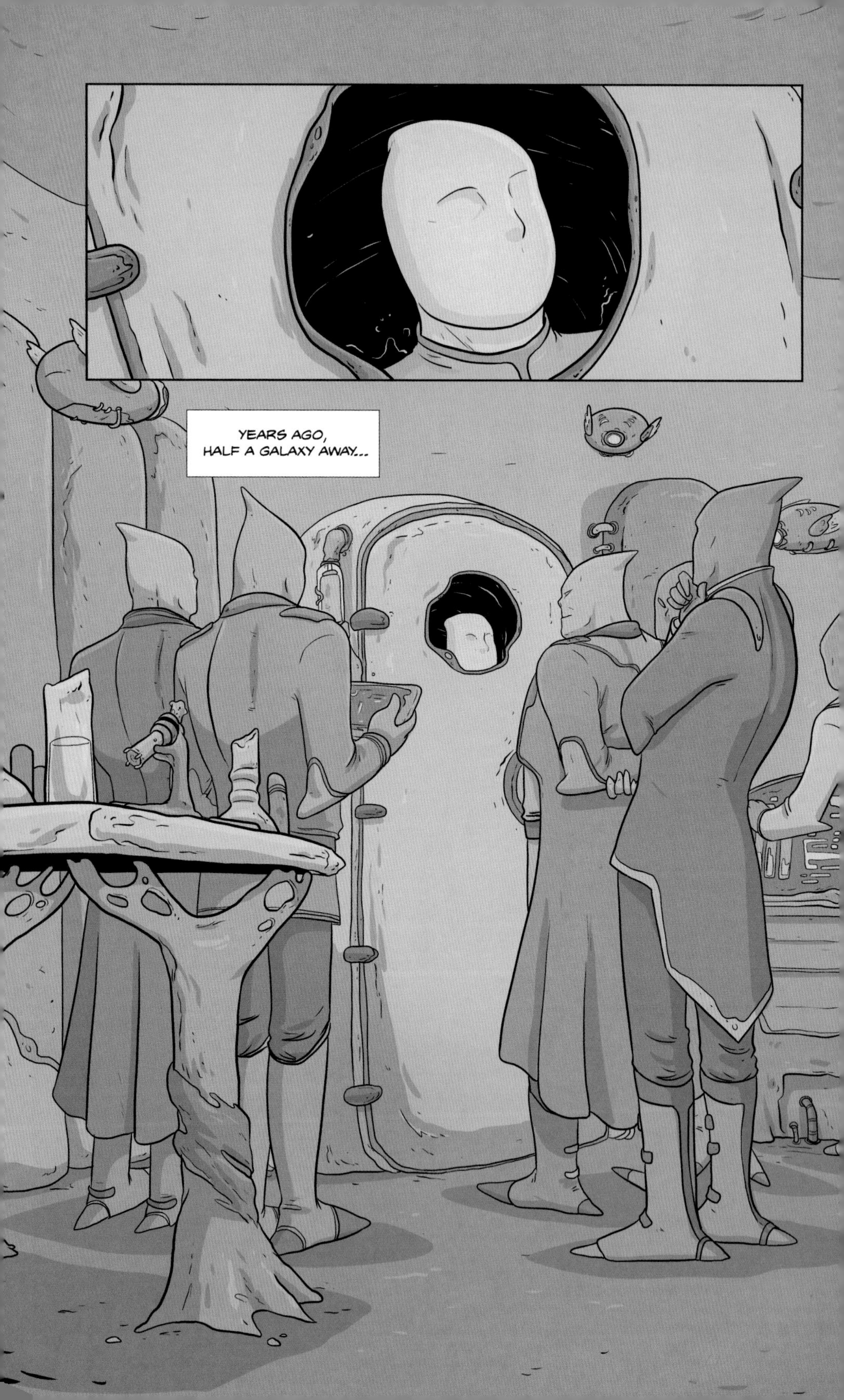
YEARS AGO,
HALF A GALAXY AWAY...

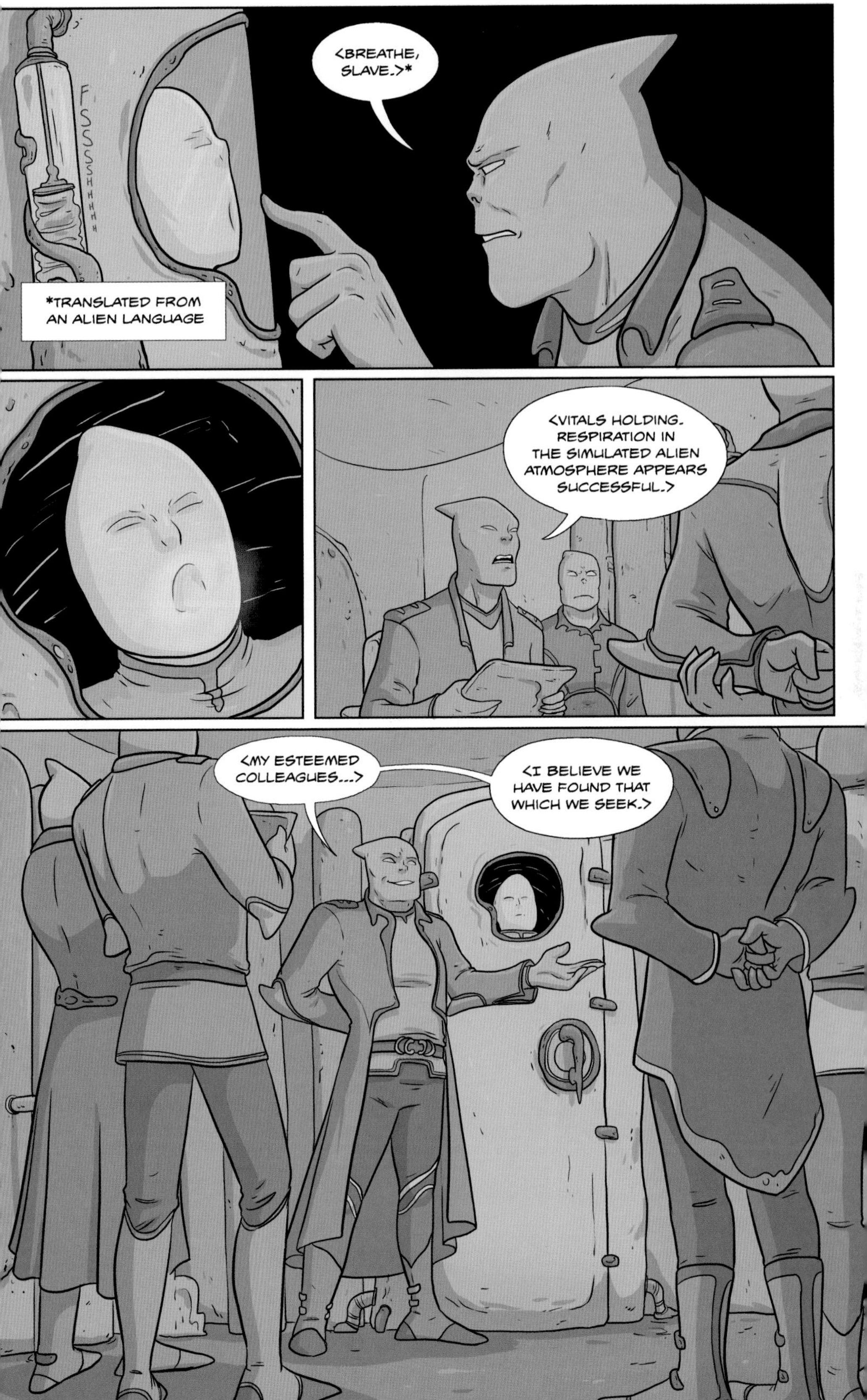
<BREATHE, SLAVE.>*
FSSSSHHHHHH
*TRANSLATED FROM AN ALIEN LANGUAGE
<VITALS HOLDING. RESPIRATION IN THE SIMULATED ALIEN ATMOSPHERE APPEARS SUCCESSFUL.>
<MY ESTEEMED COLLEAGUES...>
<I BELIEVE WE HAVE FOUND THAT WHICH WE SEEK.>

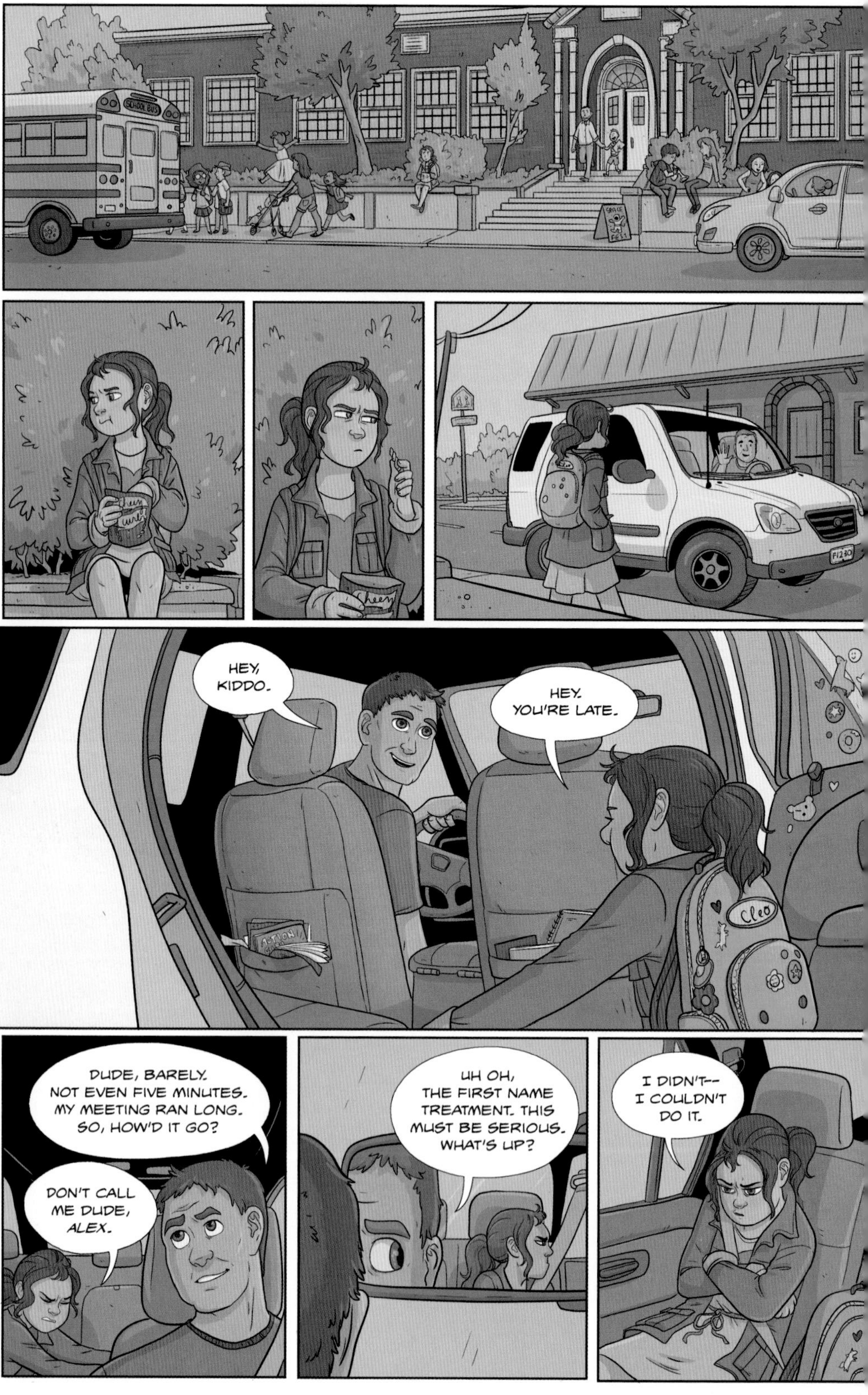
SCHOOL BUS
HEY, KIDDO.
HEY. YOU'RE LATE.
Cleo
DUDE, BARELY. NOT EVEN FIVE MINUTES. MY MEETING RAN LONG. SO, HOW'D IT GO?
DON'T CALL ME DUDE, ALEX.
UH OH, THE FIRST NAME TREATMENT. THIS MUST BE SERIOUS. WHAT'S UP?
I DIDN'T-- I COULDN'T DO IT.

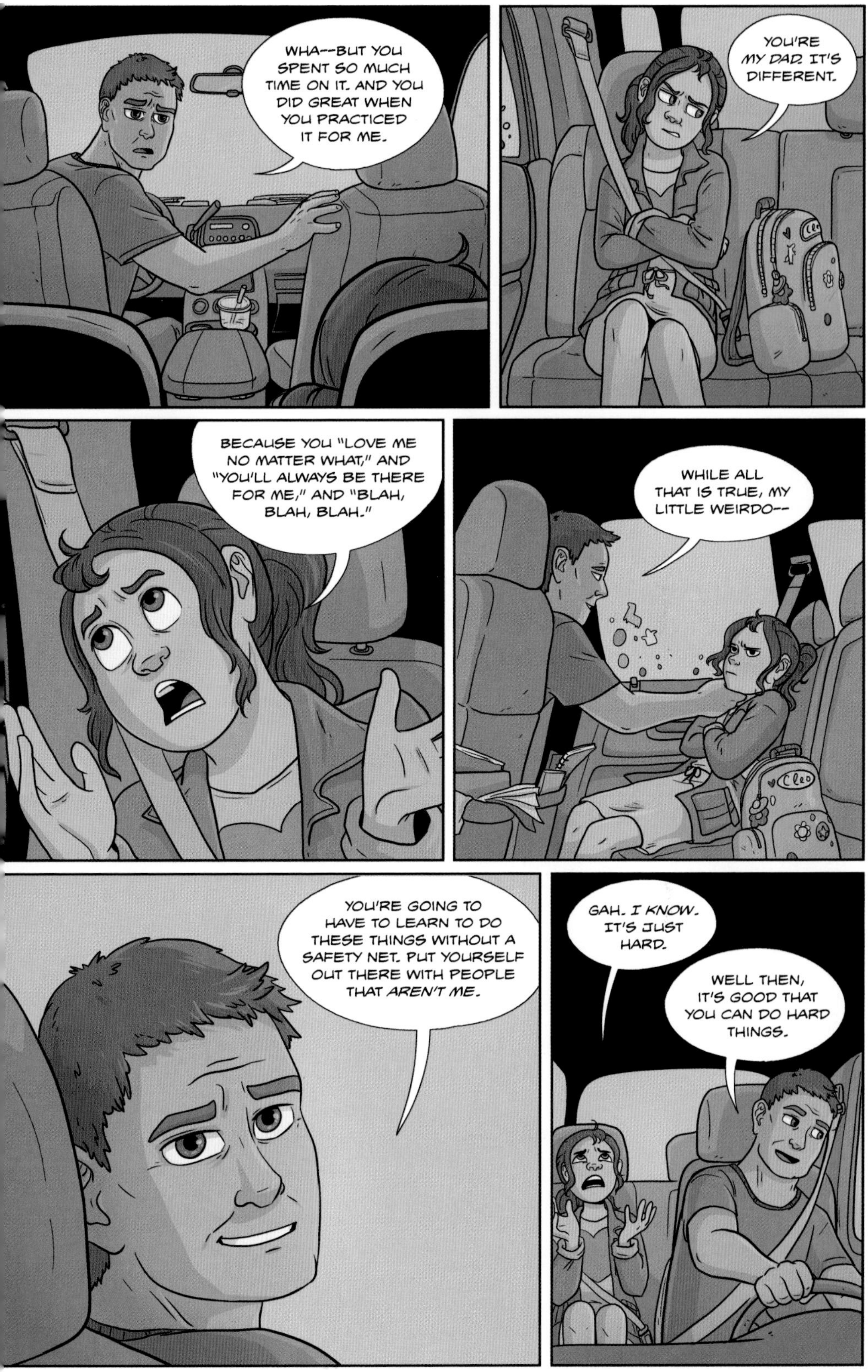
WHA--BUT YOU SPENT SO MUCH TIME ON IT. AND YOU DID GREAT WHEN YOU PRACTICED IT FOR ME.
YOU'RE *MY DAD*. IT'S DIFFERENT.
BECAUSE YOU "LOVE ME NO MATTER WHAT," AND "YOU'LL ALWAYS BE THERE FOR ME," AND "BLAH, BLAH, BLAH."
WHILE ALL THAT IS TRUE, MY LITTLE WEIRDO--
YOU'RE GOING TO HAVE TO LEARN TO DO THESE THINGS WITHOUT A SAFETY NET. PUT YOURSELF OUT THERE WITH PEOPLE THAT *AREN'T ME*.
GAH. *I KNOW*. IT'S JUST HARD.
WELL THEN, IT'S GOOD THAT YOU CAN DO HARD THINGS.

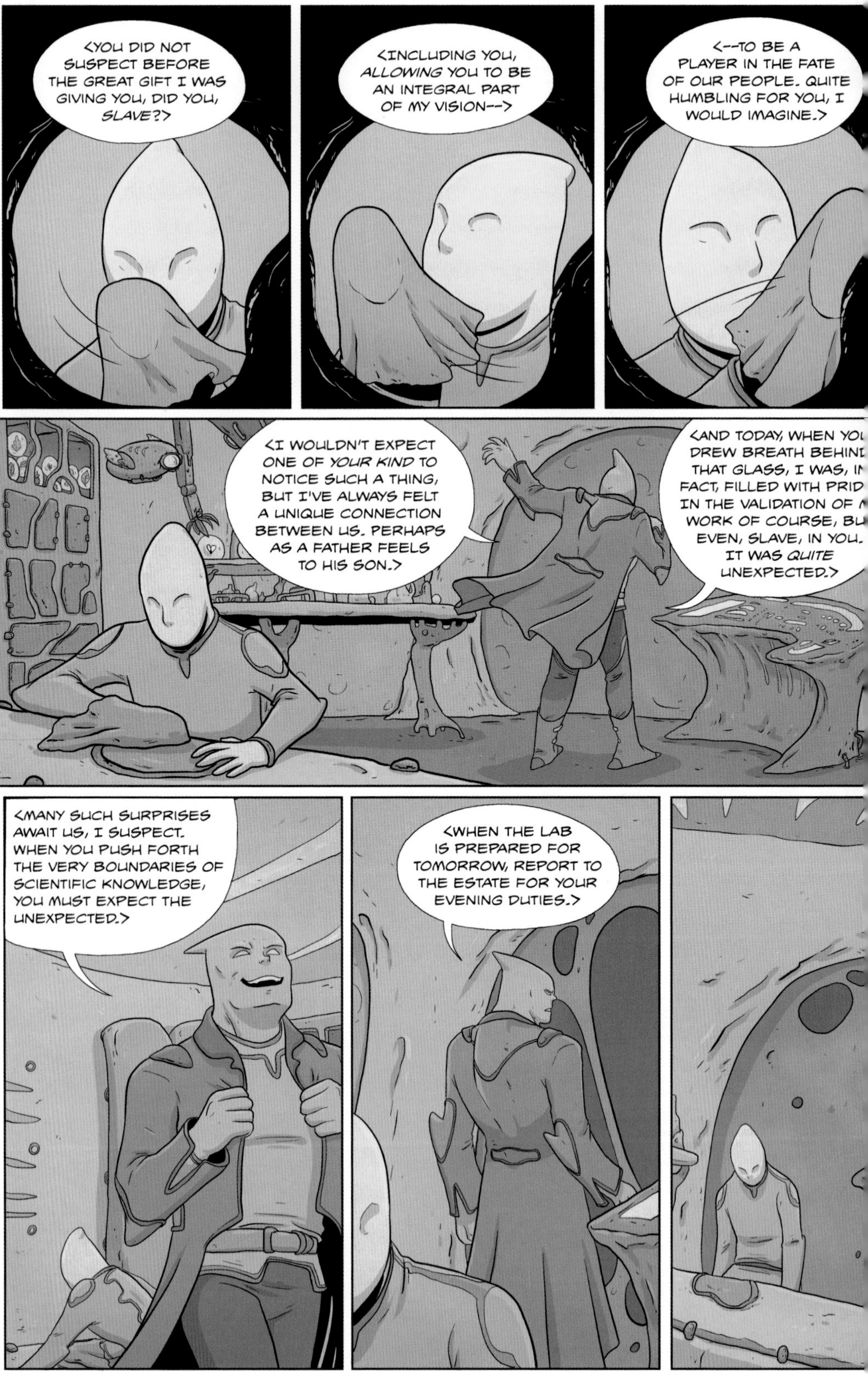

<YOU DID NOT SUSPECT BEFORE THE GREAT GIFT I WAS GIVING YOU, DID YOU, *SLAVE*?>
<INCLUDING YOU, *ALLOWING* YOU TO BE AN INTEGRAL PART OF MY VISION-->
<--TO BE A PLAYER IN THE FATE OF OUR PEOPLE. QUITE HUMBLING FOR YOU, I WOULD IMAGINE.>
<I WOULDN'T EXPECT ONE OF *YOUR KIND* TO NOTICE SUCH A THING, BUT I'VE ALWAYS FELT A UNIQUE CONNECTION BETWEEN US. PERHAPS AS A FATHER FEELS TO HIS SON.>
<AND TODAY, WHEN YOU DREW BREATH BEHIND THAT GLASS, I WAS, IN FACT, FILLED WITH PRIDE IN THE VALIDATION OF MY WORK OF COURSE, BUT EVEN, SLAVE, IN YOU. IT WAS *QUITE* UNEXPECTED.>
<MANY SUCH SURPRISES AWAIT US, I SUSPECT. WHEN YOU PUSH FORTH THE VERY BOUNDARIES OF SCIENTIFIC KNOWLEDGE, YOU MUST EXPECT THE UNEXPECTED.>
<WHEN THE LAB IS PREPARED FOR TOMORROW, REPORT TO THE ESTATE FOR YOUR EVENING DUTIES.>

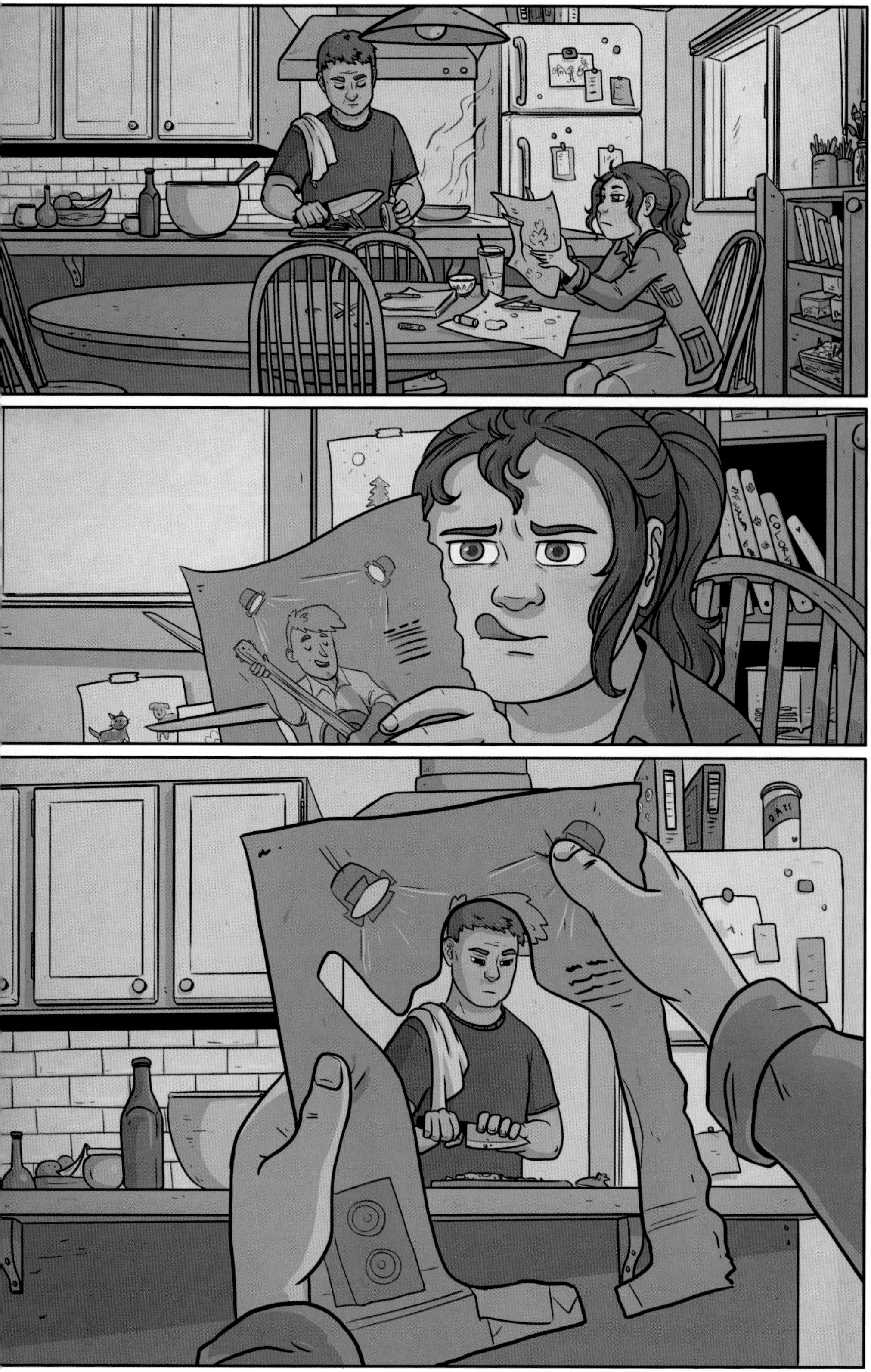
OATS

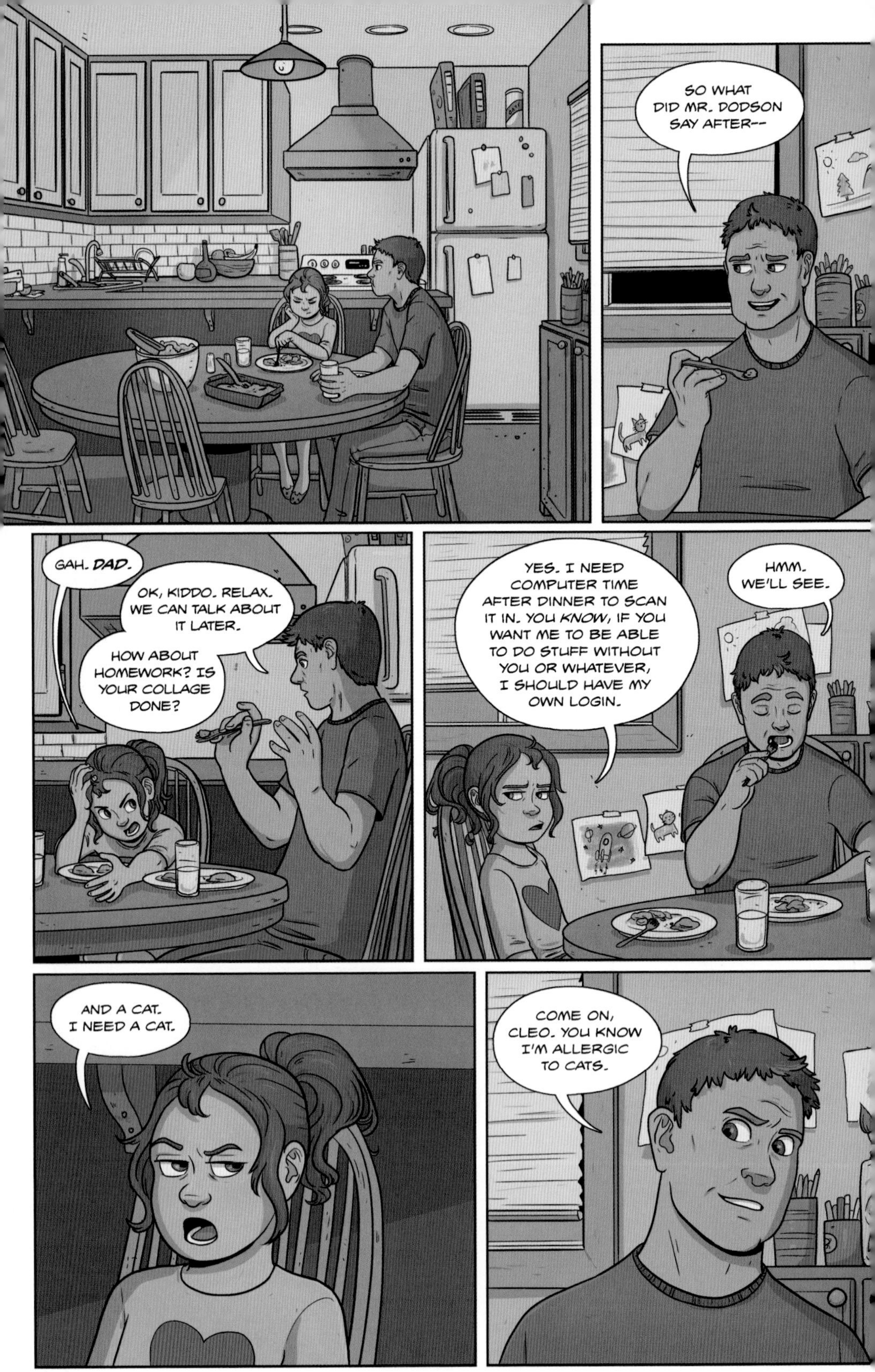
SO WHAT DID MR. DODSON SAY AFTER--
GAH. DAD.
OK, KIDDO. RELAX. WE CAN TALK ABOUT IT LATER.
HOW ABOUT HOMEWORK? IS YOUR COLLAGE DONE?
YES. I NEED COMPUTER TIME AFTER DINNER TO SCAN IT IN. YOU KNOW, IF YOU WANT ME TO BE ABLE TO DO STUFF WITHOUT YOU OR WHATEVER, I SHOULD HAVE MY OWN LOGIN.
HMM. WE'LL SEE.
AND A CAT. I NEED A CAT.
COME ON, CLEO. YOU KNOW I'M ALLERGIC TO CATS.

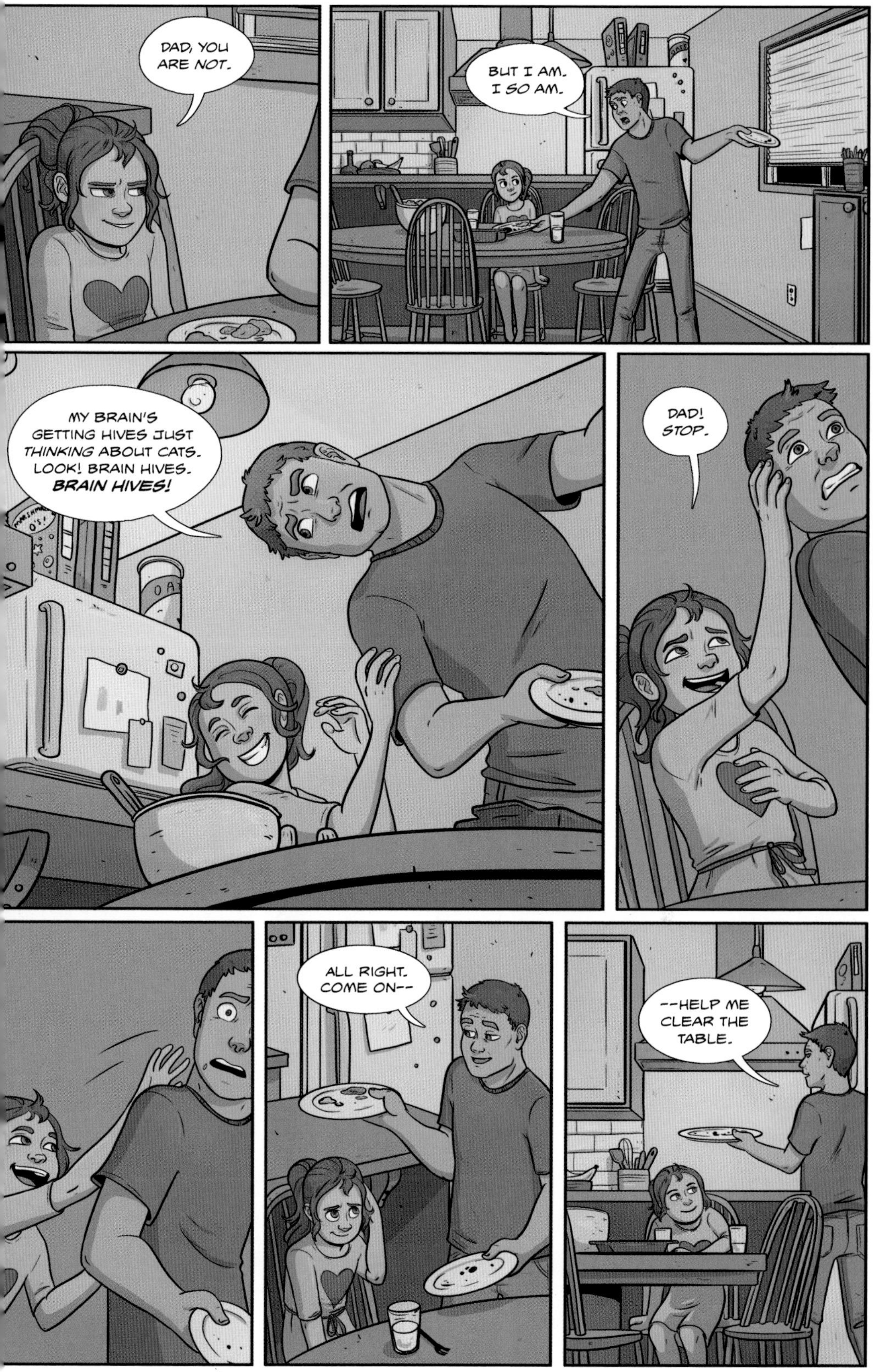
DAD, YOU ARE *NOT*.
BUT I AM. I SO AM.
MY BRAIN'S GETTING HIVES JUST *THINKING* ABOUT CATS. LOOK! BRAIN HIVES. ***BRAIN HIVES!***
DAD! *STOP*.
ALL RIGHT. COME ON--
--HELP ME CLEAR THE TABLE.

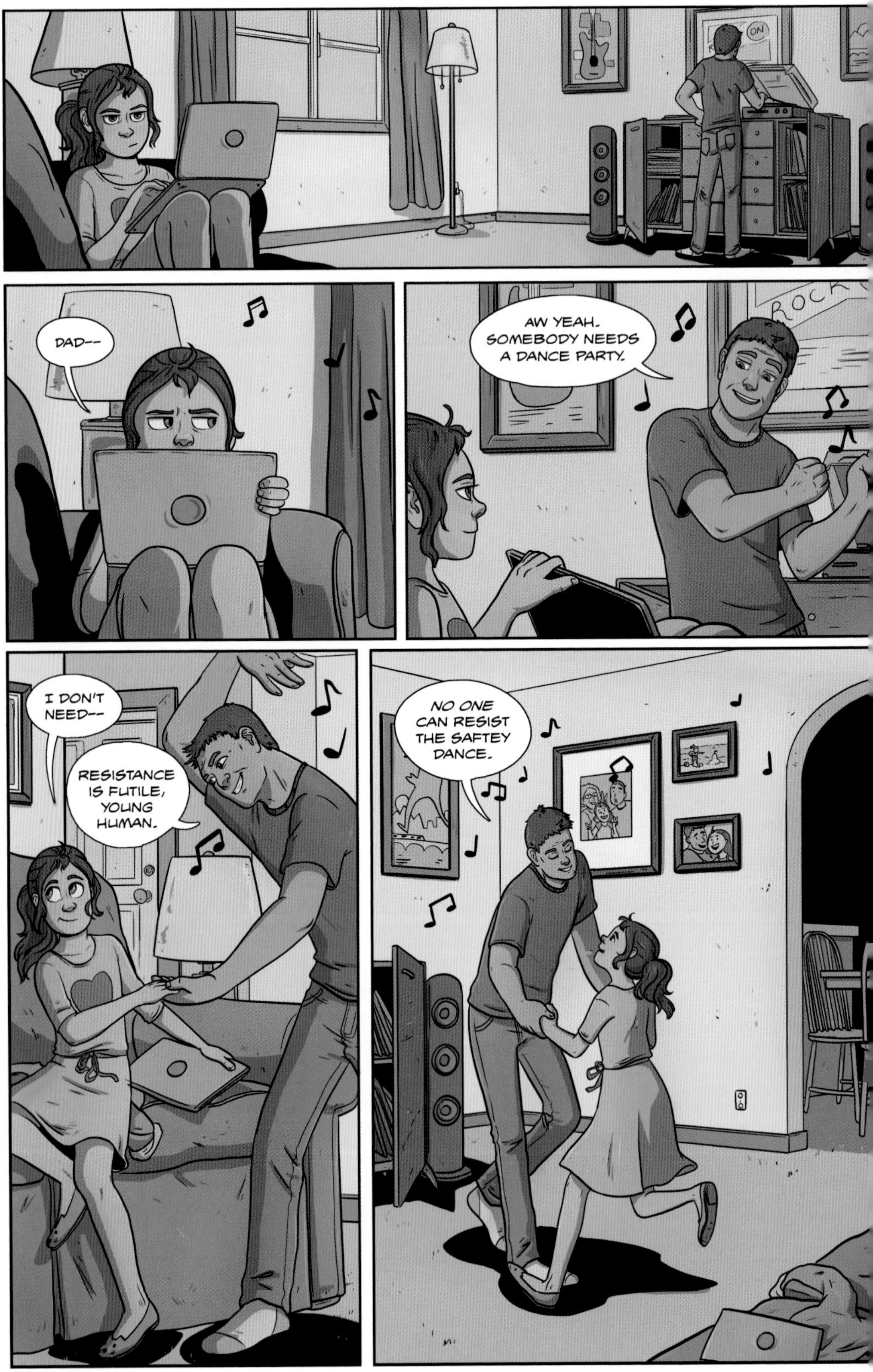

DAD--
AW YEAH. SOMEBODY NEEDS A DANCE PARTY.
I DON'T NEED--
RESISTANCE IS FUTILE, YOUNG HUMAN.
NO ONE CAN RESIST THE SAFTEY DANCE.

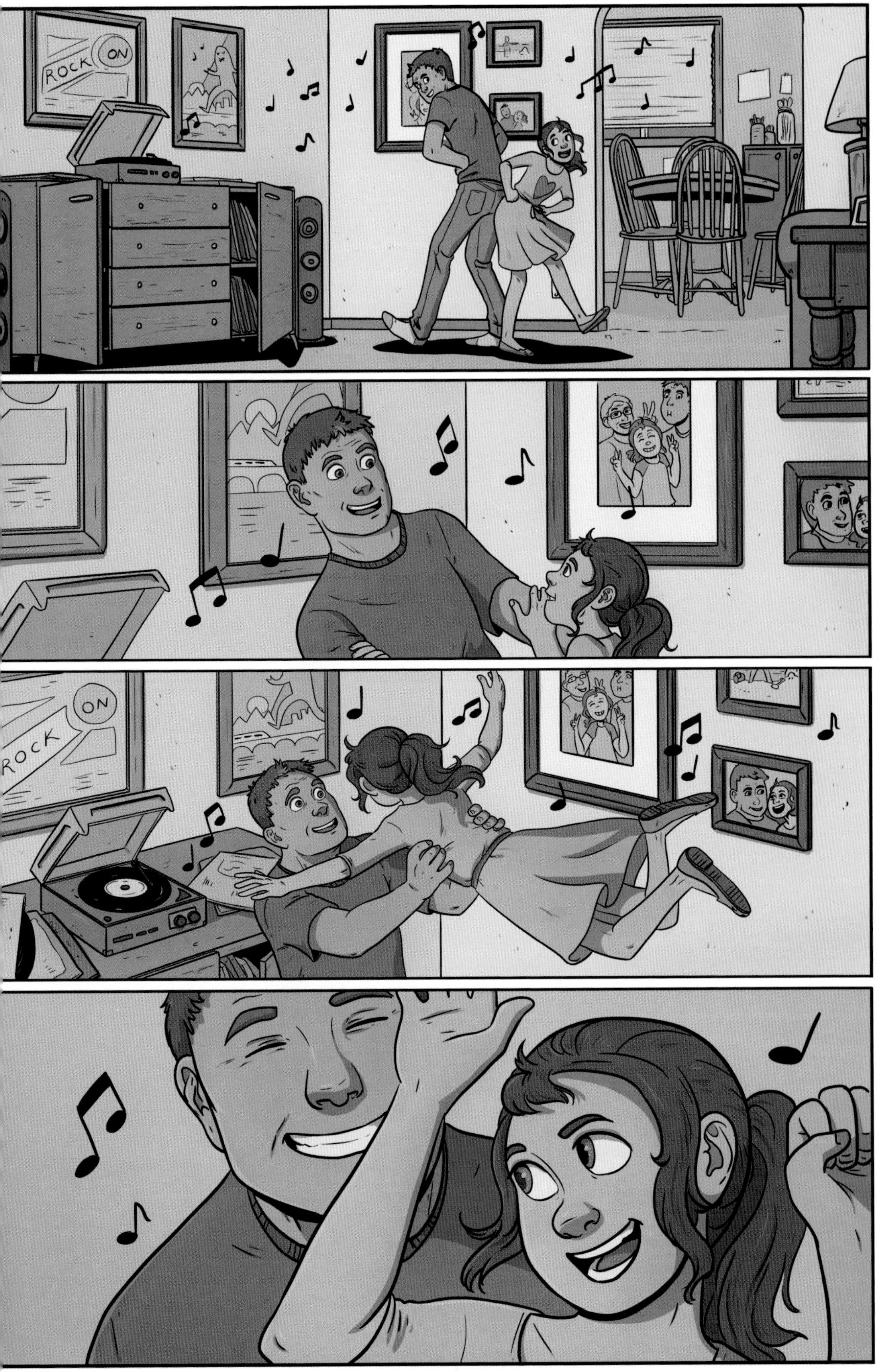
ROCK
ON
ROCK
ON

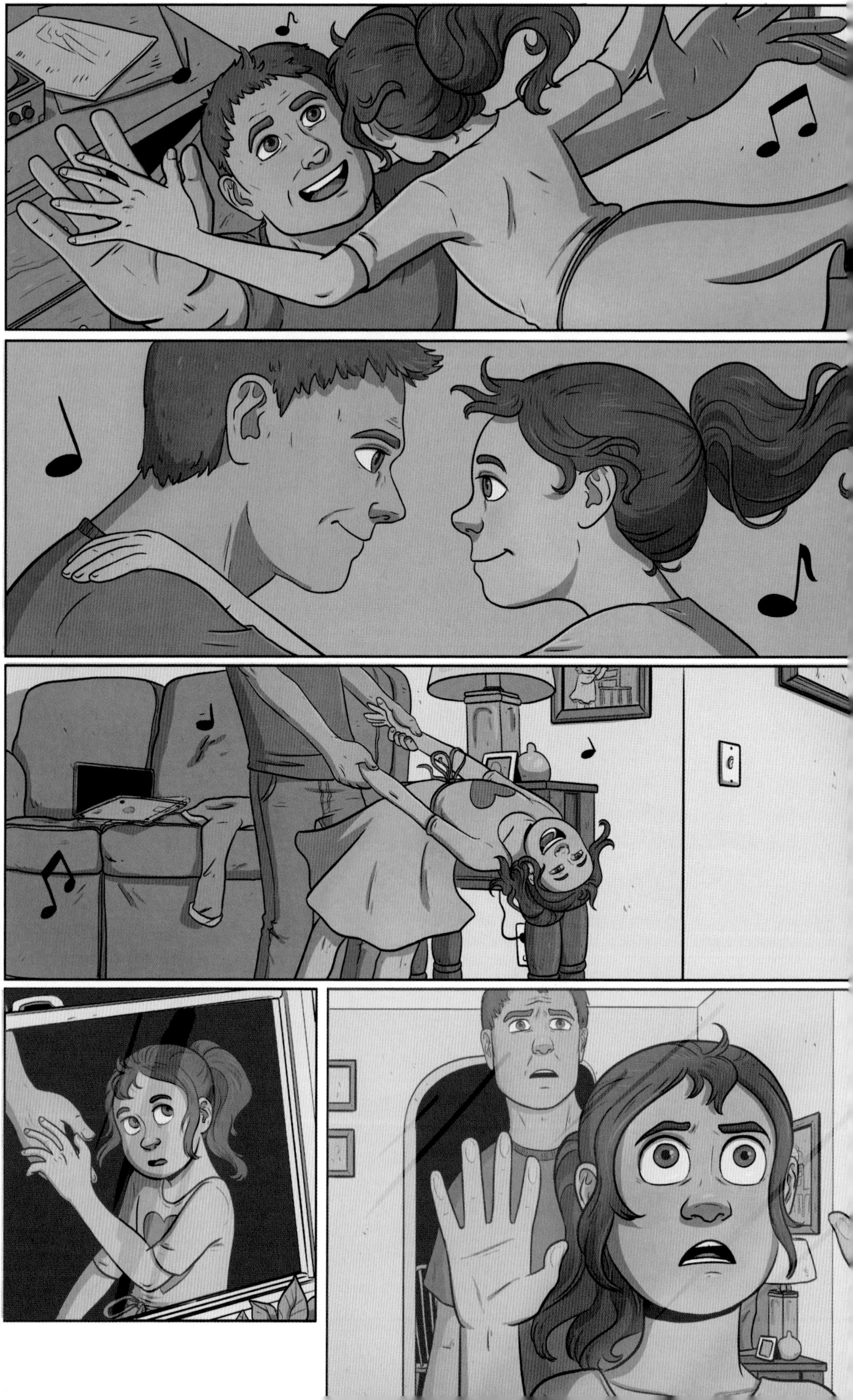

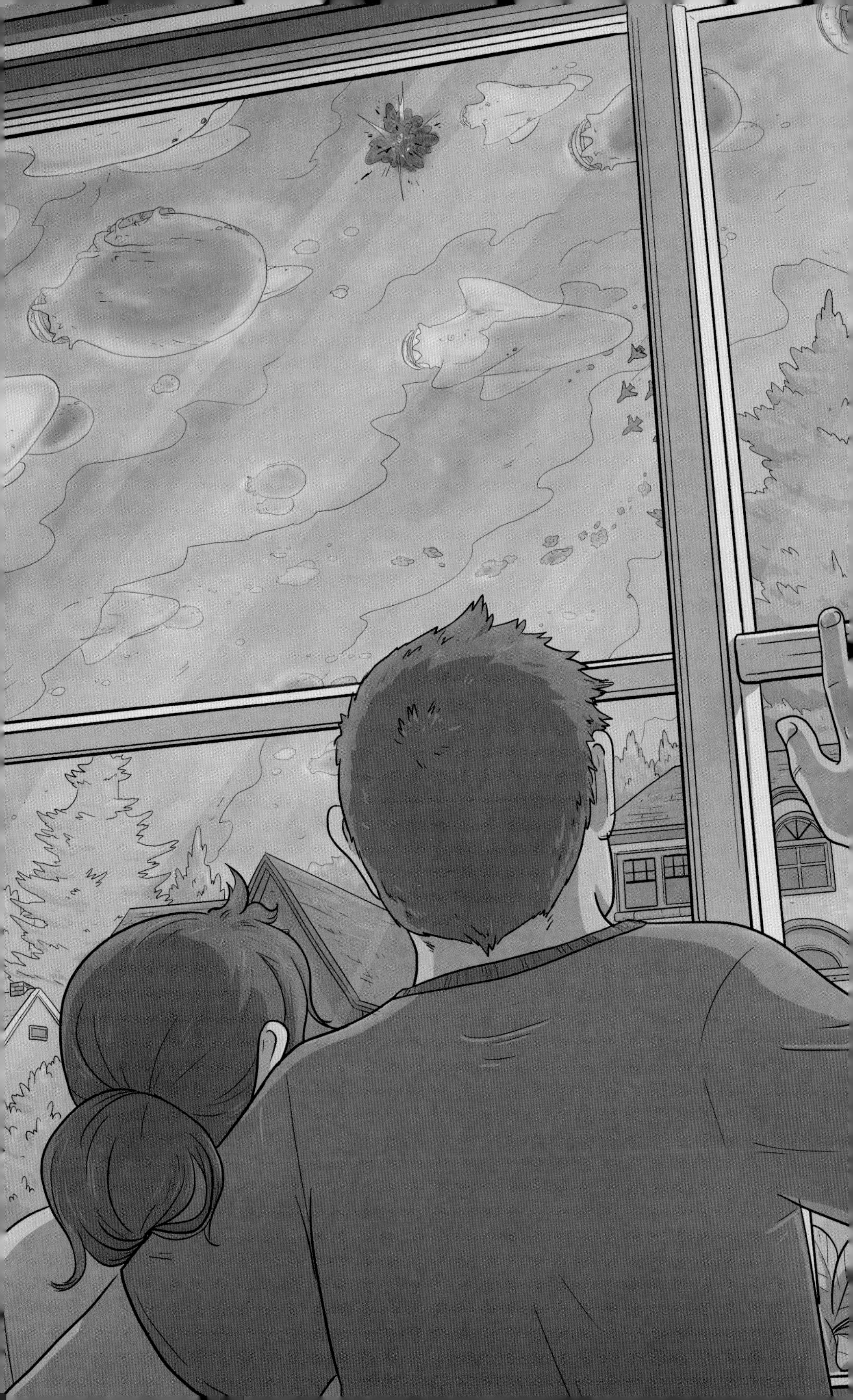

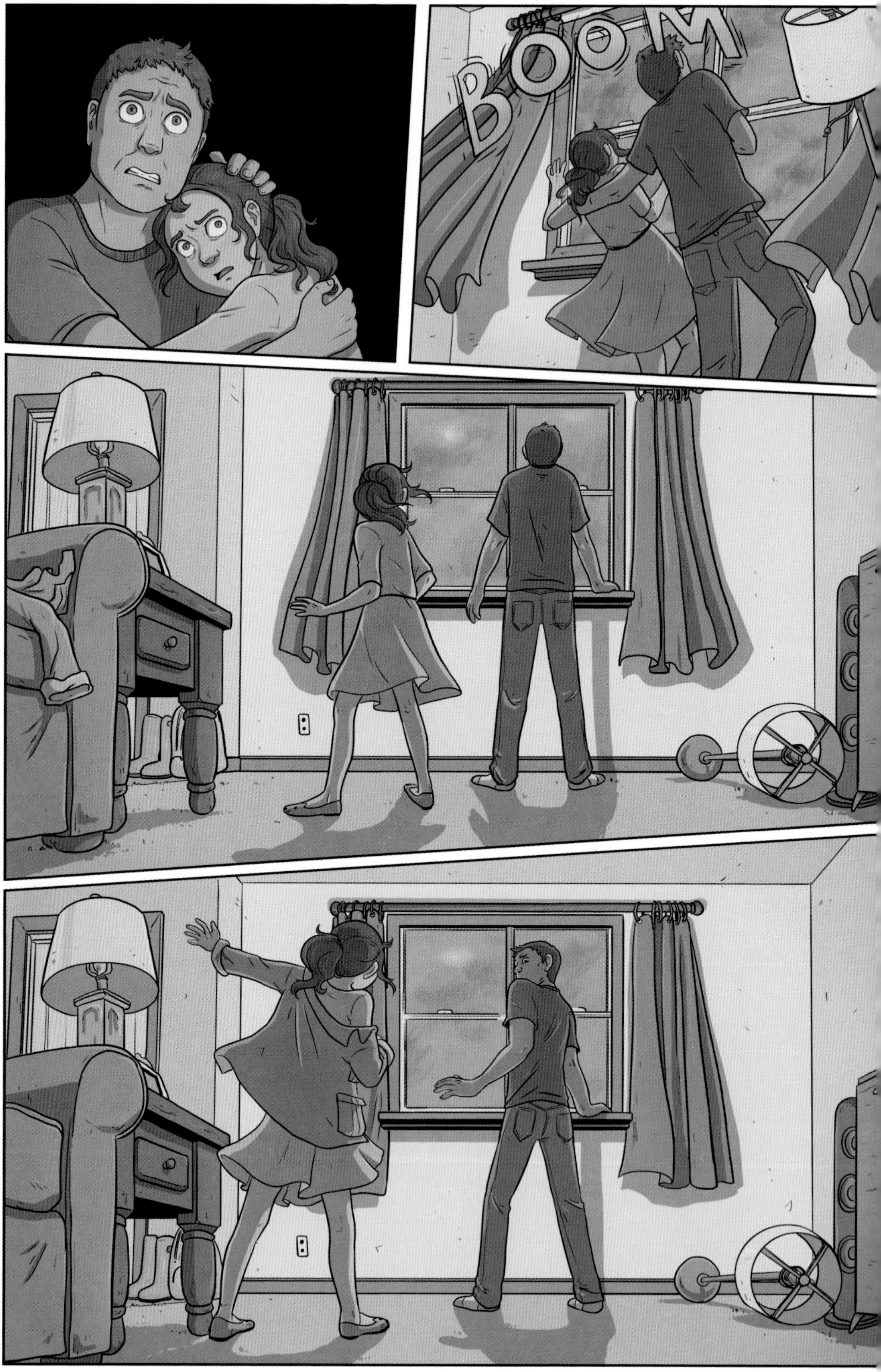
BOOM

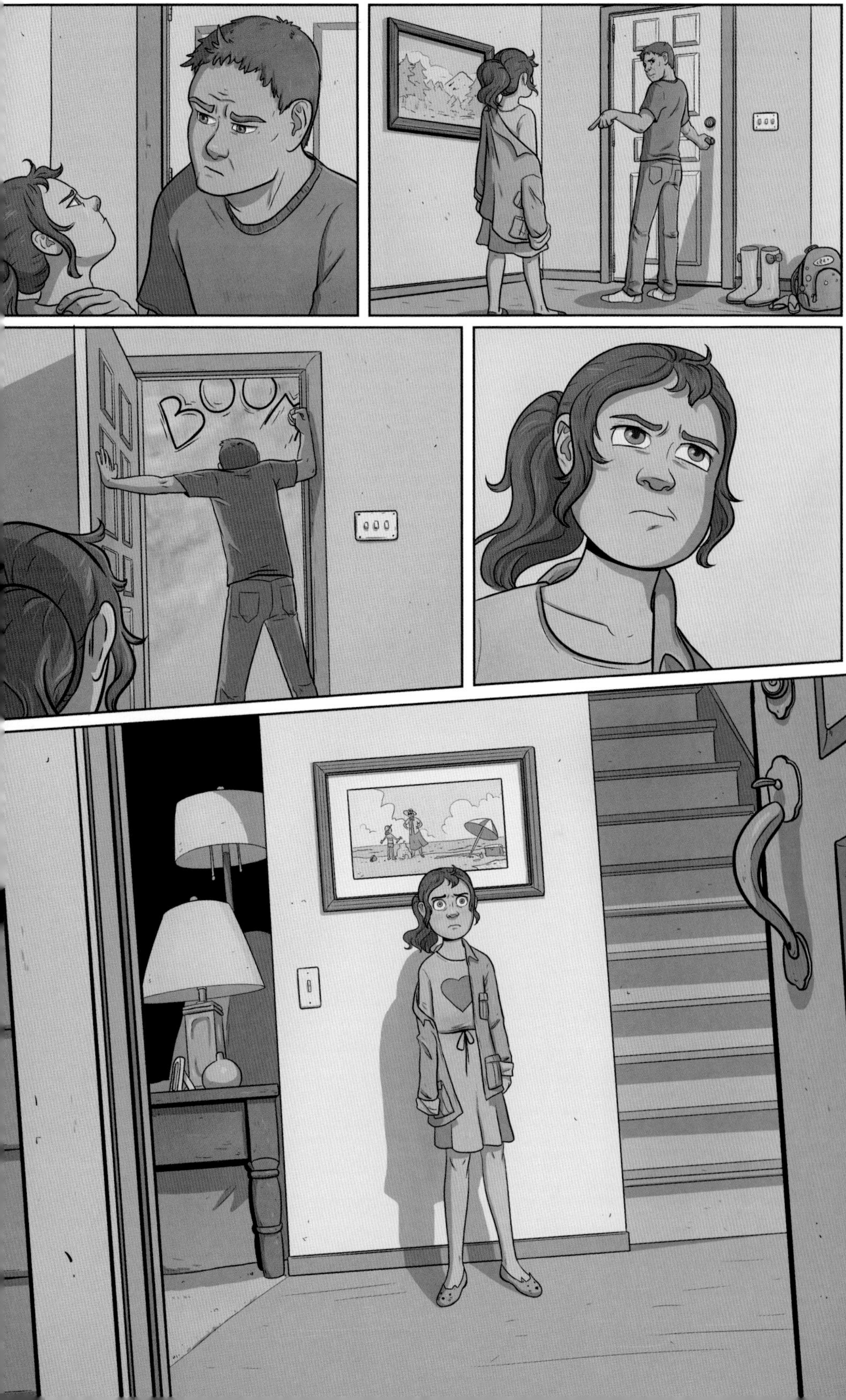
BOO

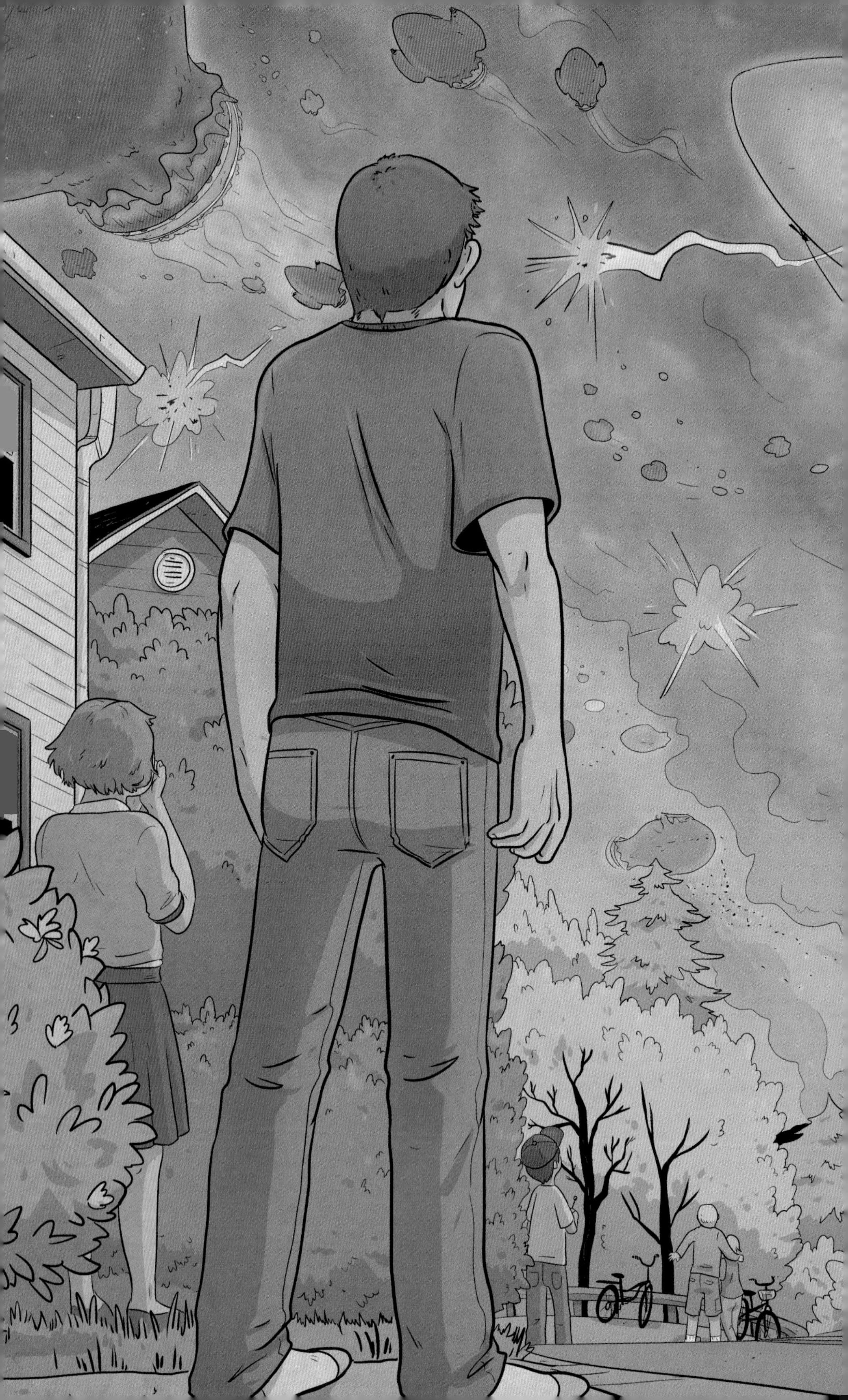

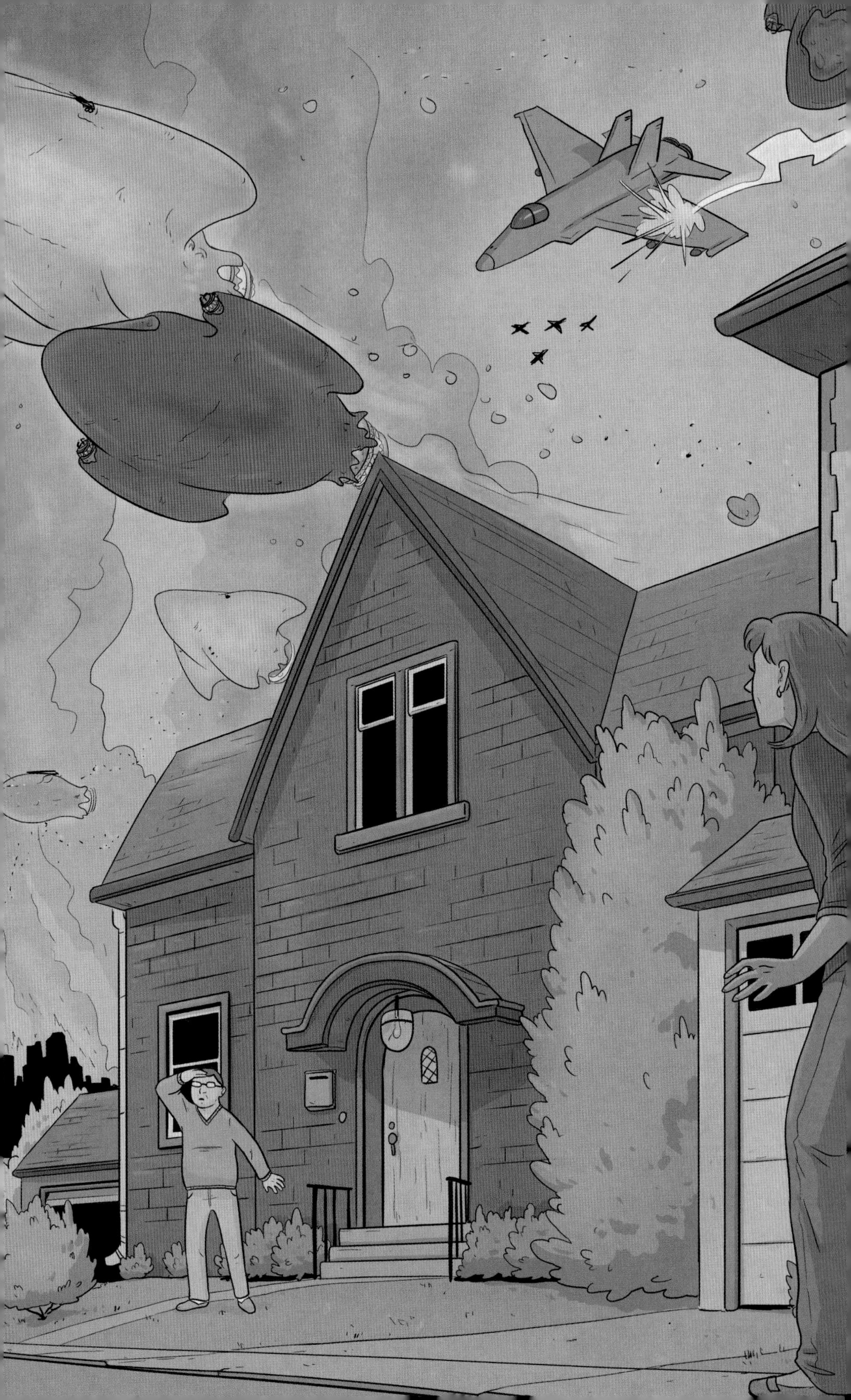

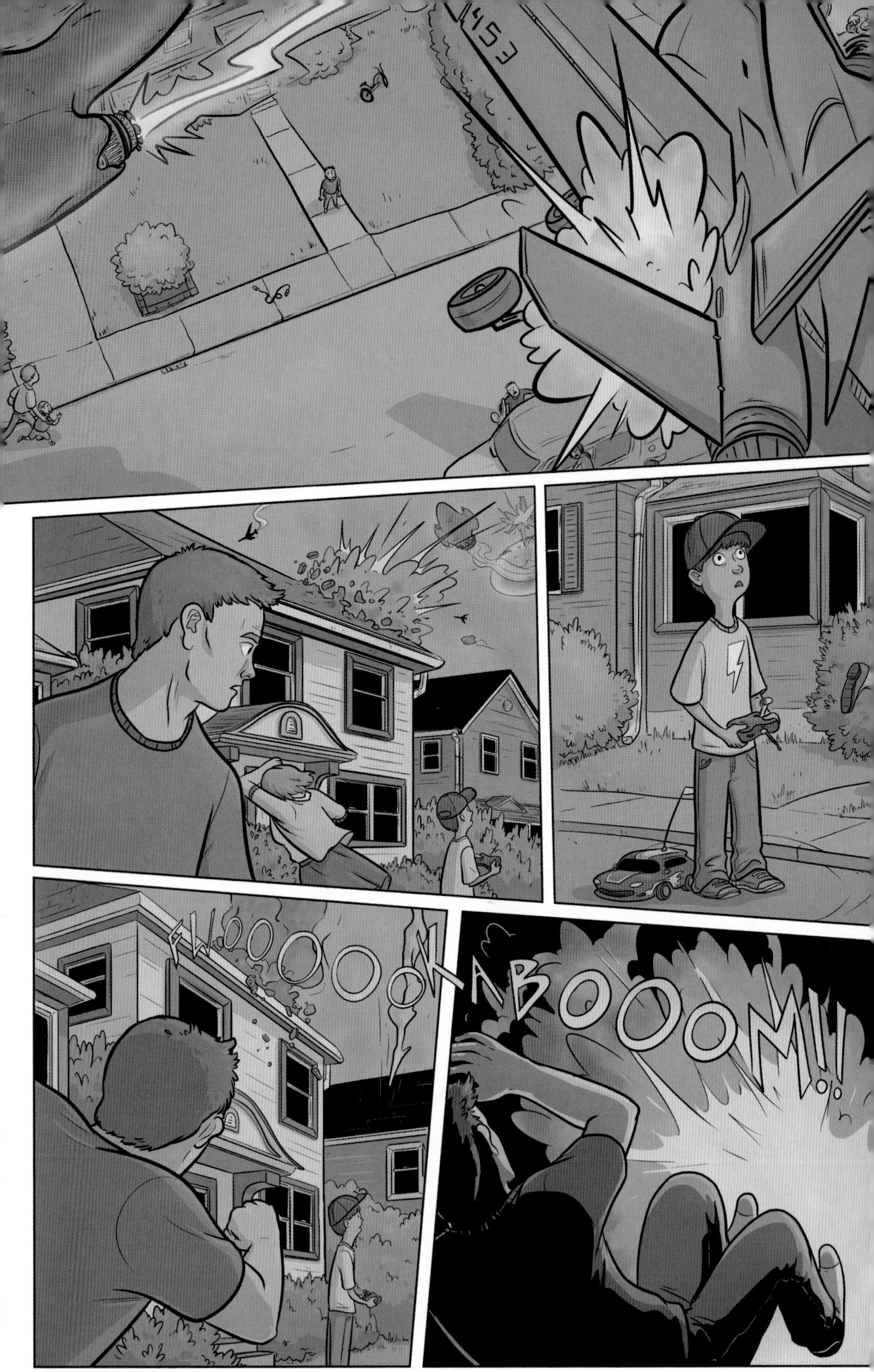
FWOOOOOKABOOOOM!!

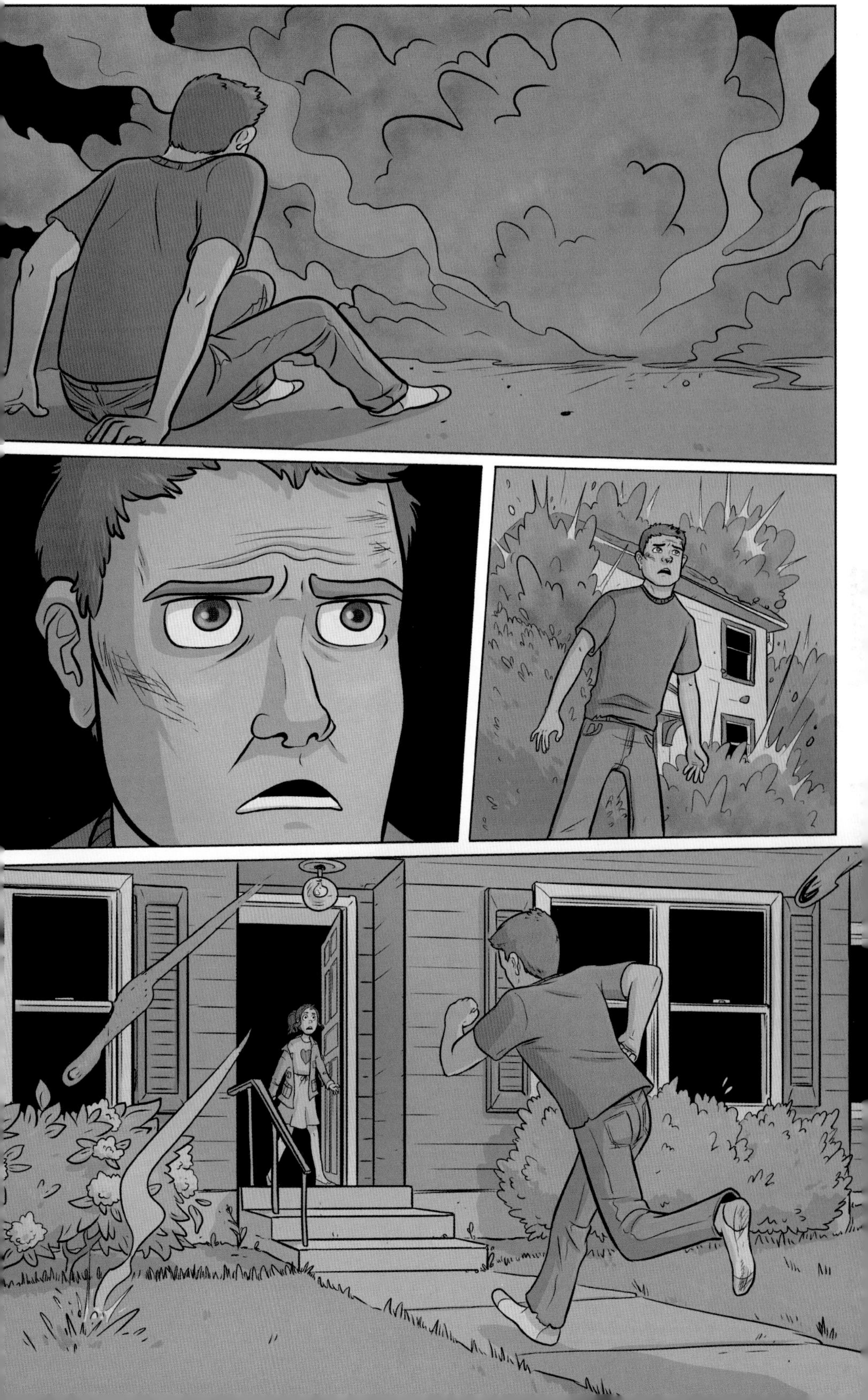

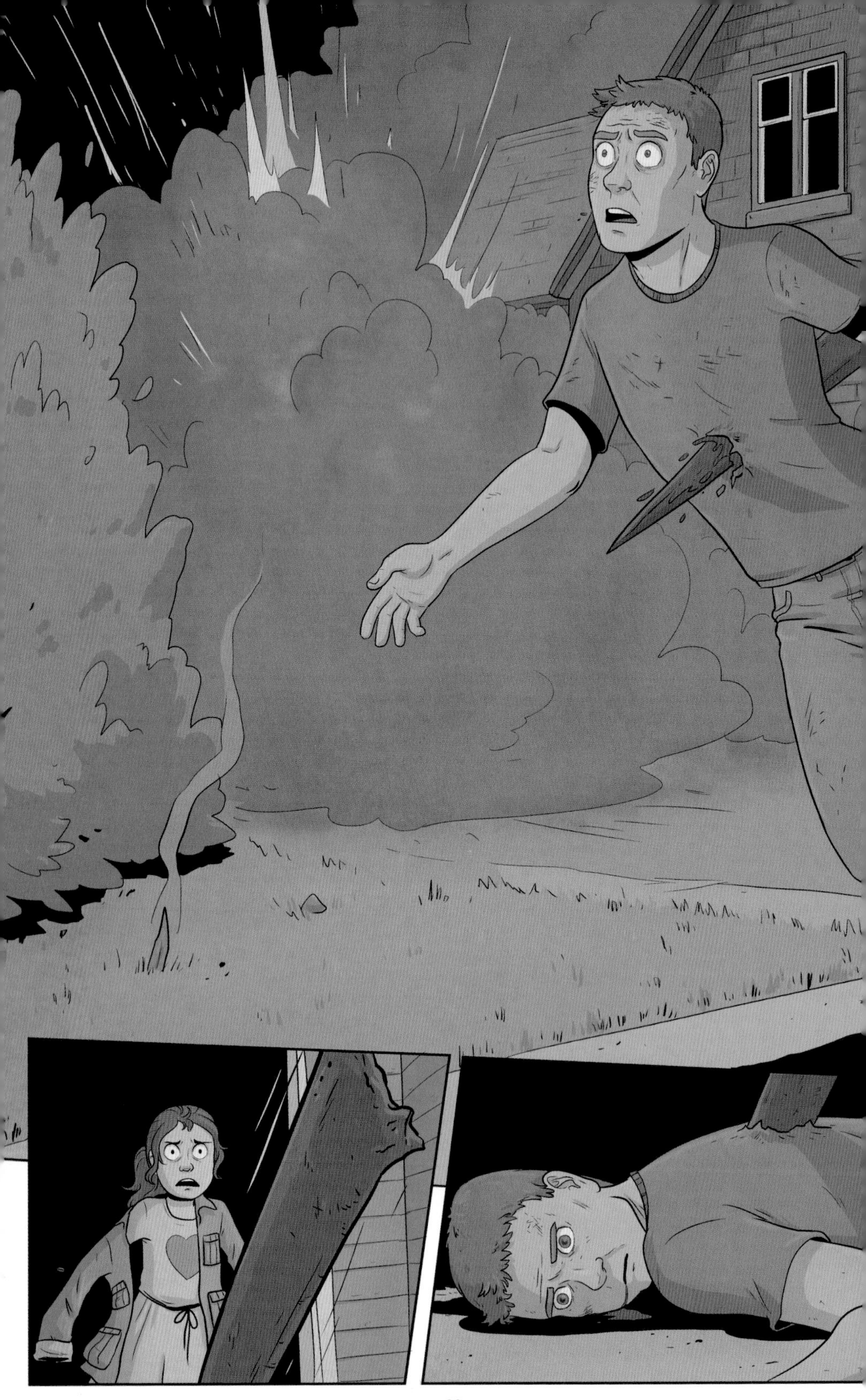

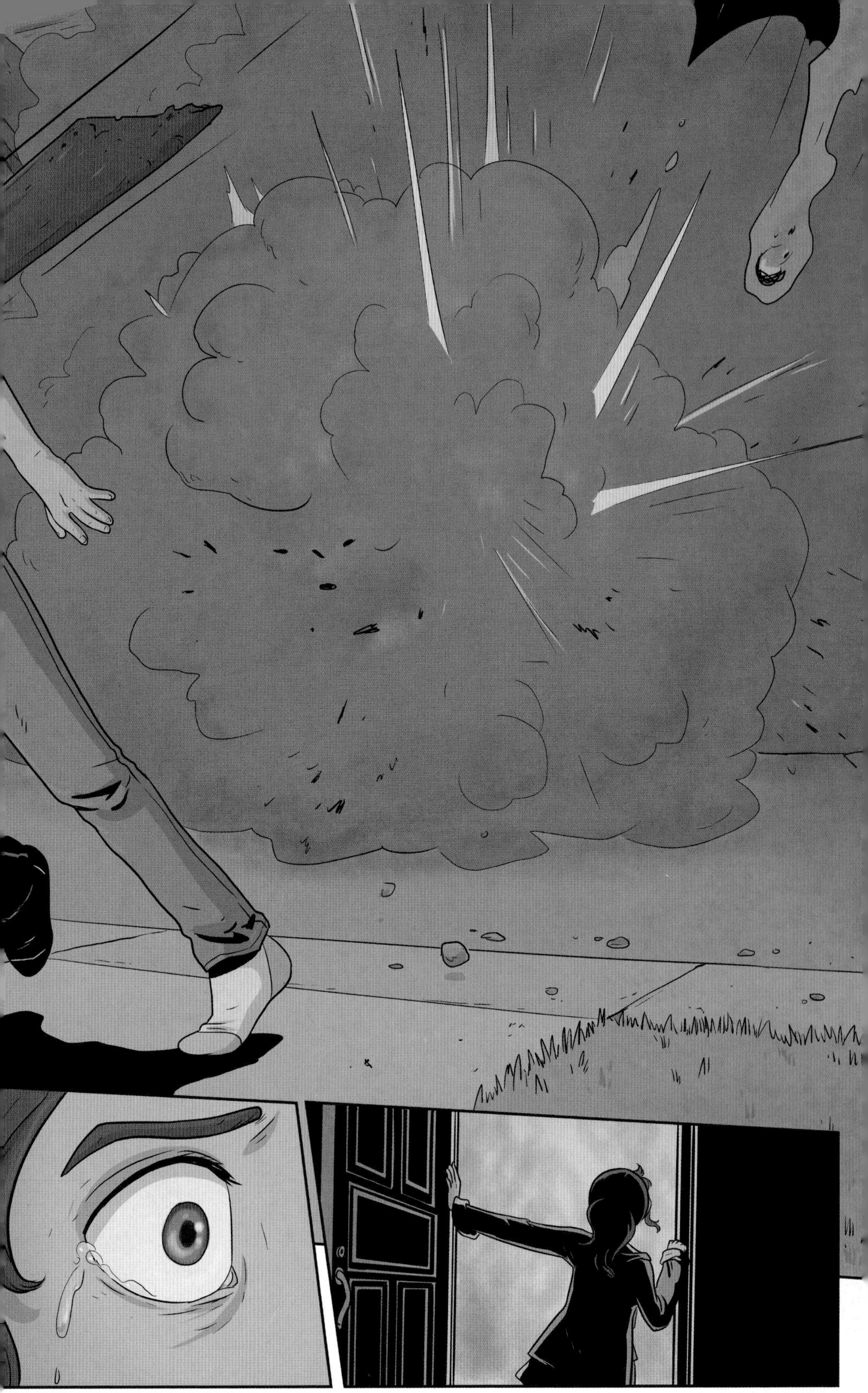

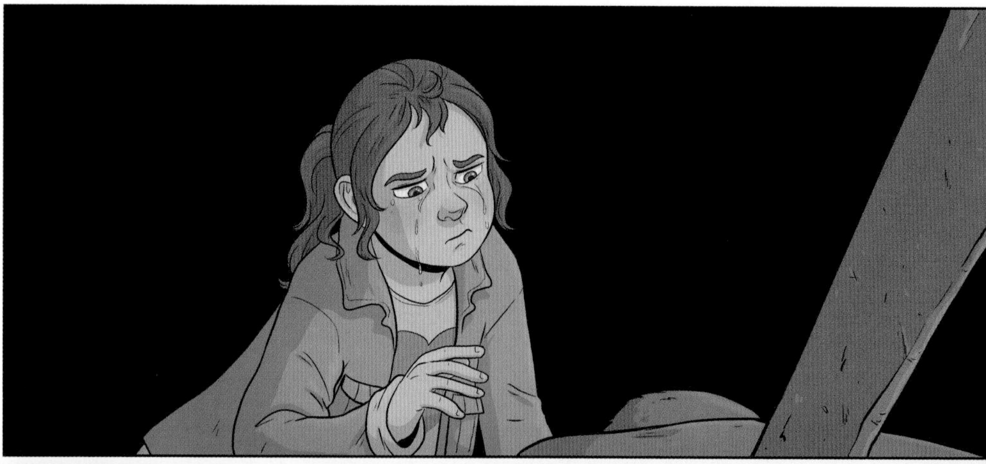
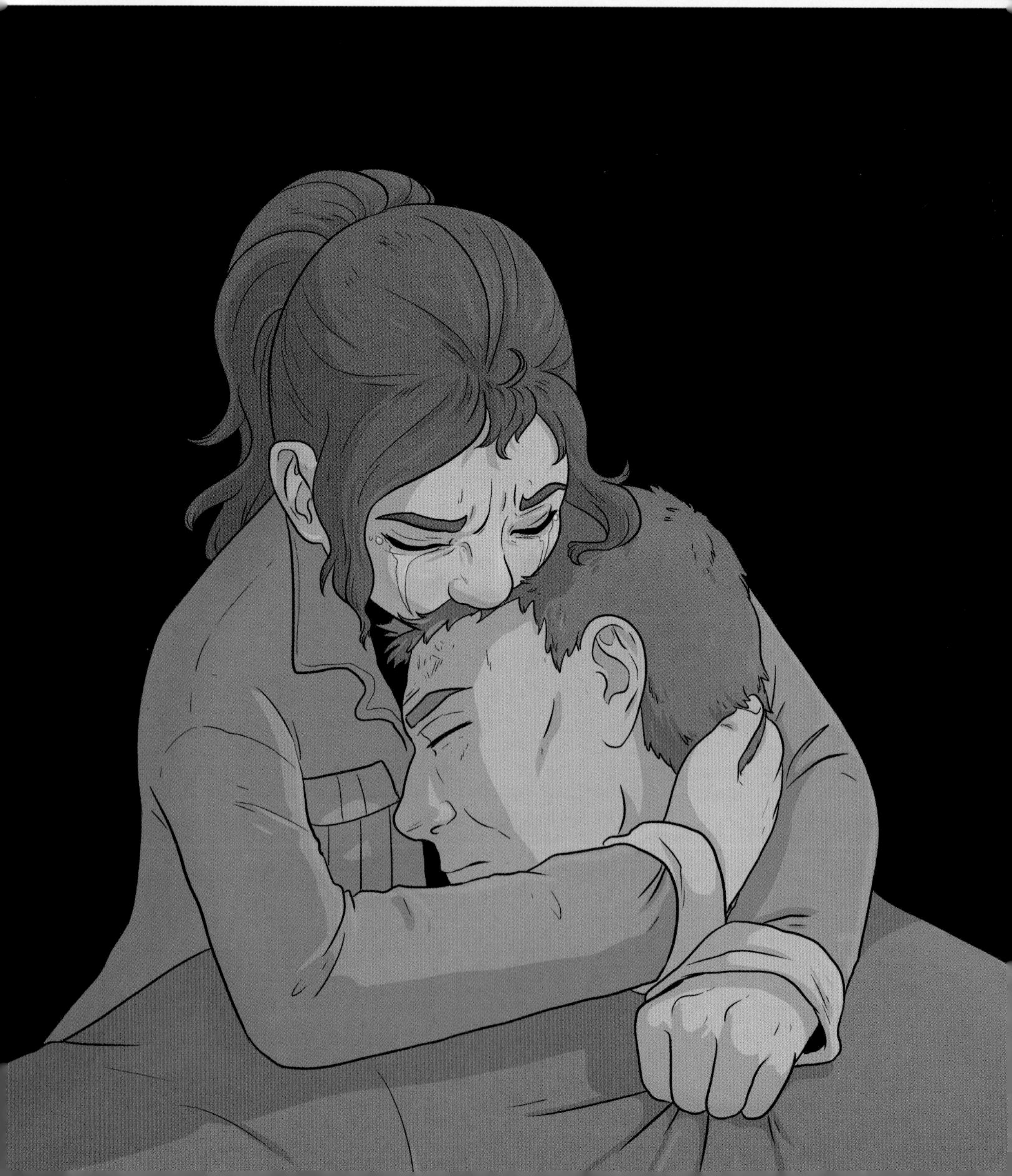

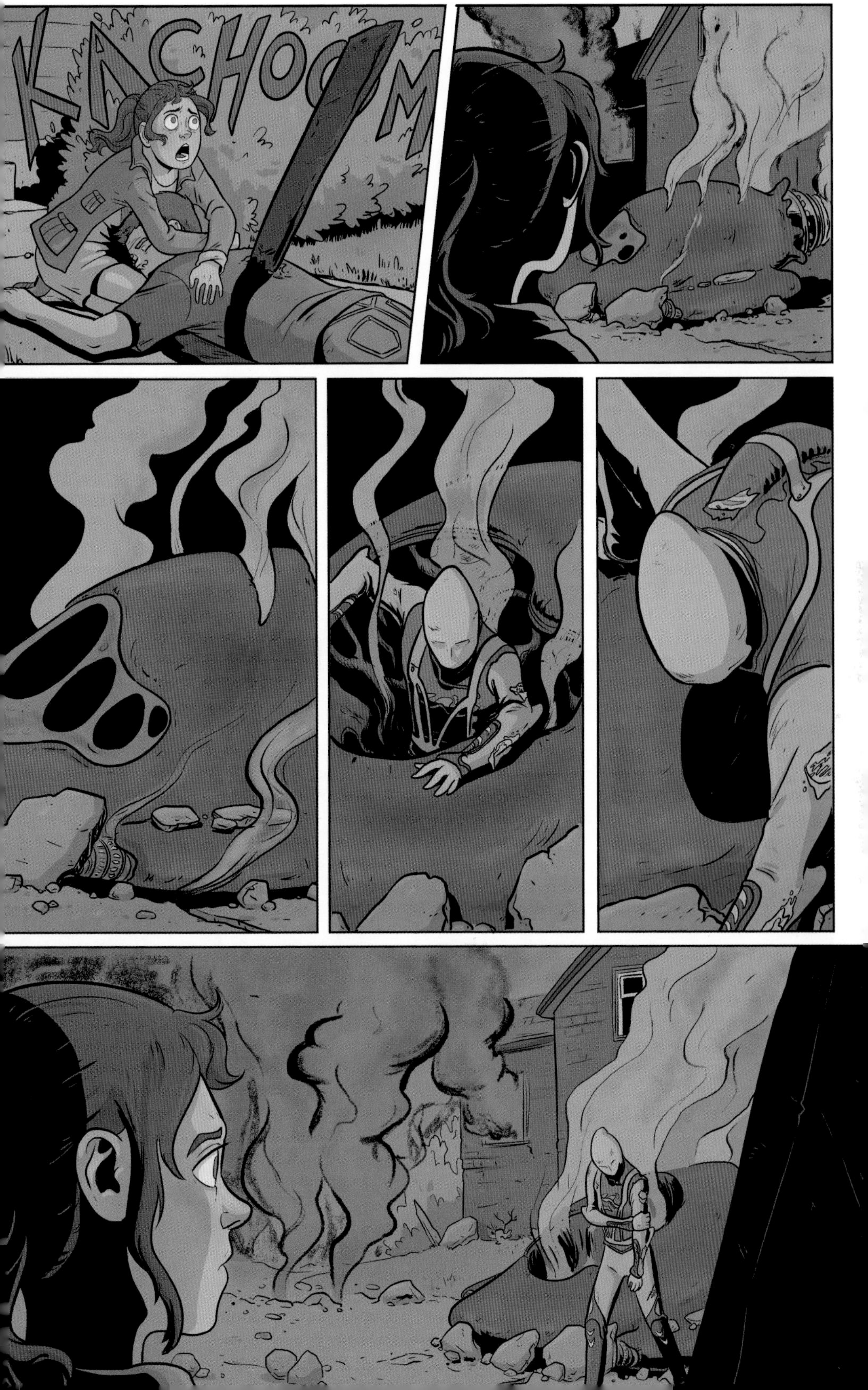
KACHOOM

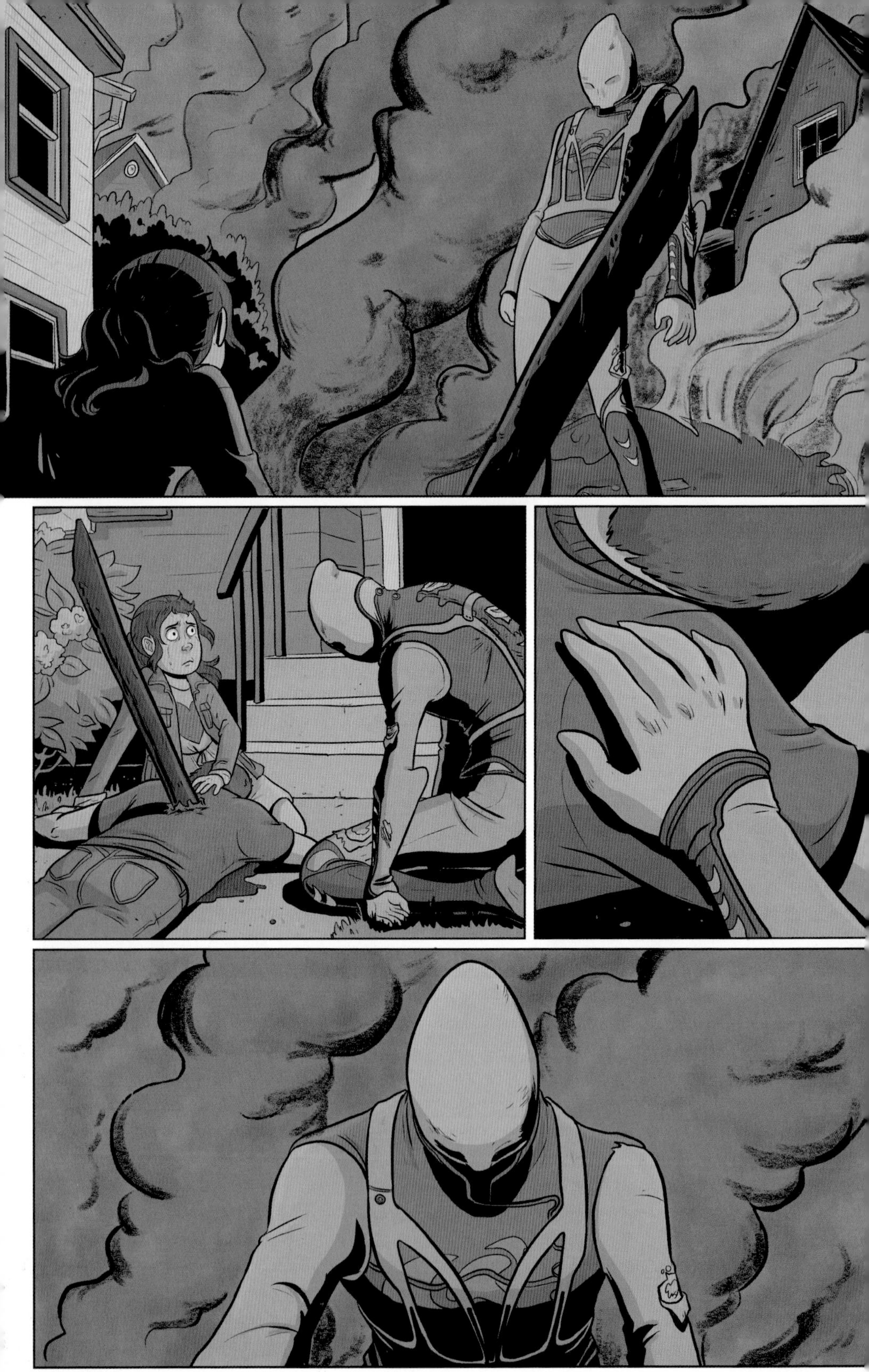

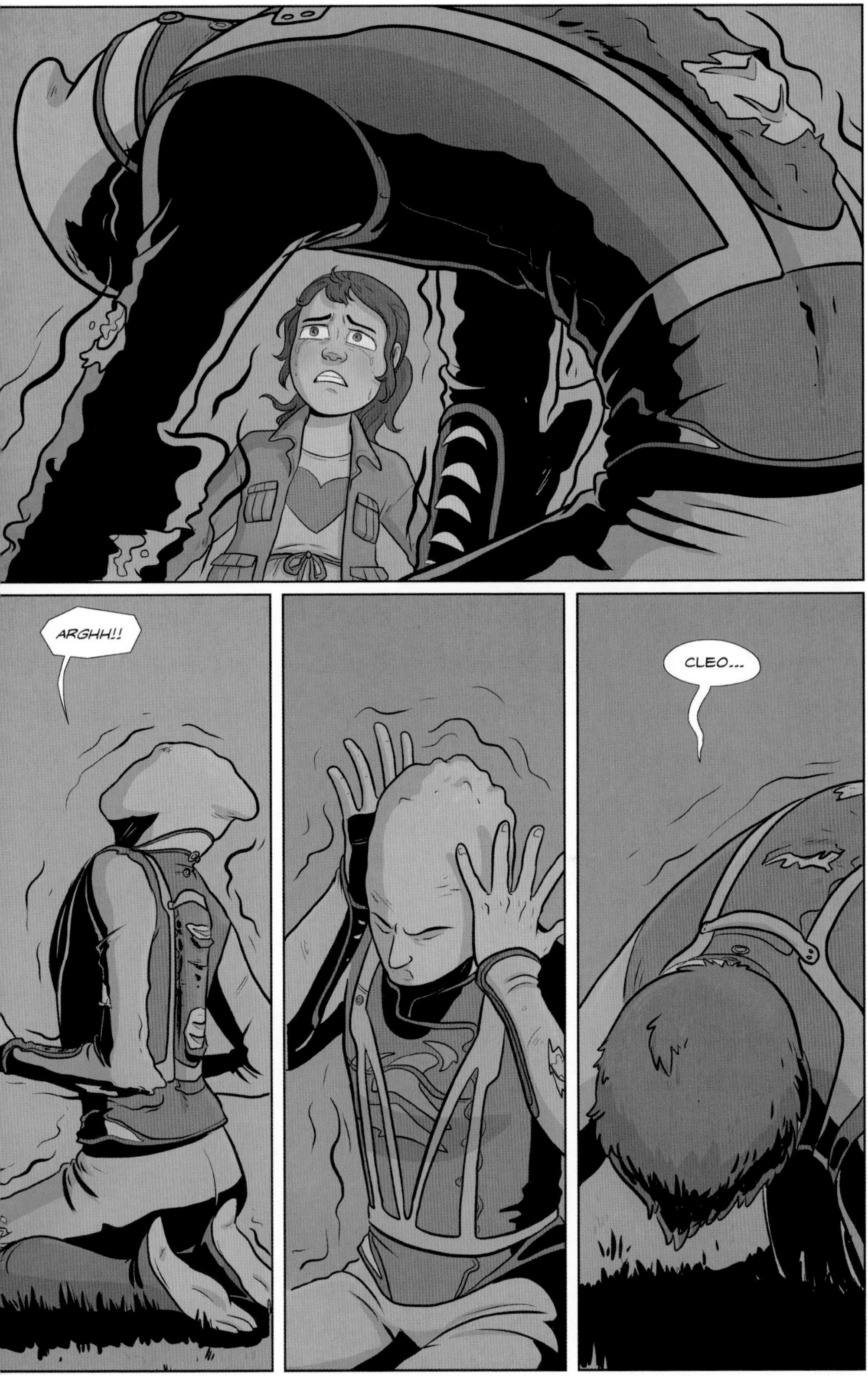
ARGHH!!
CLEO...

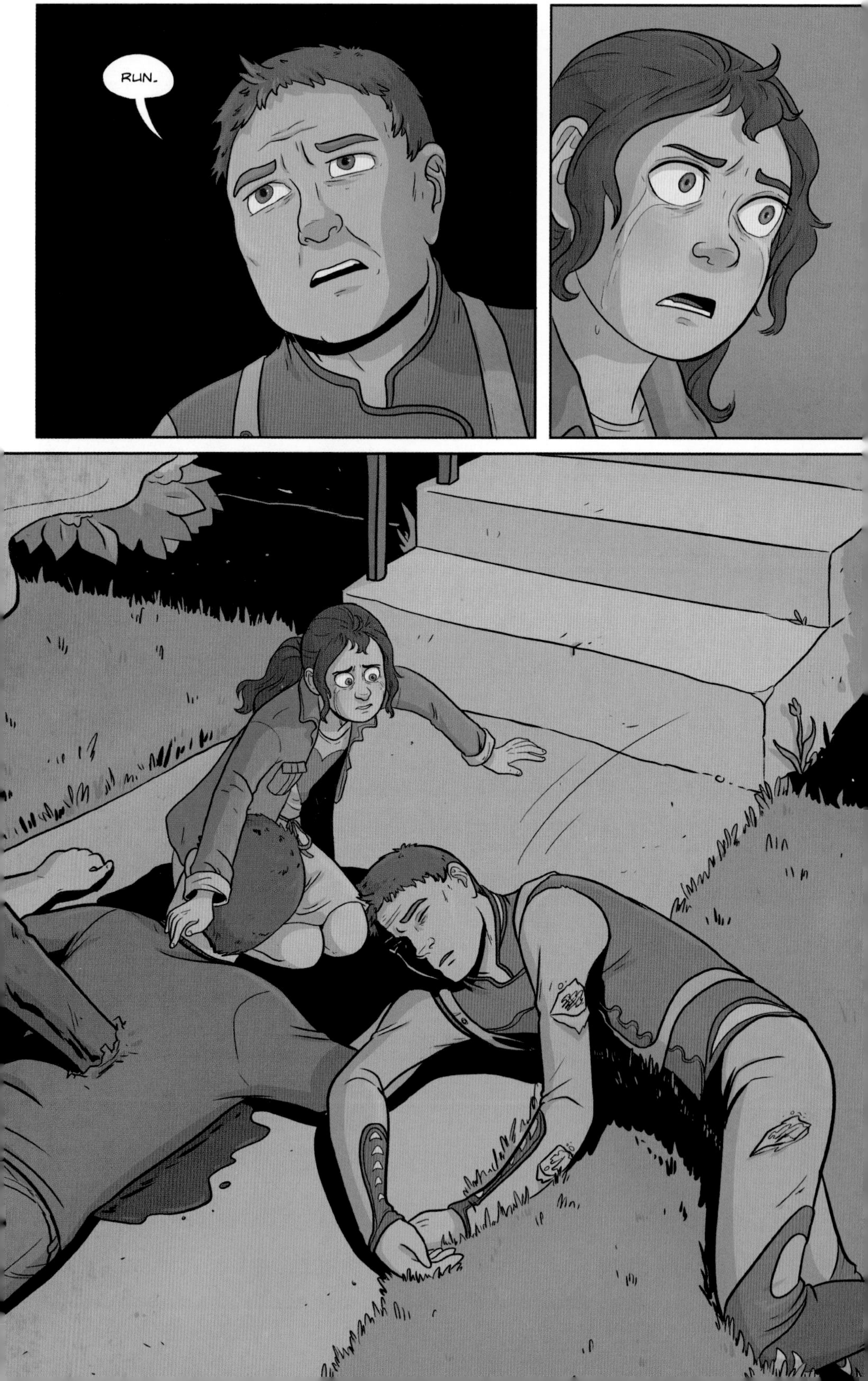
RUN.

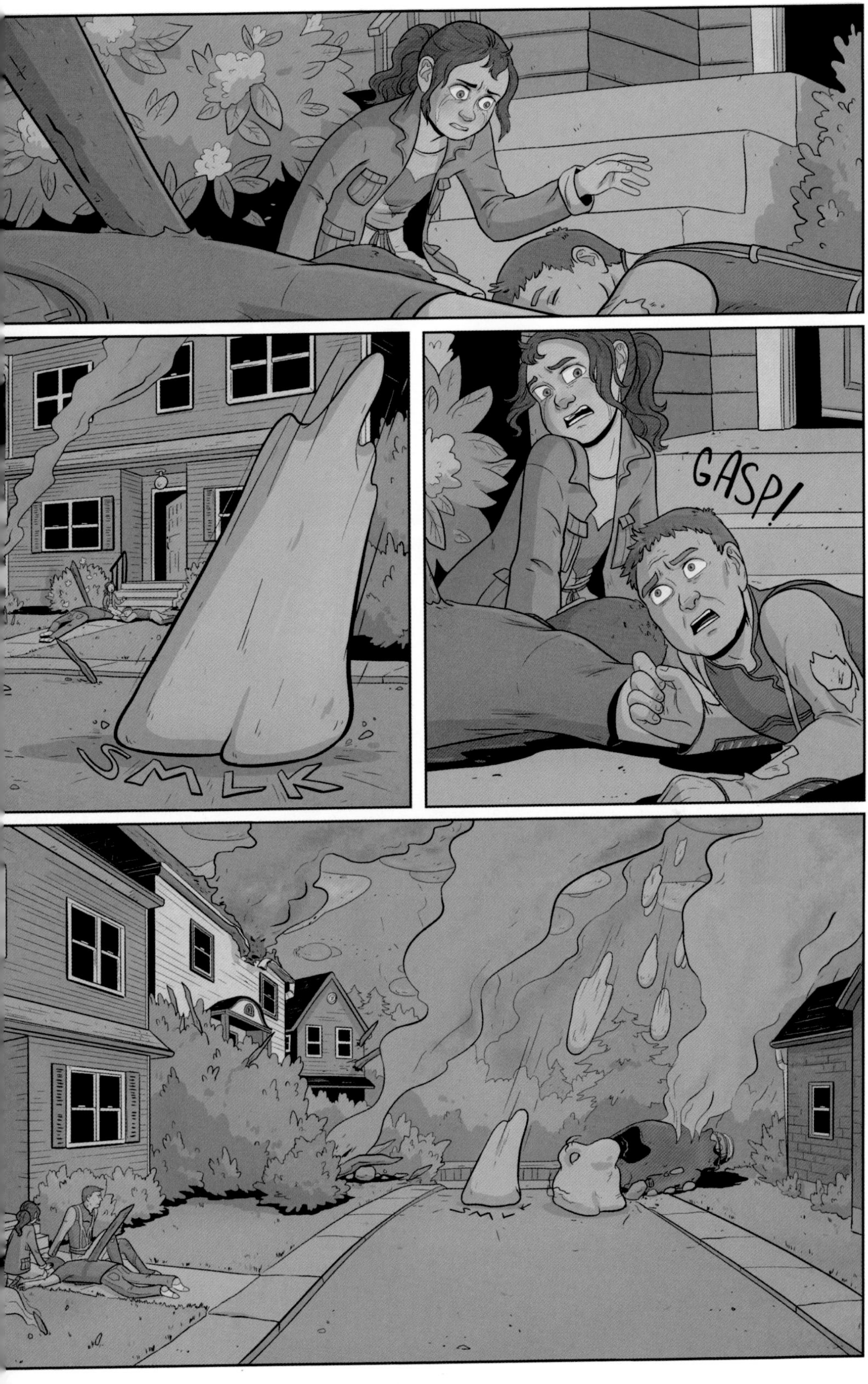
SMLK
GASP!
SMLK

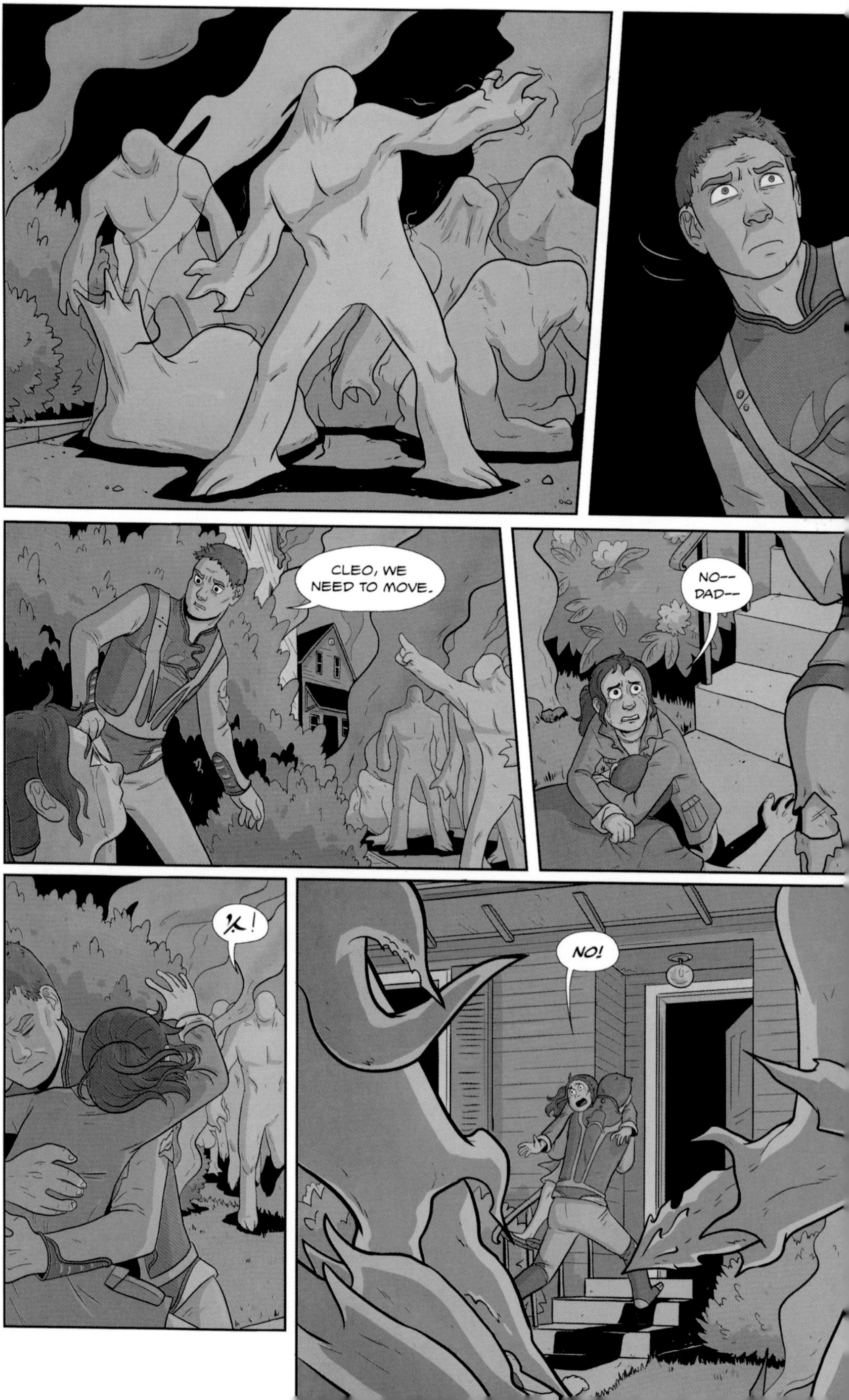
CLEO, WE NEED TO MOVE.
NO-- DAD--
NO!

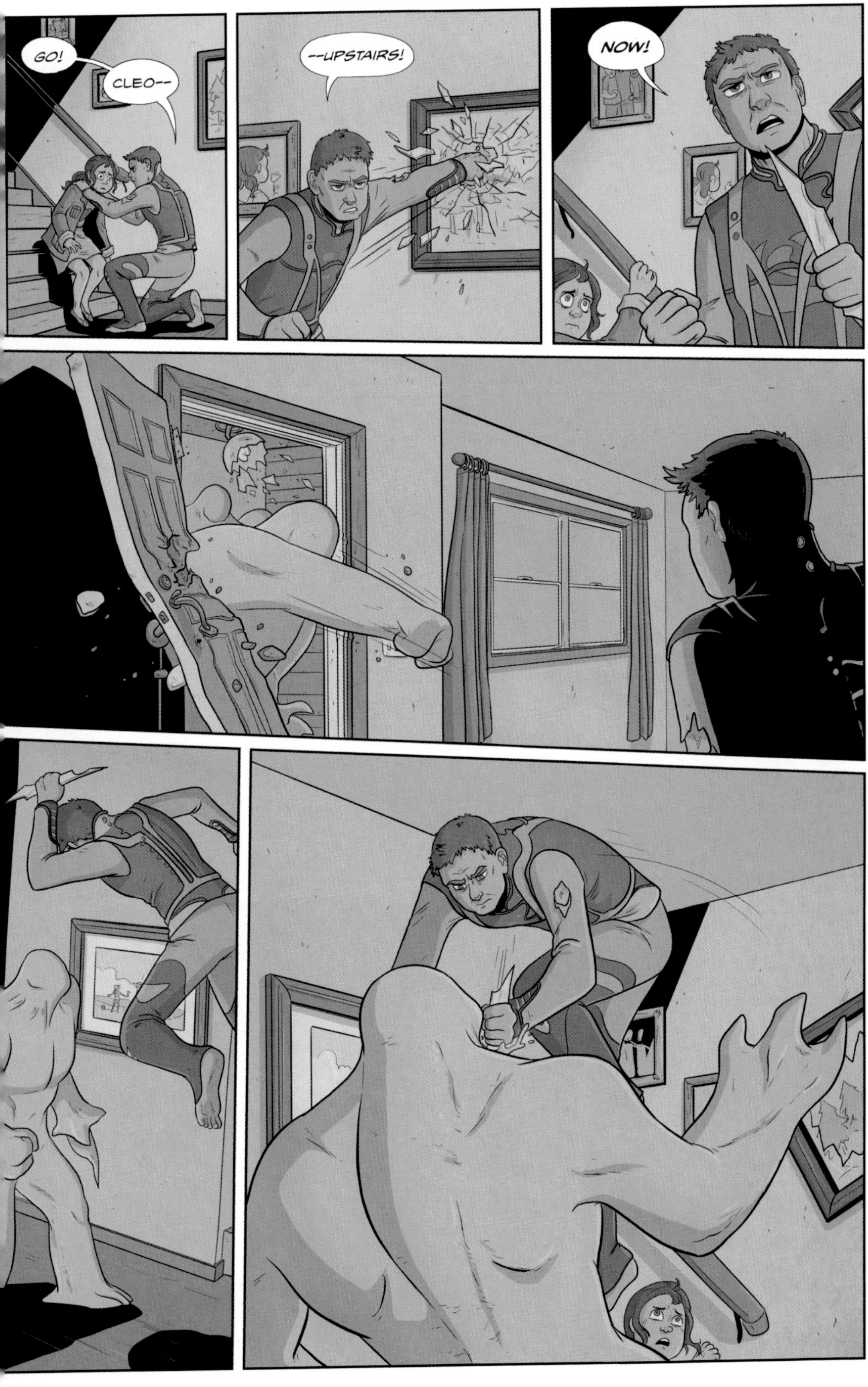
GO!
CLEO--
--UPSTAIRS!
NOW!

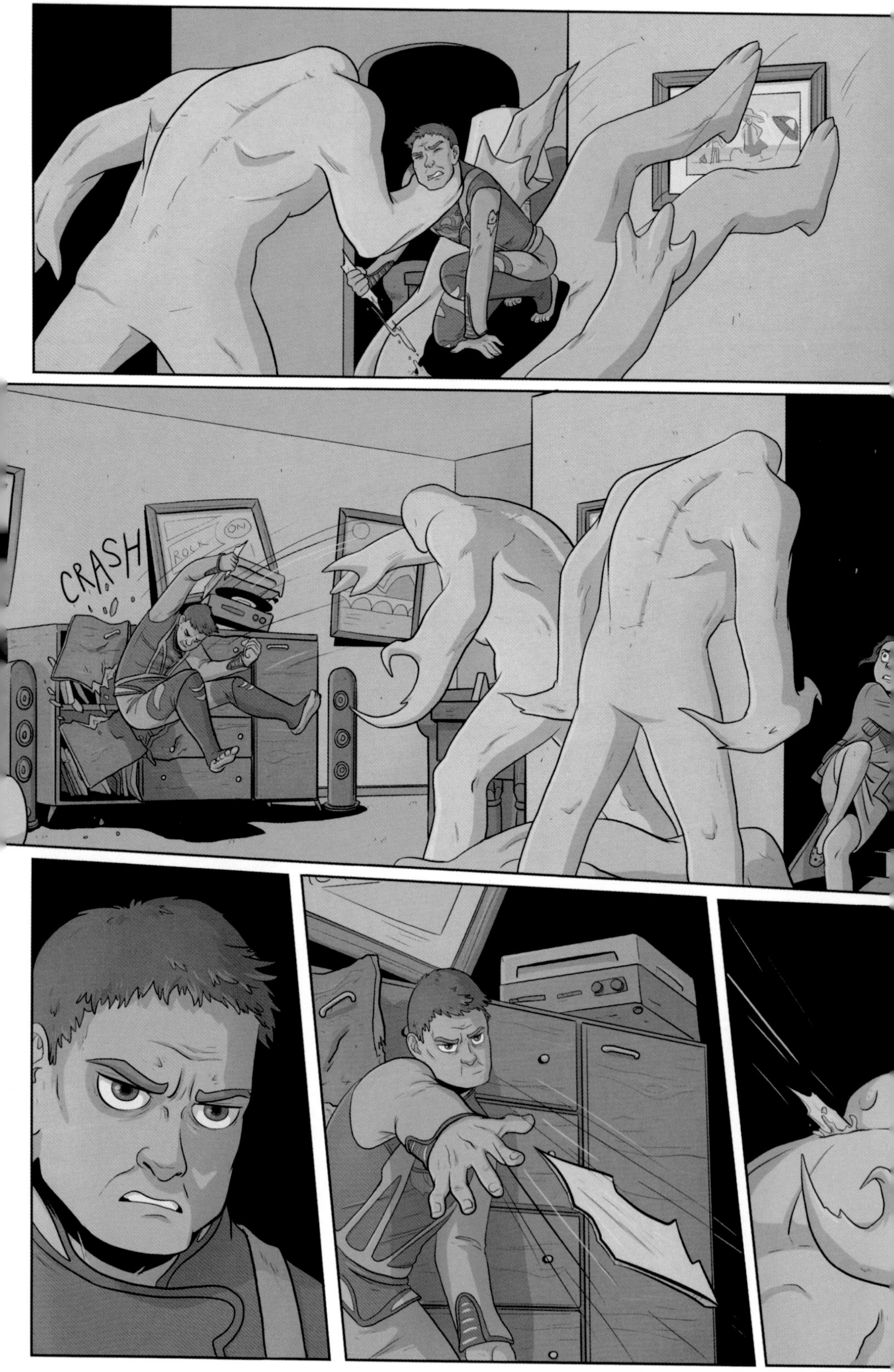
CRASH
ROCK
ON

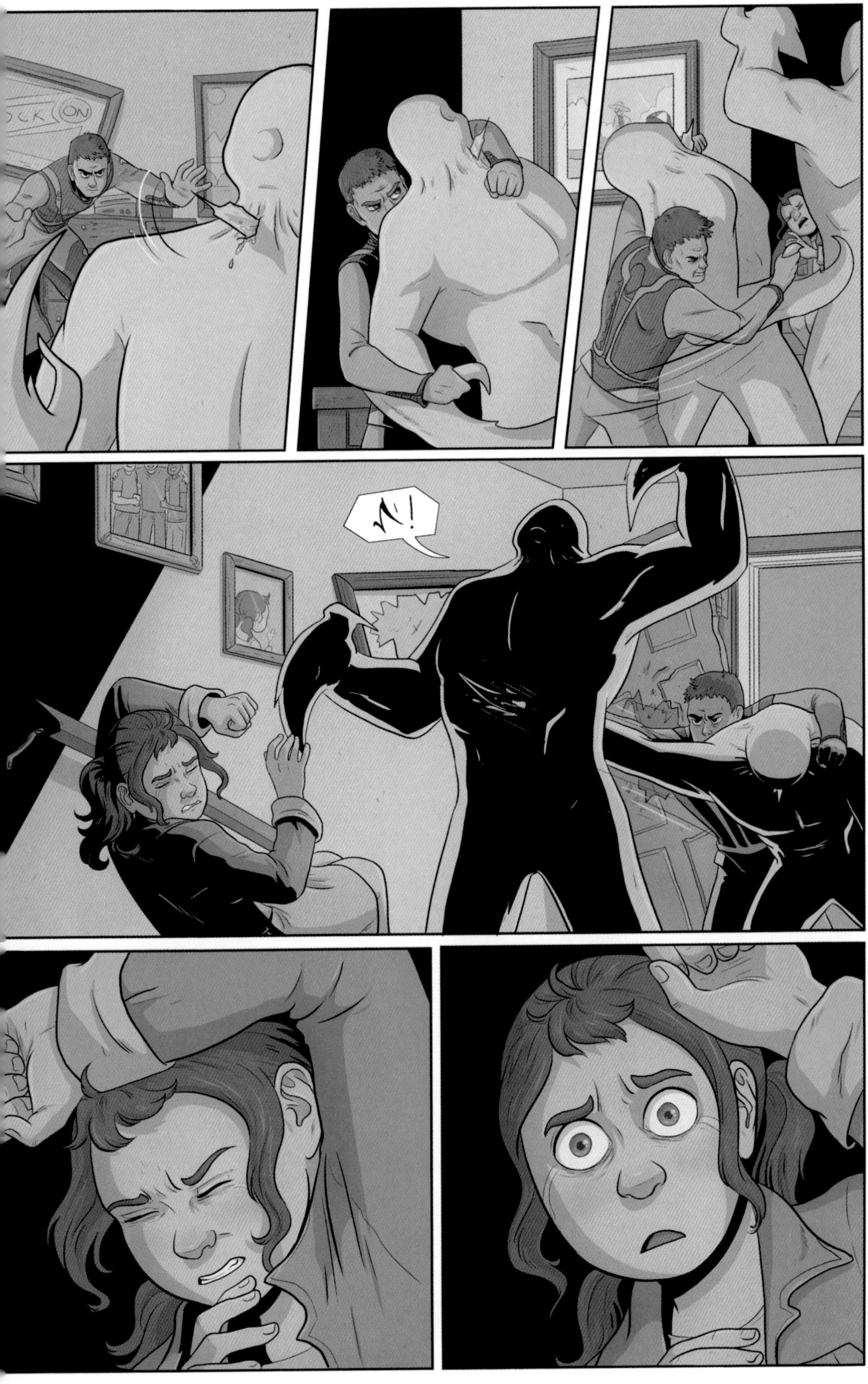

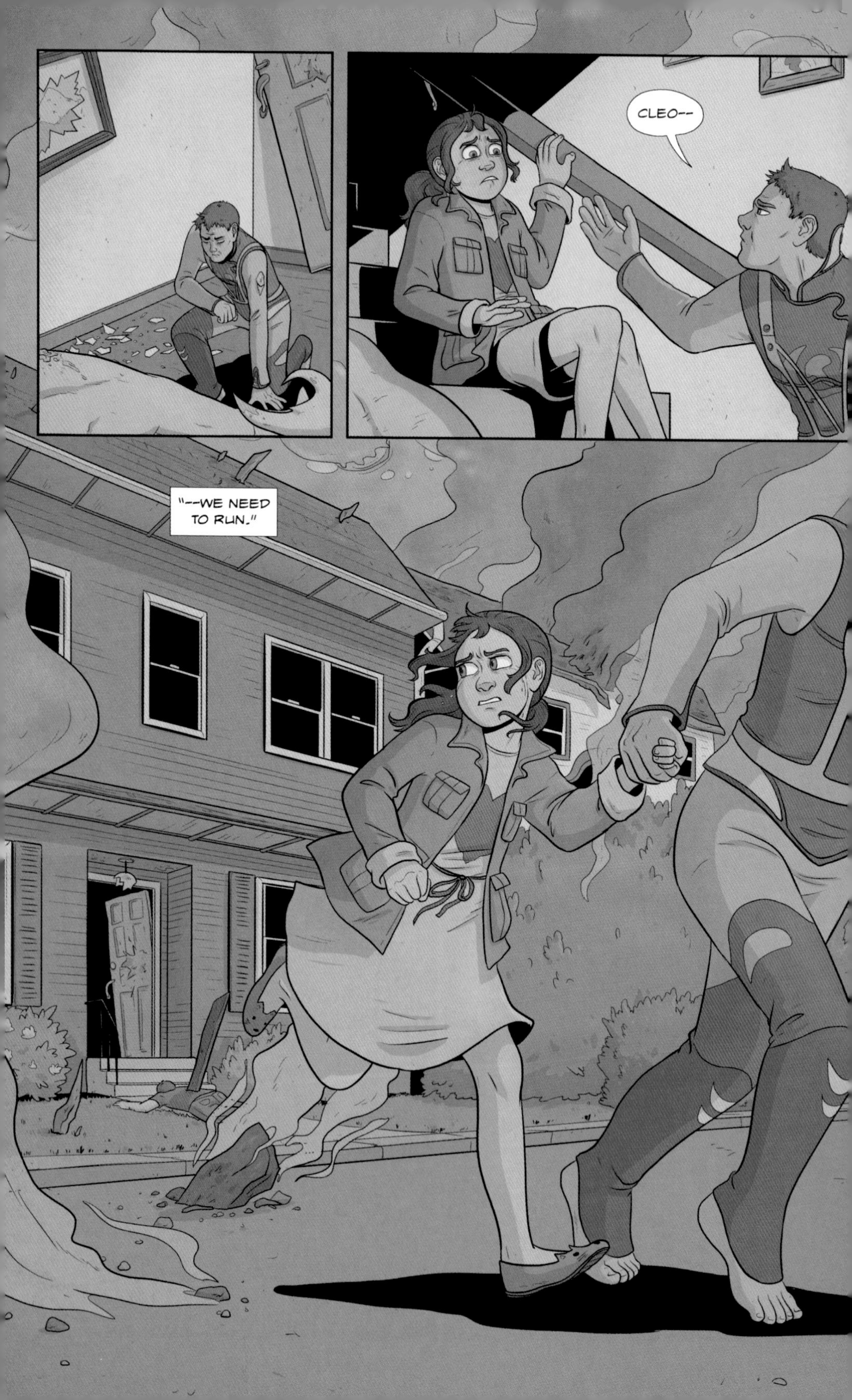
CLEO--
"--WE NEED TO RUN."

TWO

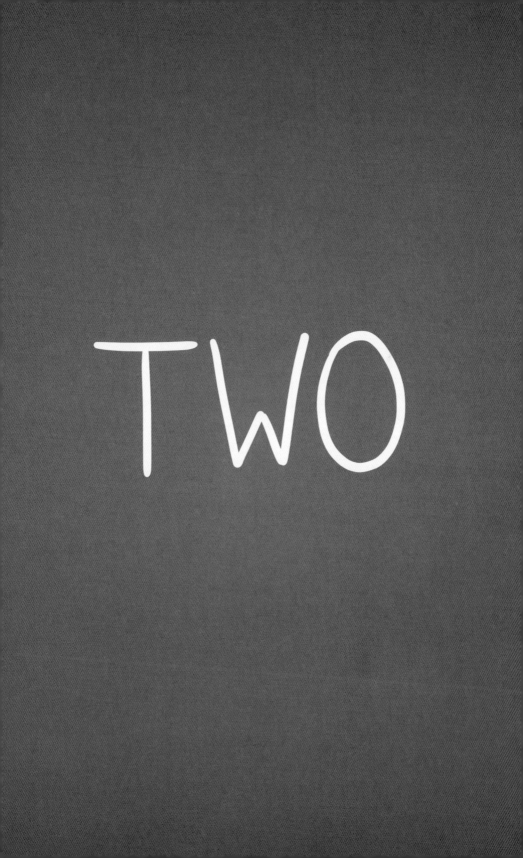

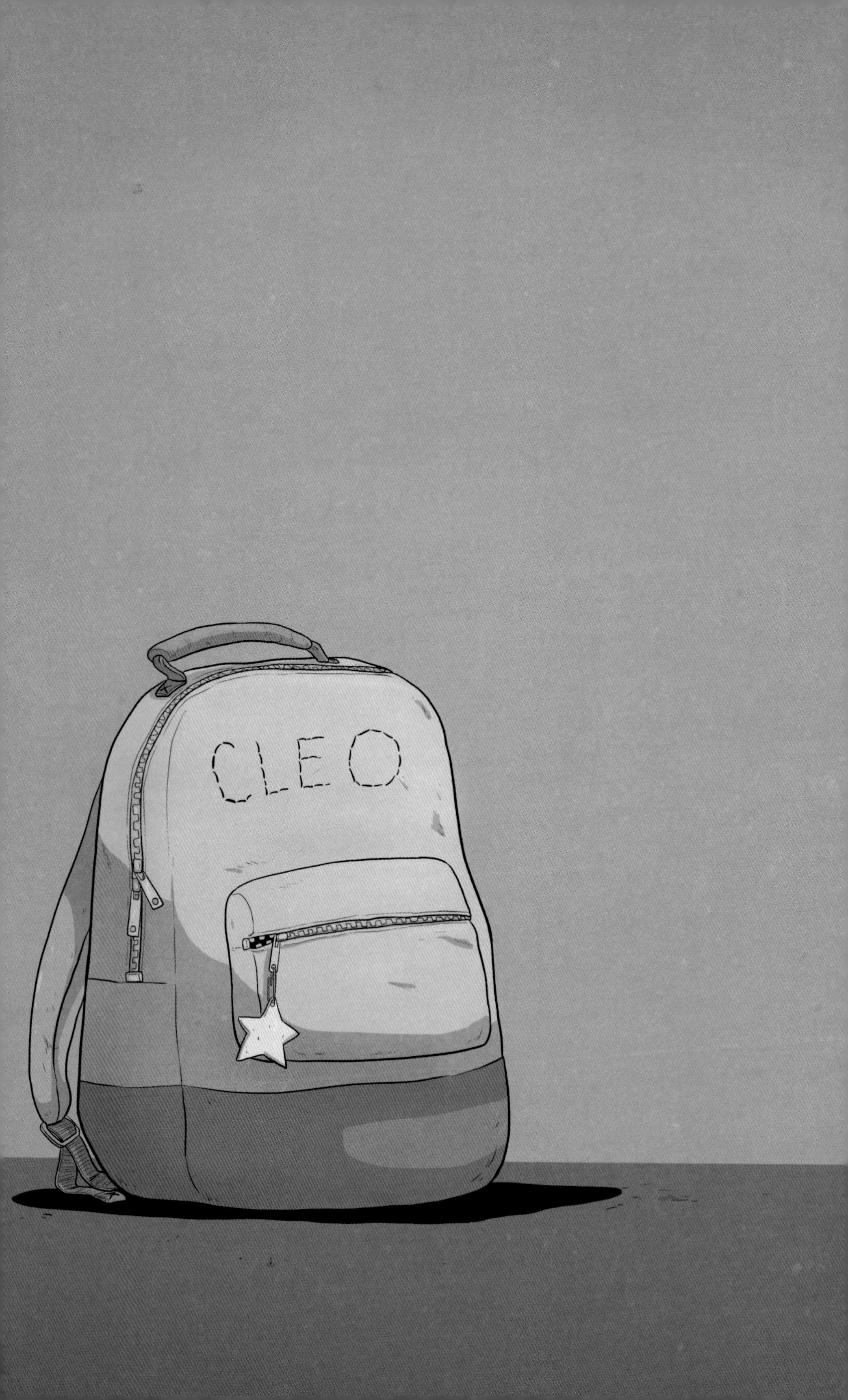
CLEO

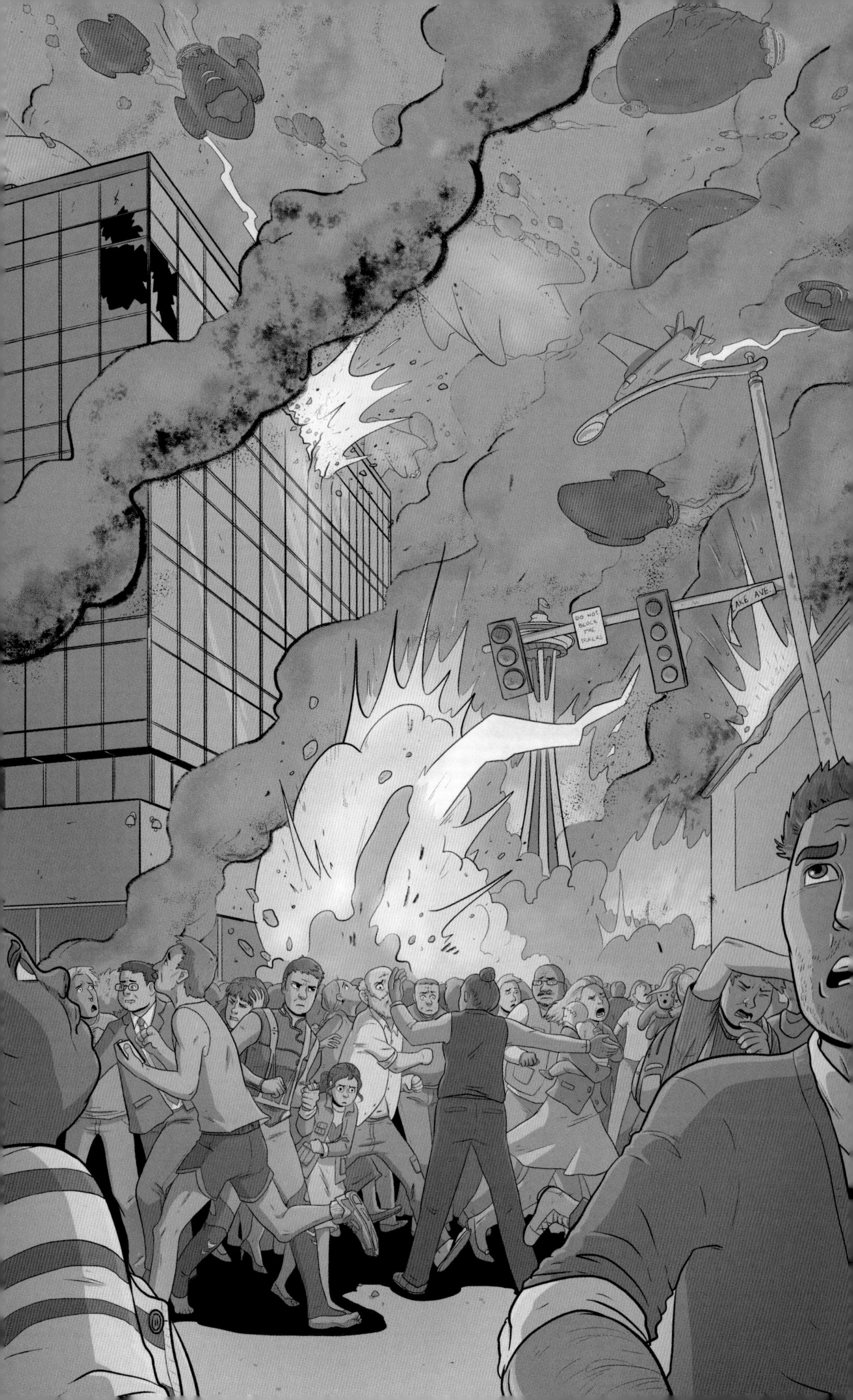
DO NOT BLOCK THE TRACKS
LAKE AVE.

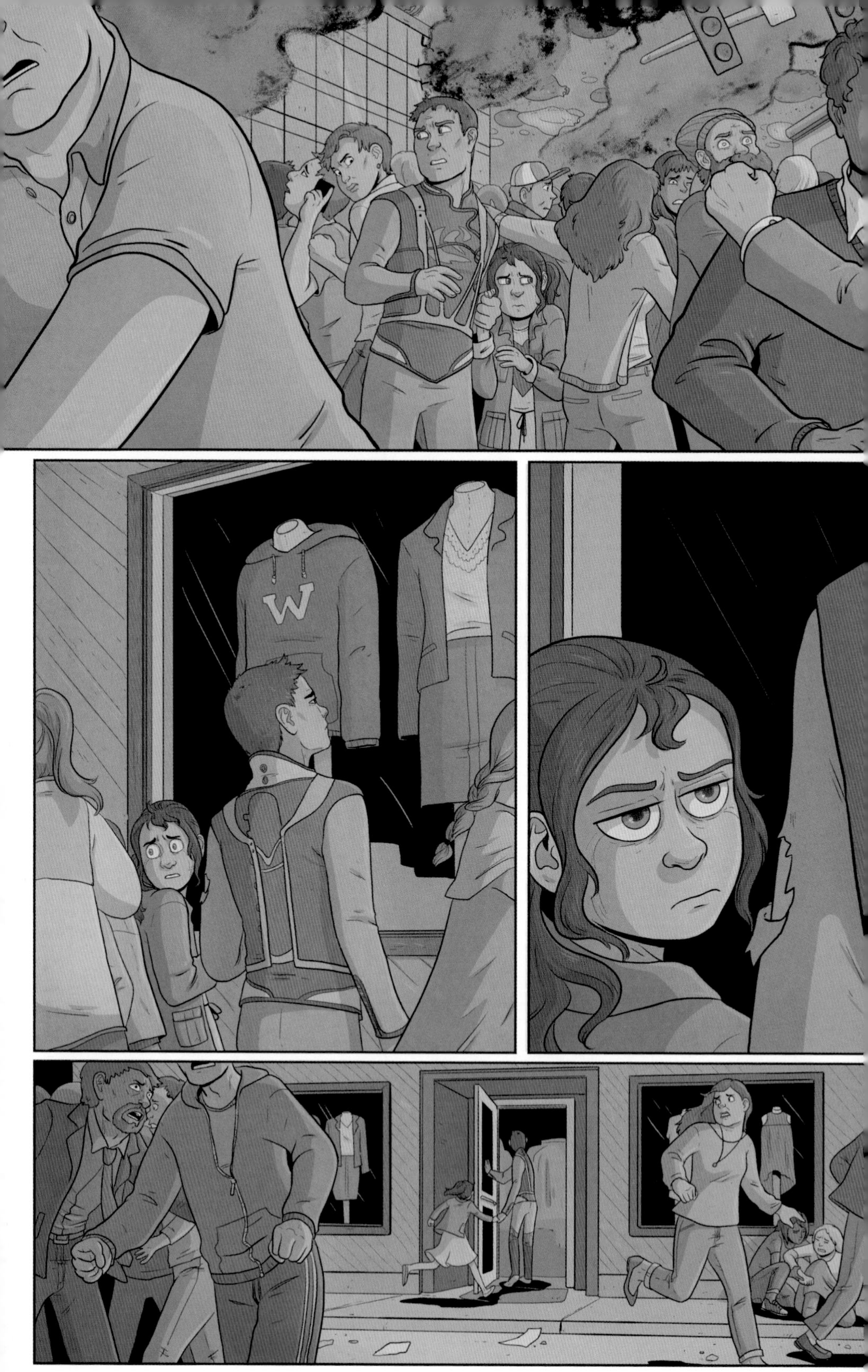
W

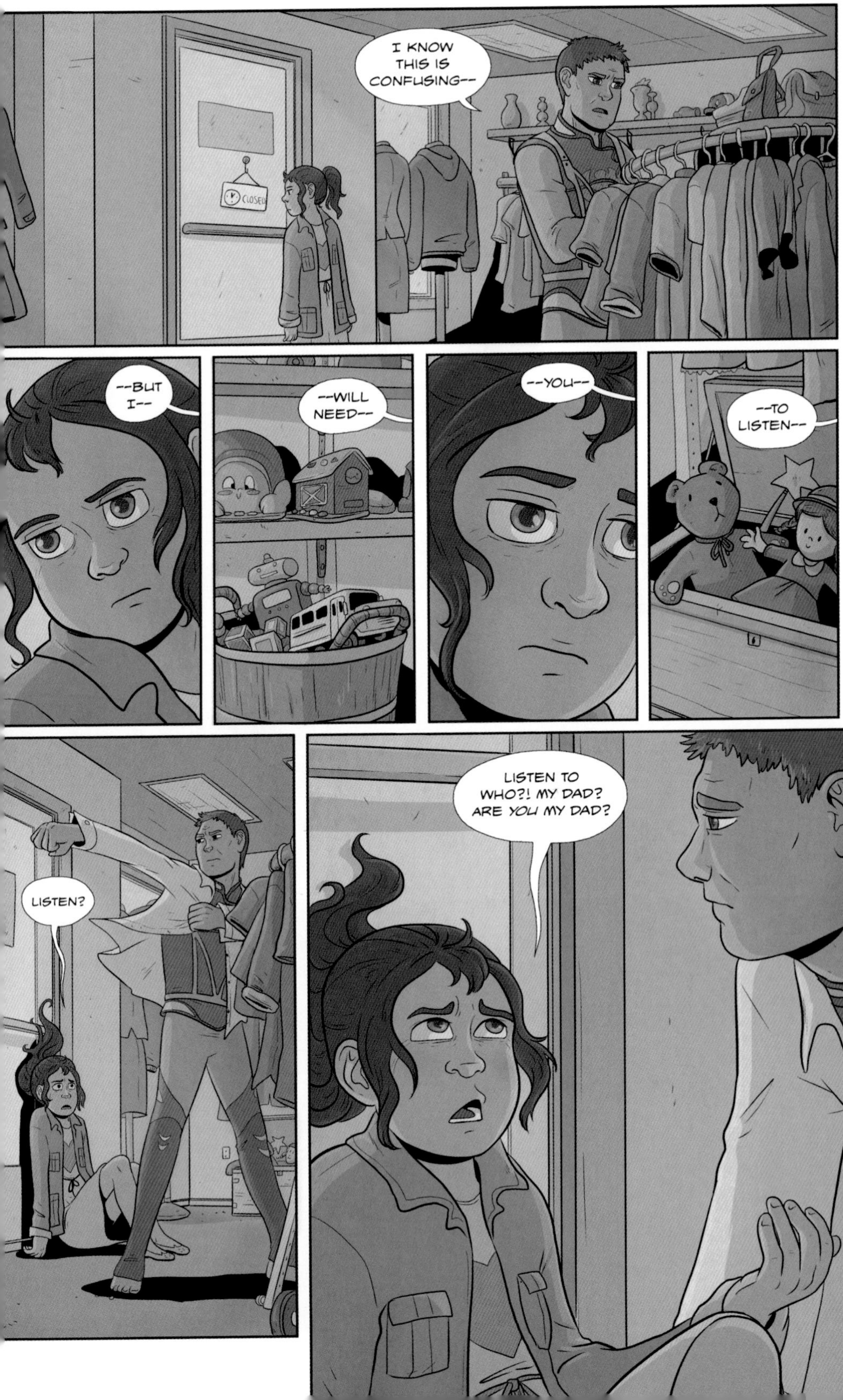
I KNOW THIS IS CONFUSING--
--BUT I--
--WILL NEED--
--YOU--
--TO LISTEN--
LISTEN?
LISTEN TO WHO?! MY DAD? ARE YOU MY DAD?
CLOSED

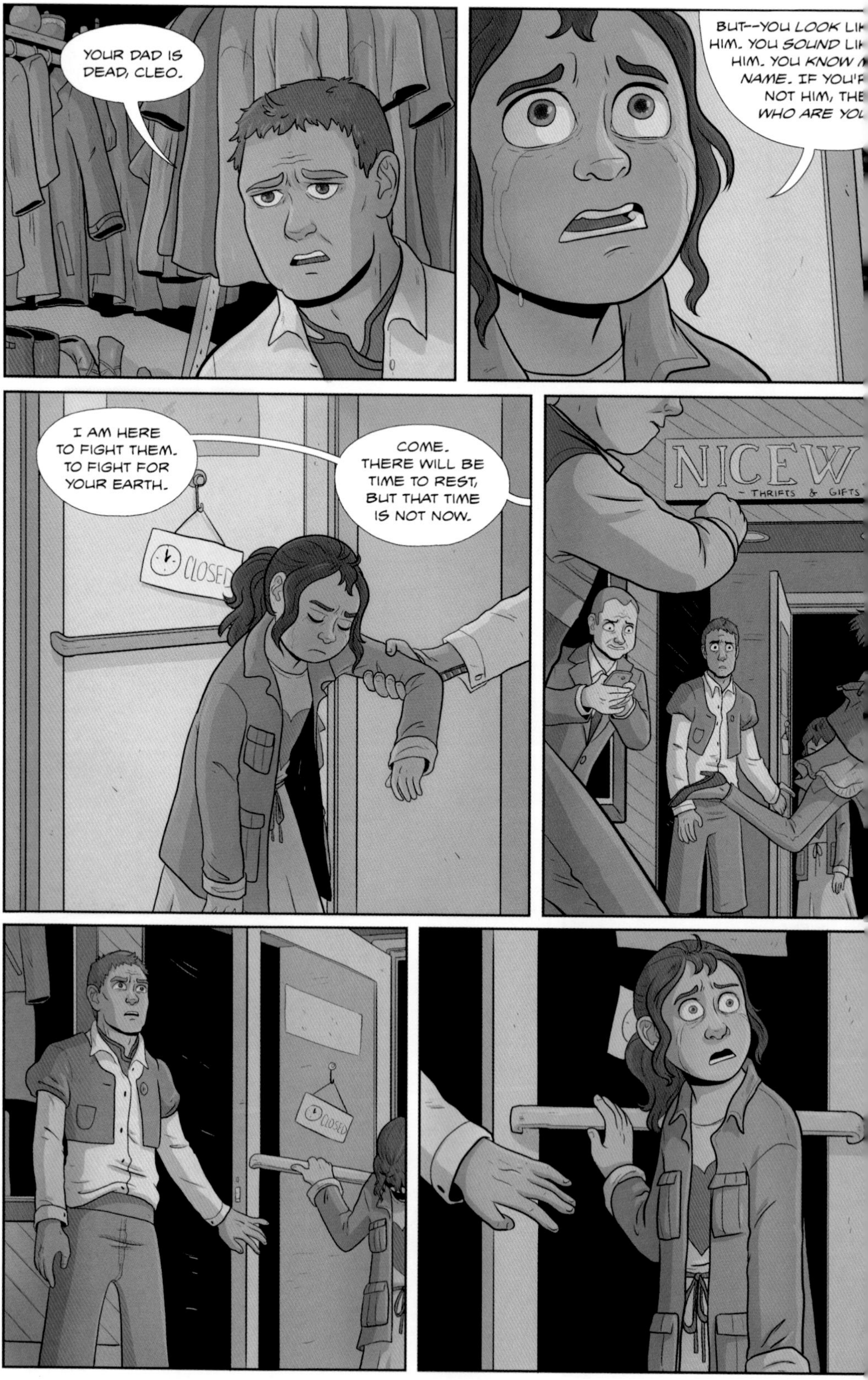
YOUR DAD IS DEAD, CLEO.
I AM HERE TO FIGHT THEM. TO FIGHT FOR YOUR EARTH.
COME. THERE WILL BE TIME TO REST, BUT THAT TIME IS NOT NOW.
NICEW
THRIFTS & GIFTS
CLOSED

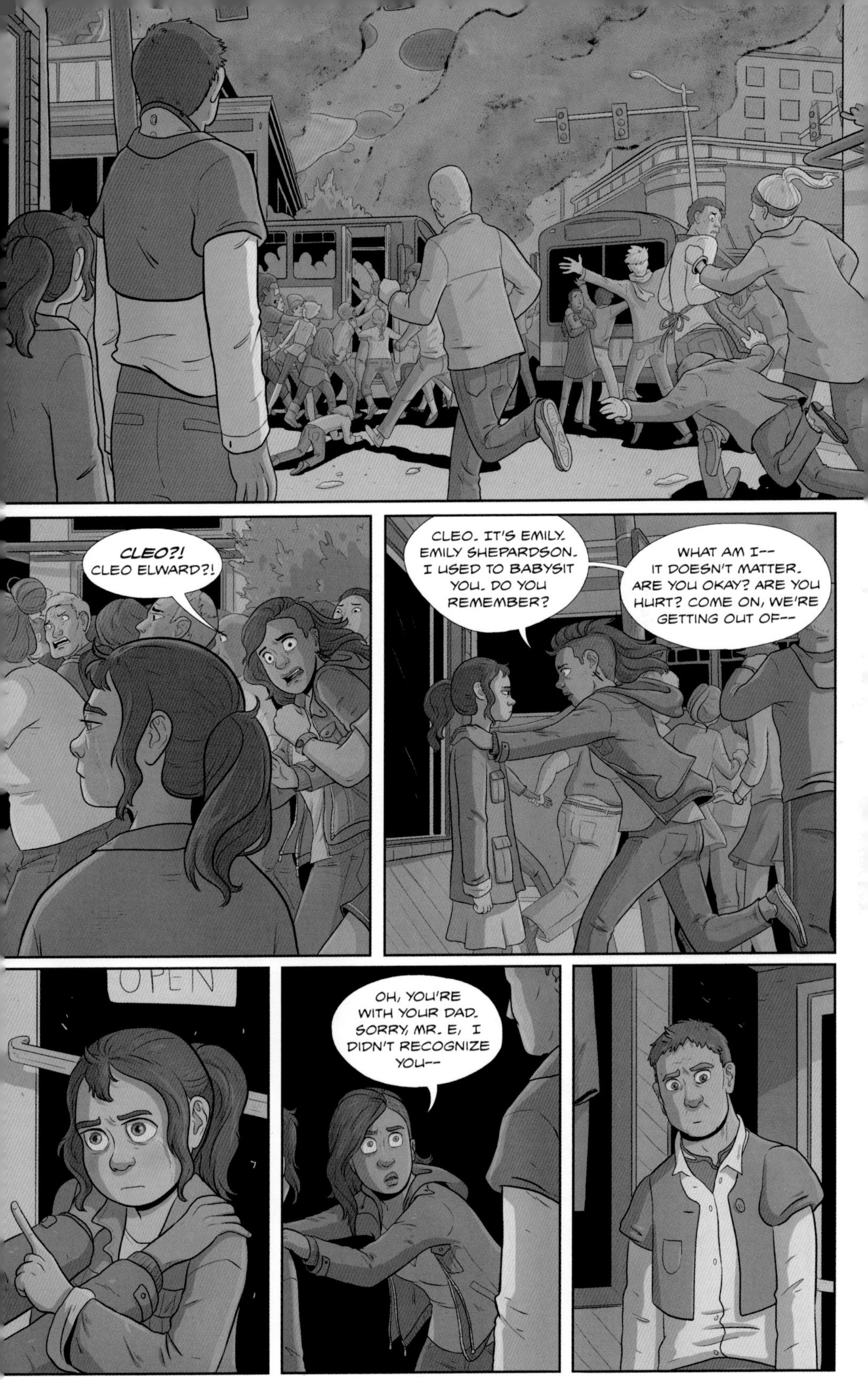
CLEO?! CLEO ELWARD?!
CLEO. IT'S EMILY. EMILY SHEPARDSON. I USED TO BABYSIT YOU. DO YOU REMEMBER?
WHAT AM I-- IT DOESN'T MATTER. ARE YOU OKAY? ARE YOU HURT? COME ON, WE'RE GETTING OUT OF--
OPEN
OH, YOU'RE WITH YOUR DAD. SORRY, MR. E, I DIDN'T RECOGNIZE YOU--

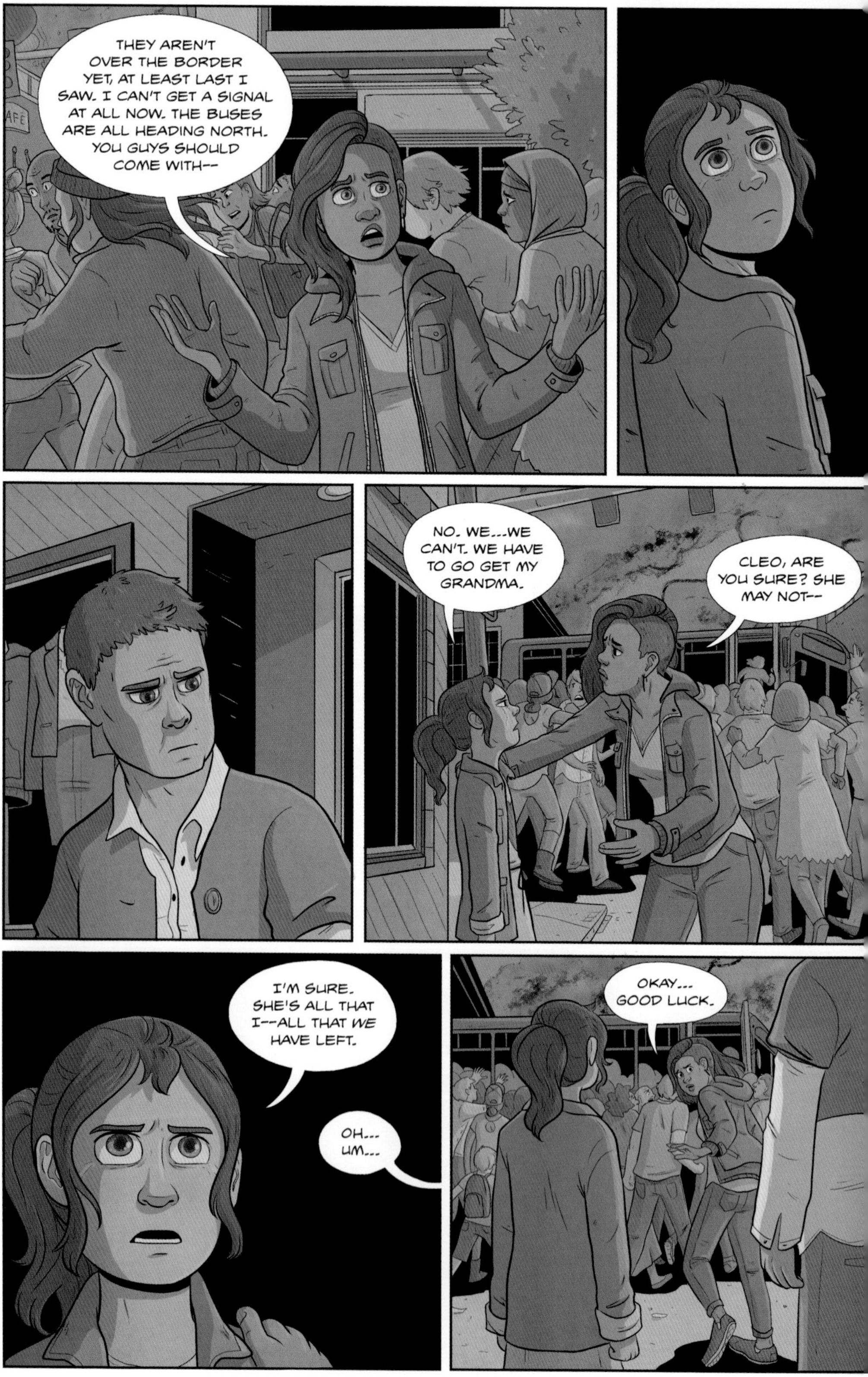
THEY AREN'T OVER THE BORDER YET, AT LEAST LAST I SAW. I CAN'T GET A SIGNAL AT ALL NOW. THE BUSES ARE ALL HEADING NORTH. YOU GUYS SHOULD COME WITH--
AFÉ
NO. WE...WE CAN'T. WE HAVE TO GO GET MY GRANDMA.
CLEO, ARE YOU SURE? SHE MAY NOT--
I'M SURE. SHE'S ALL THAT I--ALL THAT *WE* HAVE LEFT.
OH... UM...
OKAY... GOOD LUCK.

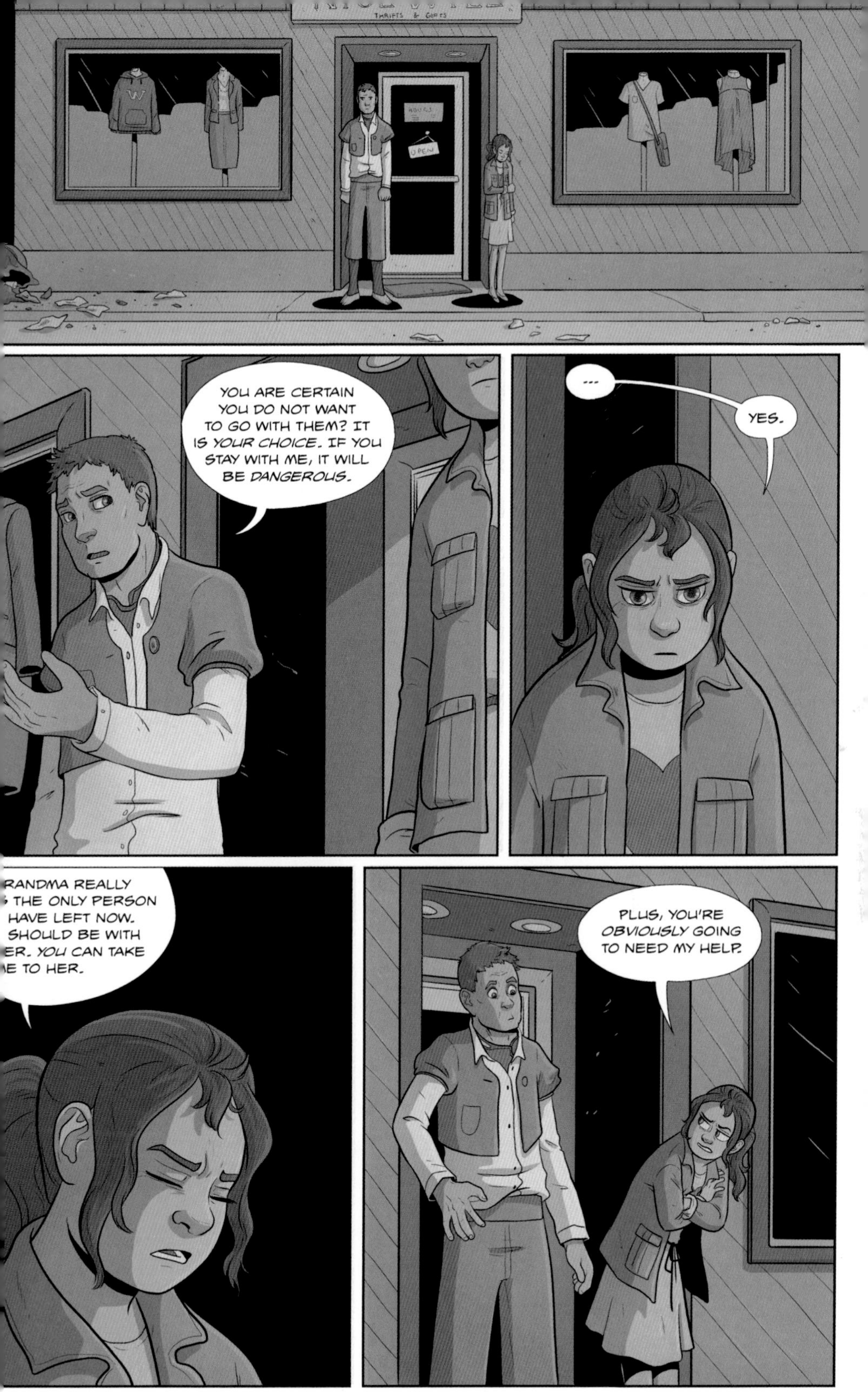
THRIFTS & GIFTS
HOURS
OPEN
YOU ARE CERTAIN YOU DO NOT WANT TO GO WITH THEM? IT IS *YOUR CHOICE*. IF YOU STAY WITH ME, IT WILL BE *DANGEROUS*.
...
YES.
RANDMA REALLY
THE ONLY PERSON
HAVE LEFT NOW.
SHOULD BE WITH
ER. *YOU* CAN TAKE
E TO HER.
PLUS, YOU'RE *OBVIOUSLY* GOING TO NEED MY HELP.

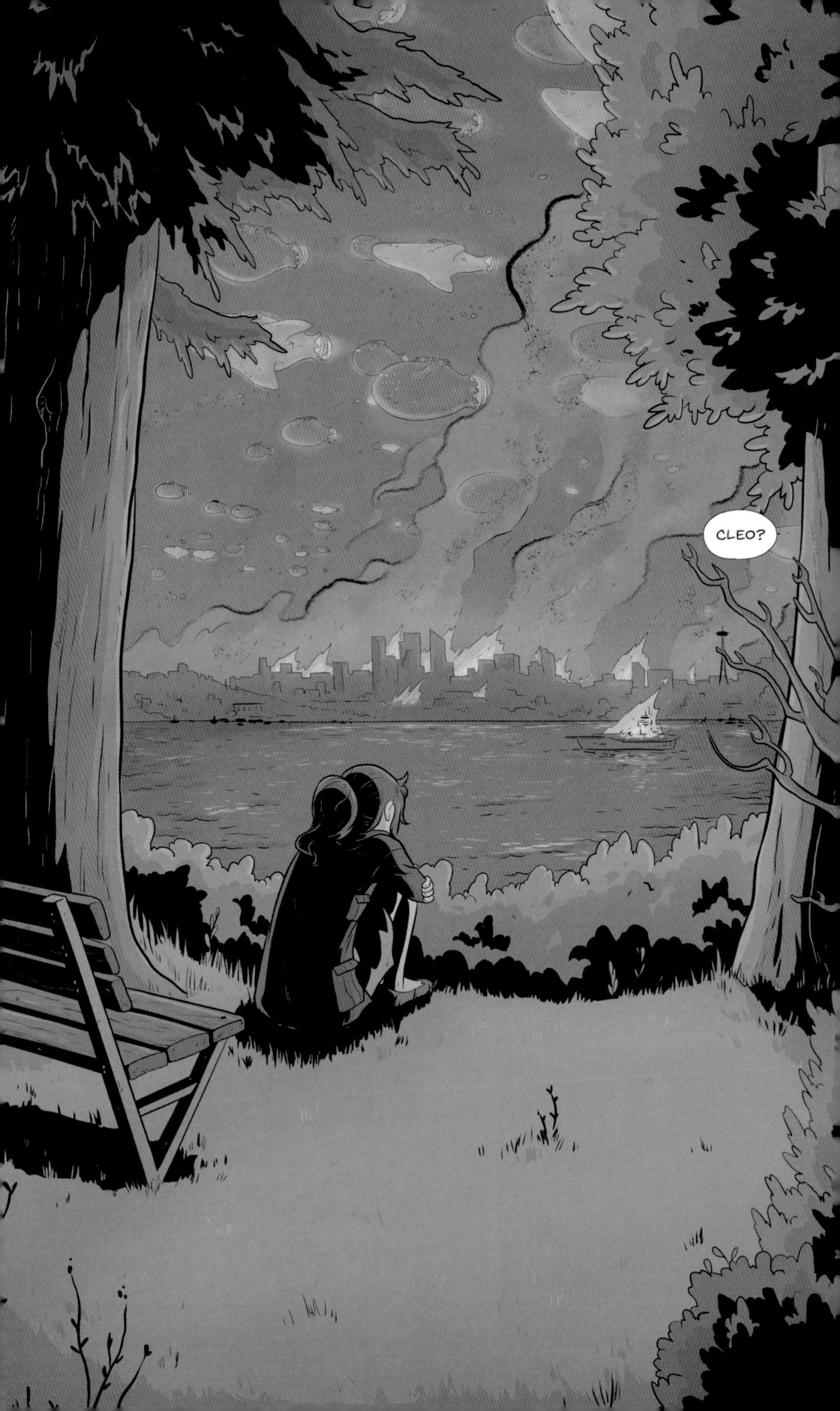
CLEO?

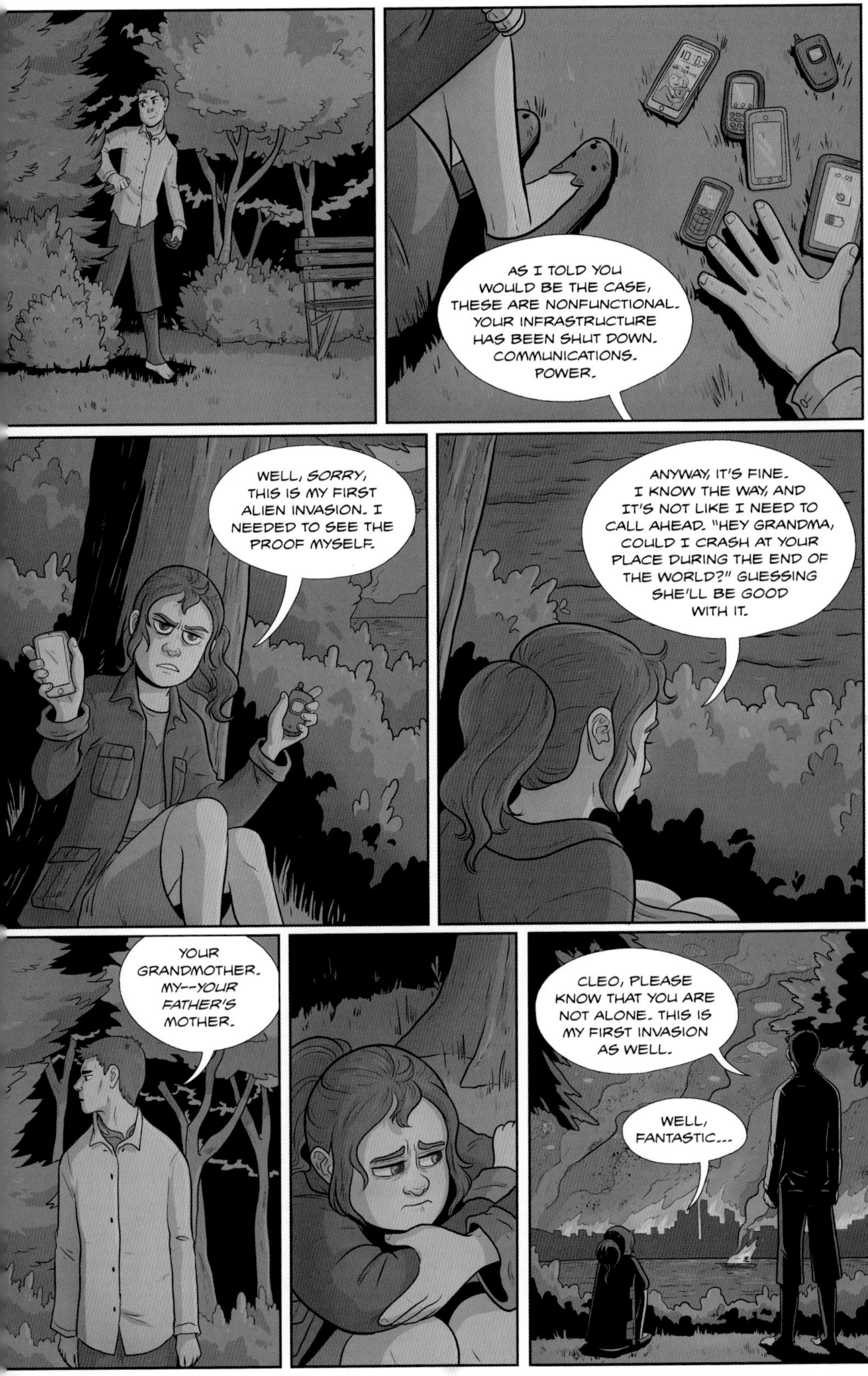
AS I TOLD YOU WOULD BE THE CASE, THESE ARE NONFUNCTIONAL. YOUR INFRASTRUCTURE HAS BEEN SHUT DOWN. COMMUNICATIONS. POWER.
WELL, *SORRY*, THIS IS MY FIRST ALIEN INVASION. I NEEDED TO SEE THE PROOF MYSELF.
ANYWAY, IT'S FINE. I KNOW THE WAY, AND IT'S NOT LIKE I NEED TO CALL AHEAD. "HEY GRANDMA, COULD I CRASH AT YOUR PLACE DURING THE END OF THE WORLD?" GUESSING SHE'LL BE GOOD WITH IT.
YOUR GRANDMOTHER. *MY--YOUR FATHER'S* MOTHER.
CLEO, PLEASE KNOW THAT YOU ARE NOT ALONE. THIS IS MY FIRST INVASION AS WELL.
WELL, FANTASTIC...

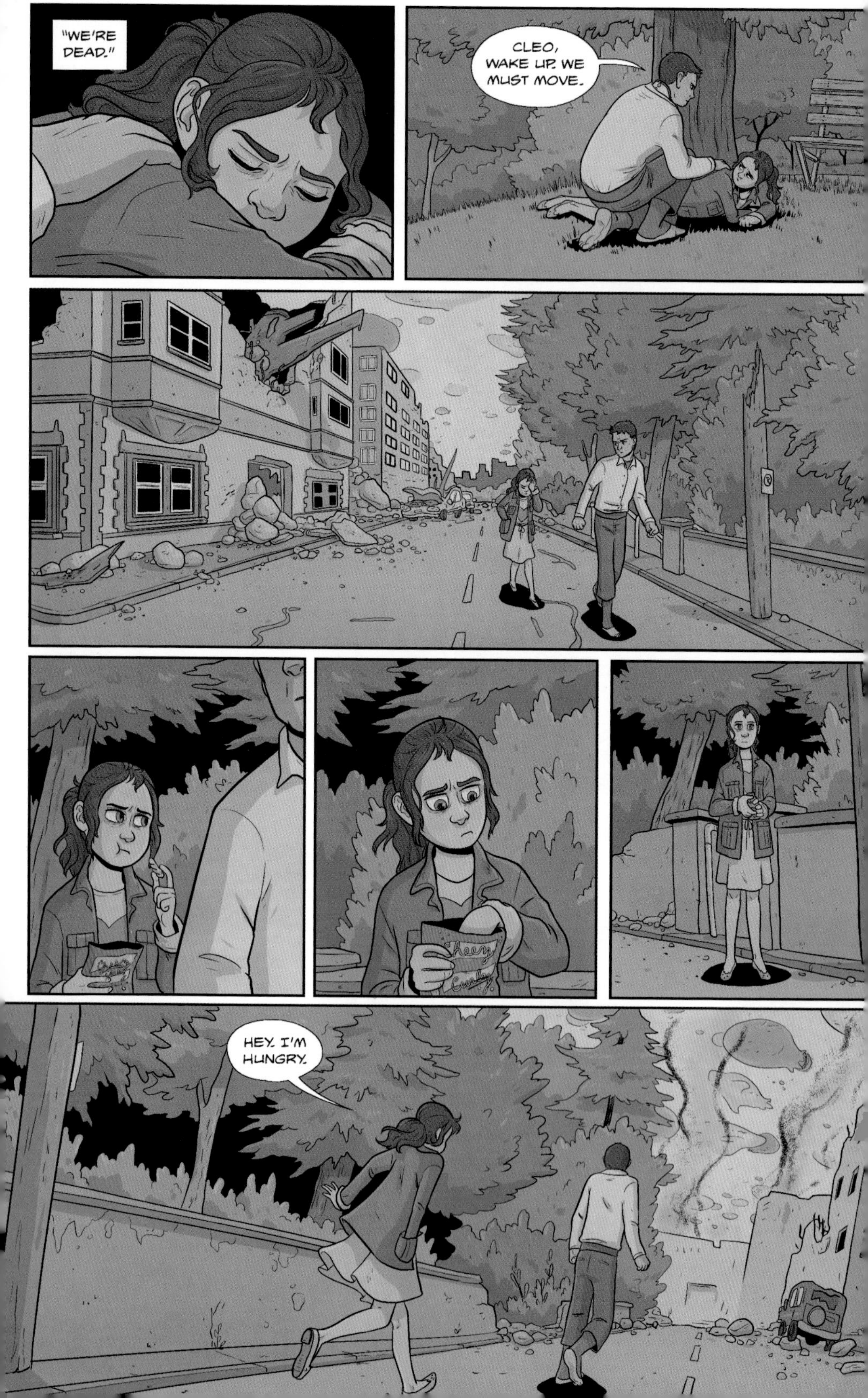
"WE'RE DEAD."
CLEO, WAKE UP. WE MUST MOVE.
HEY. I'M HUNGRY.

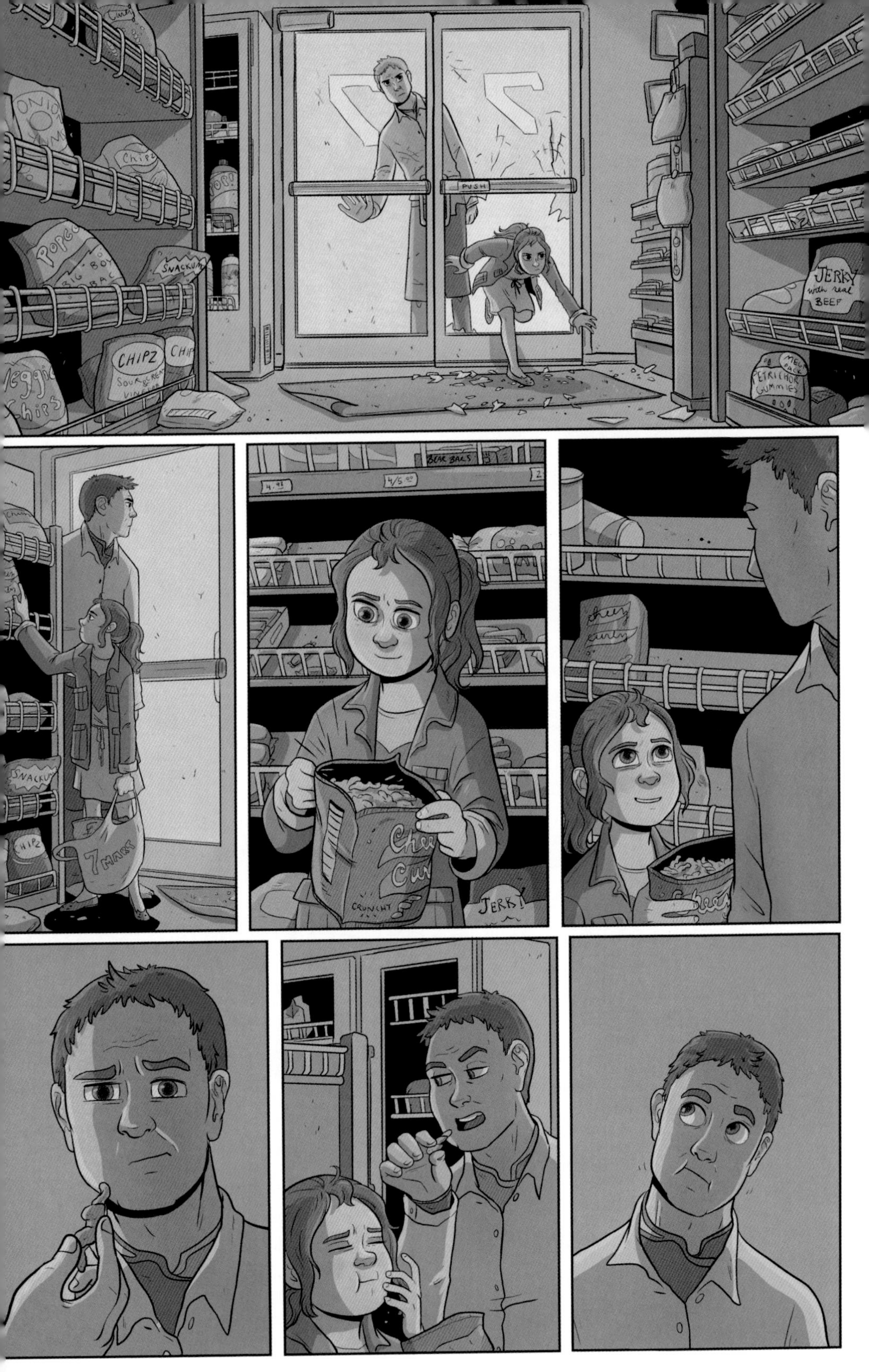
PUSH
CHIPZ
JERKY with real BEEF
PETRICHOR GUMMIES
7 MART
BEAR BARS
4/5.00
CRUNCHY
JERKY!

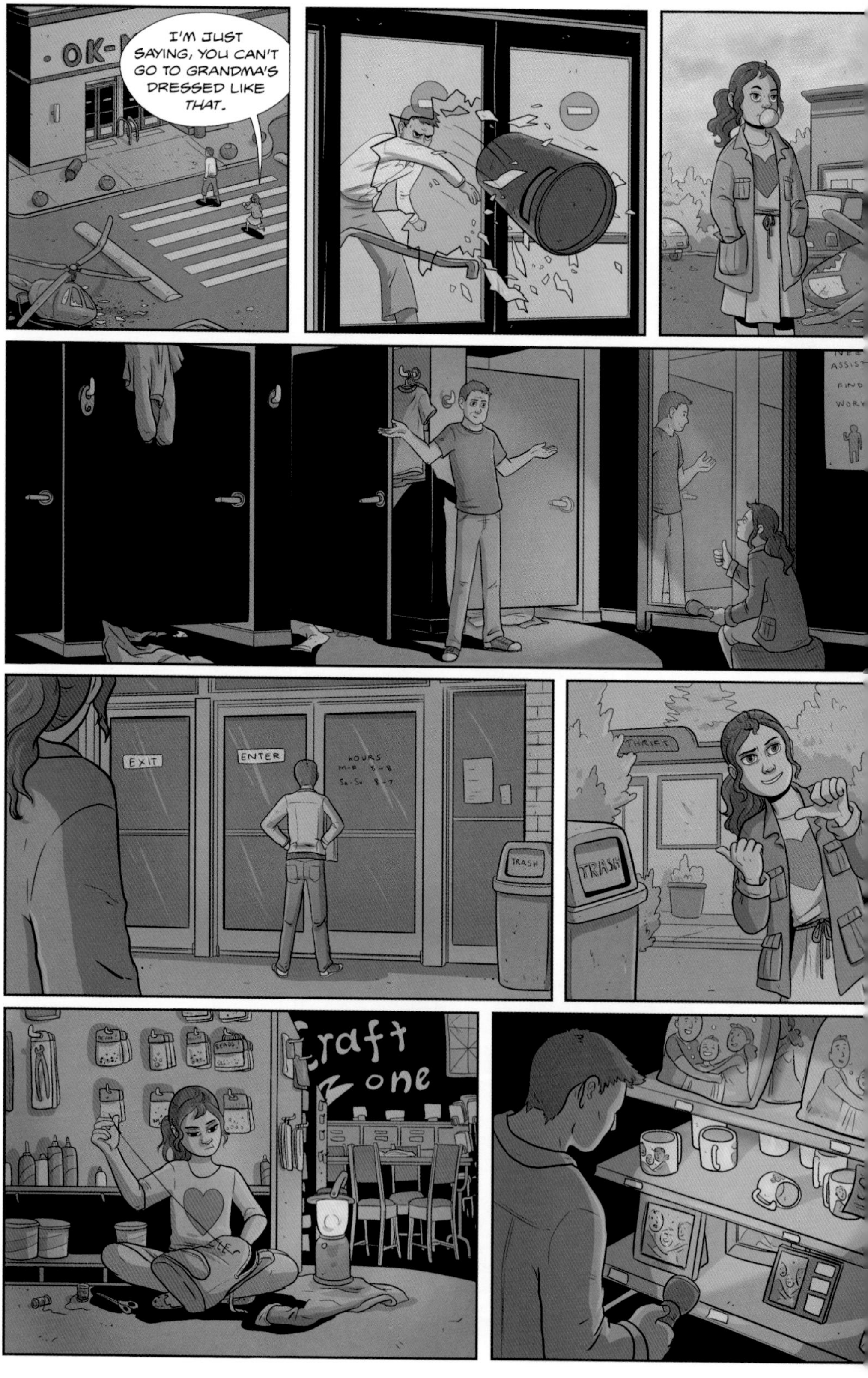
I'M JUST SAYING, YOU CAN'T GO TO GRANDMA'S DRESSED LIKE THAT.
EXIT
ENTER
TRASH
TRASH
Craft Zone

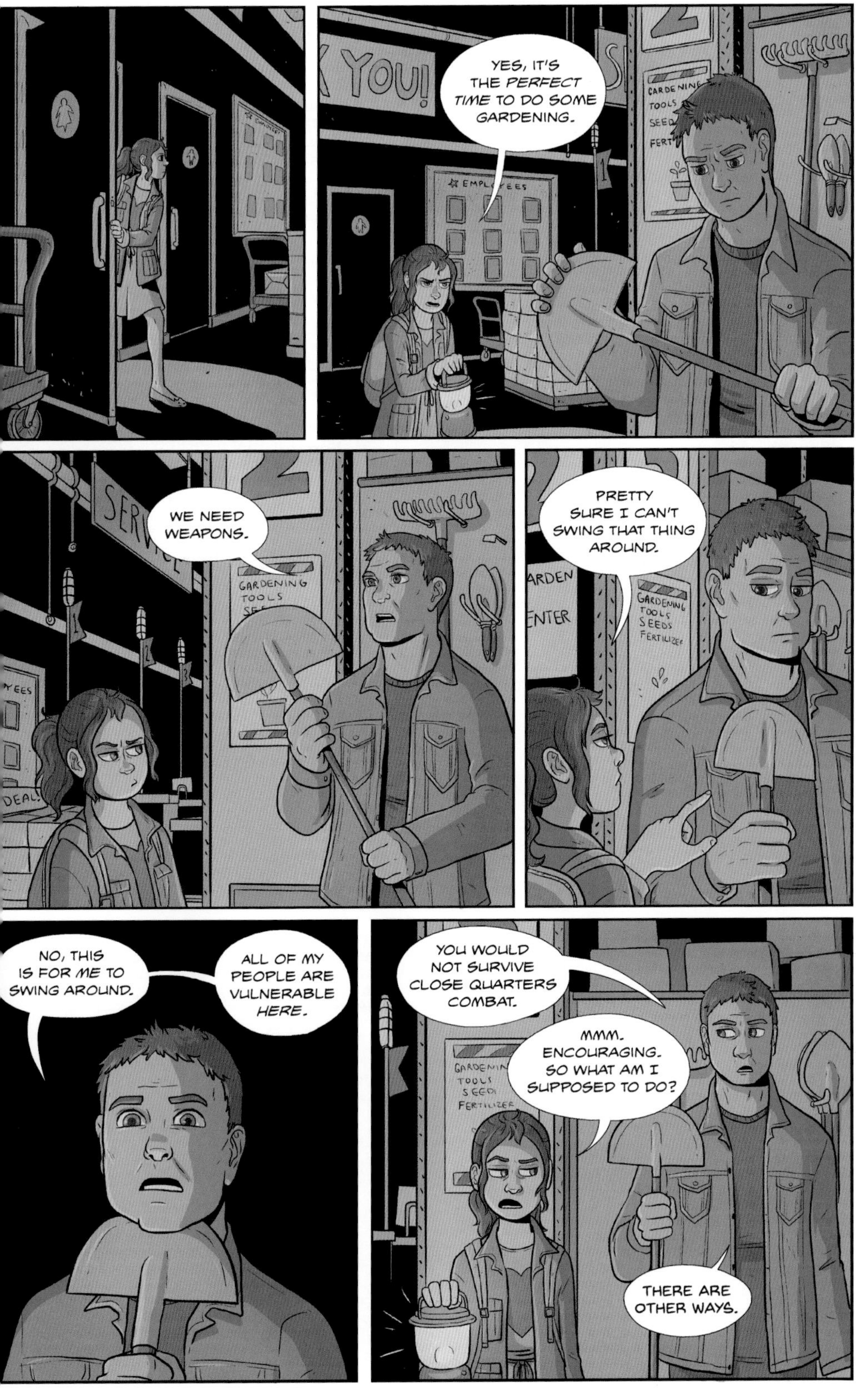

YOU!
YES, IT'S THE *PERFECT* *TIME* TO DO SOME GARDENING.
GARDENING TOOLS SEED FERT
EMPLOYEES
SERVICE
WE NEED WEAPONS.
GARDENING TOOLS
PRETTY SURE I CAN'T SWING THAT THING AROUND.
ARDEN ENTER
GARDENING TOOLS SEEDS FERTILIZER
DEAL!
NO, THIS IS FOR *ME* TO SWING AROUND.
ALL OF MY PEOPLE ARE VULNERABLE *HERE*.
YOU WOULD NOT SURVIVE CLOSE QUARTERS COMBAT.
MMM. ENCOURAGING. SO WHAT AM I SUPPOSED TO DO?
GARDENING TOOLS SEEDS FERTILIZER
THERE ARE OTHER WAYS.

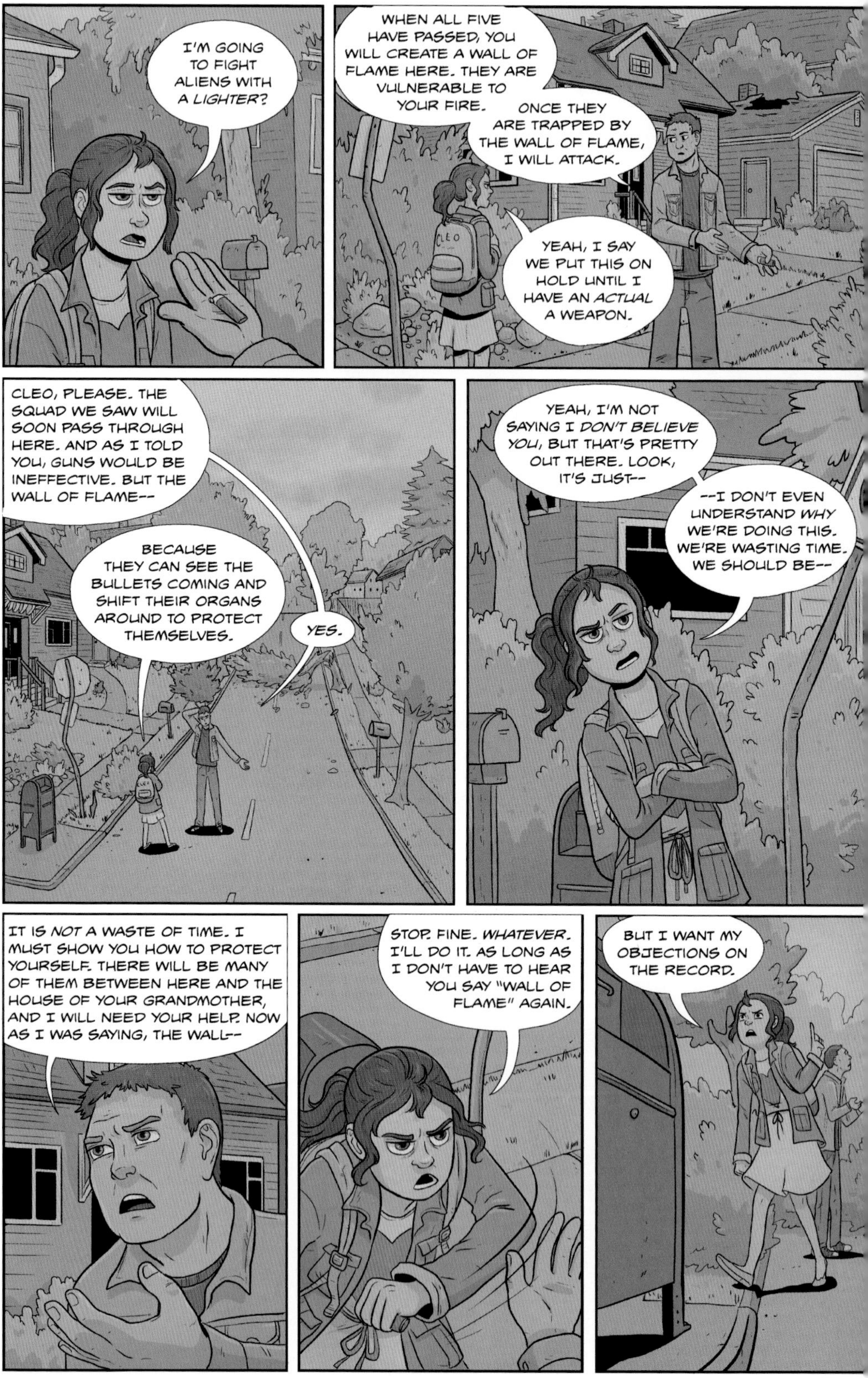
I'M GOING TO FIGHT ALIENS WITH A *LIGHTER*?
WHEN ALL FIVE HAVE PASSED, YOU WILL CREATE A WALL OF FLAME HERE. THEY ARE VULNERABLE TO YOUR FIRE.
ONCE THEY ARE TRAPPED BY THE WALL OF FLAME, I WILL ATTACK.
CLEO
YEAH, I SAY WE PUT THIS ON HOLD UNTIL I HAVE AN *ACTUAL* A WEAPON.
CLEO, PLEASE. THE SQUAD WE SAW WILL SOON PASS THROUGH HERE. AND AS I TOLD YOU, GUNS WOULD BE INEFFECTIVE. BUT THE WALL OF FLAME--
BECAUSE THEY CAN SEE THE BULLETS COMING AND SHIFT THEIR ORGANS AROUND TO PROTECT THEMSELVES.
YES.
YEAH, I'M NOT SAYING I *DON'T BELIEVE YOU*, BUT THAT'S PRETTY OUT THERE. LOOK, IT'S JUST--
--I DON'T EVEN UNDERSTAND *WHY* WE'RE DOING THIS. WE'RE WASTING TIME. WE SHOULD BE--
IT IS *NOT* A WASTE OF TIME. I MUST SHOW YOU HOW TO PROTECT YOURSELF. THERE WILL BE MANY OF THEM BETWEEN HERE AND THE HOUSE OF YOUR GRANDMOTHER, AND I WILL NEED YOUR HELP. NOW AS I WAS SAYING, THE WALL--
STOP. FINE. *WHATEVER*. I'LL DO IT. AS LONG AS I DON'T HAVE TO HEAR YOU SAY "WALL OF FLAME" AGAIN.
BUT I WANT MY OBJECTIONS ON THE RECORD.

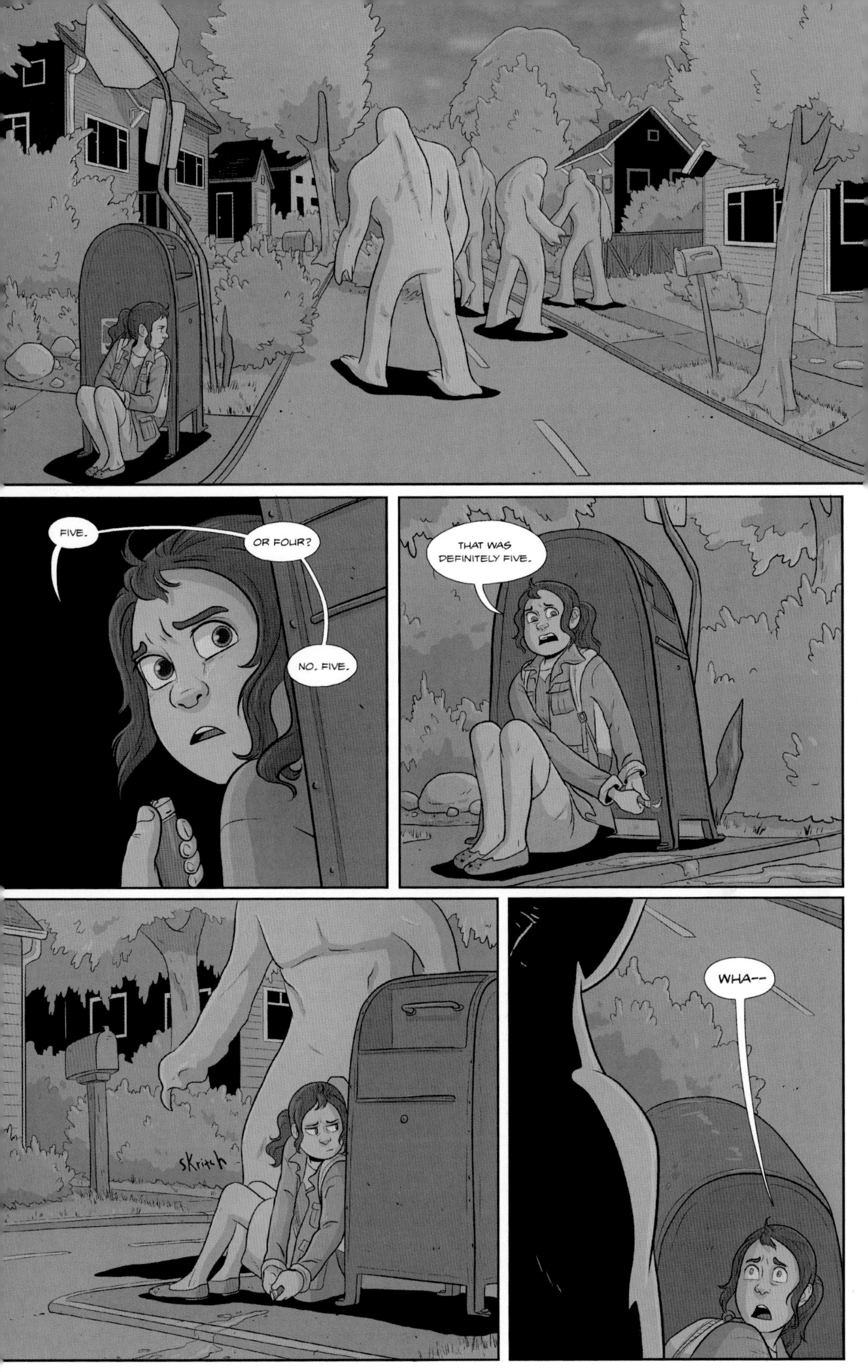
FIVE.
OR FOUR?
NO. FIVE.
THAT WAS DEFINITELY FIVE.
sKritch
WHA--

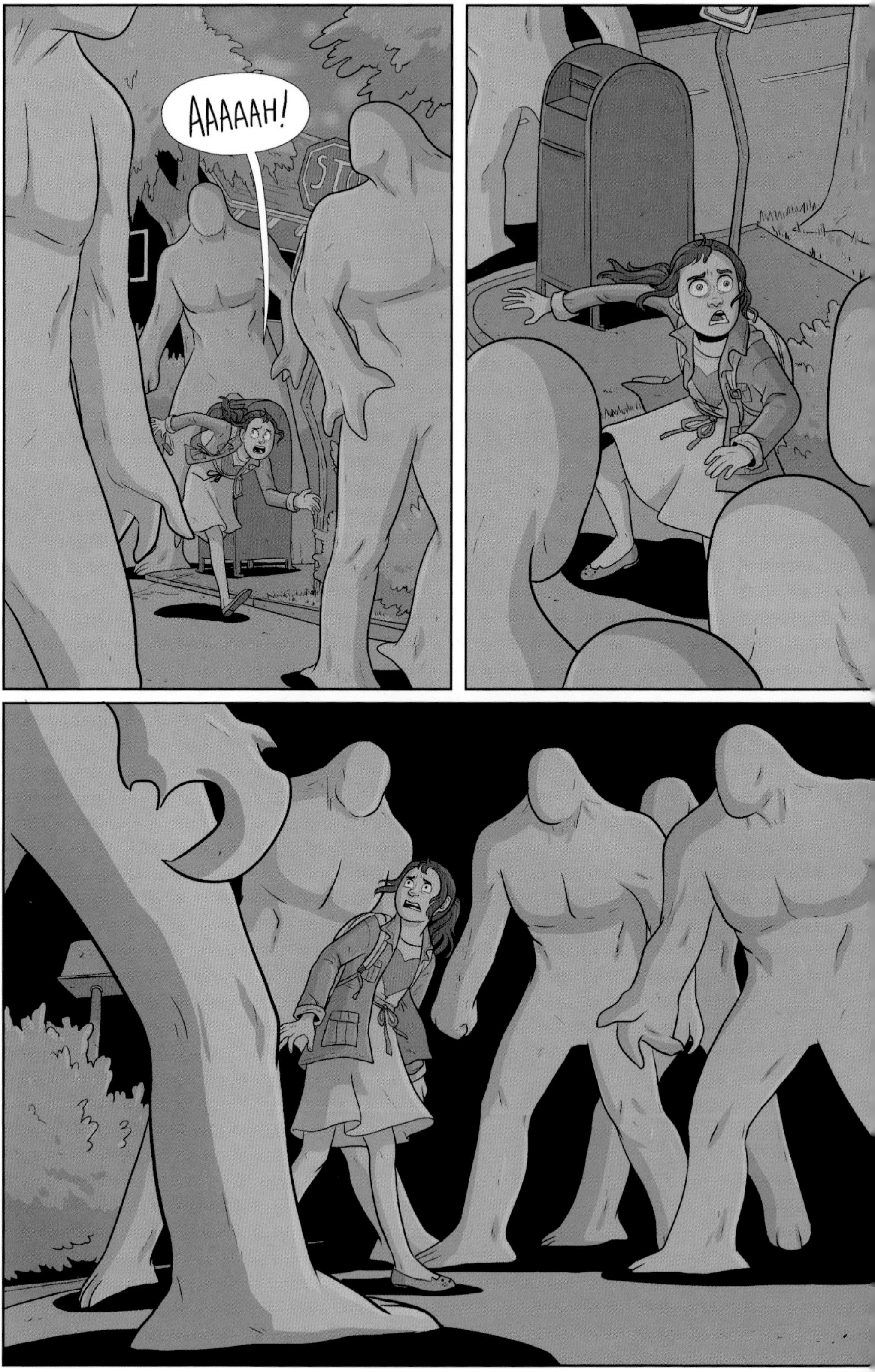
AAAAAH!
STO

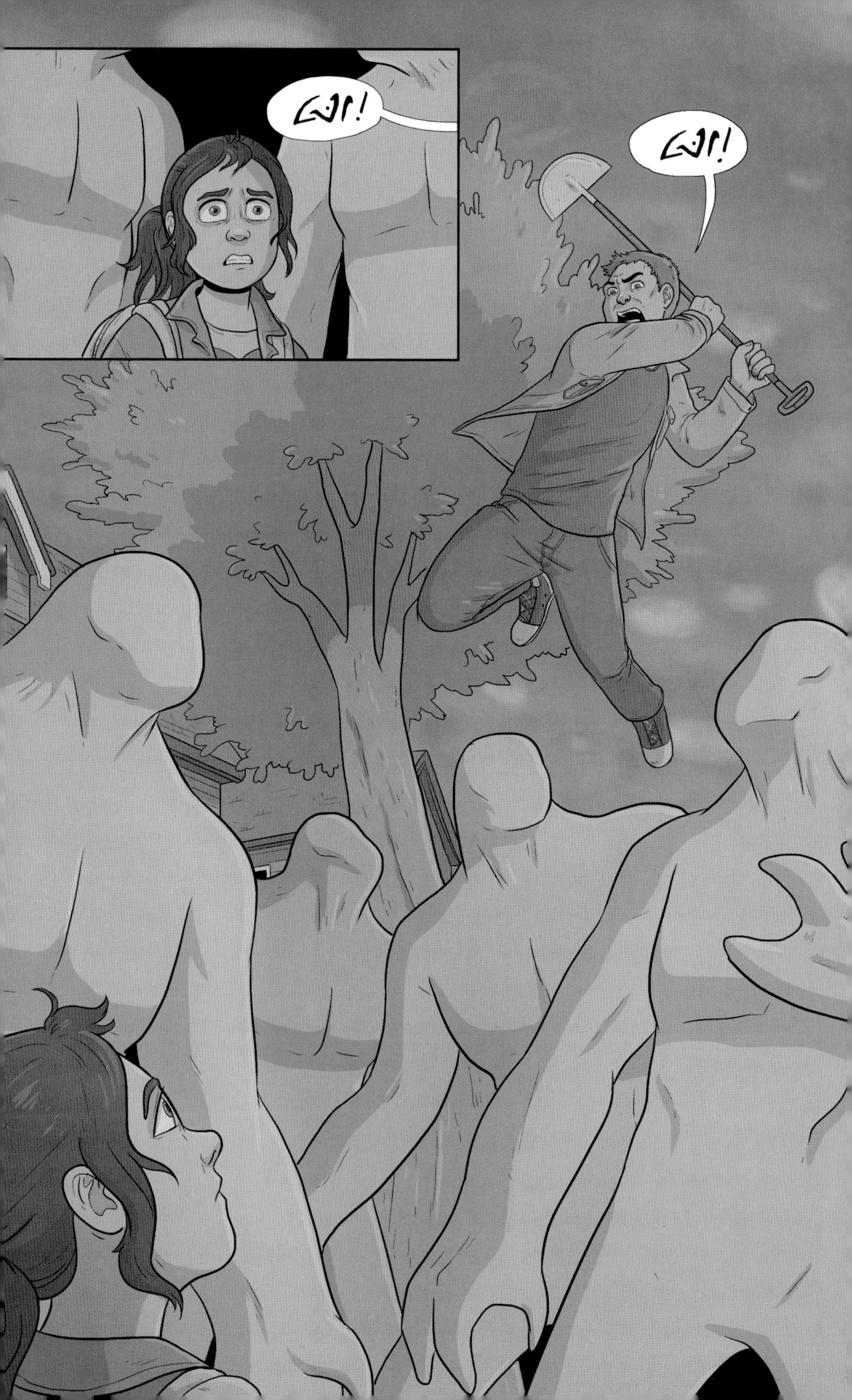

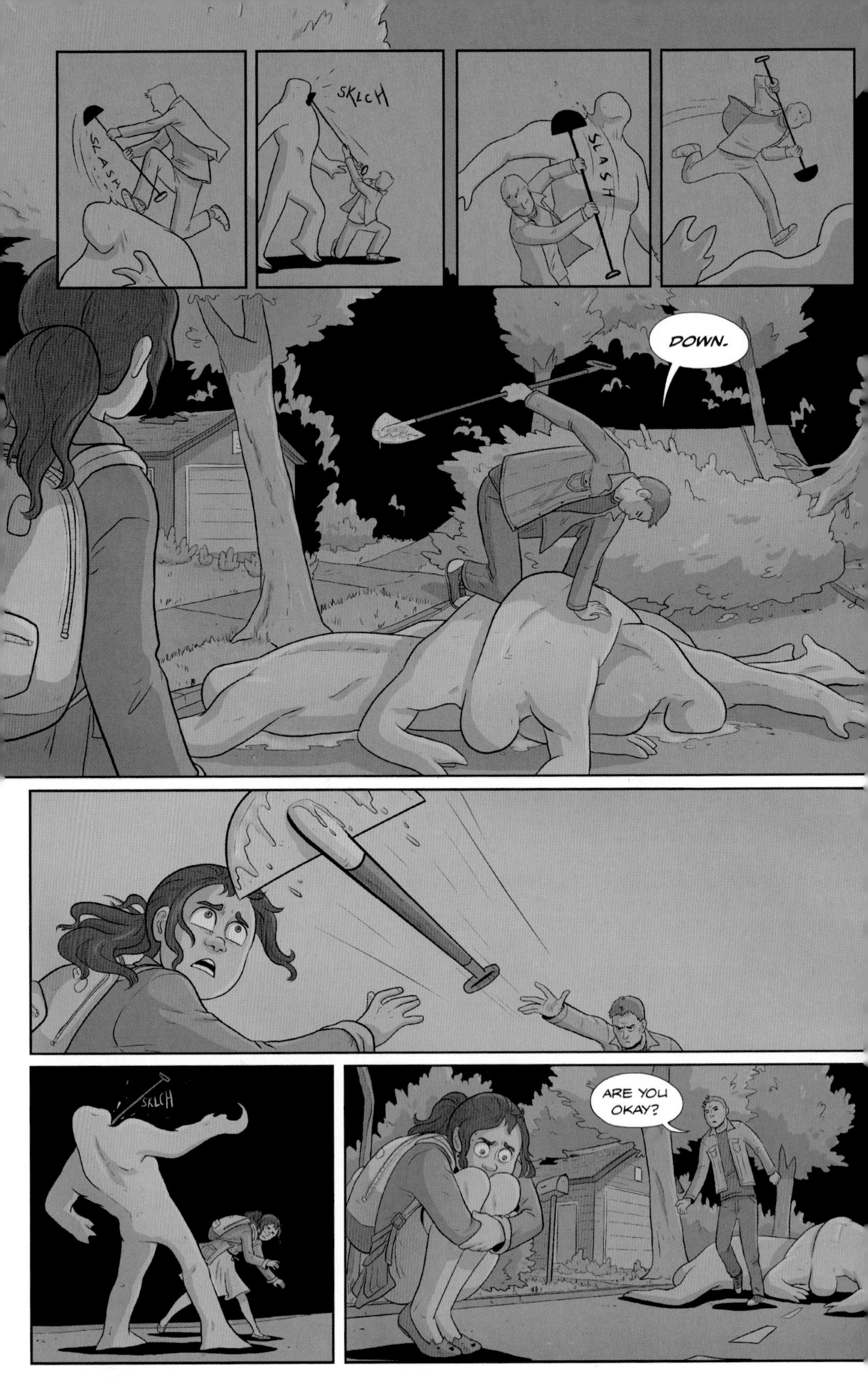
SLASH
SKLCH
SLASH
DOWN.
SKLCH
ARE YOU OKAY?

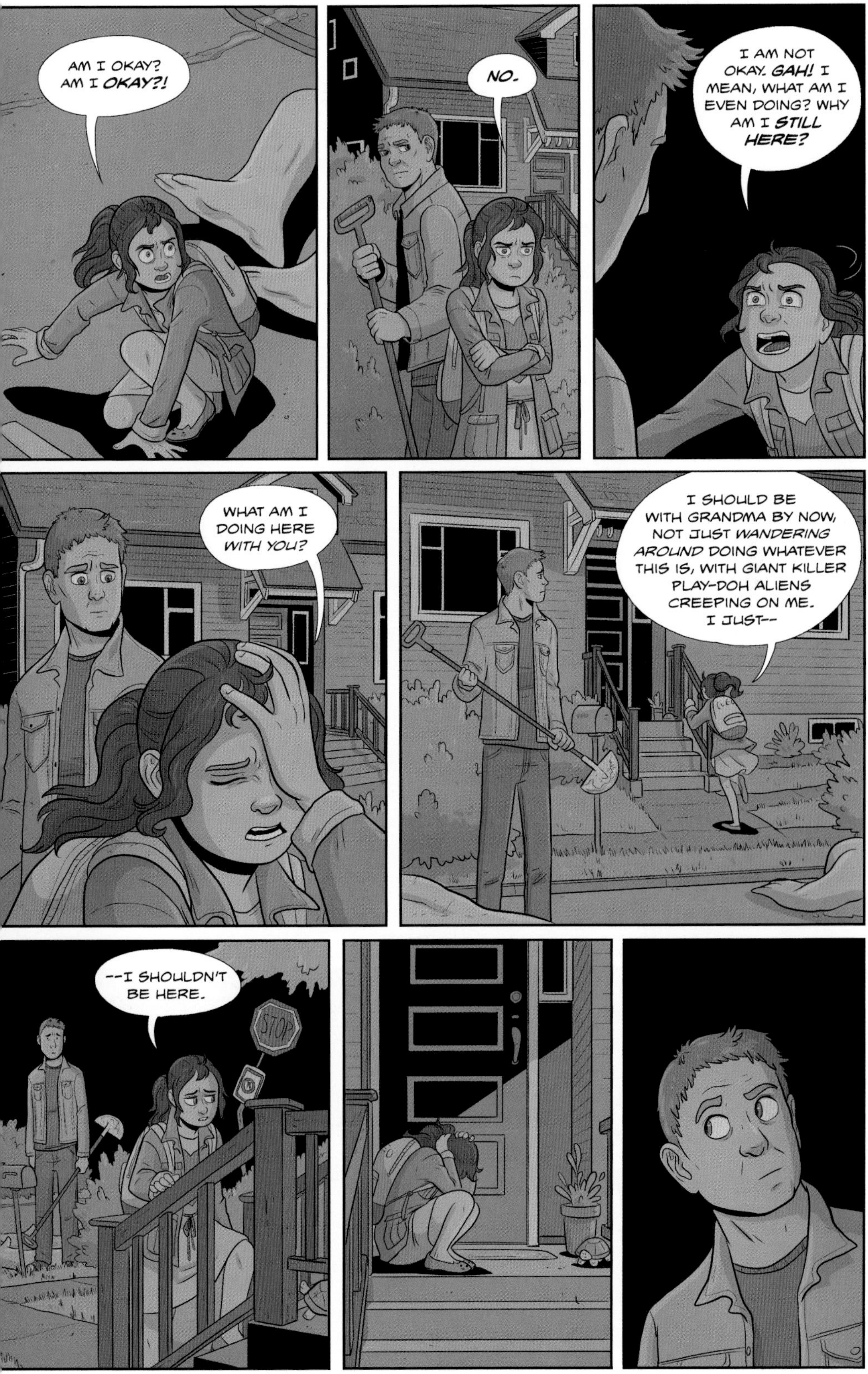
AM I OKAY? AM I OKAY?!
NO.
I AM NOT OKAY. GAH! I MEAN, WHAT AM I EVEN DOING? WHY AM I STILL HERE?
WHAT AM I DOING HERE WITH YOU?
I SHOULD BE WITH GRANDMA BY NOW, NOT JUST WANDERING AROUND DOING WHATEVER THIS IS, WITH GIANT KILLER PLAY-DOH ALIENS CREEPING ON ME. I JUST--
--I SHOULDN'T BE HERE.
STOP

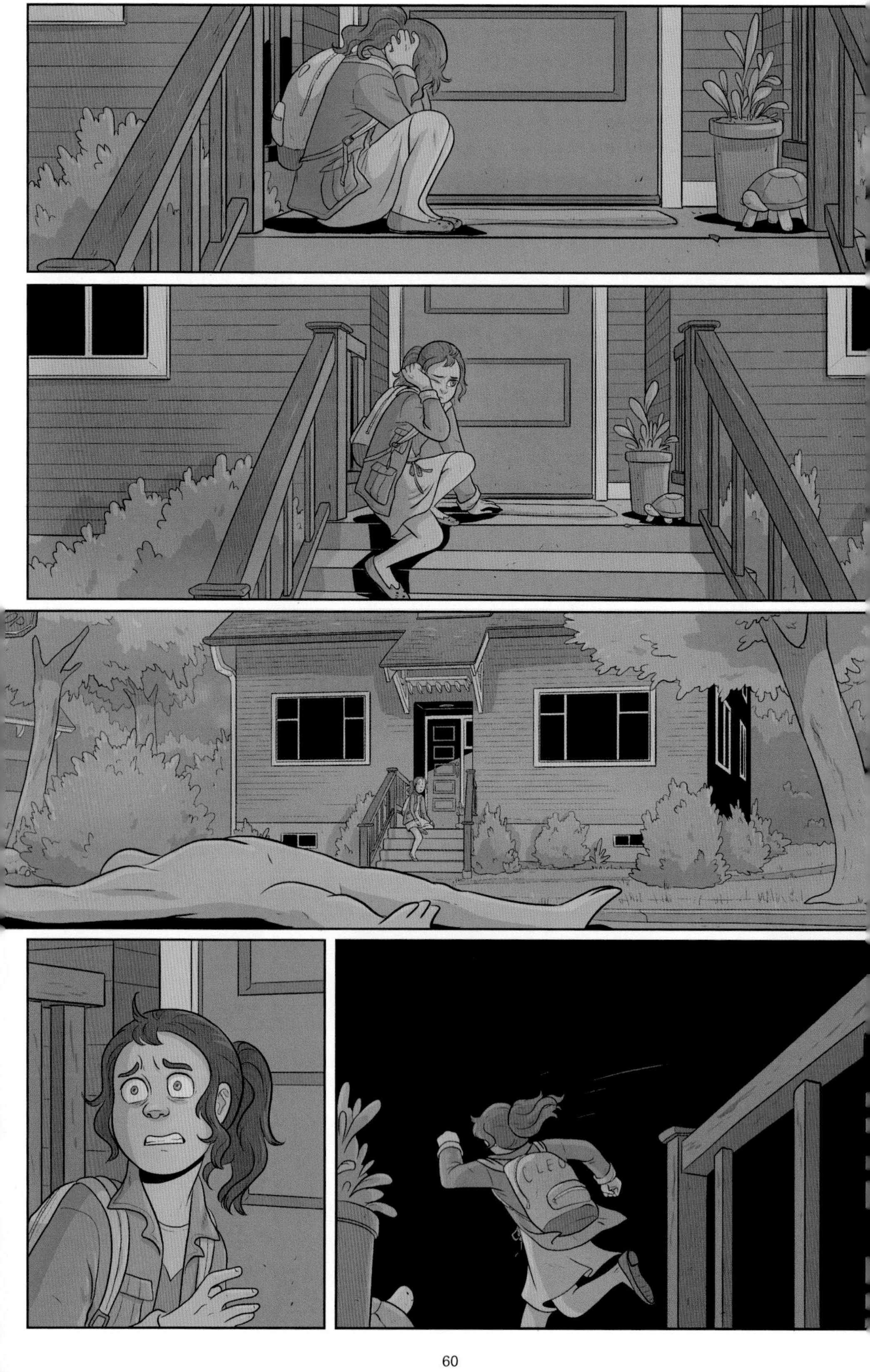

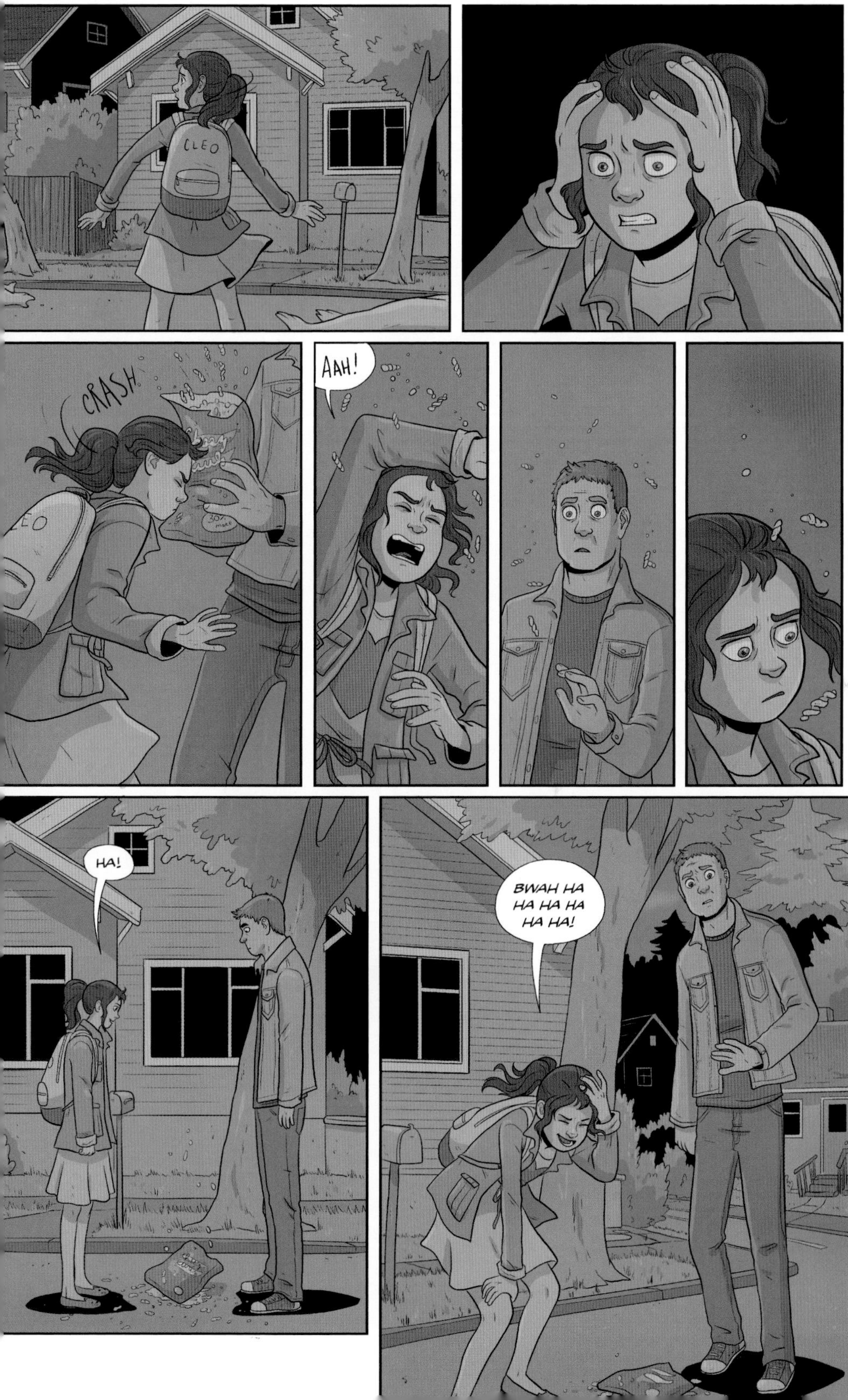
CLEO
CRASH
AAH!
HA!
BWAH HA HA HA HA HA HA!

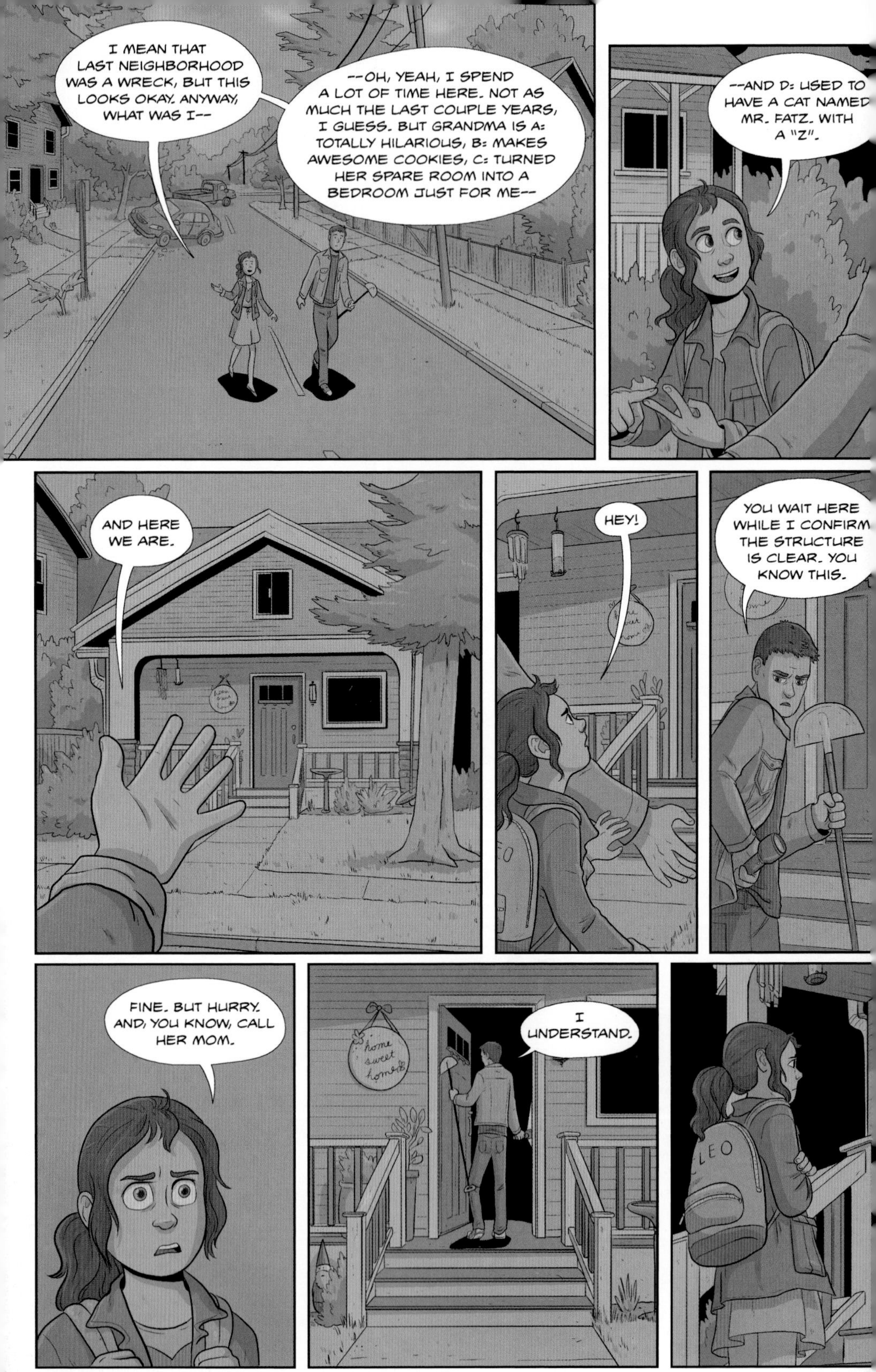
I MEAN THAT LAST NEIGHBORHOOD WAS A WRECK, BUT THIS LOOKS OKAY. ANYWAY, WHAT WAS I--
--OH, YEAH, I SPEND A LOT OF TIME HERE. NOT AS MUCH THE LAST COUPLE YEARS, I GUESS. BUT GRANDMA IS A: TOTALLY HILARIOUS, B: MAKES AWESOME COOKIES, C: TURNED HER SPARE ROOM INTO A BEDROOM JUST FOR ME--
--AND D: USED TO HAVE A CAT NAMED MR. FATZ. WITH A "Z".
AND HERE WE ARE.
HEY!
YOU WAIT HERE WHILE I CONFIRM THE STRUCTURE IS CLEAR. YOU KNOW THIS.
FINE. BUT HURRY. AND, YOU KNOW, CALL HER MOM.
home sweet home
I UNDERSTAND.
LEO

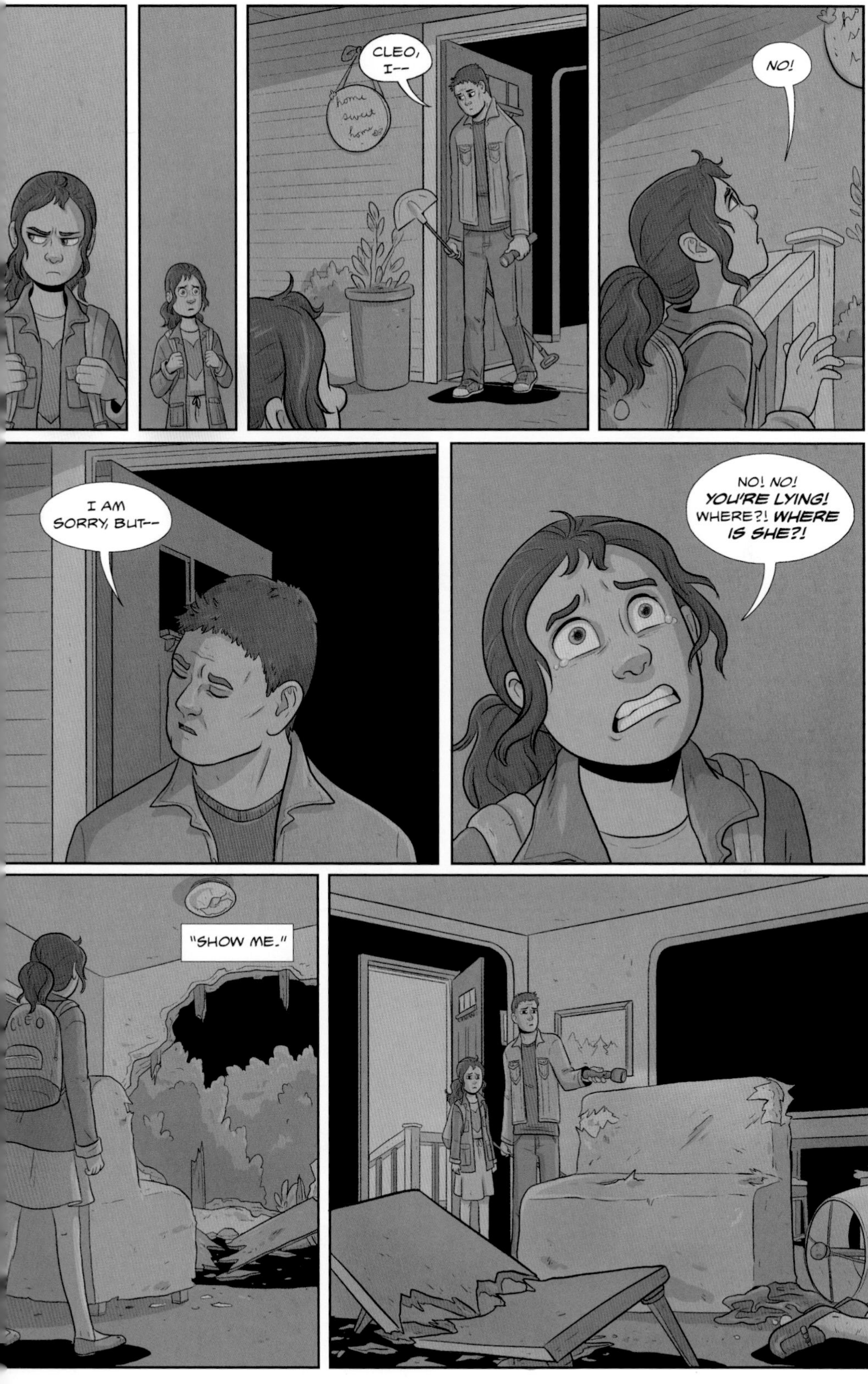
CLEO, I--
NO!
I AM SORRY, BUT--
NO! NO! YOU'RE LYING! WHERE?! WHERE IS SHE?!
"SHOW ME."

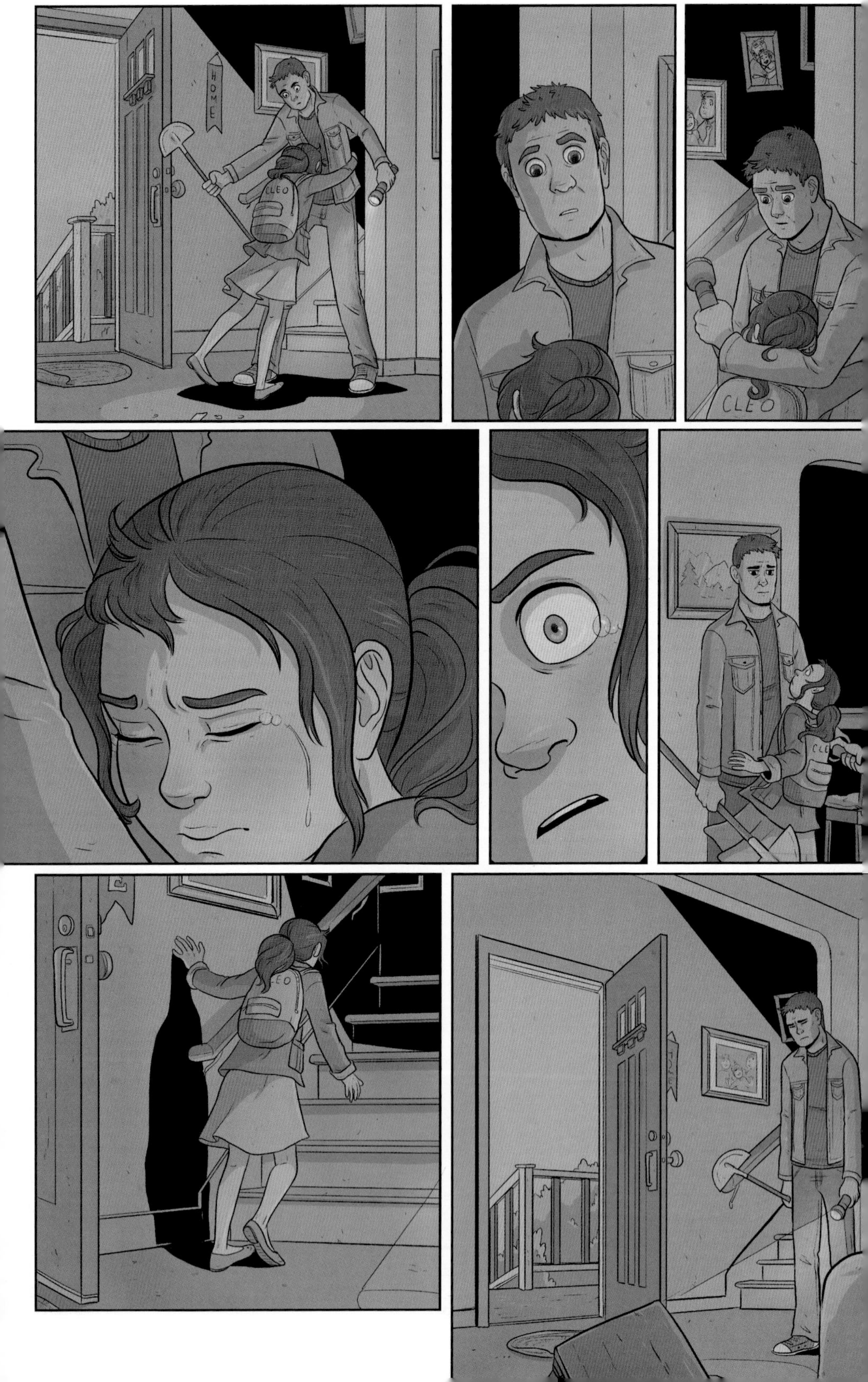
HOME
CLEO
CLEO
CLEO

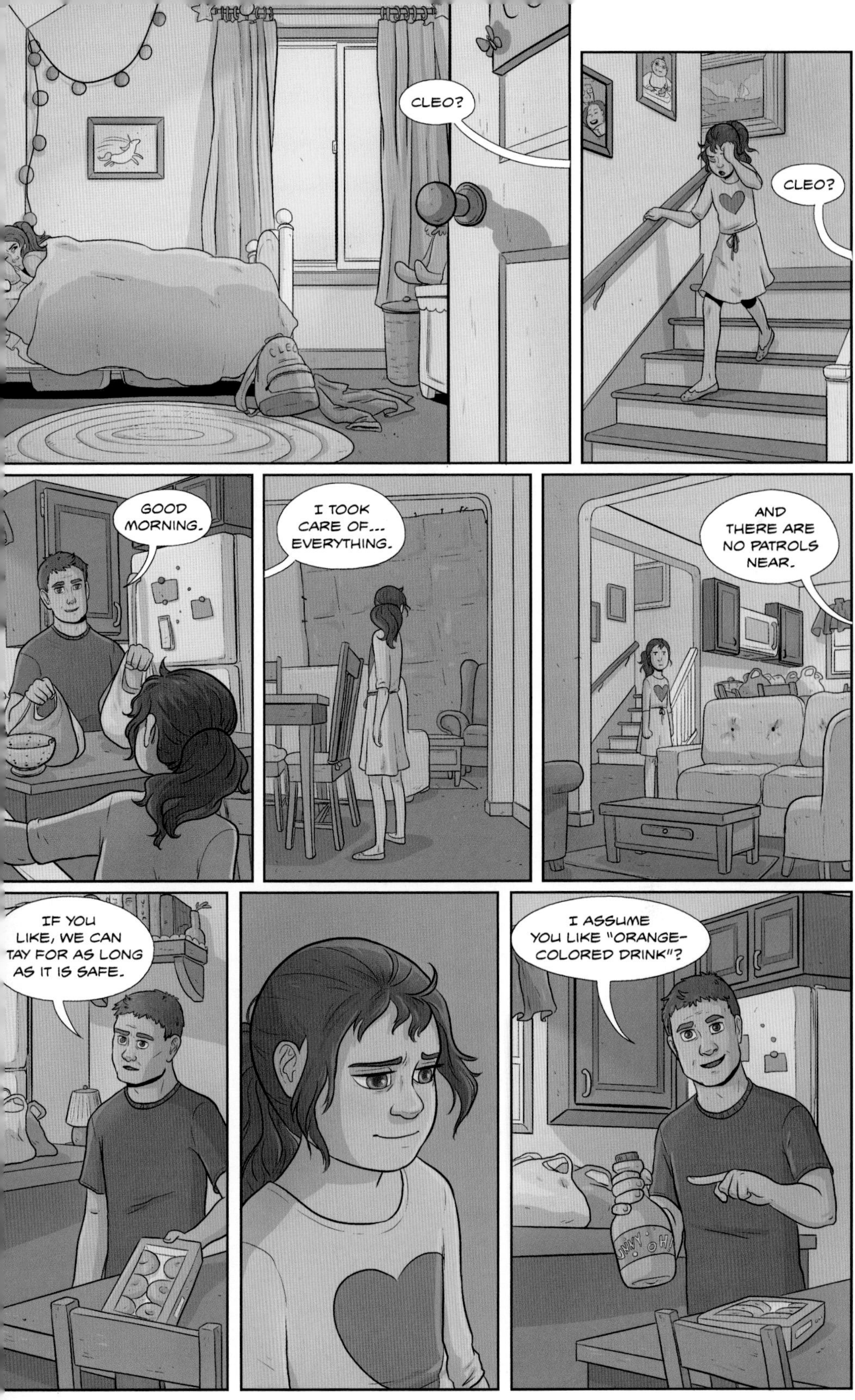
CLEO?
CLEO?
GOOD MORNING.
I TOOK CARE OF... EVERYTHING.
AND THERE ARE NO PATROLS NEAR.
IF YOU LIKE, WE CAN TAY FOR AS LONG AS IT IS SAFE.
I ASSUME YOU LIKE "ORANGE-COLORED DRINK"?

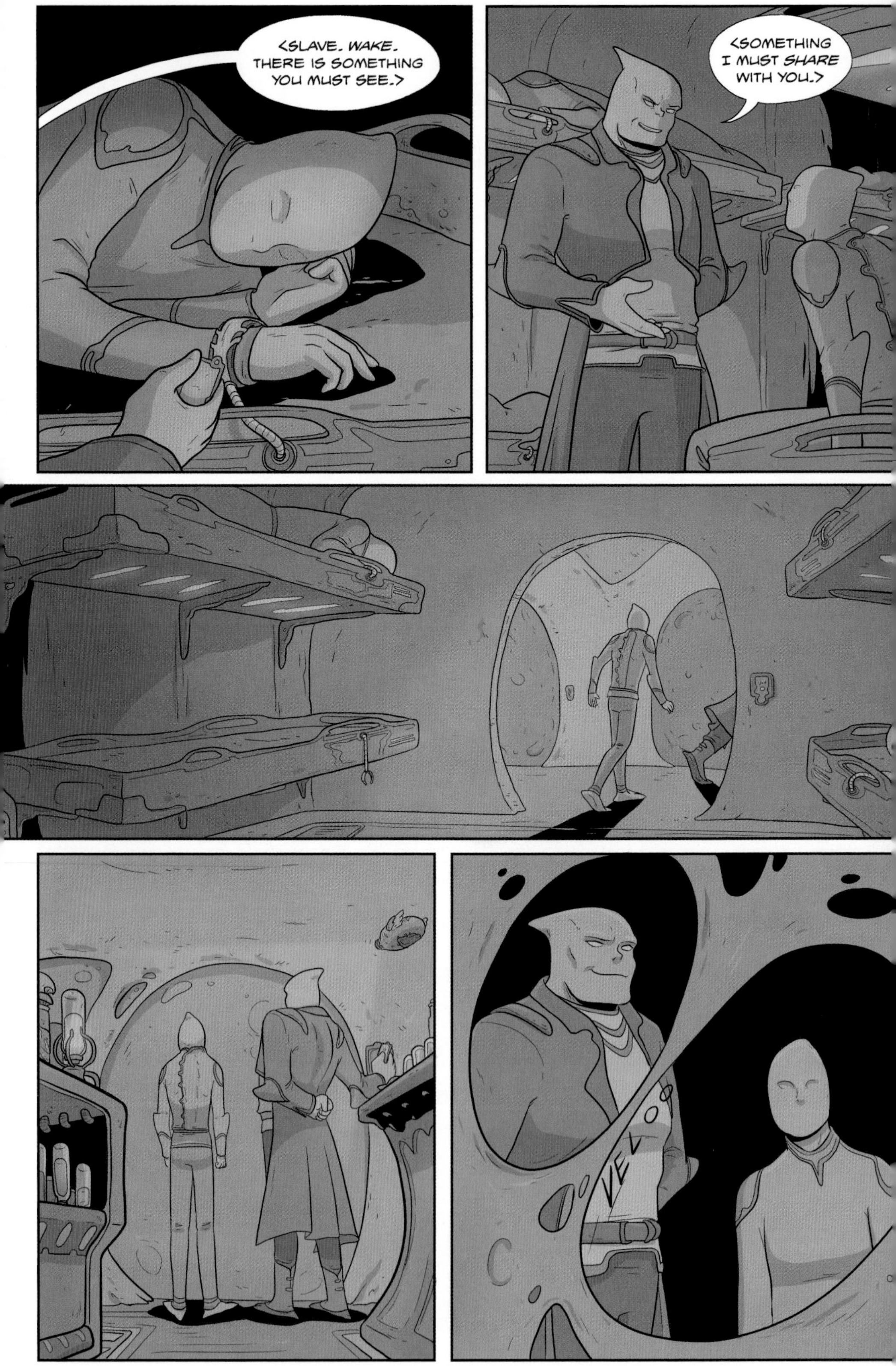
<SLAVE. WAKE. THERE IS SOMETHING YOU MUST SEE.>
<SOMETHING I MUST SHARE WITH YOU.>

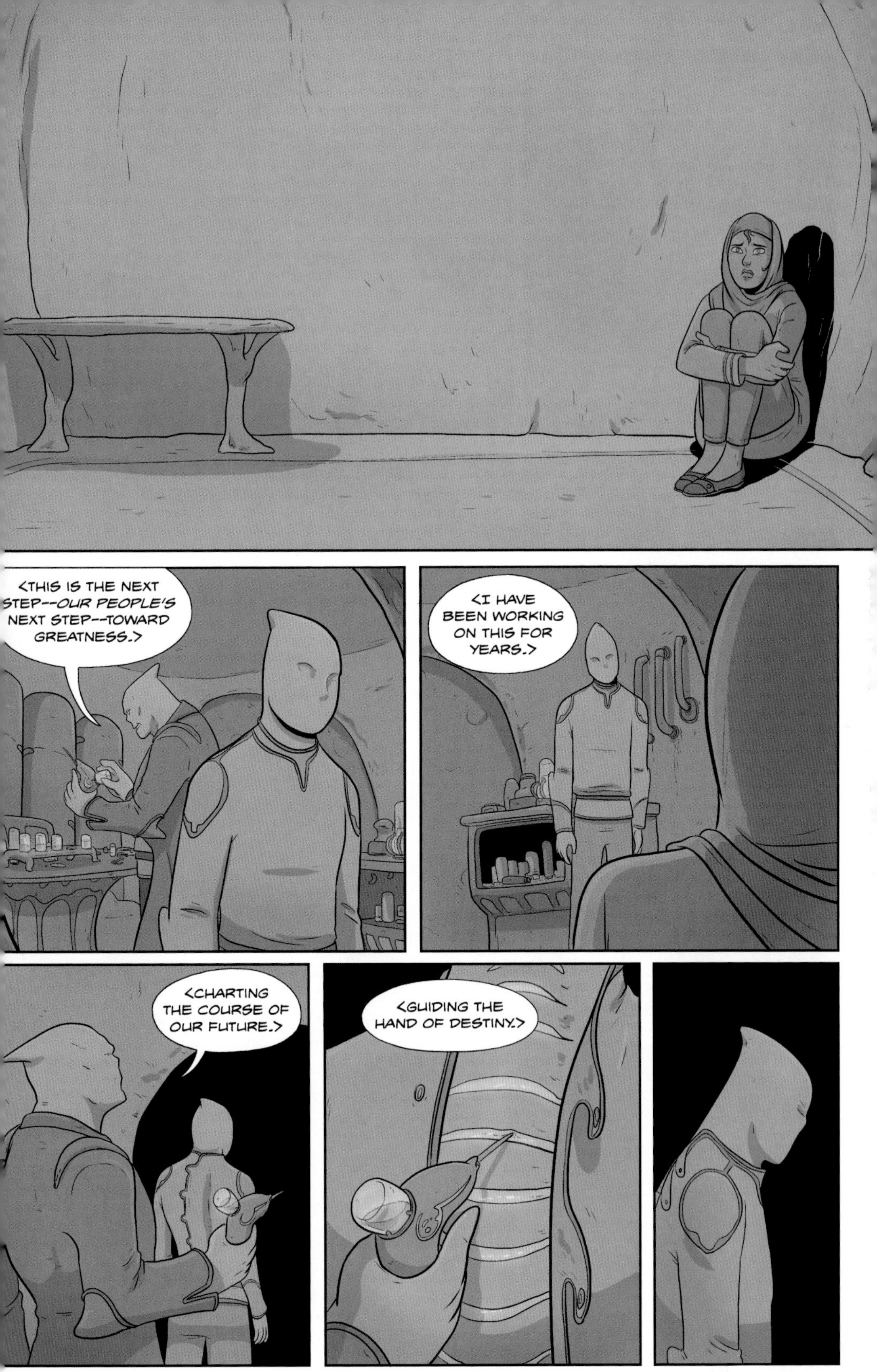
<THIS IS THE NEXT STEP--OUR PEOPLE'S NEXT STEP--TOWARD GREATNESS.>
<I HAVE BEEN WORKING ON THIS FOR YEARS.>
<CHARTING THE COURSE OF OUR FUTURE.>
<GUIDING THE HAND OF DESTINY.>

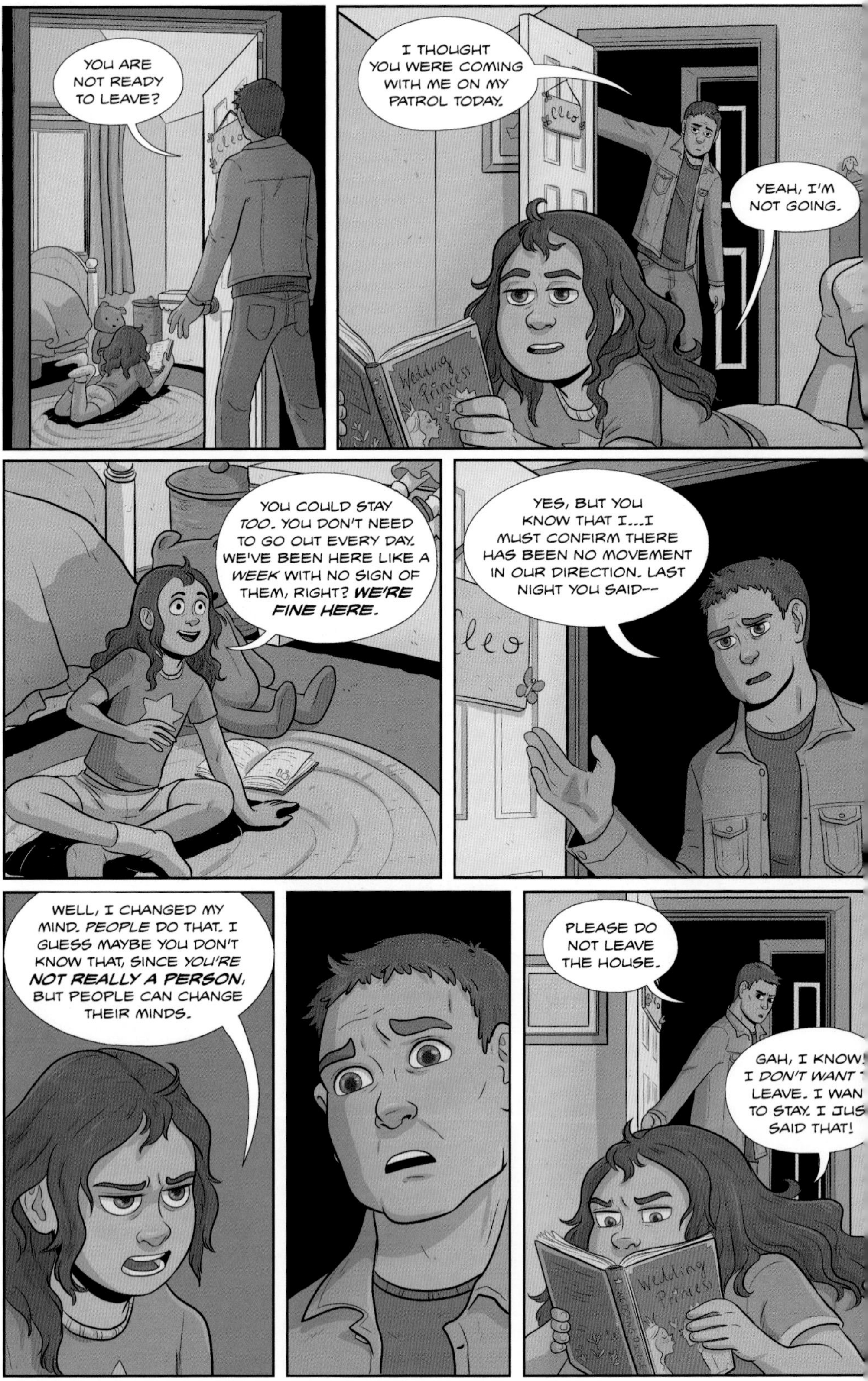
YOU ARE NOT READY TO LEAVE?
I THOUGHT YOU WERE COMING WITH ME ON MY PATROL TODAY.
YEAH, I'M NOT GOING.
YOU COULD STAY *TOO*. YOU DON'T NEED TO GO OUT EVERY DAY. WE'VE BEEN HERE LIKE A *WEEK* WITH NO SIGN OF THEM, RIGHT? ***WE'RE FINE HERE.***
YES, BUT YOU KNOW THAT I...I MUST CONFIRM THERE HAS BEEN NO MOVEMENT IN OUR DIRECTION. LAST NIGHT YOU SAID--
WELL, I CHANGED MY MIND. *PEOPLE* DO THAT. I GUESS MAYBE YOU DON'T KNOW THAT, SINCE *YOU'RE* ***NOT REALLY A PERSON***, BUT PEOPLE CAN CHANGE THEIR MINDS.
PLEASE DO NOT LEAVE THE HOUSE.
GAH, I KNOW! I *DON'T WANT* LEAVE. I WAN TO STAY. I JUS SAID THAT!

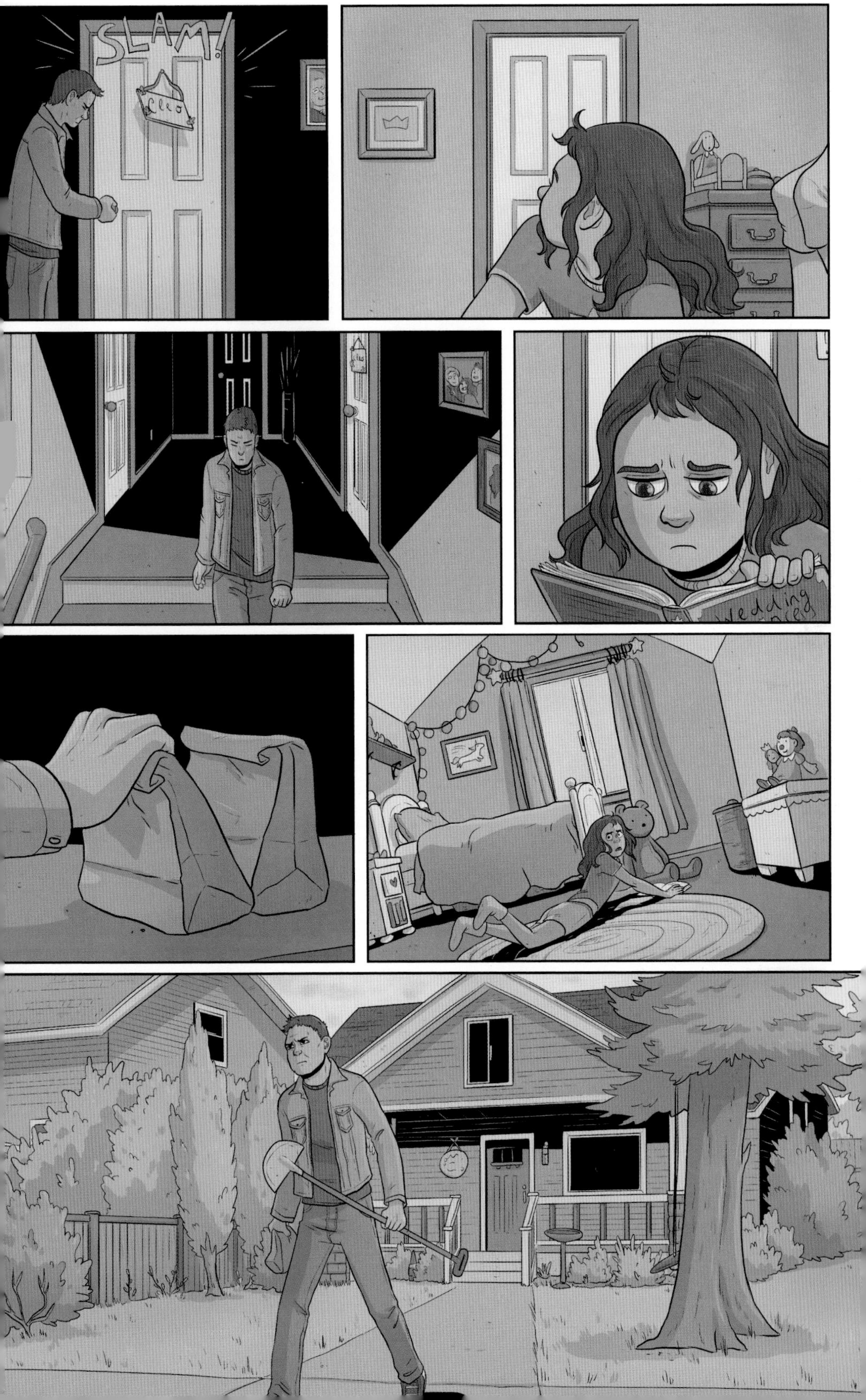
SLAM!
Cleo
Wedding

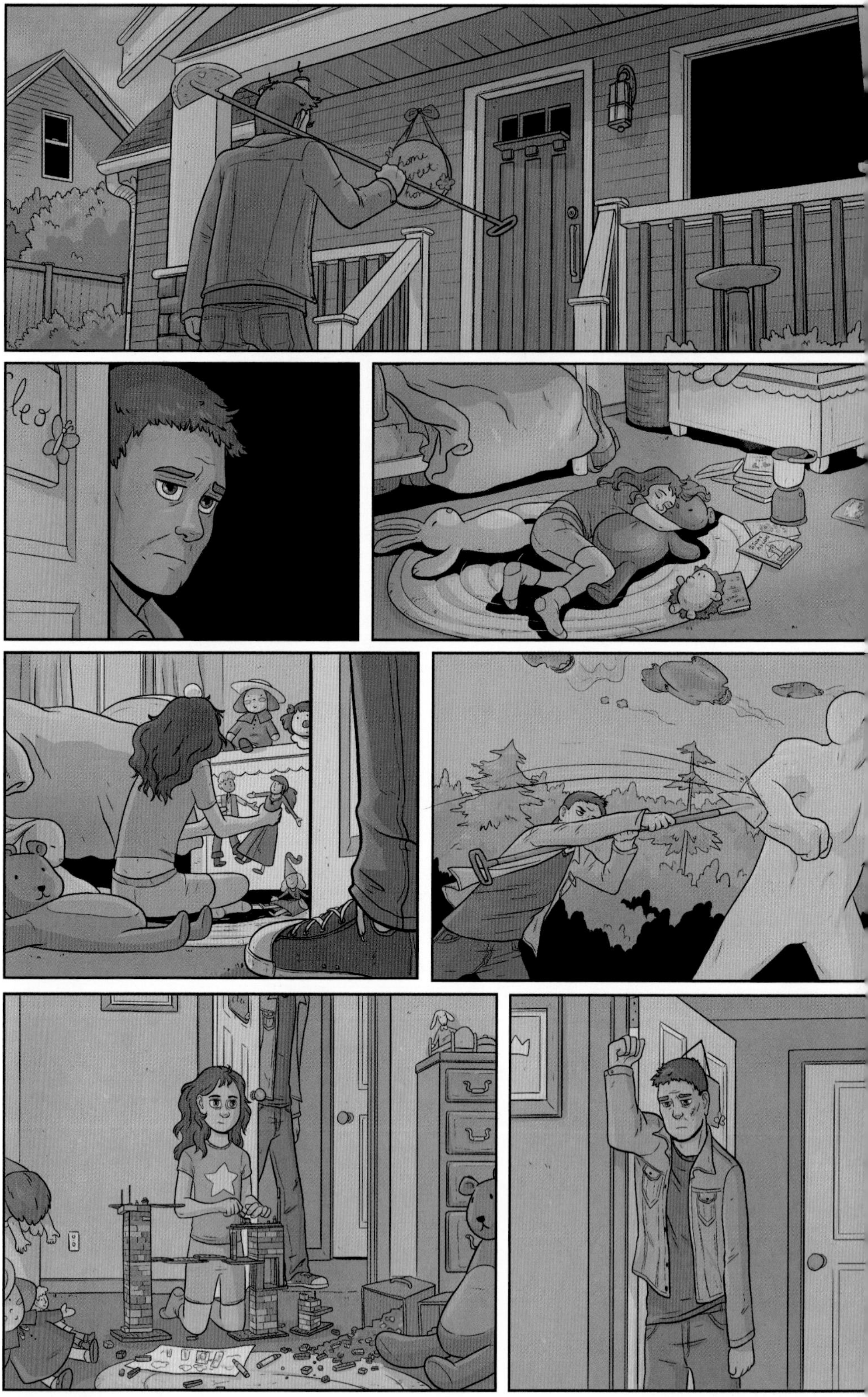

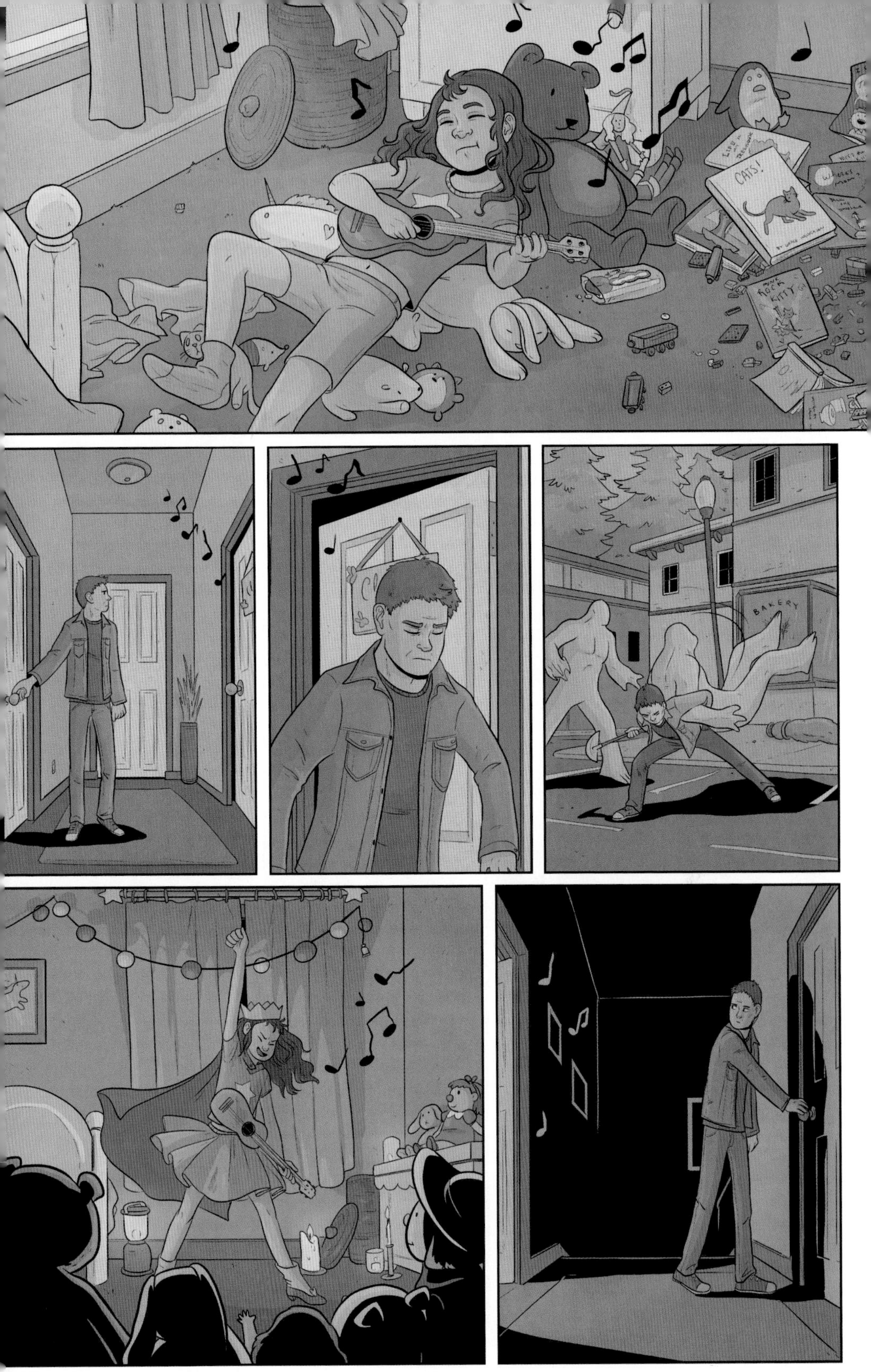
CATS!
PUNK ROCK KITTY
Where's Mom?
BAKERY

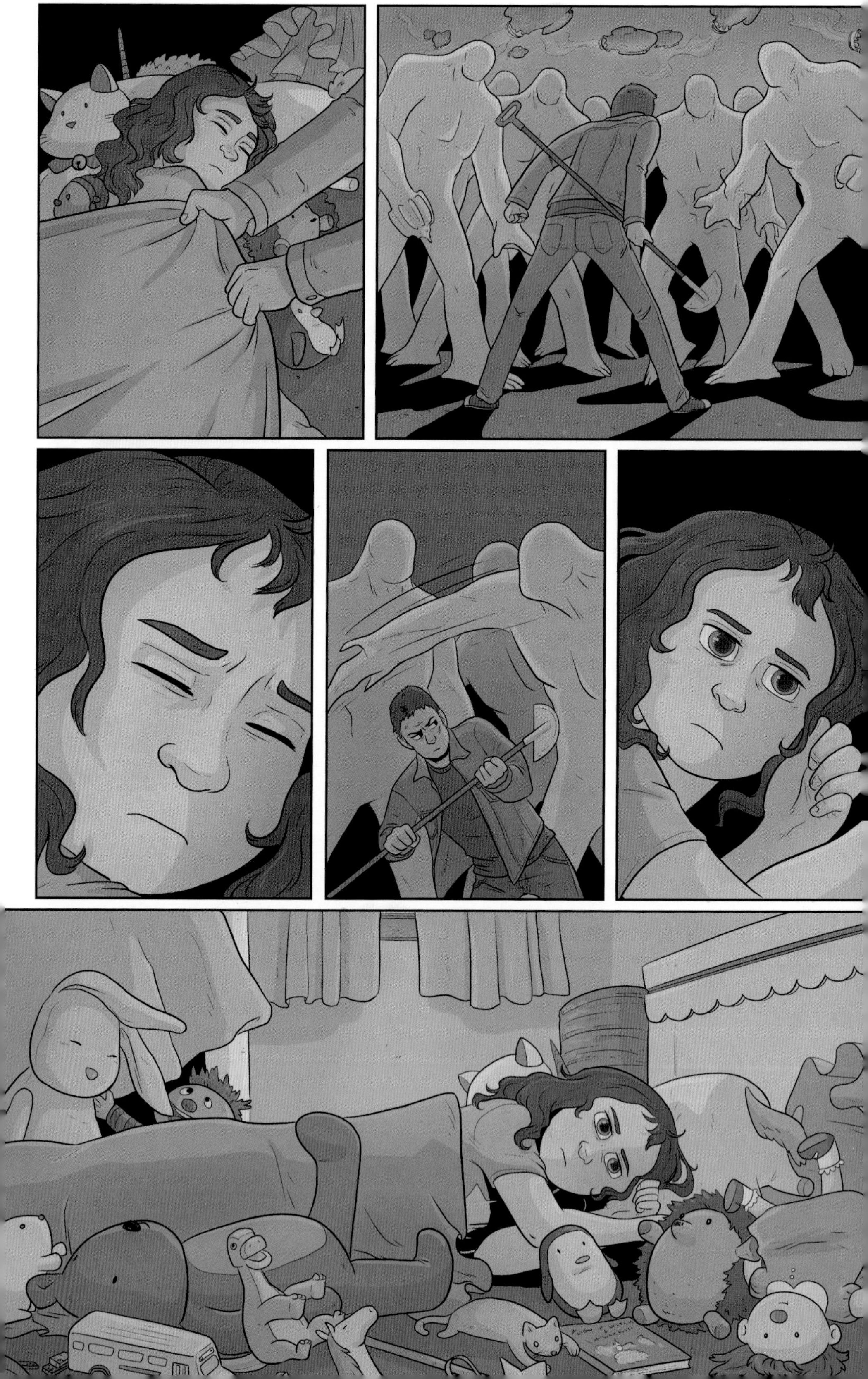

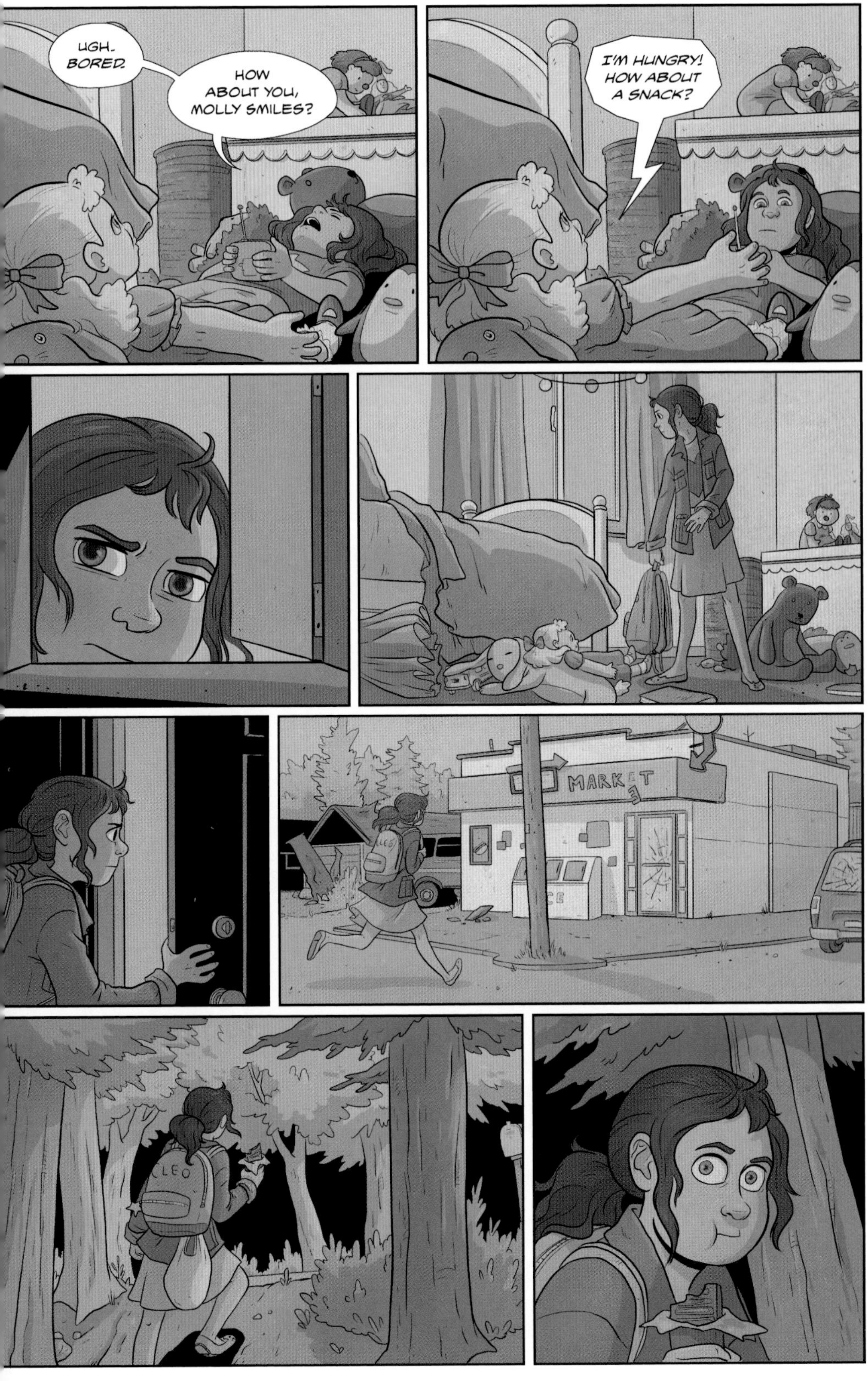
UGH. BORED.
HOW ABOUT YOU, MOLLY SMILES?
I'M HUNGRY! HOW ABOUT A SNACK?
MARKET
LEO
LEO

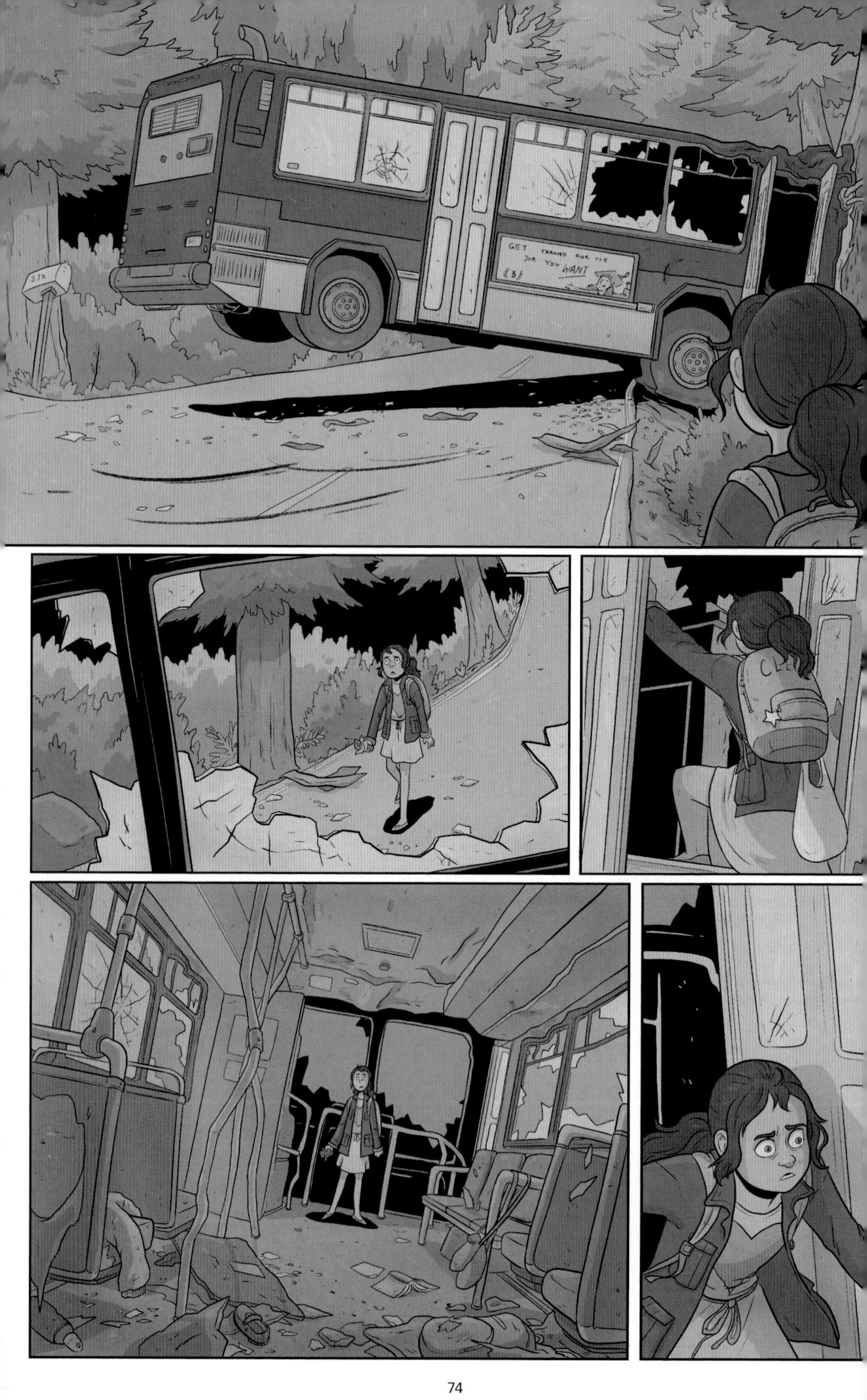
GET TRAINED FOR THE JOB YOU WANT

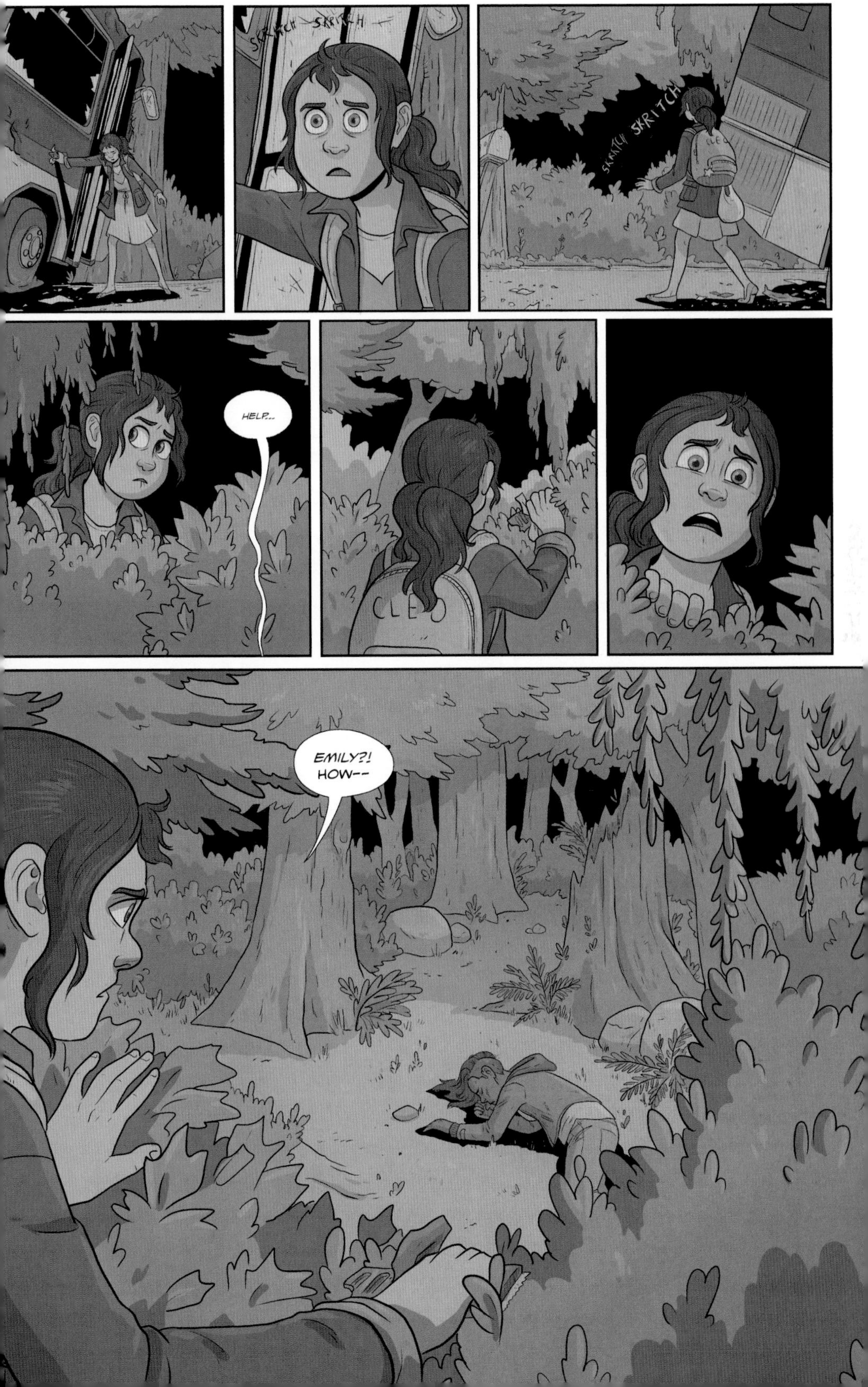
SKRITCH SKRITCH
SKRITCH SKRITCH
HELP...
EMILY?! HOW--

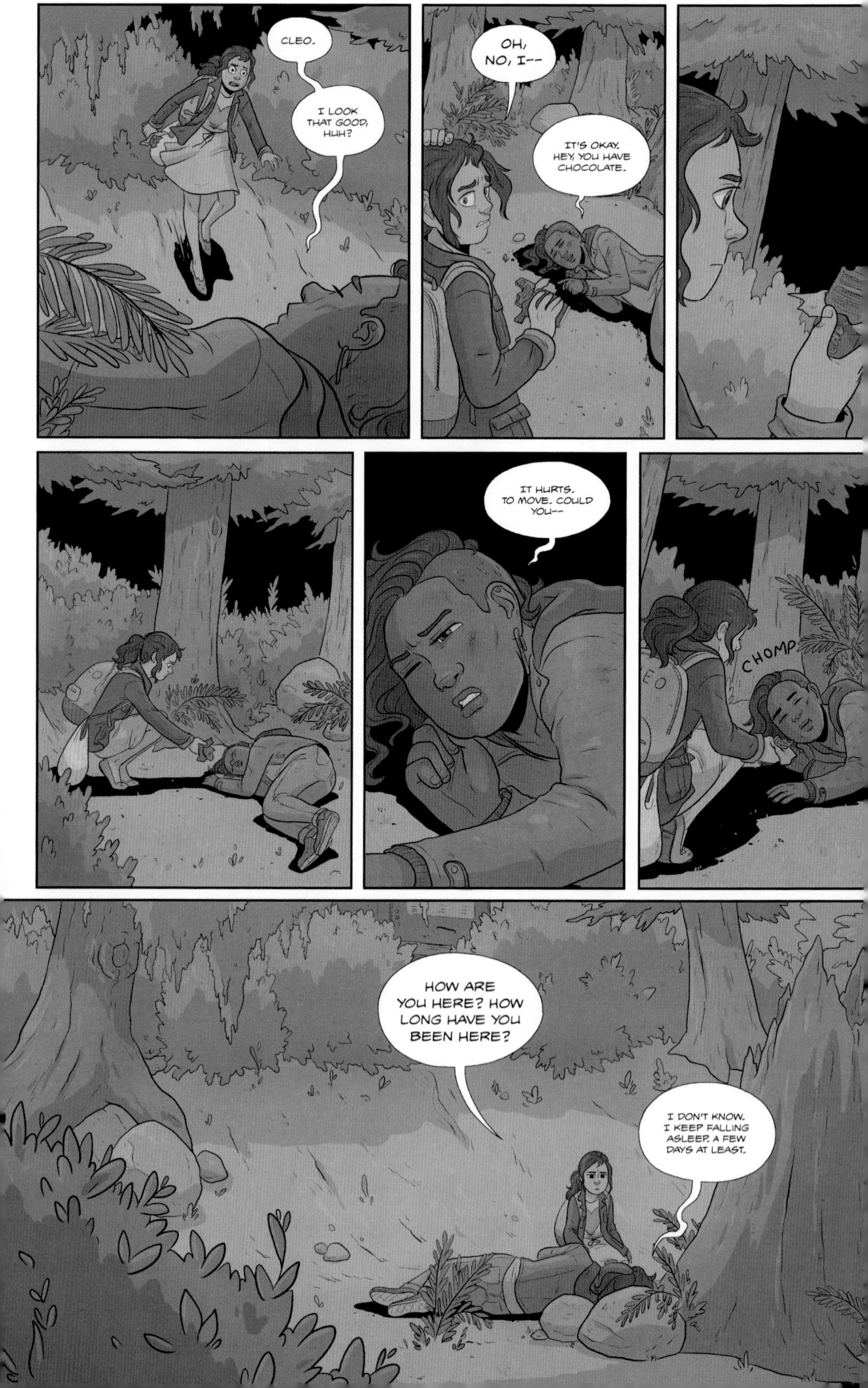
CLEO.
I LOOK THAT GOOD, HUH?
OH, NO, I--
IT'S OKAY. HEY, YOU HAVE CHOCOLATE.
IT HURTS. TO MOVE. COULD YOU--
CHOMP
HOW ARE YOU HERE? HOW LONG HAVE YOU BEEN HERE?
I DON'T KNOW. I KEEP FALLING ASLEEP. A FEW DAYS AT LEAST.

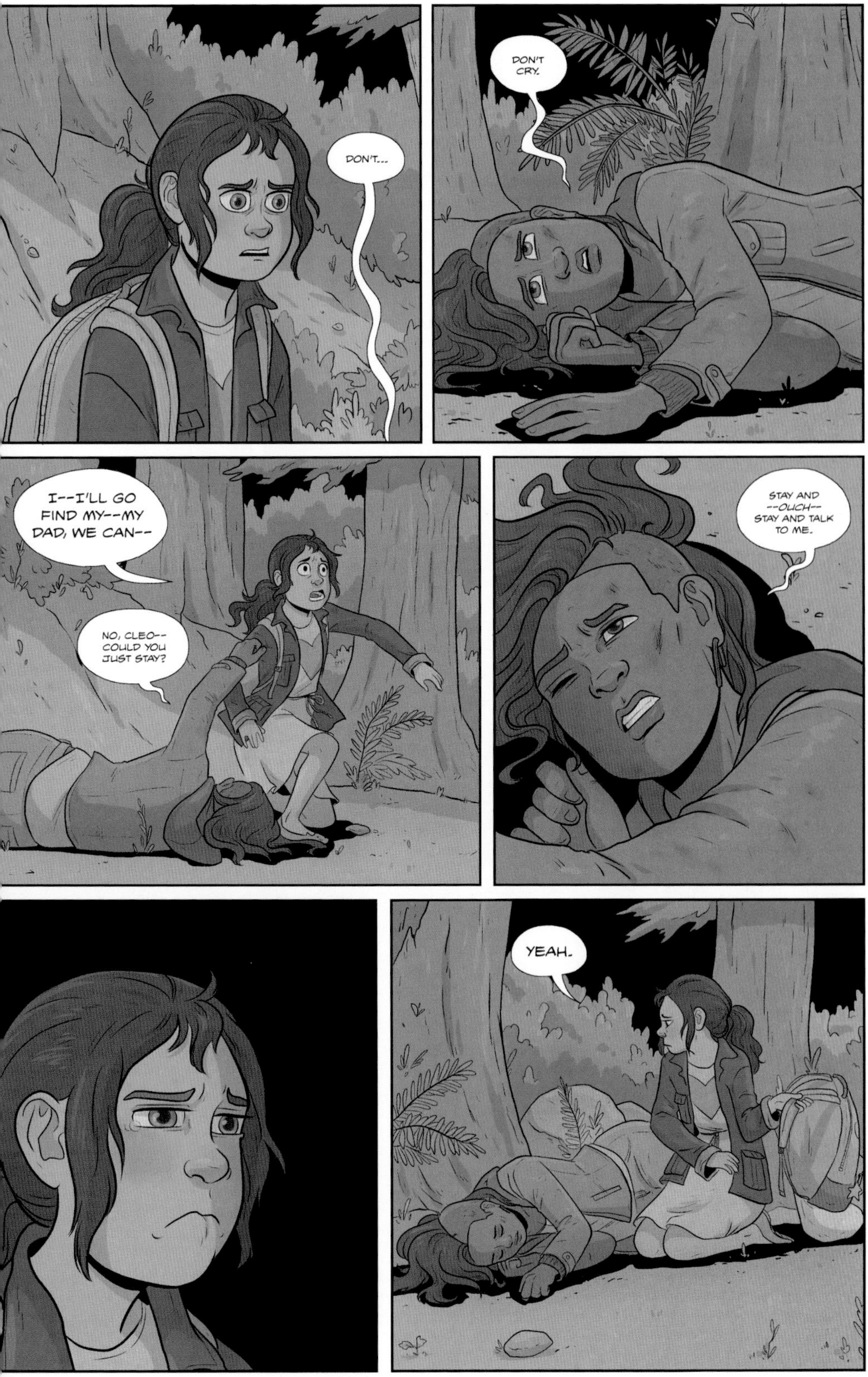
DON'T...
DON'T CRY.
I--I'LL GO FIND MY--MY DAD, WE CAN--
NO, CLEO-- COULD YOU JUST STAY?
STAY AND --OUCH-- STAY AND TALK TO ME.
YEAH.

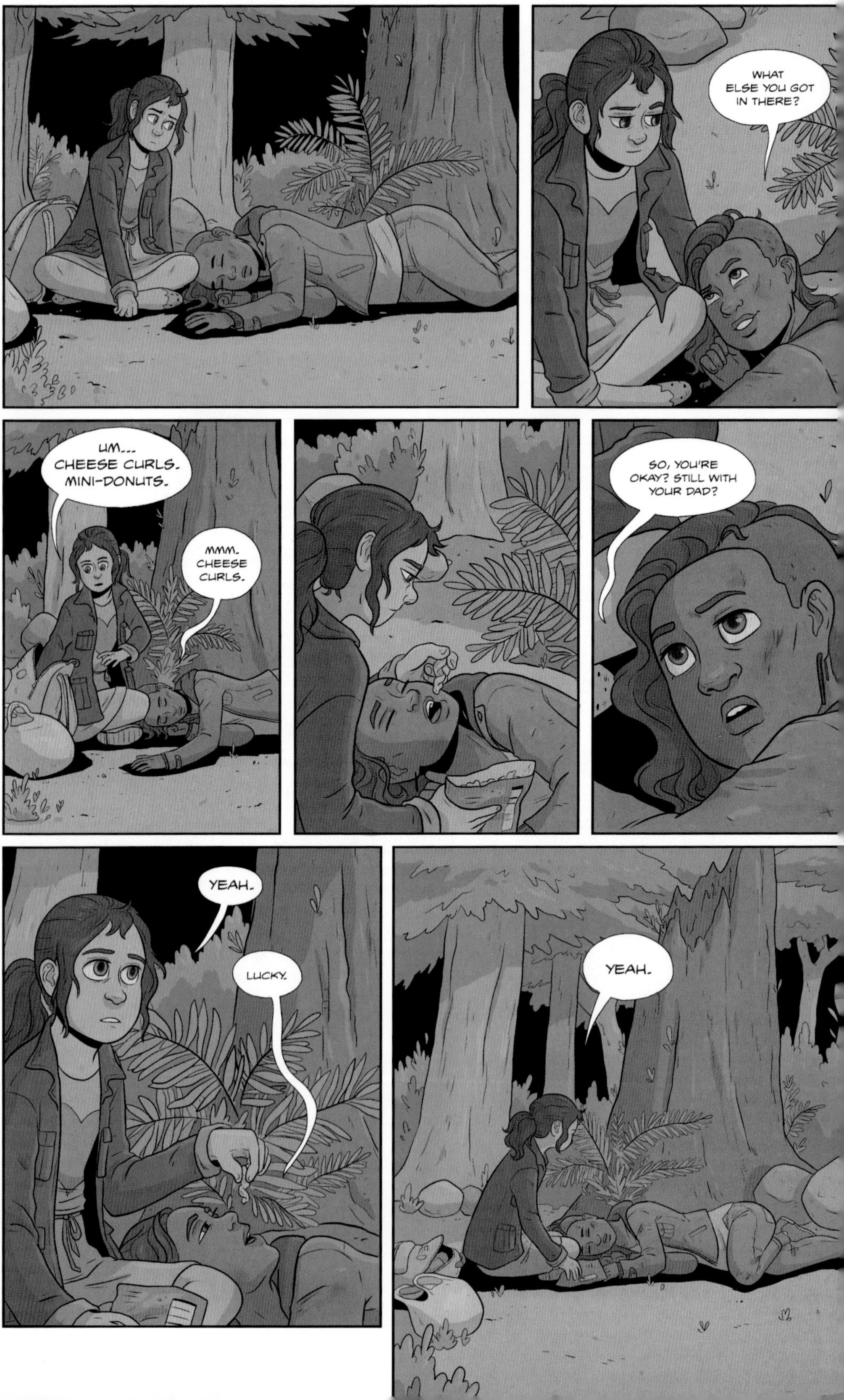
WHAT ELSE YOU GOT IN THERE?
UM... CHEESE CURLS. MINI-DONUTS.
MMM. CHEESE CURLS.
SO, YOU'RE OKAY? STILL WITH YOUR DAD?
YEAH.
LUCKY.
YEAH.

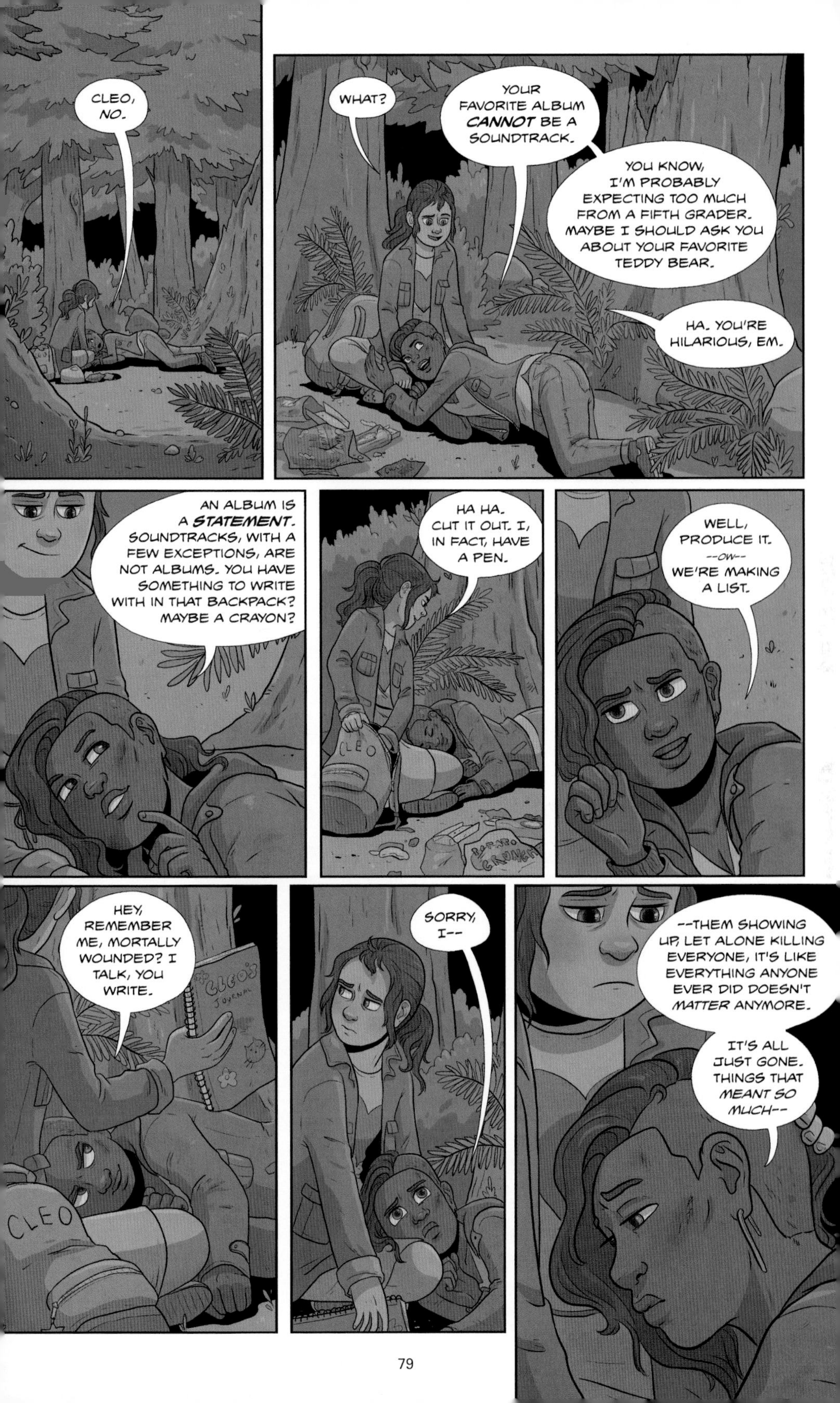
CLEO, NO.
WHAT?
YOUR FAVORITE ALBUM CANNOT BE A SOUNDTRACK.
YOU KNOW, I'M PROBABLY EXPECTING TOO MUCH FROM A FIFTH GRADER. MAYBE I SHOULD ASK YOU ABOUT YOUR FAVORITE TEDDY BEAR.
HA. YOU'RE HILARIOUS, EM.
AN ALBUM IS A STATEMENT. SOUNDTRACKS, WITH A FEW EXCEPTIONS, ARE NOT ALBUMS. YOU HAVE SOMETHING TO WRITE WITH IN THAT BACKPACK? MAYBE A CRAYON?
HA HA. CUT IT OUT. I, IN FACT, HAVE A PEN.
WELL, PRODUCE IT. --OW-- WE'RE MAKING A LIST.
HEY, REMEMBER ME, MORTALLY WOUNDED? I TALK, YOU WRITE.
CLEO'S JOURNAL
SORRY, I--
--THEM SHOWING UP, LET ALONE KILLING EVERYONE, IT'S LIKE EVERYTHING ANYONE EVER DID DOESN'T MATTER ANYMORE.
IT'S ALL JUST GONE. THINGS THAT MEANT SO MUCH--

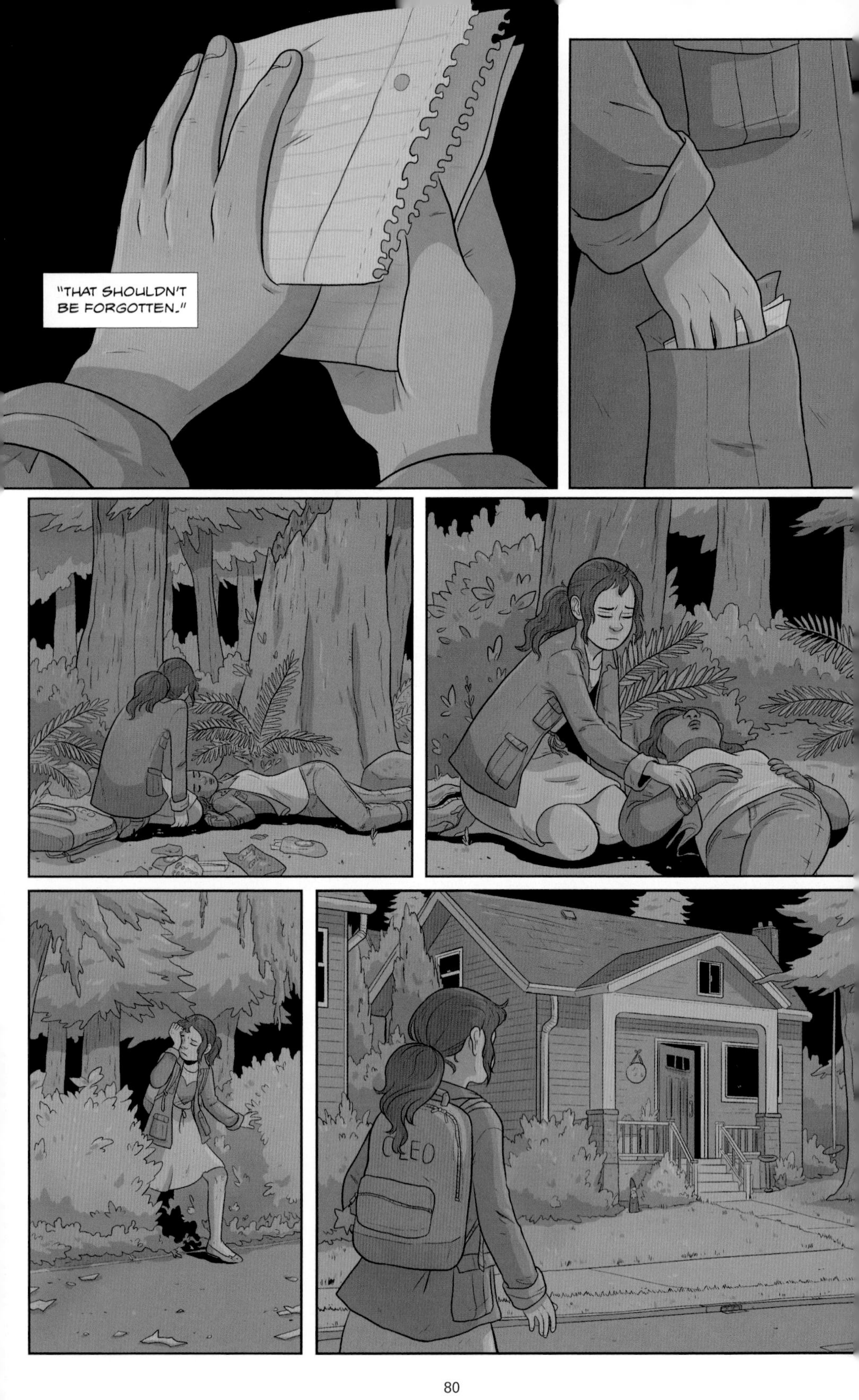
"THAT SHOULDN'T
BE FORGOTTEN."
CLEO

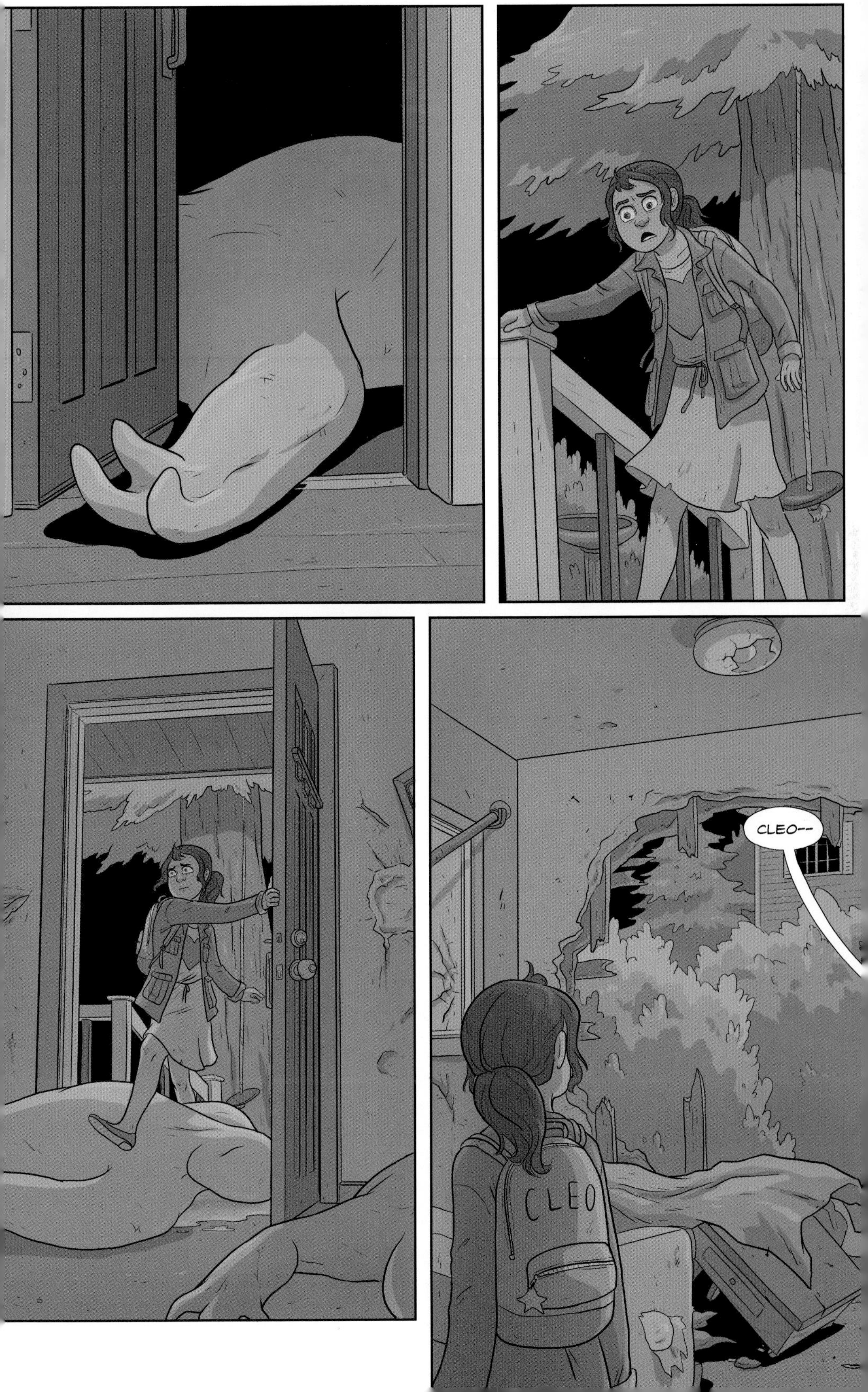

CLEO--
CLEO

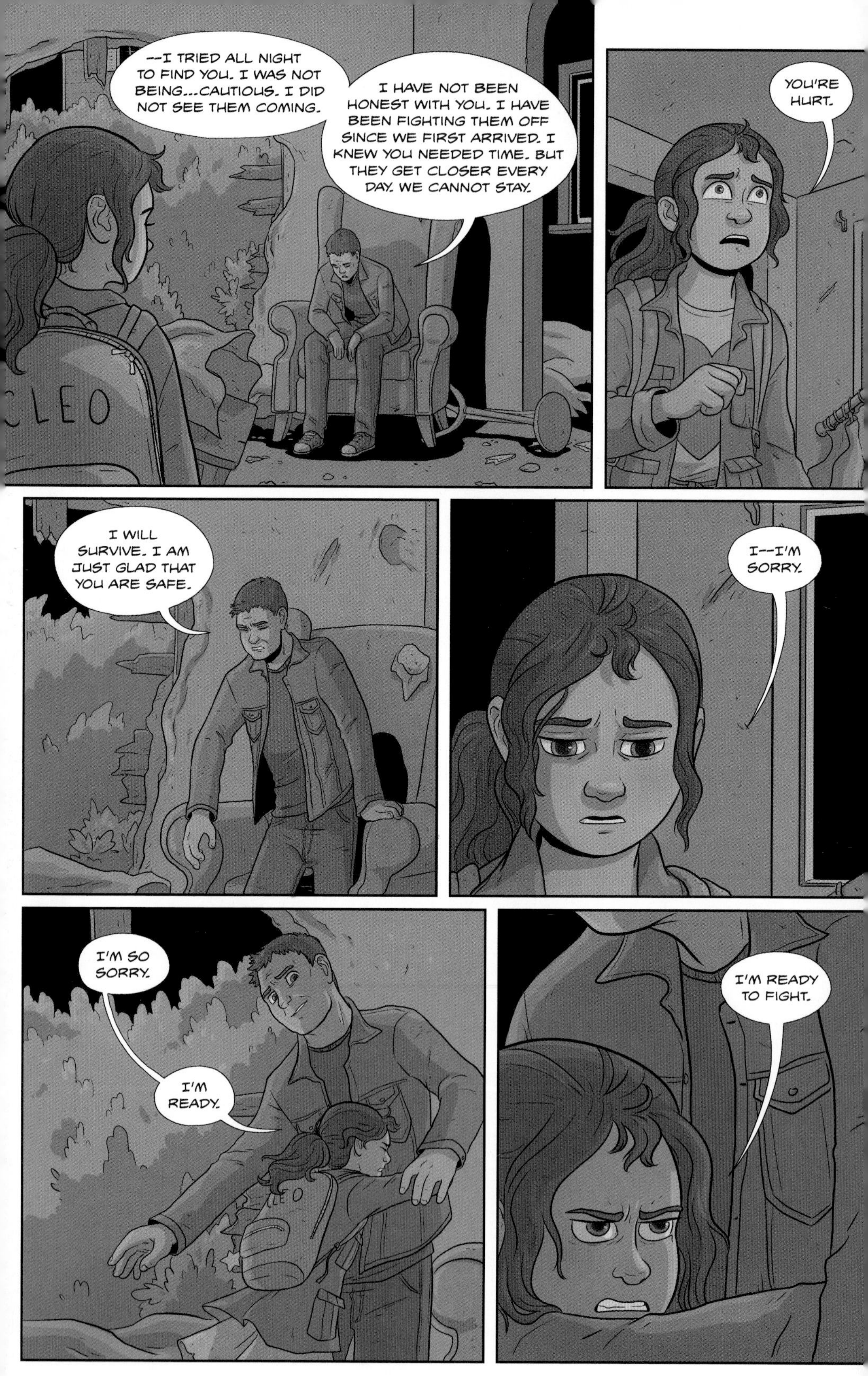
--I TRIED ALL NIGHT TO FIND YOU. I WAS NOT BEING...CAUTIOUS. I DID NOT SEE THEM COMING.
I HAVE NOT BEEN HONEST WITH YOU. I HAVE BEEN FIGHTING THEM OFF SINCE WE FIRST ARRIVED. I KNEW YOU NEEDED TIME. BUT THEY GET CLOSER EVERY DAY. WE CANNOT STAY.
CLEO
YOU'RE HURT.
I WILL SURVIVE. I AM JUST GLAD THAT YOU ARE SAFE.
I--I'M SORRY.
I'M SO SORRY.
I'M READY.
I'M READY TO FIGHT.

THREE

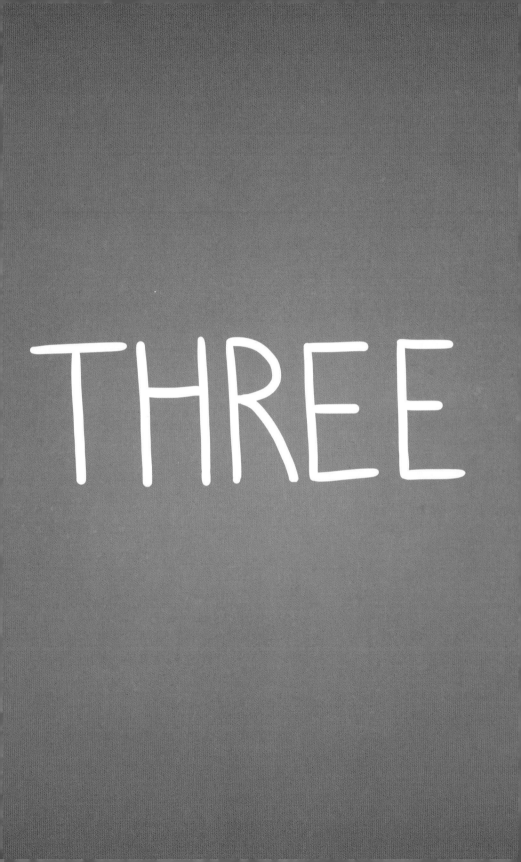

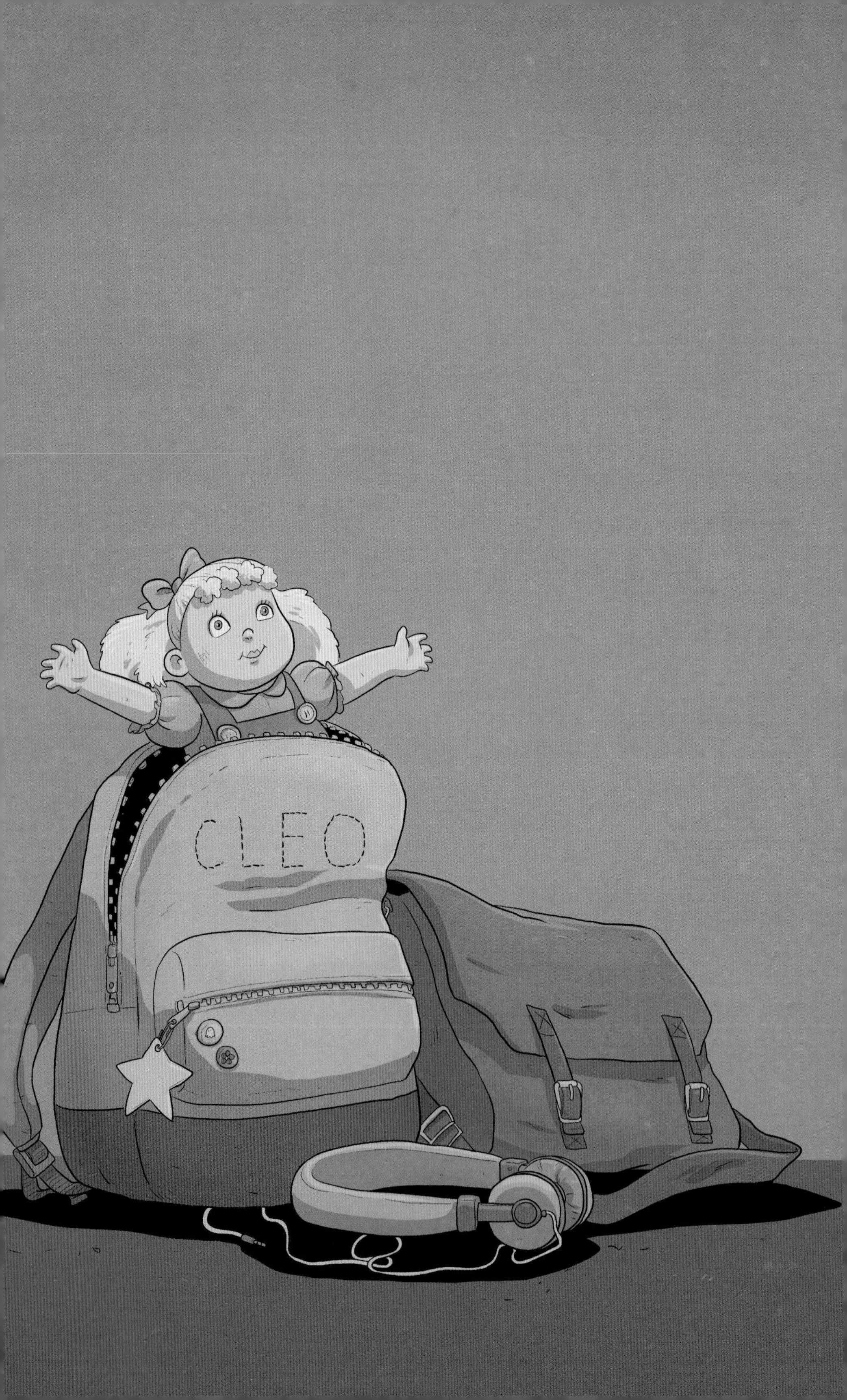
CLEO

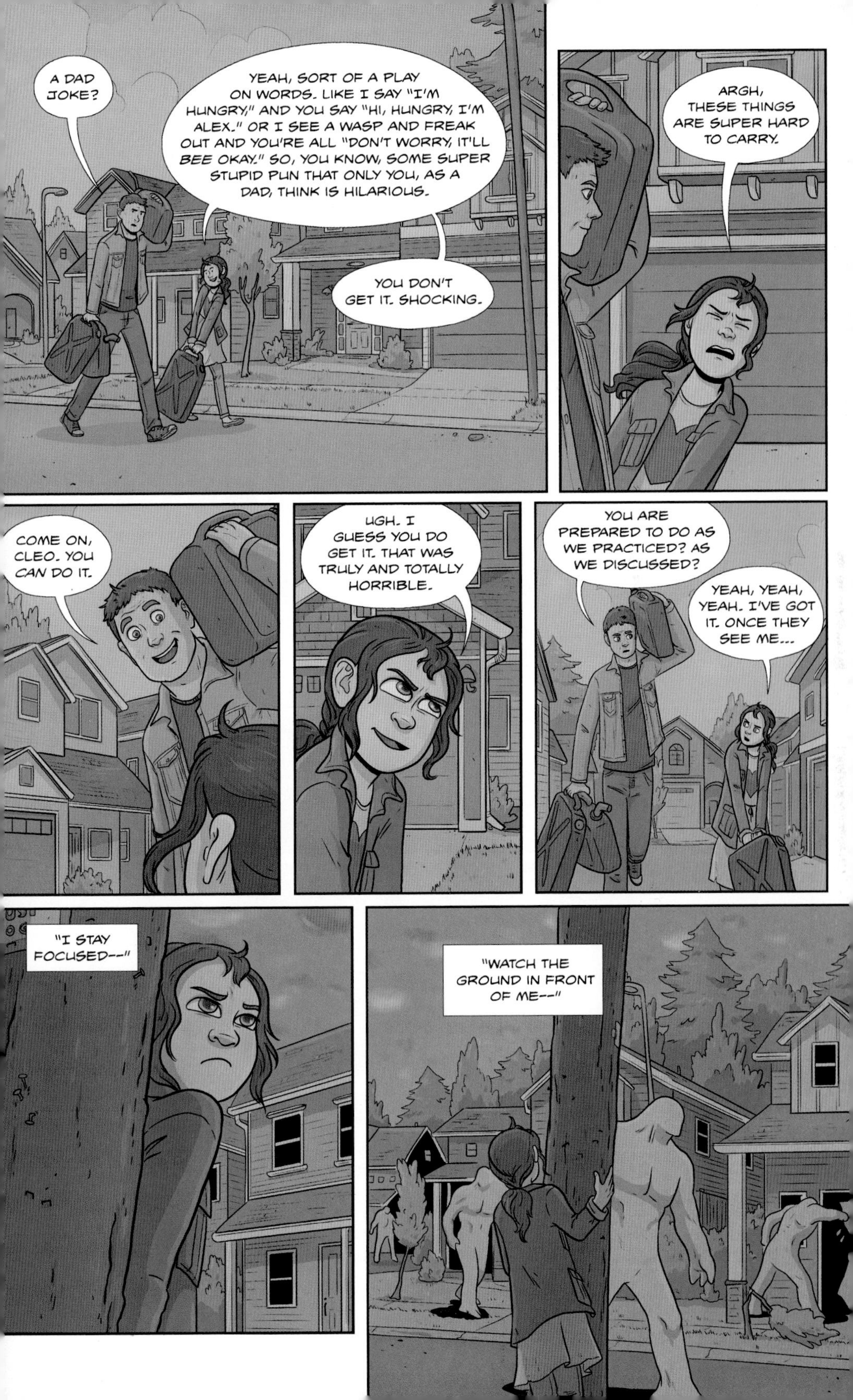
A DAD JOKE?
YEAH, SORT OF A PLAY ON WORDS. LIKE I SAY "I'M HUNGRY," AND YOU SAY "HI, HUNGRY, I'M ALEX." OR I SEE A WASP AND FREAK OUT AND YOU'RE ALL "DON'T WORRY, IT'LL BEE OKAY." SO, YOU KNOW, SOME SUPER STUPID PUN THAT ONLY YOU, AS A DAD, THINK IS HILARIOUS.
YOU DON'T GET IT. SHOCKING.
ARGH, THESE THINGS ARE SUPER HARD TO CARRY.
COME ON, CLEO. YOU CAN DO IT.
UGH. I GUESS YOU DO GET IT. THAT WAS TRULY AND TOTALLY HORRIBLE.
YOU ARE PREPARED TO DO AS WE PRACTICED? AS WE DISCUSSED?
YEAH, YEAH, YEAH. I'VE GOT IT. ONCE THEY SEE ME...
"I STAY FOCUSED--"
"WATCH THE GROUND IN FRONT OF ME--"

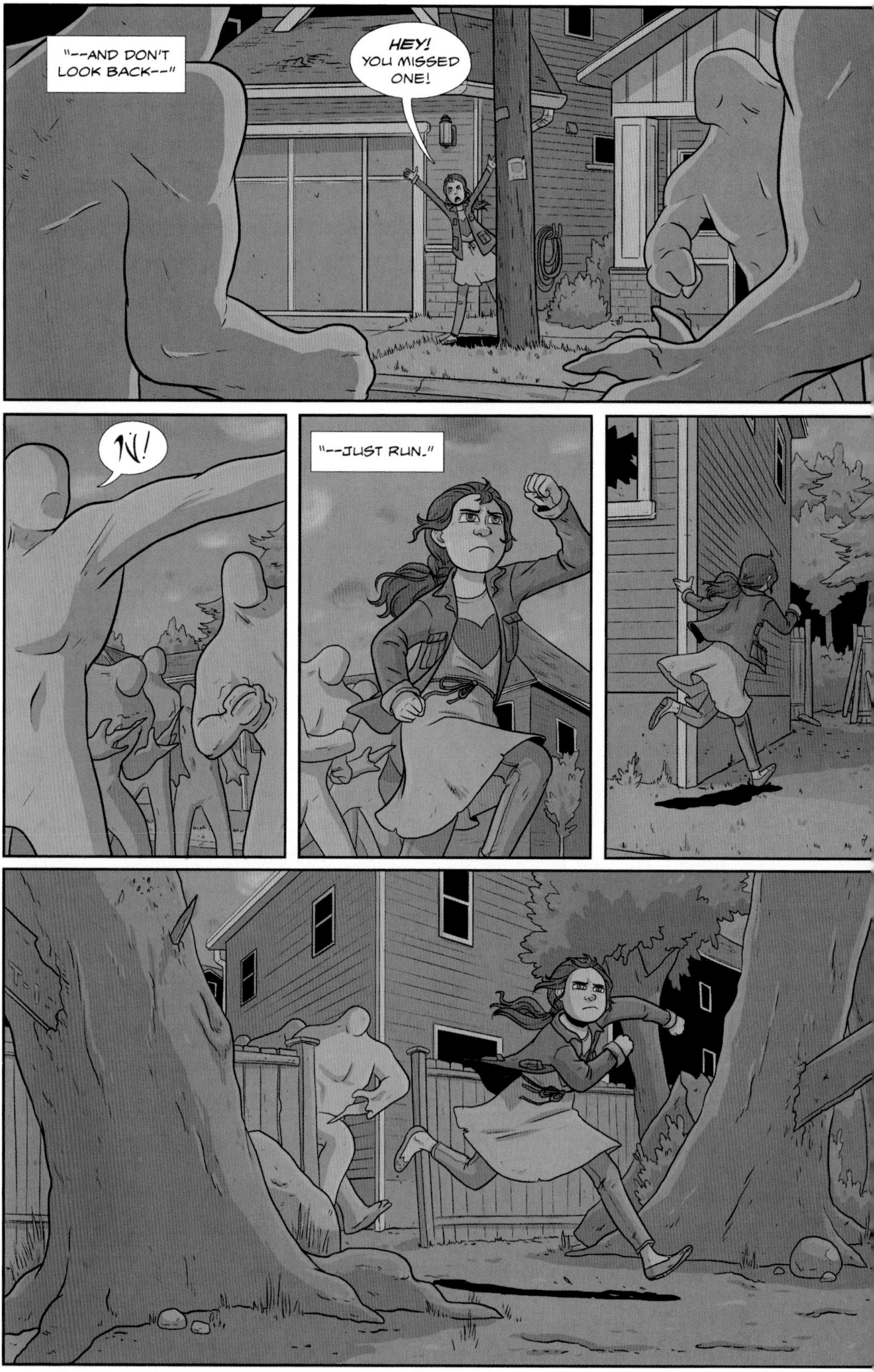
"--AND DON'T LOOK BACK--"
HEY! YOU MISSED ONE!
"--JUST RUN."

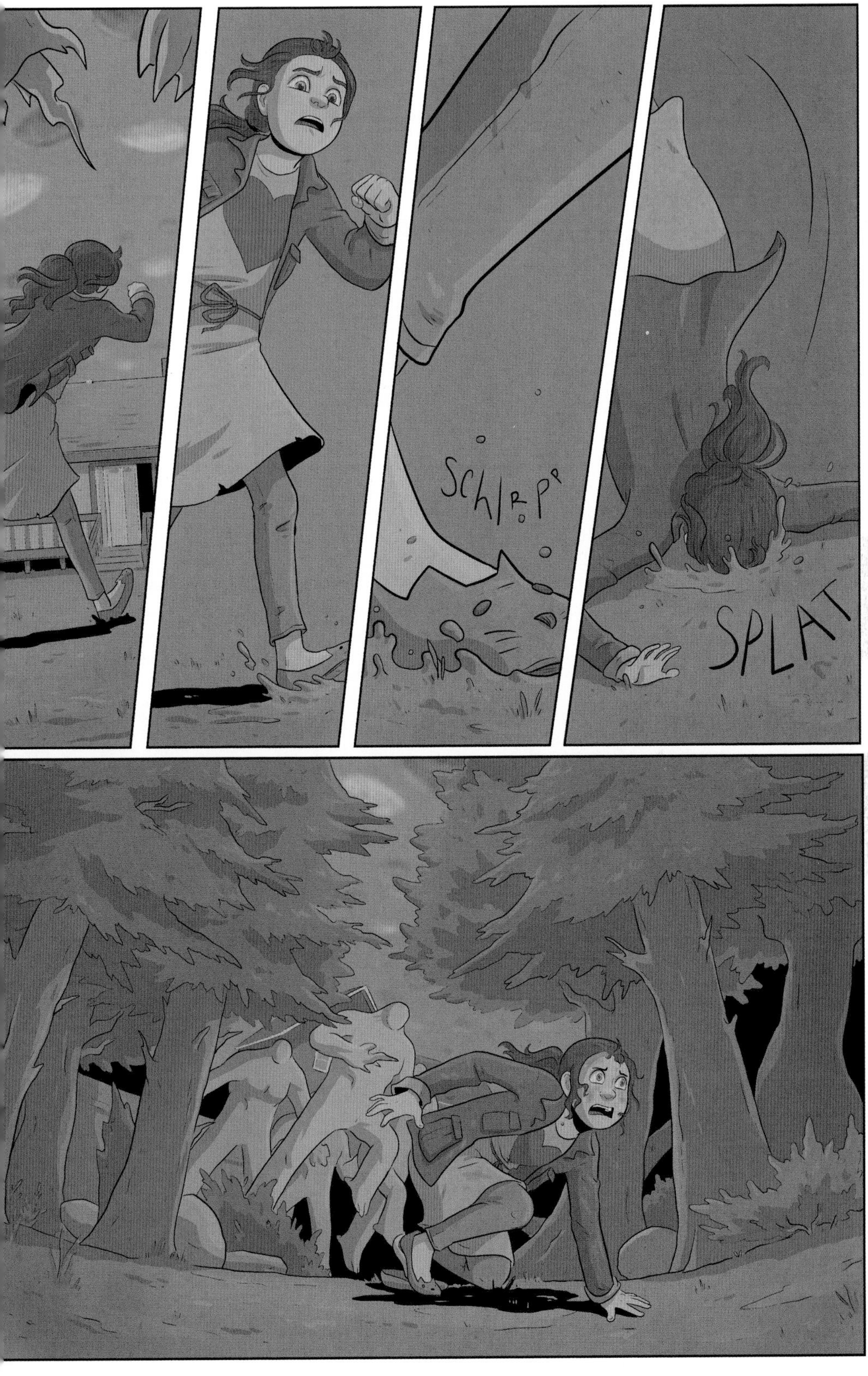
SCHIRRPP
SPLAT

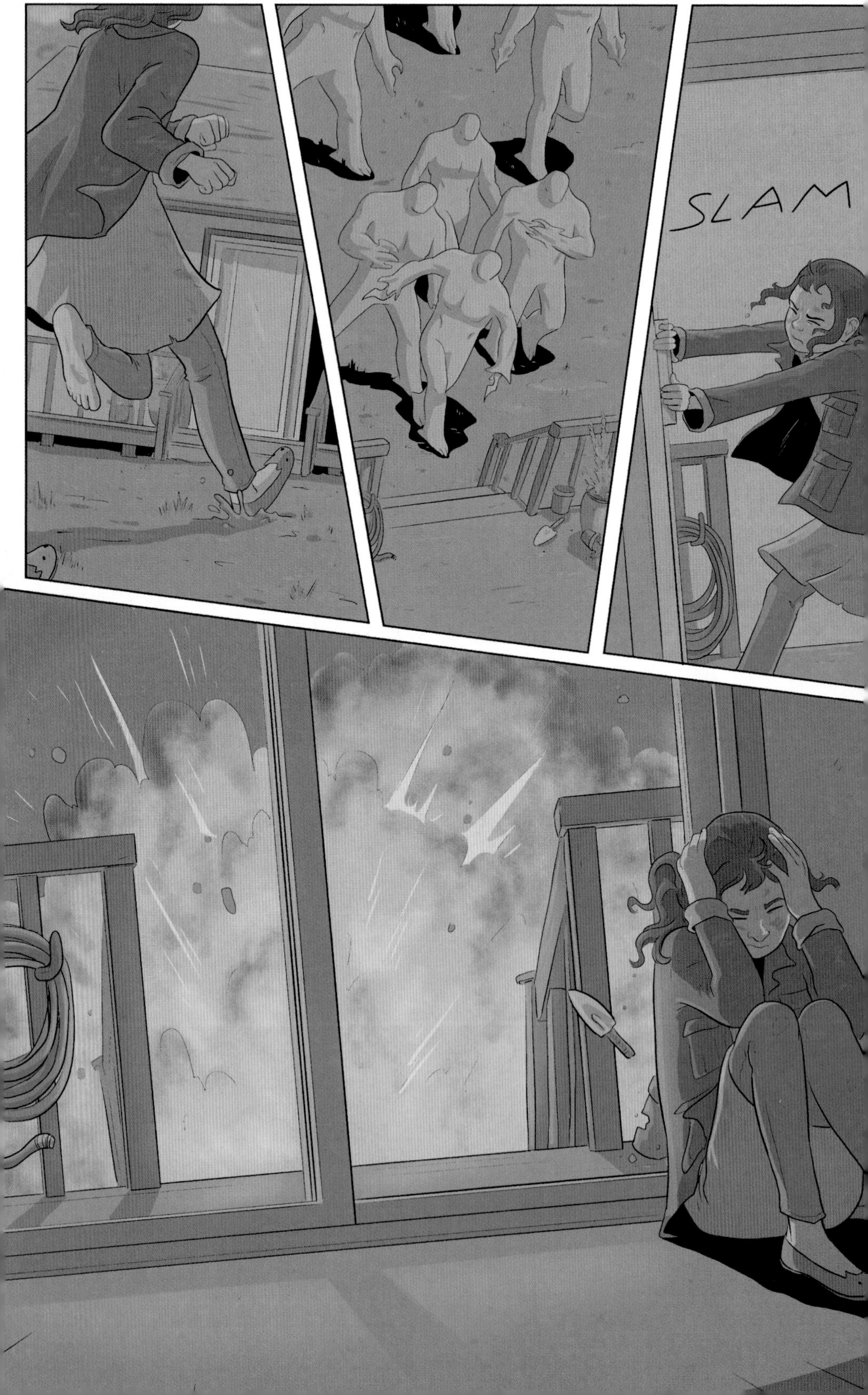
SLAM

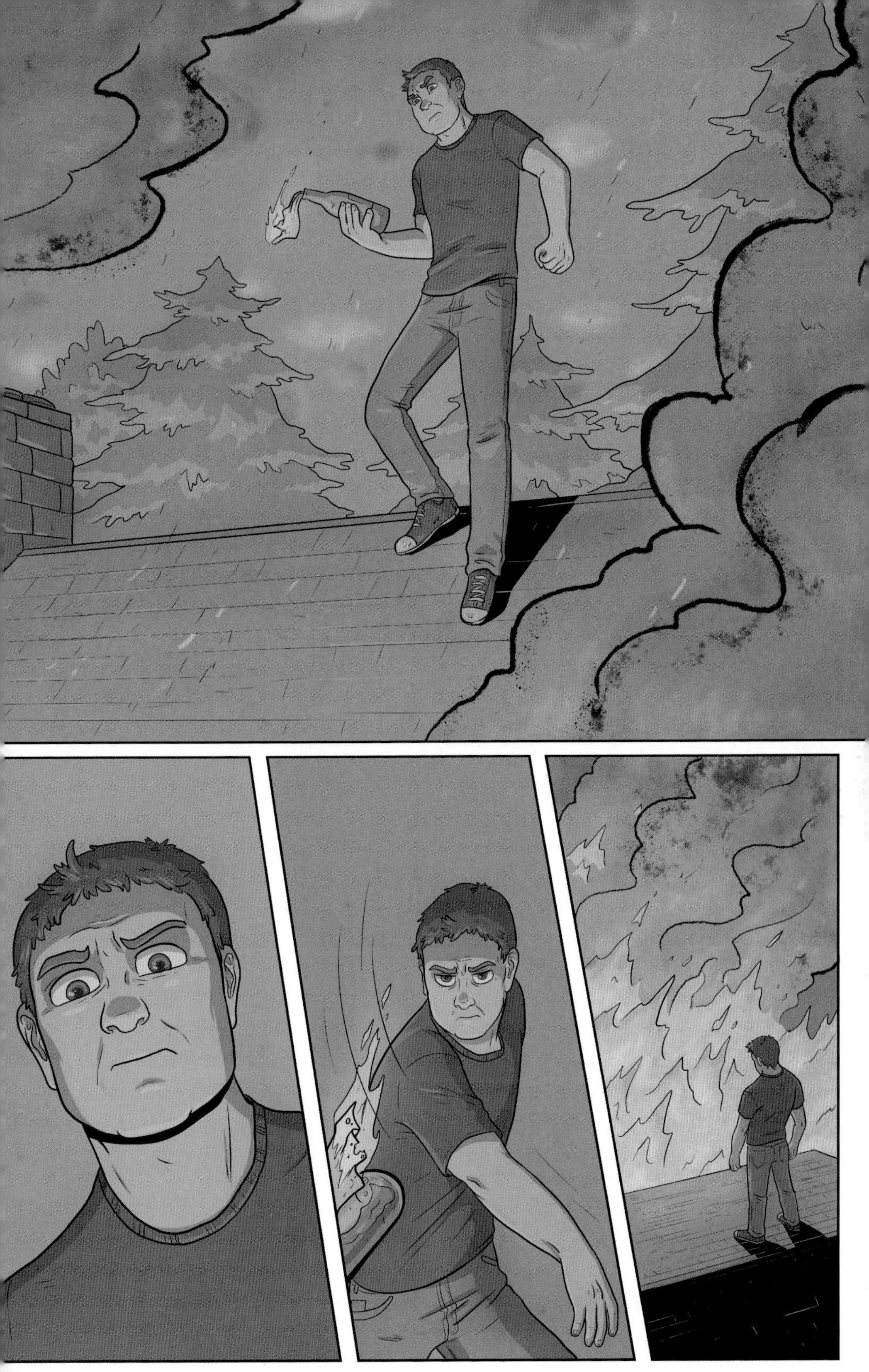

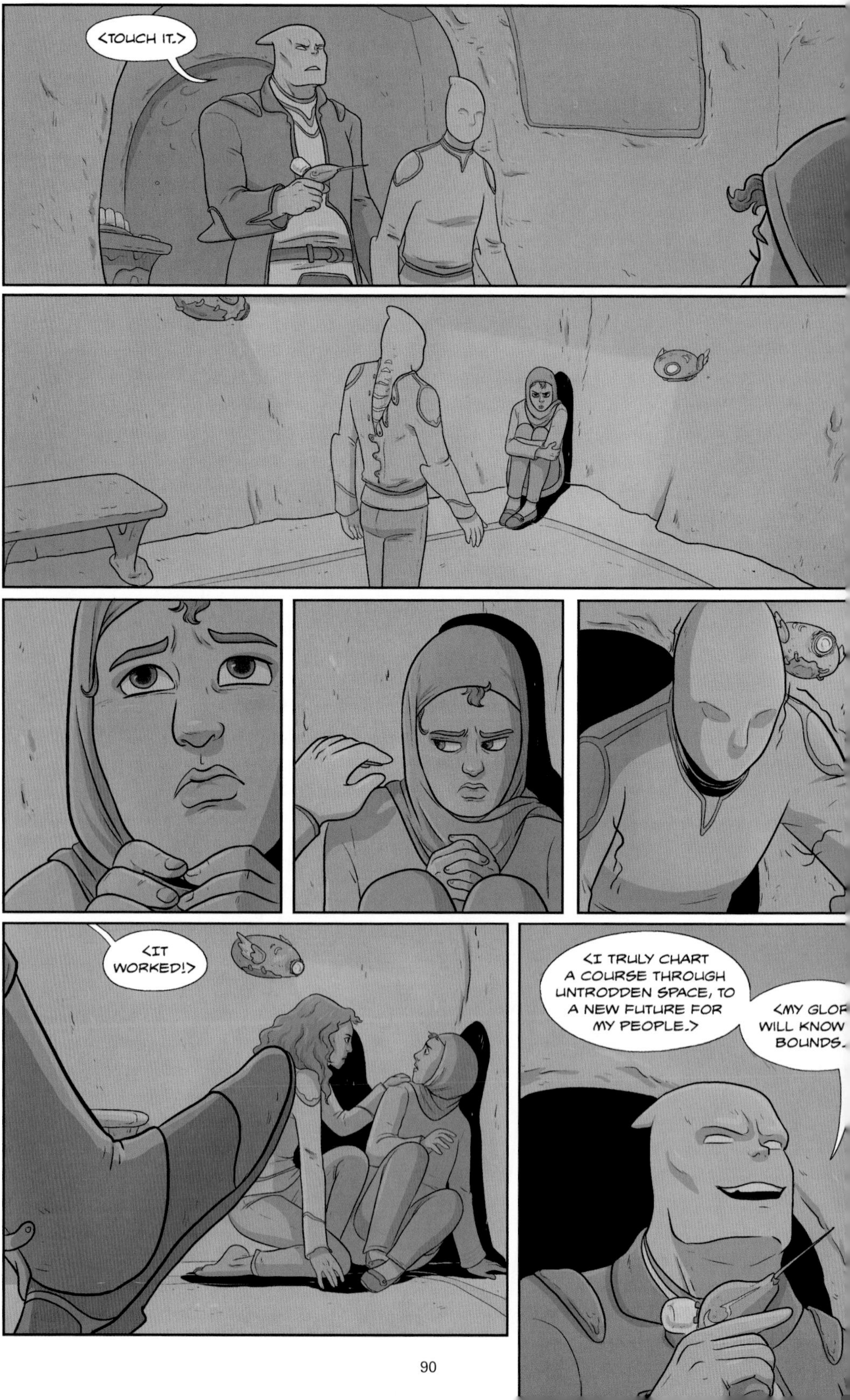
<TOUCH IT.>
<IT WORKED!>
<I TRULY CHART A COURSE THROUGH UNTRODDEN SPACE, TO A NEW FUTURE FOR MY PEOPLE.>
<MY GLOR WILL KNOW BOUNDS.

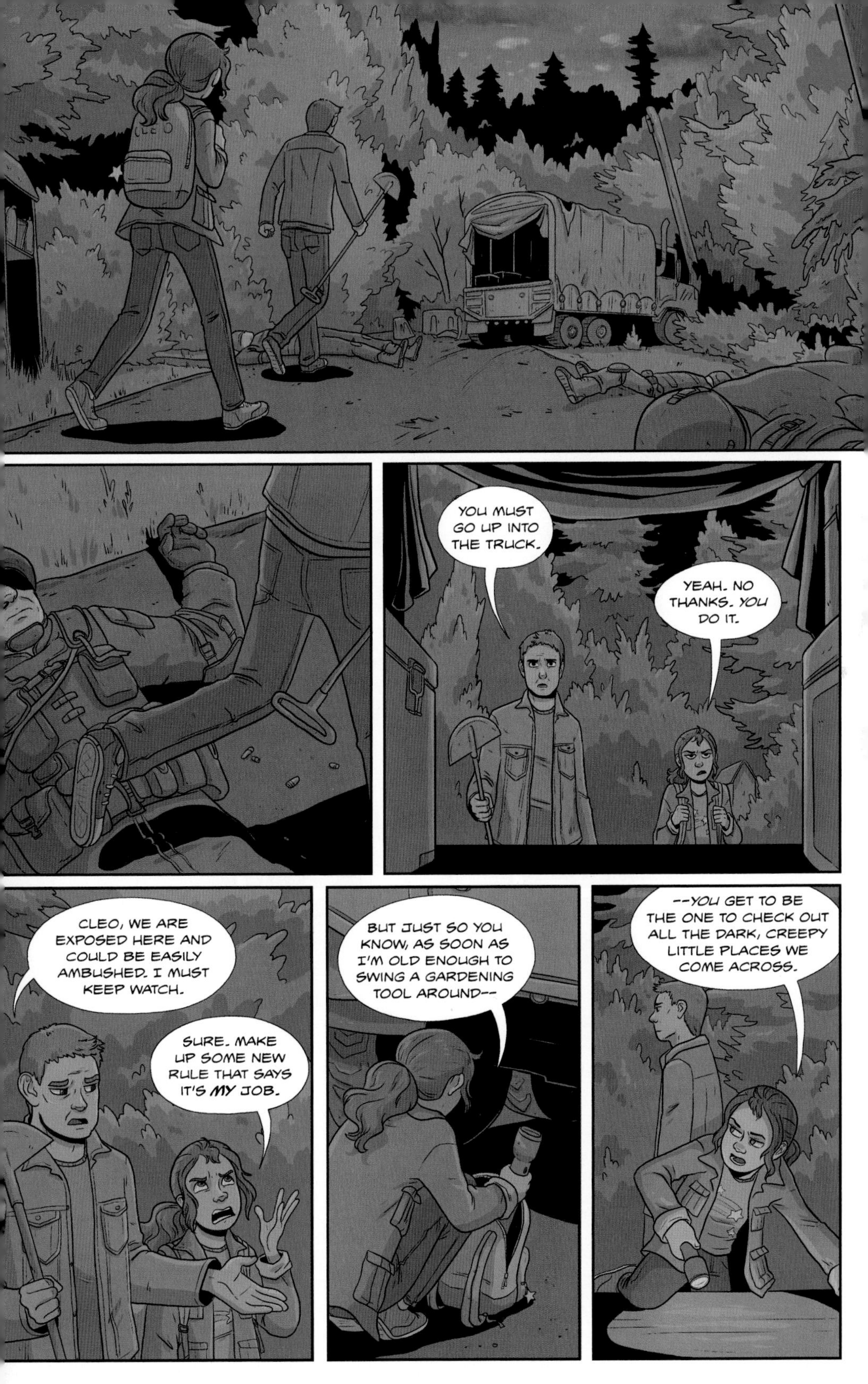

YOU MUST GO UP INTO THE TRUCK.
YEAH. NO THANKS. YOU DO IT.
CLEO, WE ARE EXPOSED HERE AND COULD BE EASILY AMBUSHED. I MUST KEEP WATCH.
SURE. MAKE UP SOME NEW RULE THAT SAYS IT'S MY JOB.
BUT JUST SO YOU KNOW, AS SOON AS I'M OLD ENOUGH TO SWING A GARDENING TOOL AROUND--
--YOU GET TO BE THE ONE TO CHECK OUT ALL THE DARK, CREEPY LITTLE PLACES WE COME ACROSS.

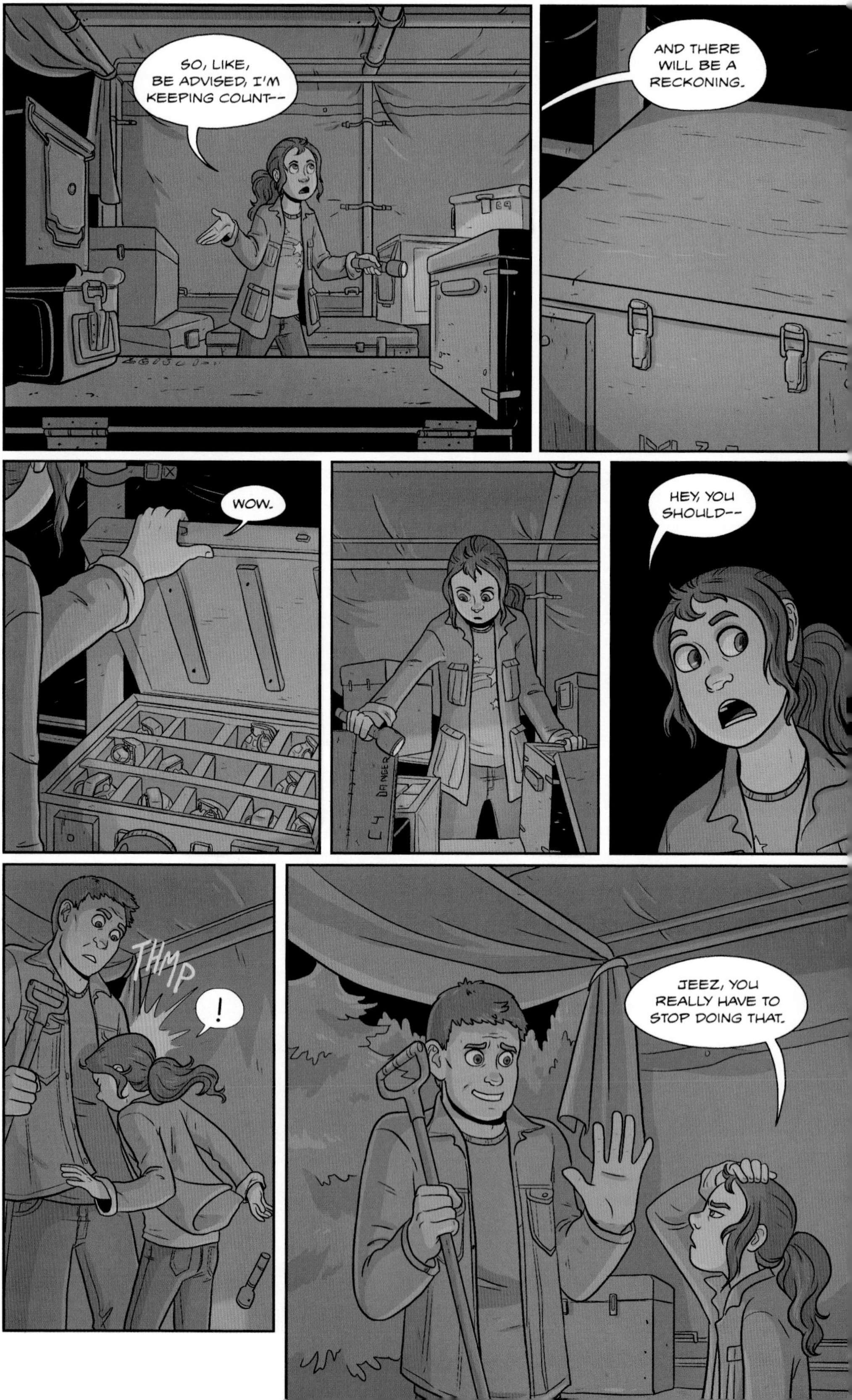
SO, LIKE, BE ADVISED, I'M KEEPING COUNT--
AND THERE WILL BE A RECKONING.
WOW.
HEY, YOU SHOULD--
THMP
!
JEEZ, YOU REALLY HAVE TO STOP DOING THAT.

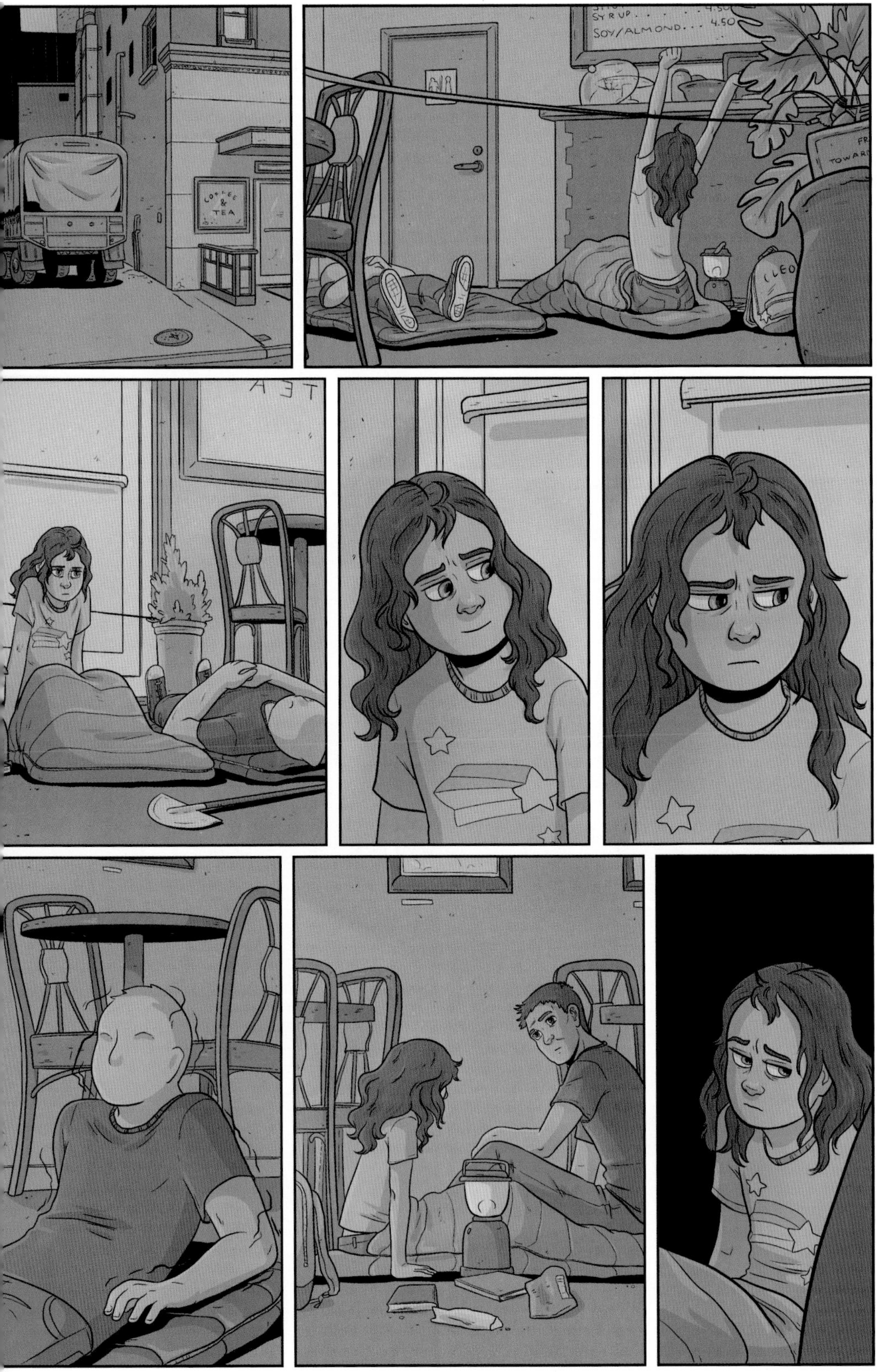
COFFEE & TEA
SYRUP . . . 4.50
SOY/ALMOND . . . 4.50

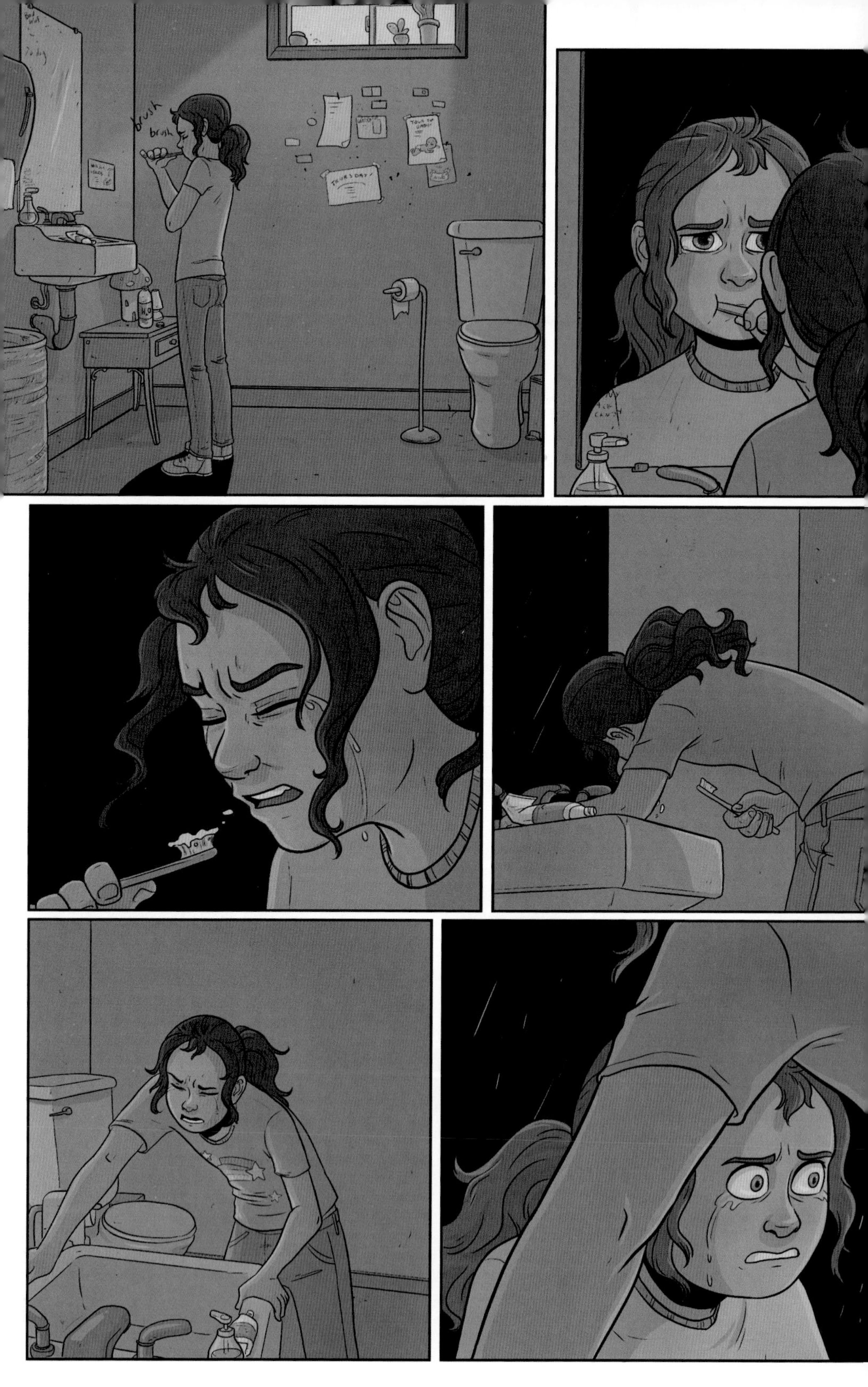
brush
brush
THURSDAY!

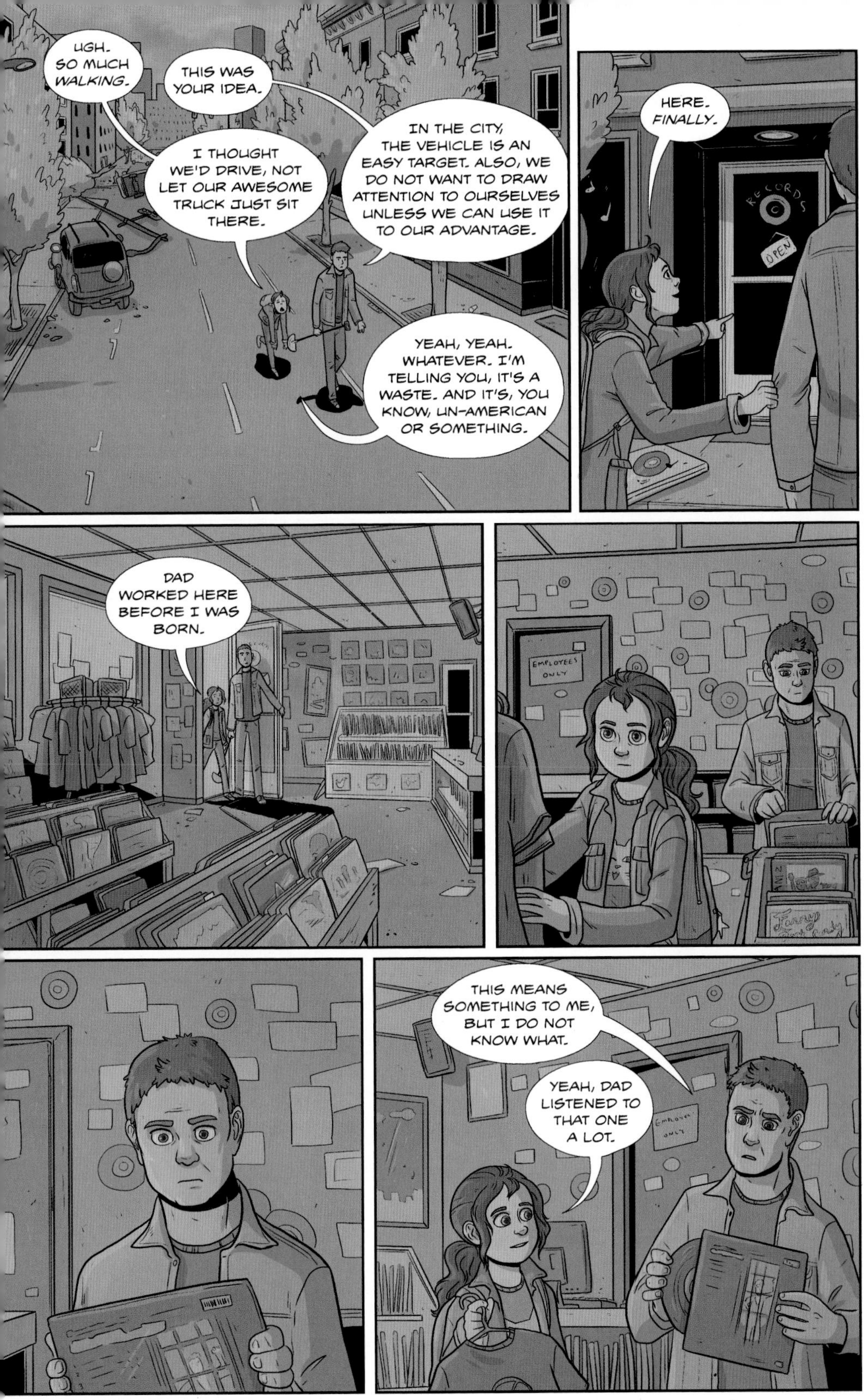
UGH. SO MUCH WALKING.
THIS WAS YOUR IDEA.
I THOUGHT WE'D DRIVE, NOT LET OUR AWESOME TRUCK JUST SIT THERE.
IN THE CITY, THE VEHICLE IS AN EASY TARGET. ALSO, WE DO NOT WANT TO DRAW ATTENTION TO OURSELVES UNLESS WE CAN USE IT TO OUR ADVANTAGE.
YEAH, YEAH. WHATEVER. I'M TELLING YOU, IT'S A WASTE. AND IT'S, YOU KNOW, UN-AMERICAN OR SOMETHING.
HERE. FINALLY.
RECORDS
OPEN
DAD WORKED HERE BEFORE I WAS BORN.
EMPLOYEES ONLY
THIS MEANS SOMETHING TO ME, BUT I DO NOT KNOW WHAT.
YEAH, DAD LISTENED TO THAT ONE A LOT.

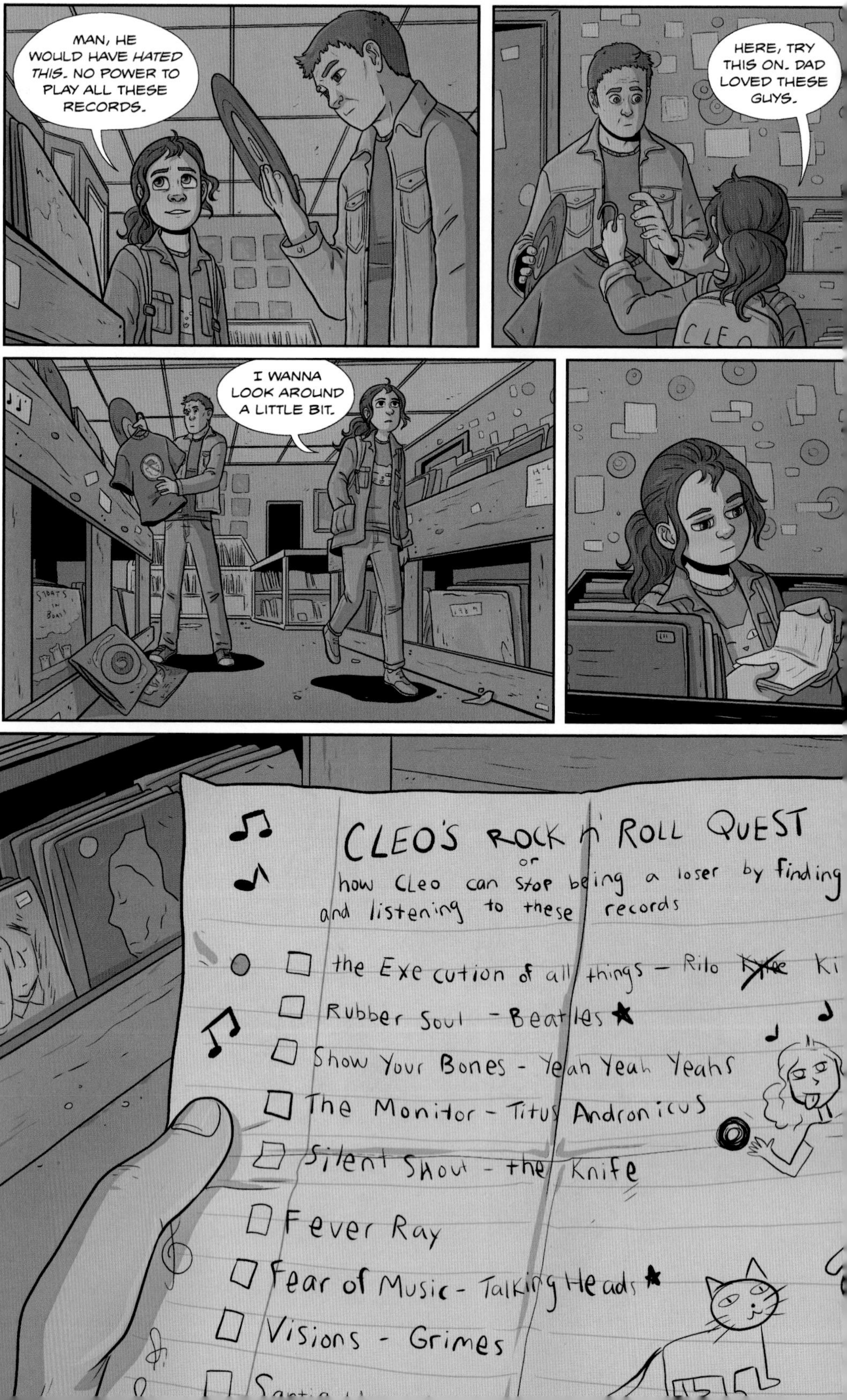

MAN, HE WOULD HAVE *HATED THIS*. NO POWER TO PLAY ALL THESE RECORDS.
HERE, TRY THIS ON. DAD LOVED THESE GUYS.
I WANNA LOOK AROUND A LITTLE BIT.
CLEO'S ROCK n' ROLL QUEST
or
how Cleo can stop being a loser by finding and listening to these records
the Execution of all things - Rilo
Rubber Soul - Beatles
Show Your Bones - Yeah Yeah Yeahs
The Monitor - Titus Andronicus
Silent Shout - the Knife
Fever Ray
Fear of Music - Talking Heads
Visions - Grimes

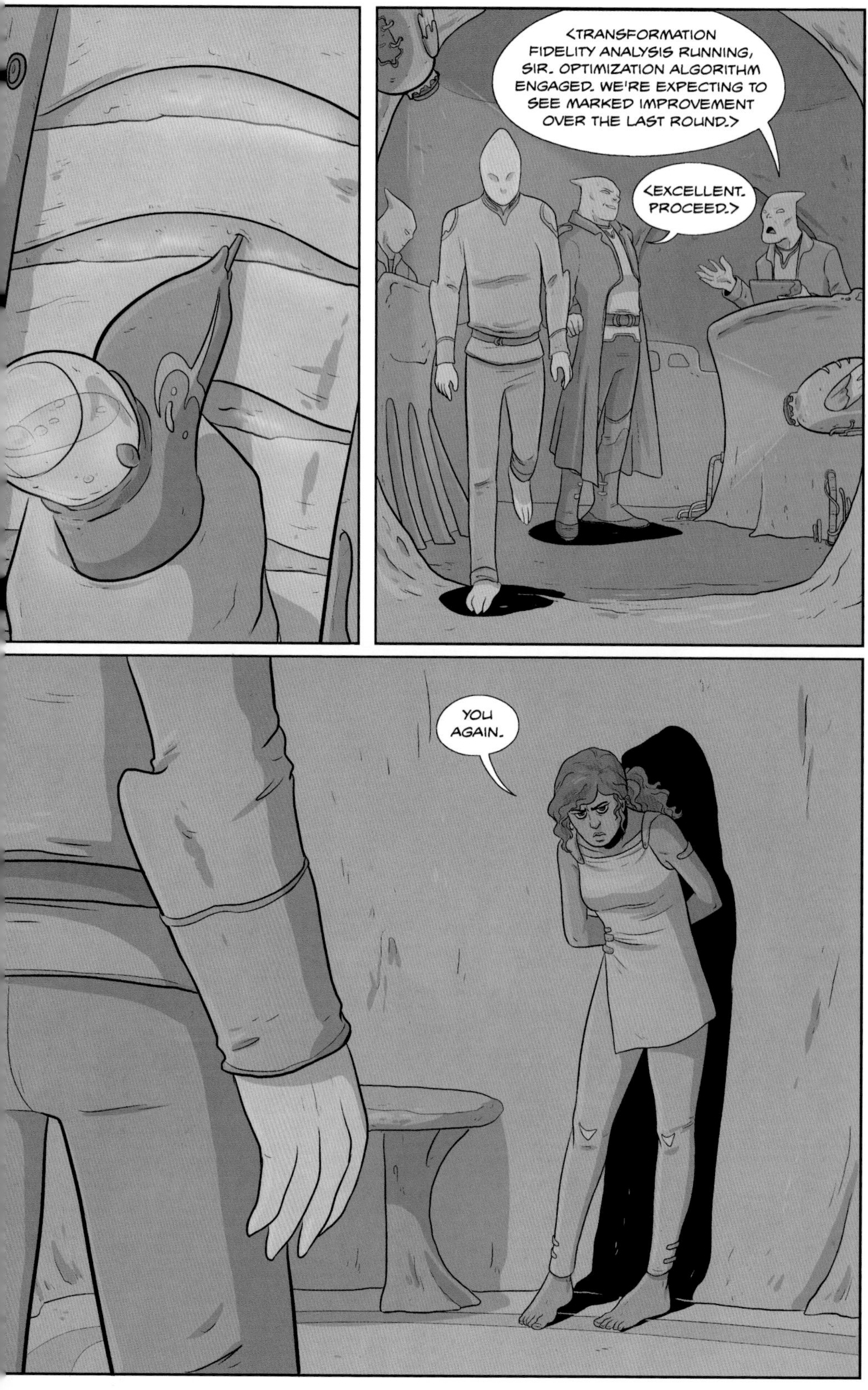
<TRANSFORMATION FIDELITY ANALYSIS RUNNING, SIR. OPTIMIZATION ALGORITHM ENGAGED. WE'RE EXPECTING TO SEE MARKED IMPROVEMENT OVER THE LAST ROUND.>
<EXCELLENT. PROCEED.>
YOU AGAIN.

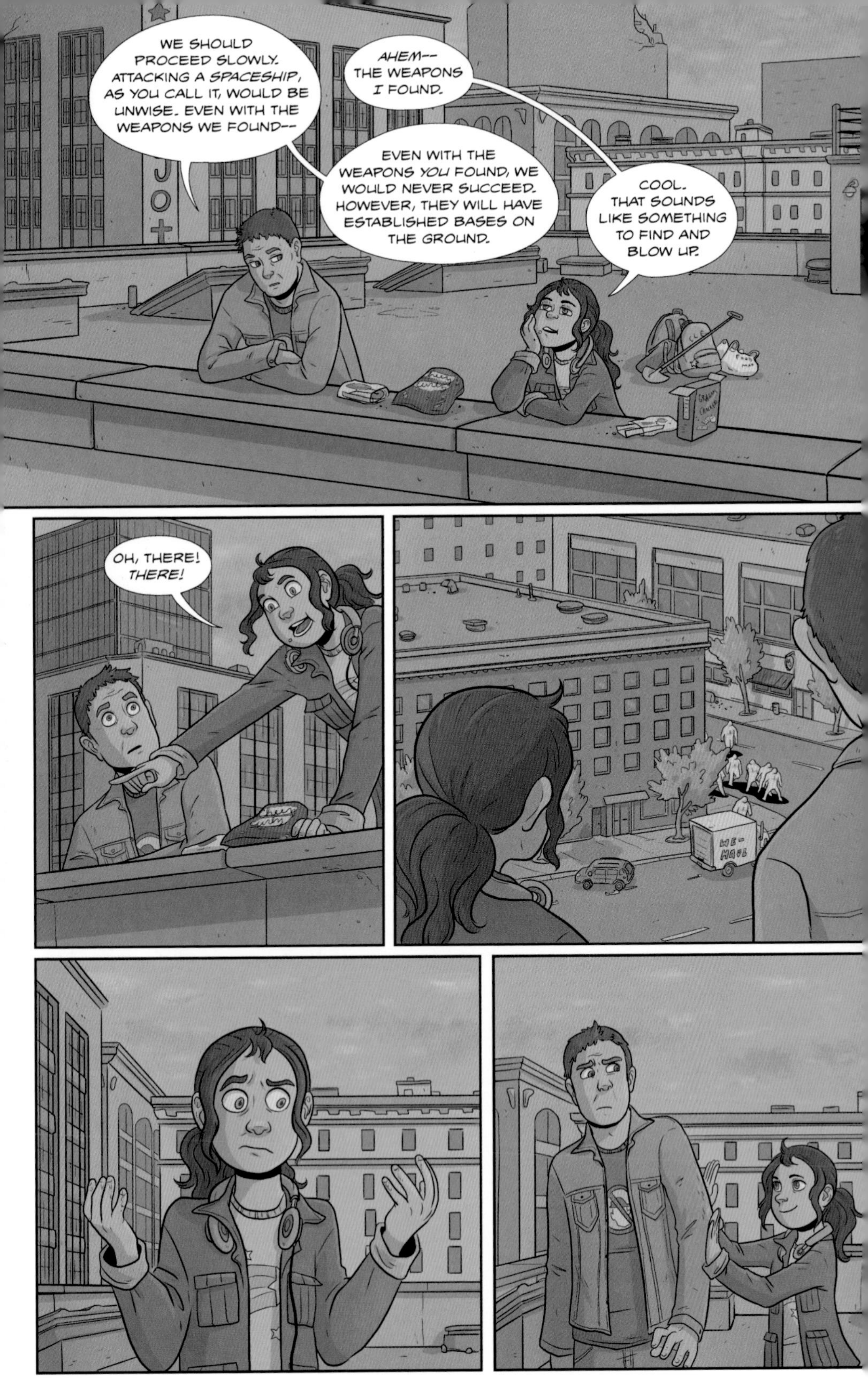
WE SHOULD PROCEED SLOWLY. ATTACKING A *SPACESHIP*, AS YOU CALL IT, WOULD BE UNWISE. EVEN WITH THE WEAPONS WE FOUND--
AHEM-- THE WEAPONS *I* FOUND.
EVEN WITH THE WEAPONS *YOU* FOUND, WE WOULD NEVER SUCCEED. HOWEVER, THEY WILL HAVE ESTABLISHED BASES ON THE GROUND.
COOL. THAT SOUNDS LIKE SOMETHING TO FIND AND BLOW UP.
OH, THERE! *THERE!*
WE-HAUL

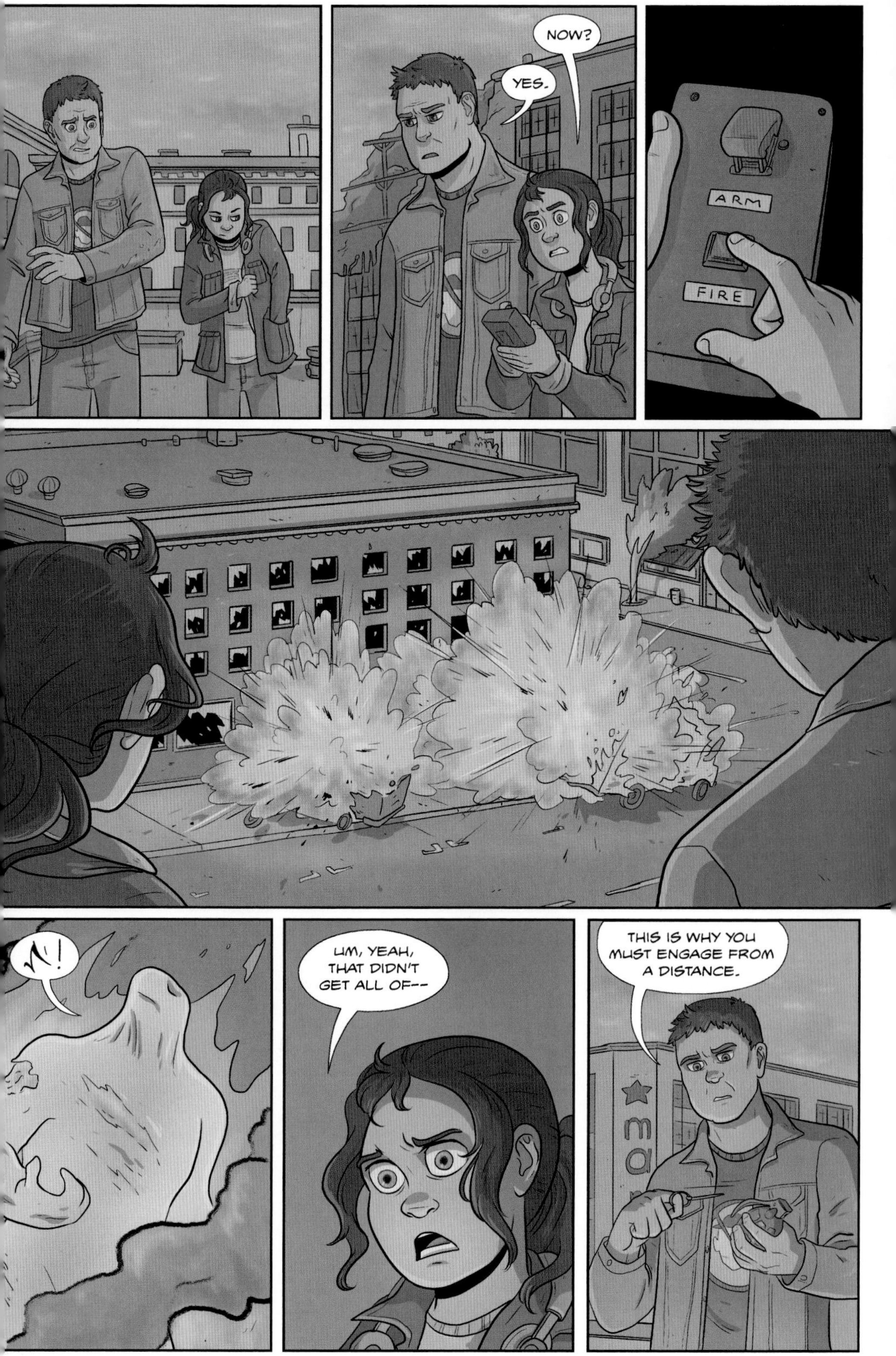
NOW?
YES.
ARM
FIRE
UM, YEAH, THAT DIDN'T GET ALL OF--
THIS IS WHY YOU MUST ENGAGE FROM A DISTANCE.

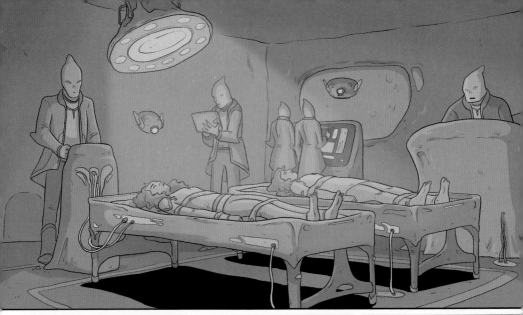

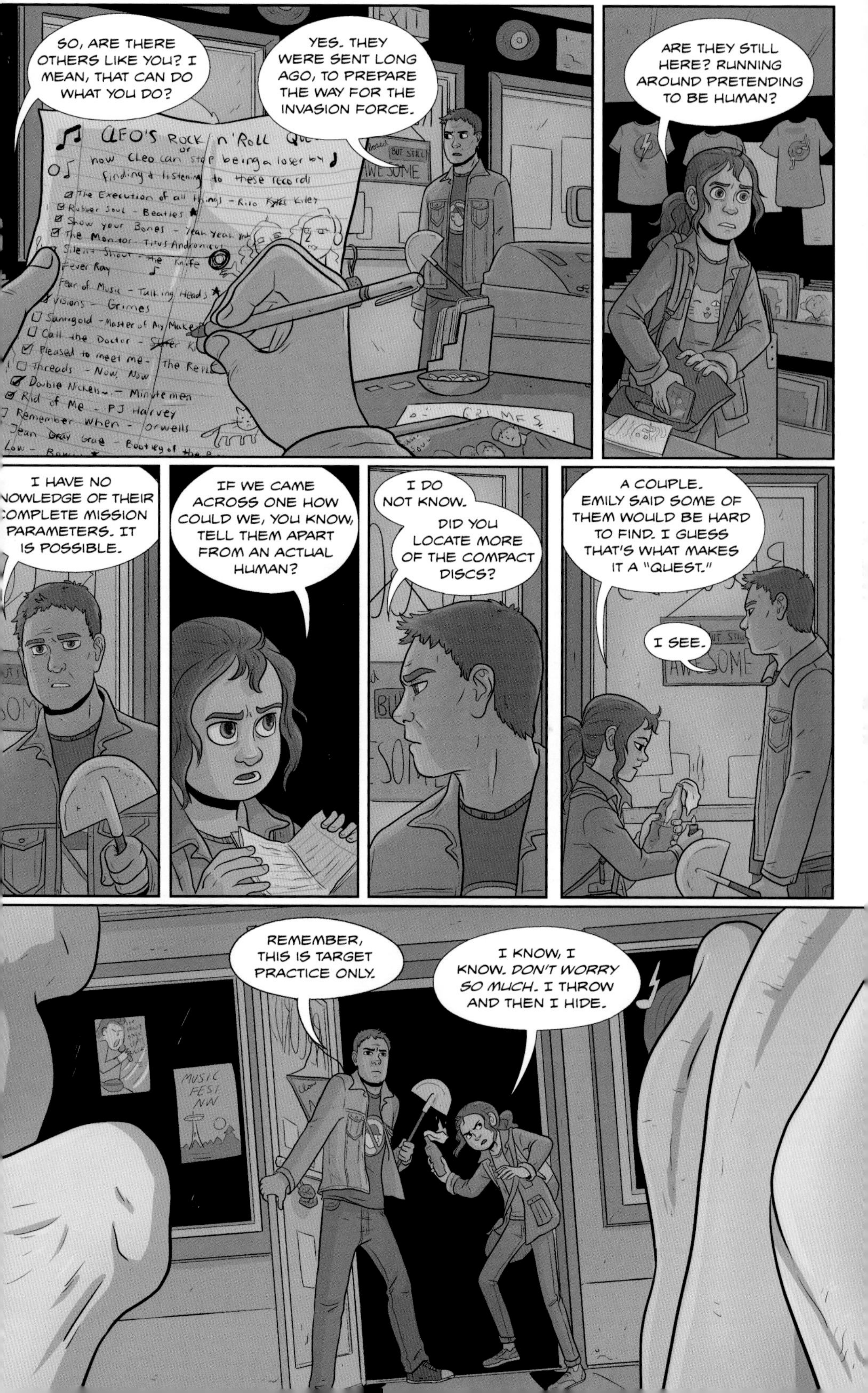
SO, ARE THERE OTHERS LIKE YOU? I MEAN, THAT CAN DO WHAT YOU DO?
YES. THEY WERE SENT LONG AGO, TO PREPARE THE WAY FOR THE INVASION FORCE.
ARE THEY STILL HERE? RUNNING AROUND PRETENDING TO BE HUMAN?
I HAVE NO KNOWLEDGE OF THEIR COMPLETE MISSION PARAMETERS. IT IS POSSIBLE.
IF WE CAME ACROSS ONE HOW COULD WE, YOU KNOW, TELL THEM APART FROM AN ACTUAL HUMAN?
I DO NOT KNOW.
DID YOU LOCATE MORE OF THE COMPACT DISCS?
A COUPLE. EMILY SAID SOME OF THEM WOULD BE HARD TO FIND. I GUESS THAT'S WHAT MAKES IT A "QUEST."
I SEE.
REMEMBER, THIS IS TARGET PRACTICE ONLY.
I KNOW, I KNOW. DON'T WORRY SO MUCH. I THROW AND THEN I HIDE.

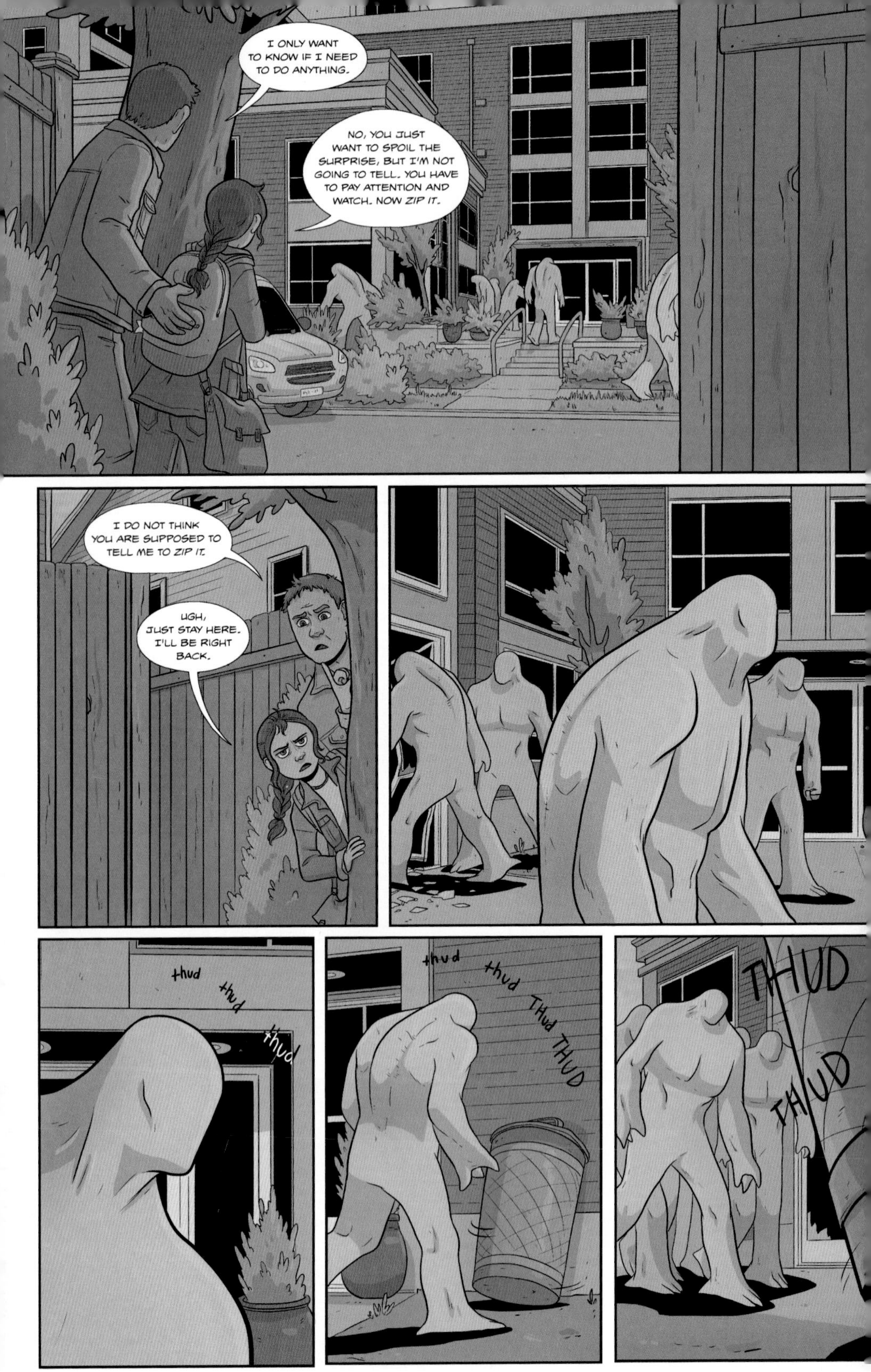
I ONLY WANT TO KNOW IF I NEED TO DO ANYTHING.
NO, YOU JUST WANT TO SPOIL THE SURPRISE, BUT I'M NOT GOING TO TELL. YOU HAVE TO PAY ATTENTION AND WATCH. NOW ZIP IT.
I DO NOT THINK YOU ARE SUPPOSED TO TELL ME TO ZIP IT.
UGH, JUST STAY HERE. I'LL BE RIGHT BACK.
thud thud thud
thud thud THud THUD
THUD THUD

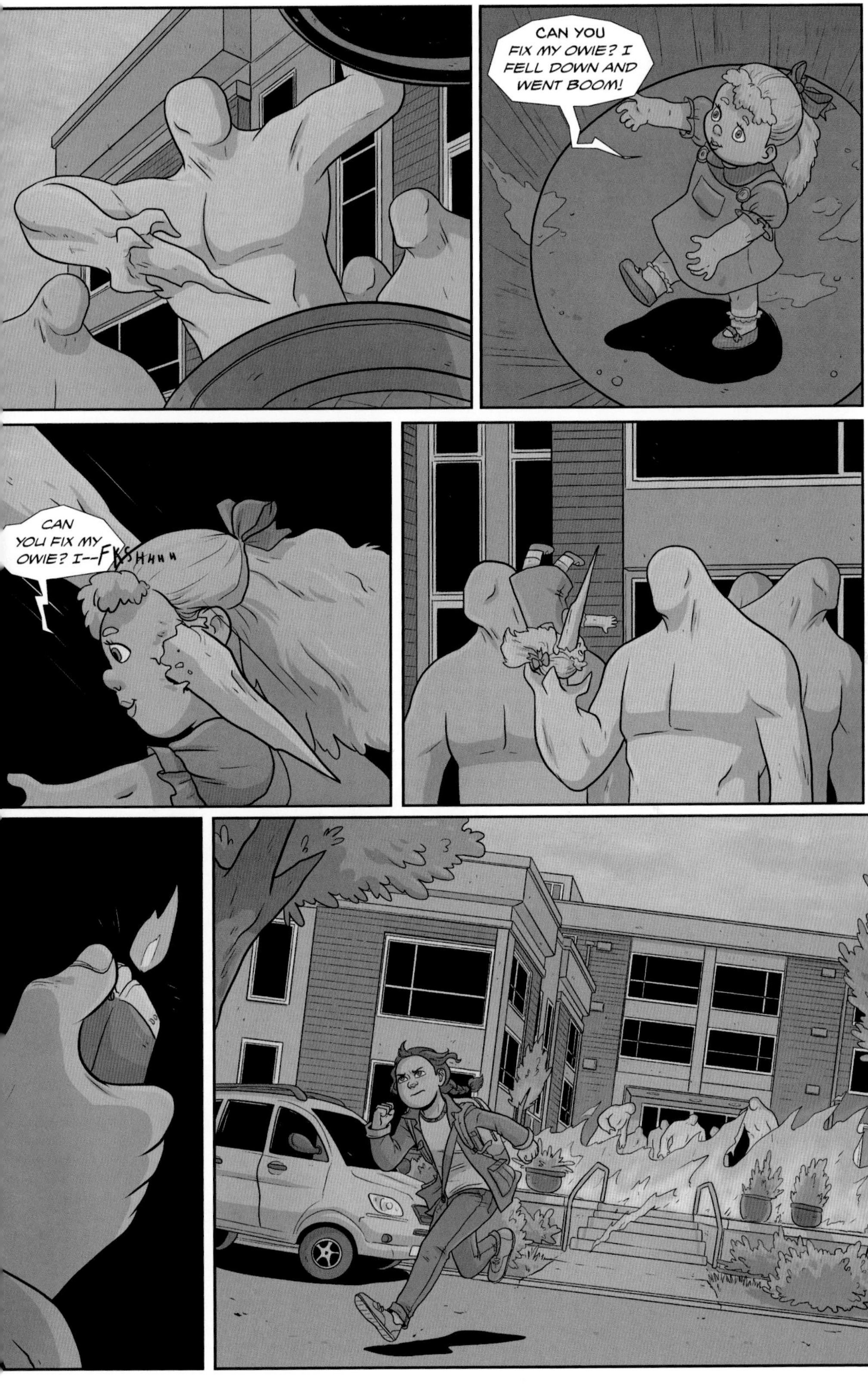
CAN YOU FIX MY OWIE? I FELL DOWN AND WENT BOOM!
CAN YOU FIX MY OWIE? I--FKSHHHH

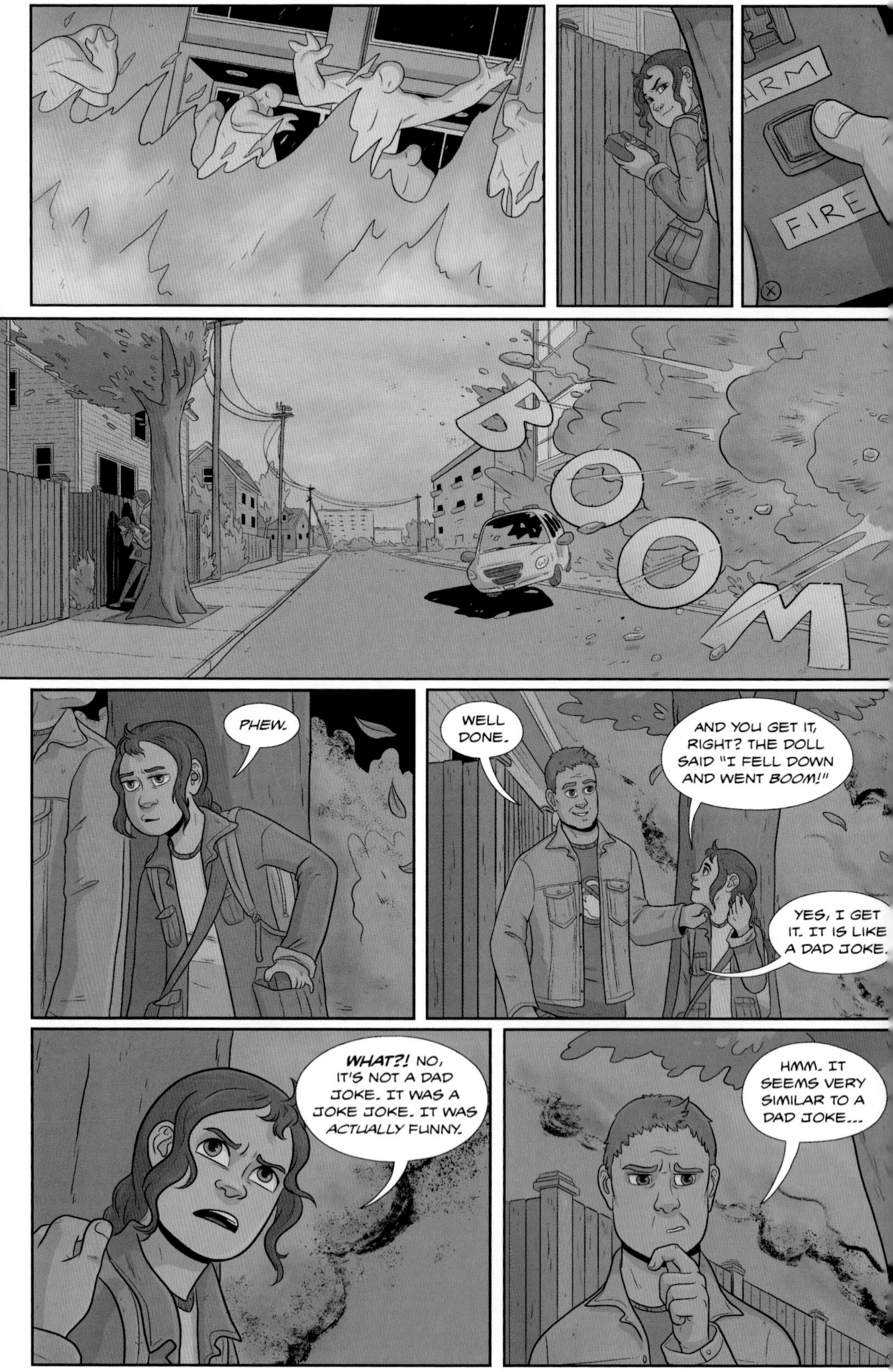
ARM
FIRE
BOOM
PHEW.
WELL DONE.
AND YOU GET IT, RIGHT? THE DOLL SAID "I FELL DOWN AND WENT BOOM!"
YES, I GET IT. IT IS LIKE A DAD JOKE.
WHAT?! NO, IT'S NOT A DAD JOKE. IT WAS A JOKE JOKE. IT WAS ACTUALLY FUNNY.
HMM. IT SEEMS VERY SIMILAR TO A DAD JOKE...

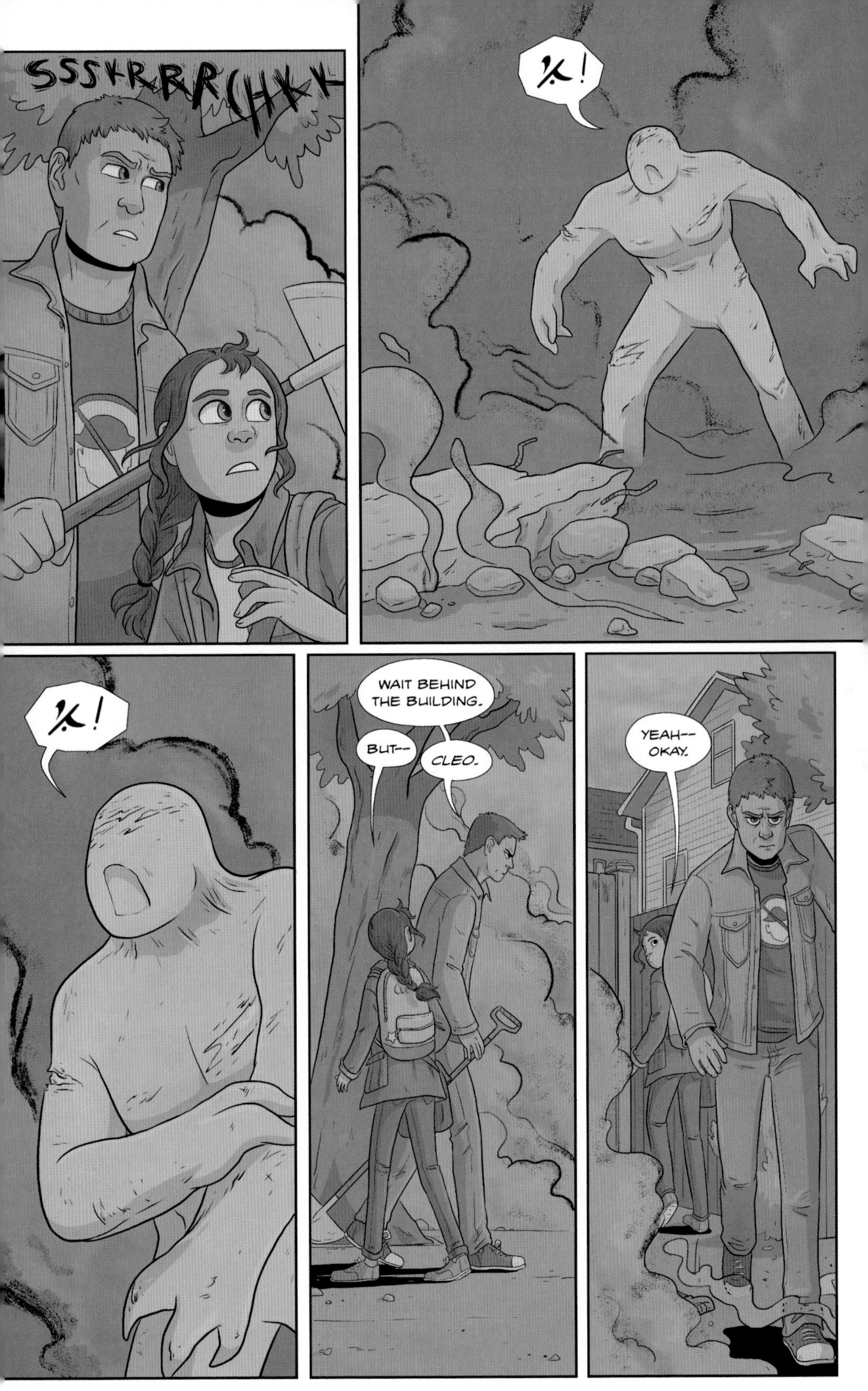
SSSKRRRCHKK
ʁ!
ʁ!
WAIT BEHIND THE BUILDING.
BUT--
CLEO.
YEAH-- OKAY.

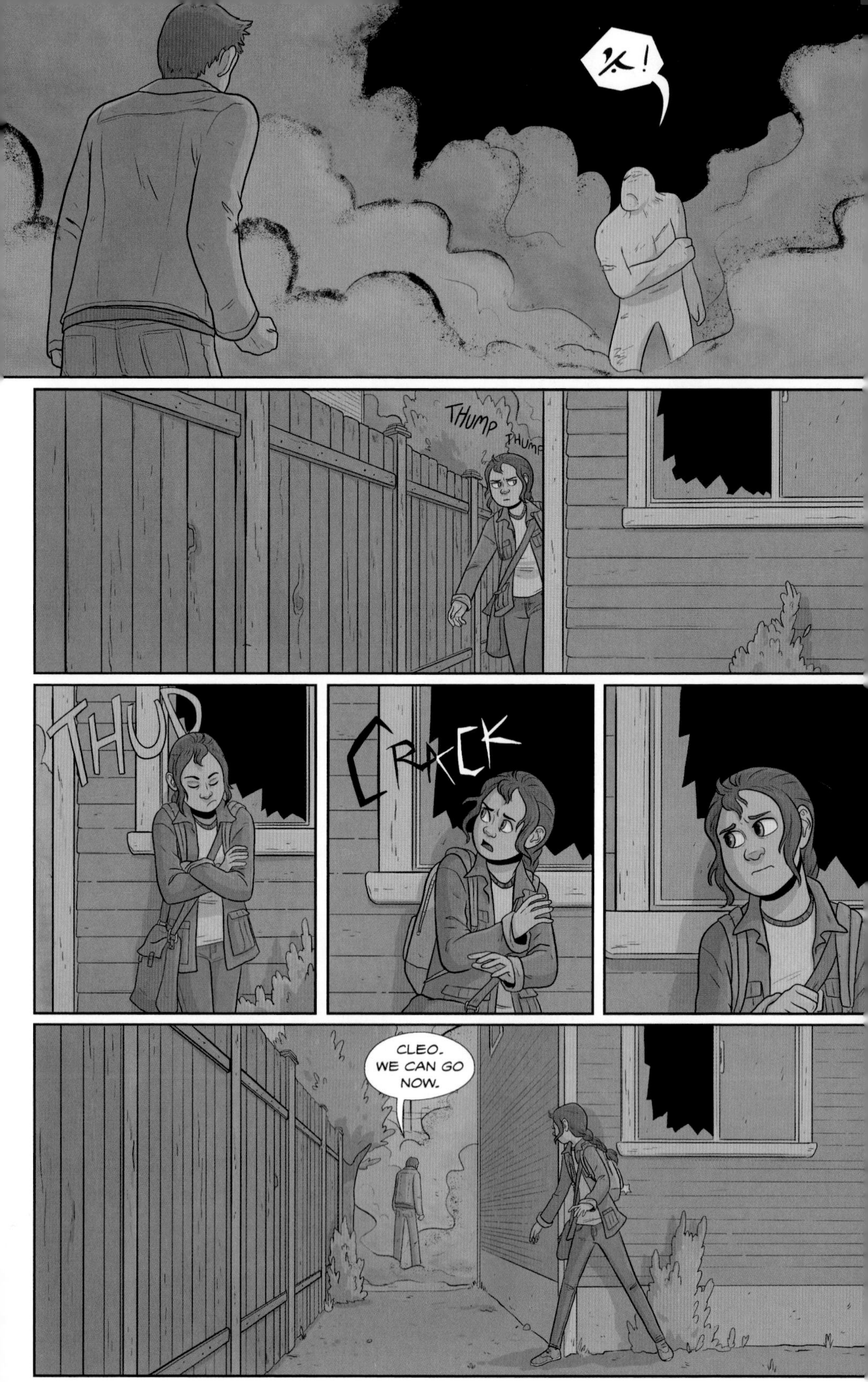
THUMP
THUMP
THUD
CRACK
CLEO. WE CAN GO NOW.

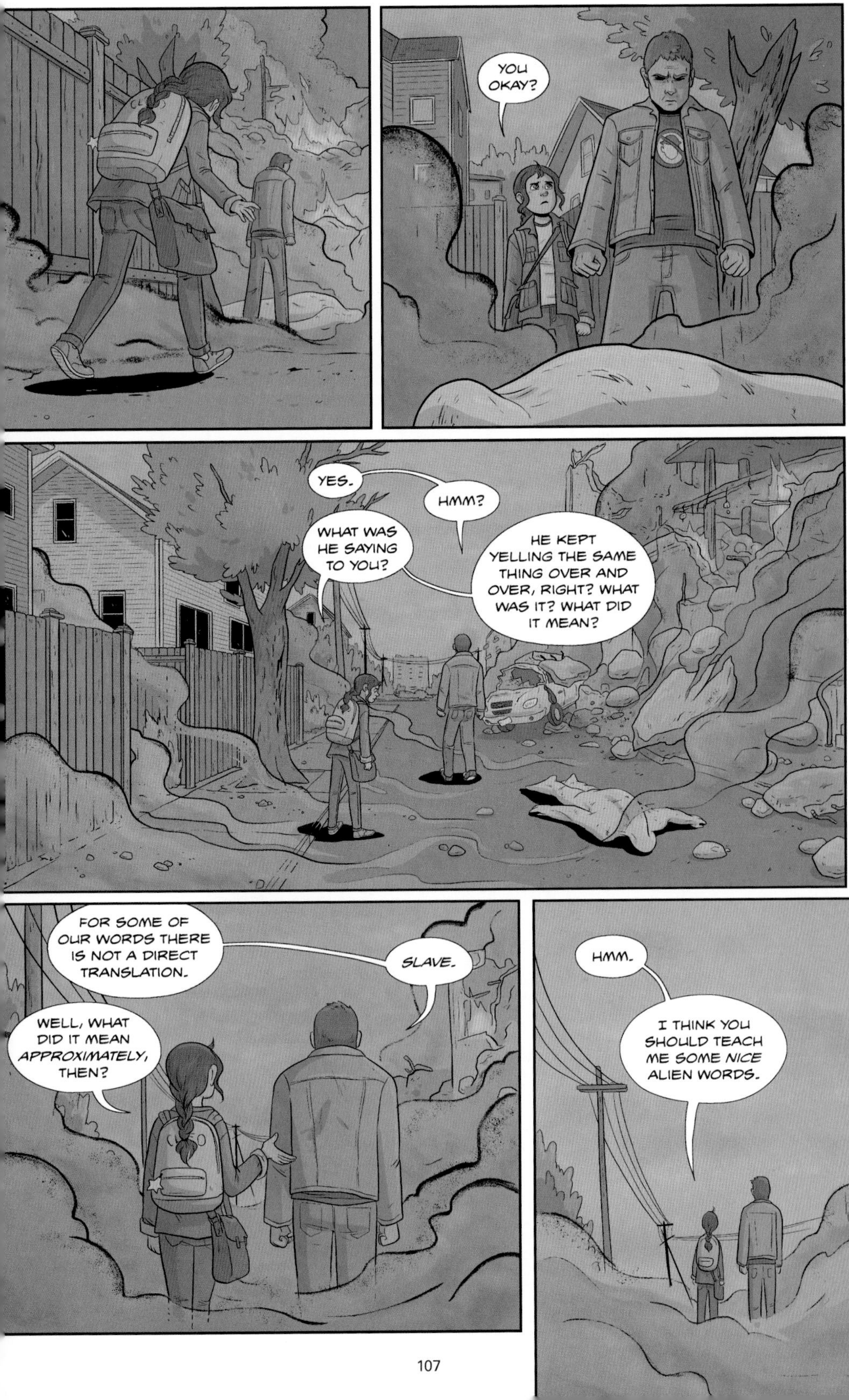
YOU OKAY?
YES.
HMM?
WHAT WAS HE SAYING TO YOU?
HE KEPT YELLING THE SAME THING OVER AND OVER, RIGHT? WHAT WAS IT? WHAT DID IT MEAN?
FOR SOME OF OUR WORDS THERE IS NOT A DIRECT TRANSLATION.
WELL, WHAT DID IT MEAN *APPROXIMATELY*, THEN?
SLAVE.
HMM.
I THINK YOU SHOULD TEACH ME SOME *NICE* ALIEN WORDS.

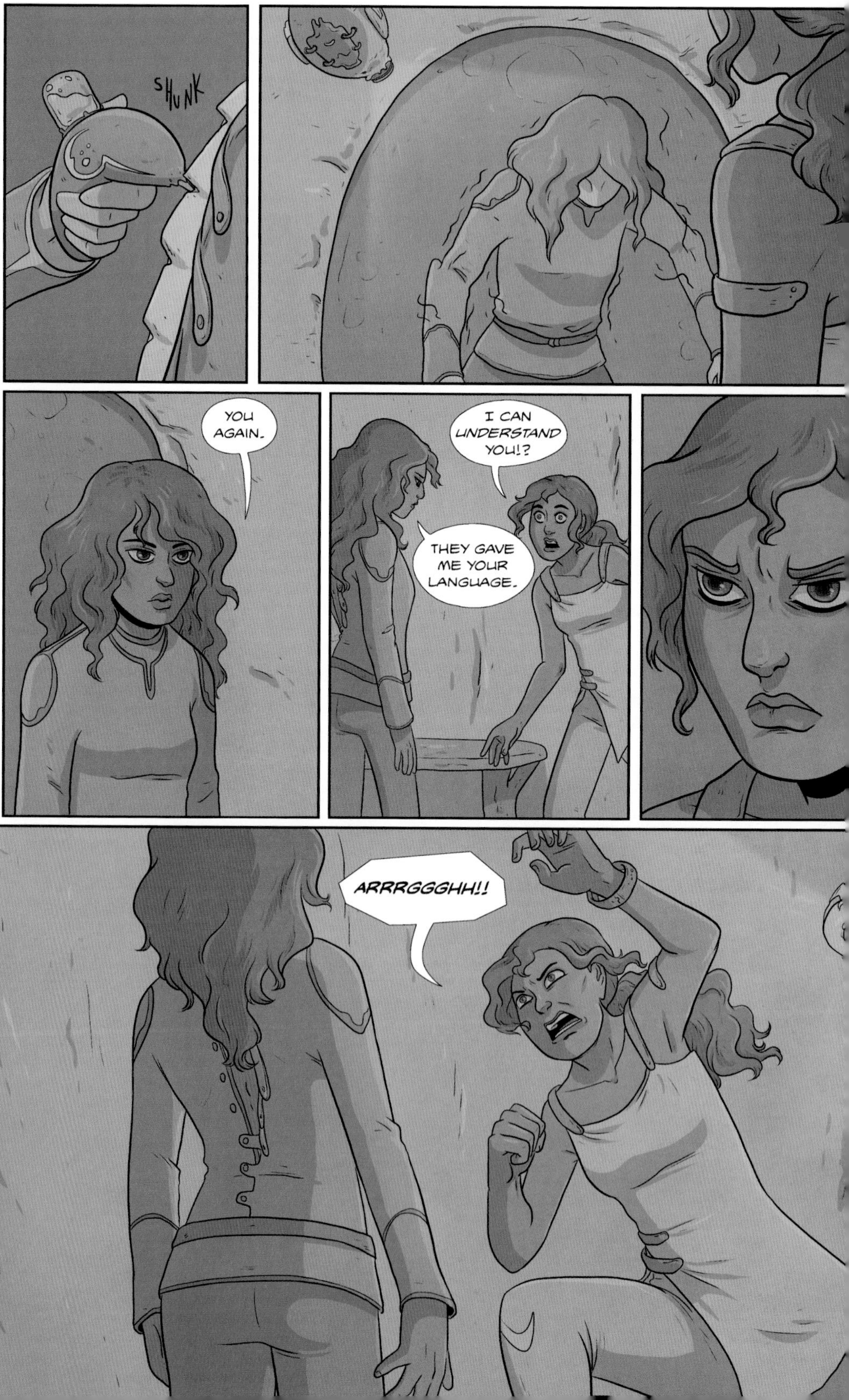
SHUNK
YOU AGAIN.
I CAN UNDERSTAND YOU!?
THEY GAVE ME YOUR LANGUAGE.
ARRRGGGHH!!

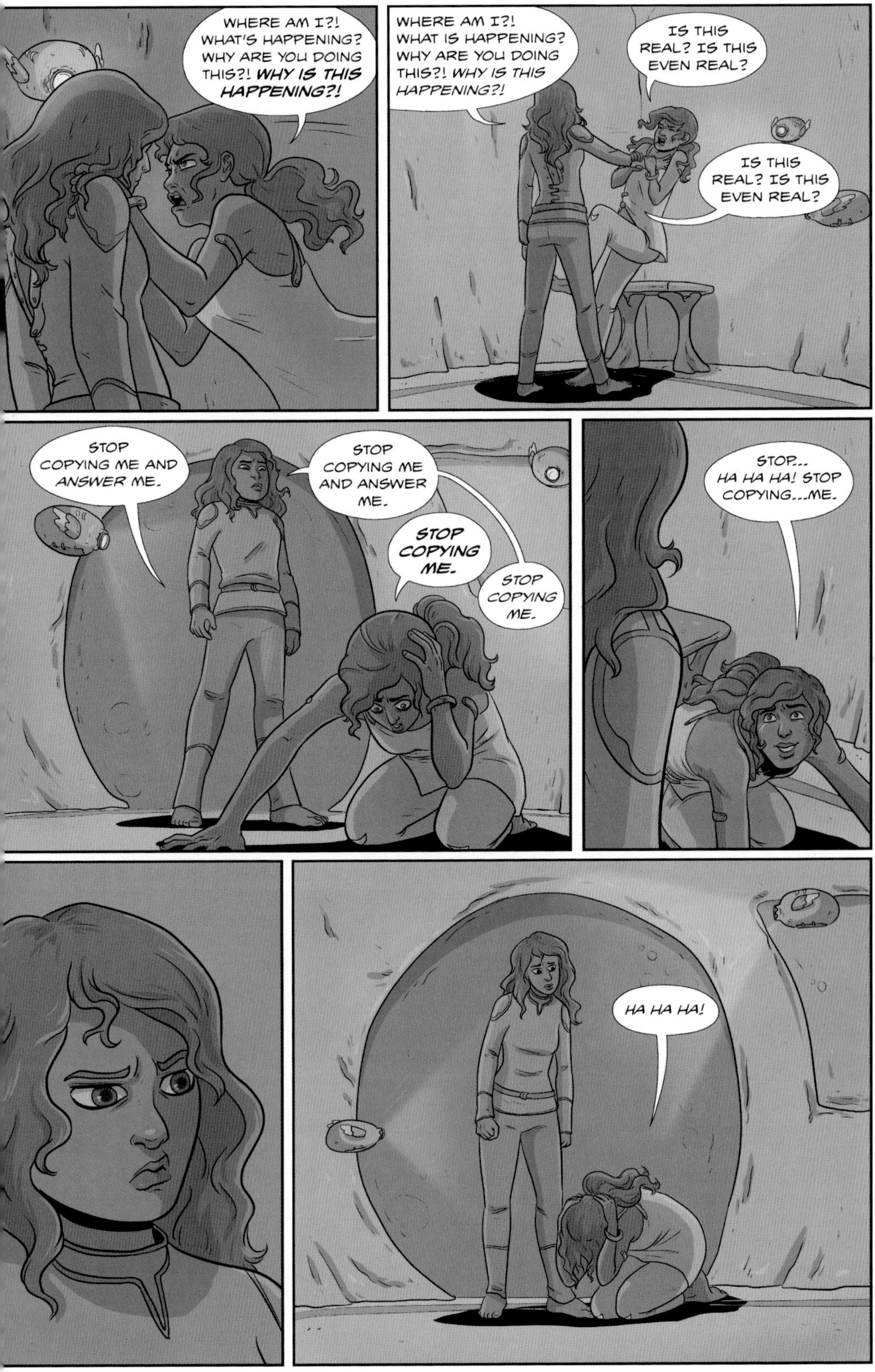
WHERE AM I?! WHAT'S HAPPENING? WHY ARE YOU DOING THIS?! *WHY IS THIS HAPPENING?!*
WHERE AM I?! WHAT IS HAPPENING? WHY ARE YOU DOING THIS?! *WHY IS THIS HAPPENING?!*
IS THIS REAL? IS THIS EVEN REAL?
IS THIS REAL? IS THIS EVEN REAL?
STOP COPYING ME AND *ANSWER ME.*
STOP COPYING ME AND ANSWER ME.
STOP COPYING ME.
STOP *COPYING* ME.
STOP... *HA HA HA!* STOP COPYING...ME.
HA HA HA!

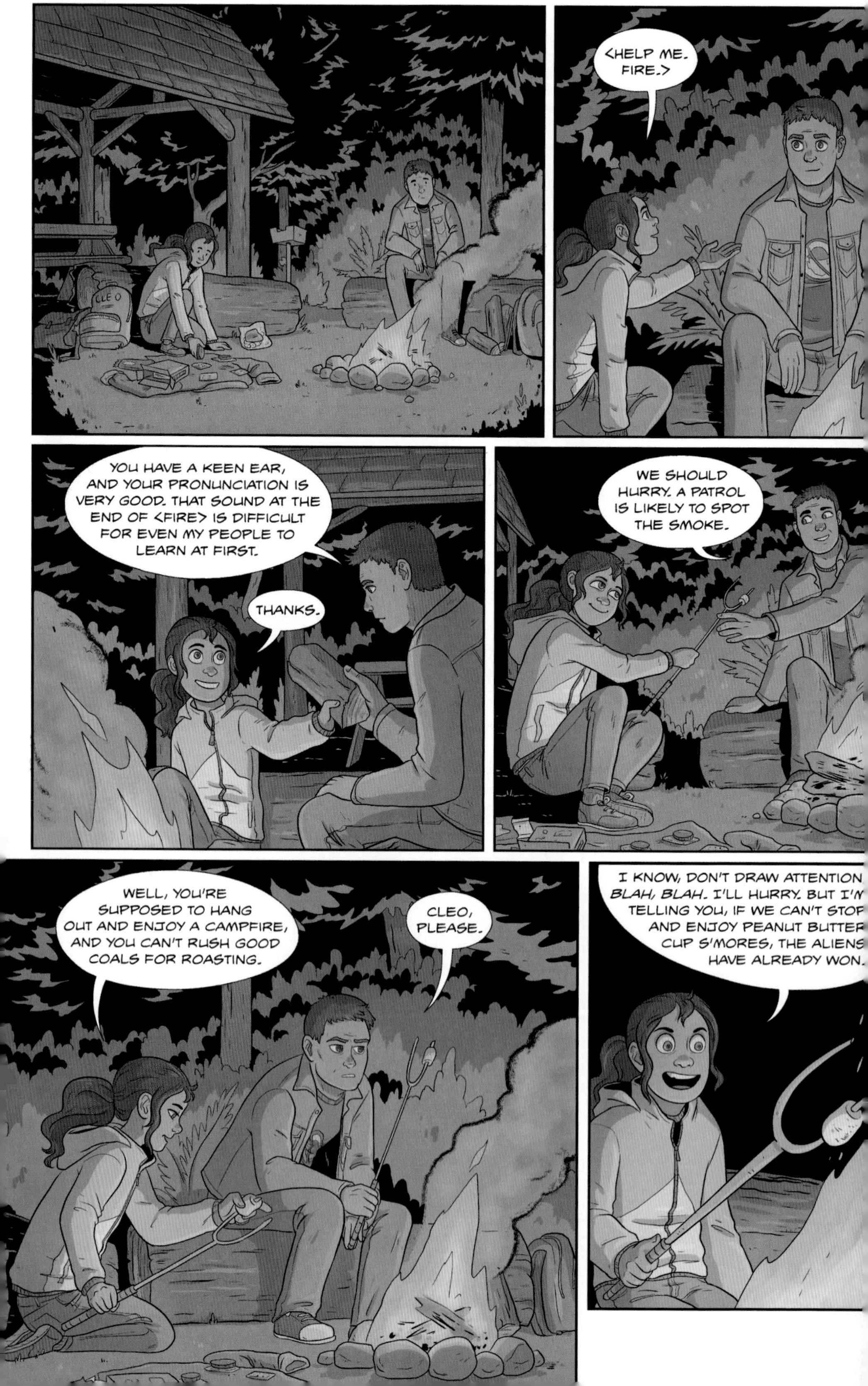
<HELP ME. FIRE.>
YOU HAVE A KEEN EAR, AND YOUR PRONUNCIATION IS VERY GOOD. THAT SOUND AT THE END OF <FIRE> IS DIFFICULT FOR EVEN MY PEOPLE TO LEARN AT FIRST.
THANKS.
WE SHOULD HURRY. A PATROL IS LIKELY TO SPOT THE SMOKE.
WELL, YOU'RE SUPPOSED TO HANG OUT AND ENJOY A CAMPFIRE, AND YOU CAN'T RUSH GOOD COALS FOR ROASTING.
CLEO, PLEASE.
I KNOW, DON'T DRAW ATTENTION, *BLAH, BLAH*. I'LL HURRY. BUT I'M TELLING YOU, IF WE CAN'T STOP AND ENJOY PEANUT BUTTER CUP S'MORES, THE ALIENS HAVE ALREADY WON.
CLEO

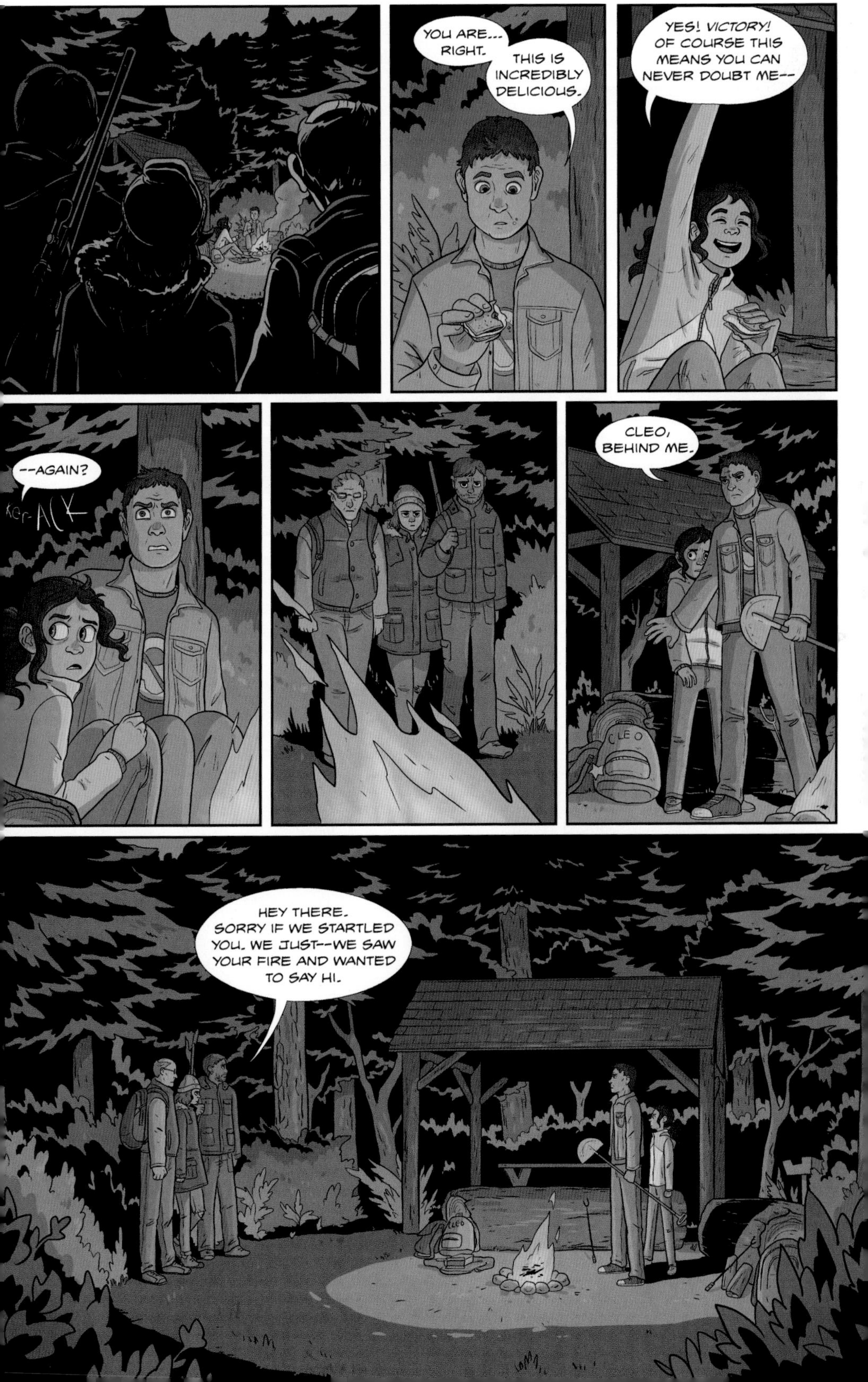
YOU ARE... RIGHT.
THIS IS INCREDIBLY DELICIOUS.
YES! VICTORY! OF COURSE THIS MEANS YOU CAN NEVER DOUBT ME--
--AGAIN?
Ker-ACK
CLEO, BEHIND ME.
CLEO
HEY THERE. SORRY IF WE STARTLED YOU. WE JUST--WE SAW YOUR FIRE AND WANTED TO SAY HI.

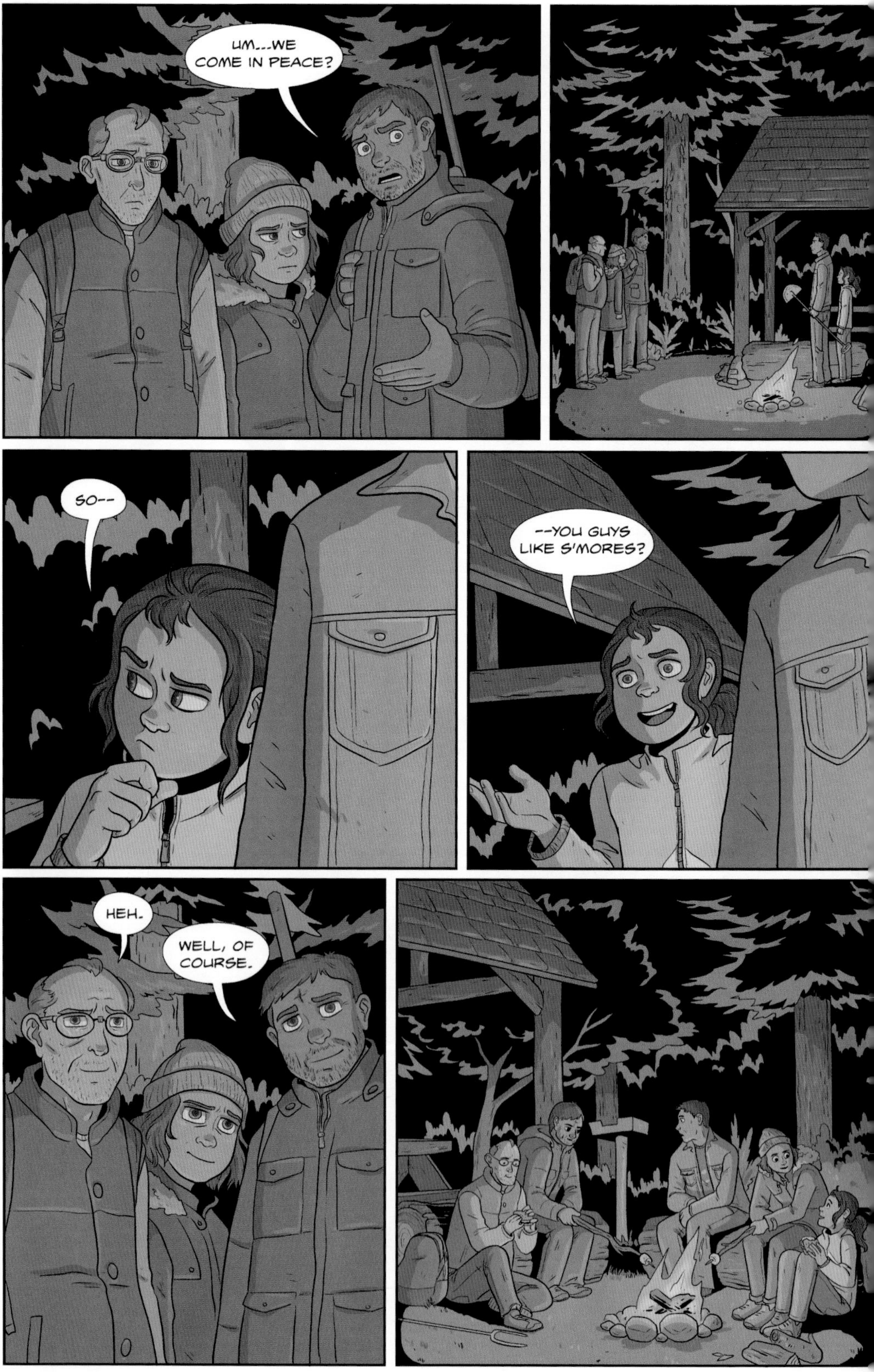
UM...WE COME IN PEACE?
SO--
--YOU GUYS LIKE S'MORES?
HEH.
WELL, OF COURSE.

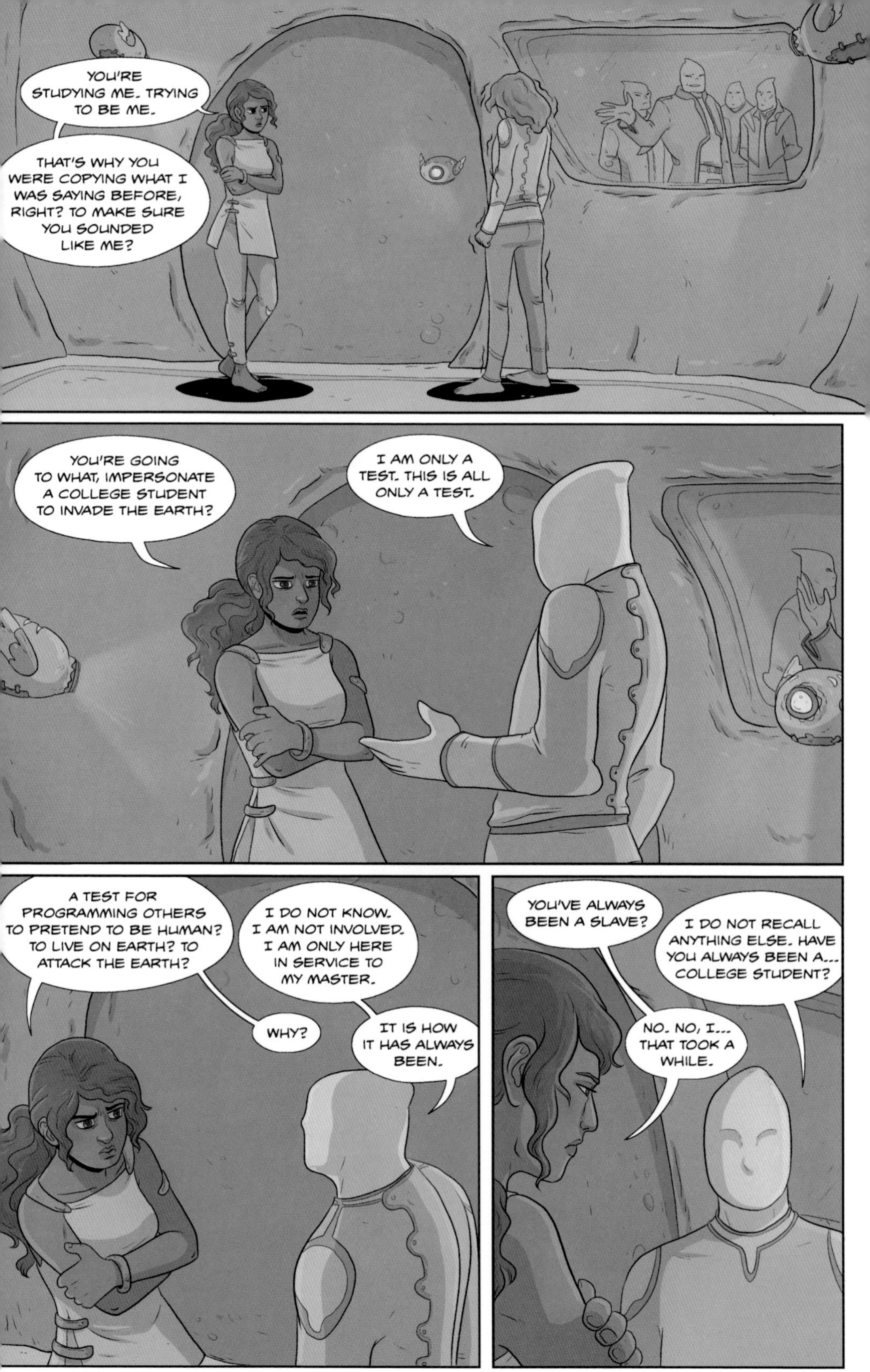
YOU'RE STUDYING ME. TRYING TO BE ME.
THAT'S WHY YOU WERE COPYING WHAT I WAS SAYING BEFORE, RIGHT? TO MAKE SURE YOU SOUNDED LIKE ME?
YOU'RE GOING TO WHAT, IMPERSONATE A COLLEGE STUDENT TO INVADE THE EARTH?
I AM ONLY A TEST. THIS IS ALL ONLY A TEST.
A TEST FOR PROGRAMMING OTHERS TO PRETEND TO BE HUMAN? TO LIVE ON EARTH? TO ATTACK THE EARTH?
I DO NOT KNOW. I AM NOT INVOLVED. I AM ONLY HERE IN SERVICE TO MY MASTER.
WHY?
IT IS HOW IT HAS ALWAYS BEEN.
YOU'VE ALWAYS BEEN A SLAVE?
I DO NOT RECALL ANYTHING ELSE. HAVE YOU ALWAYS BEEN A... COLLEGE STUDENT?
NO. NO, I... THAT TOOK A WHILE.

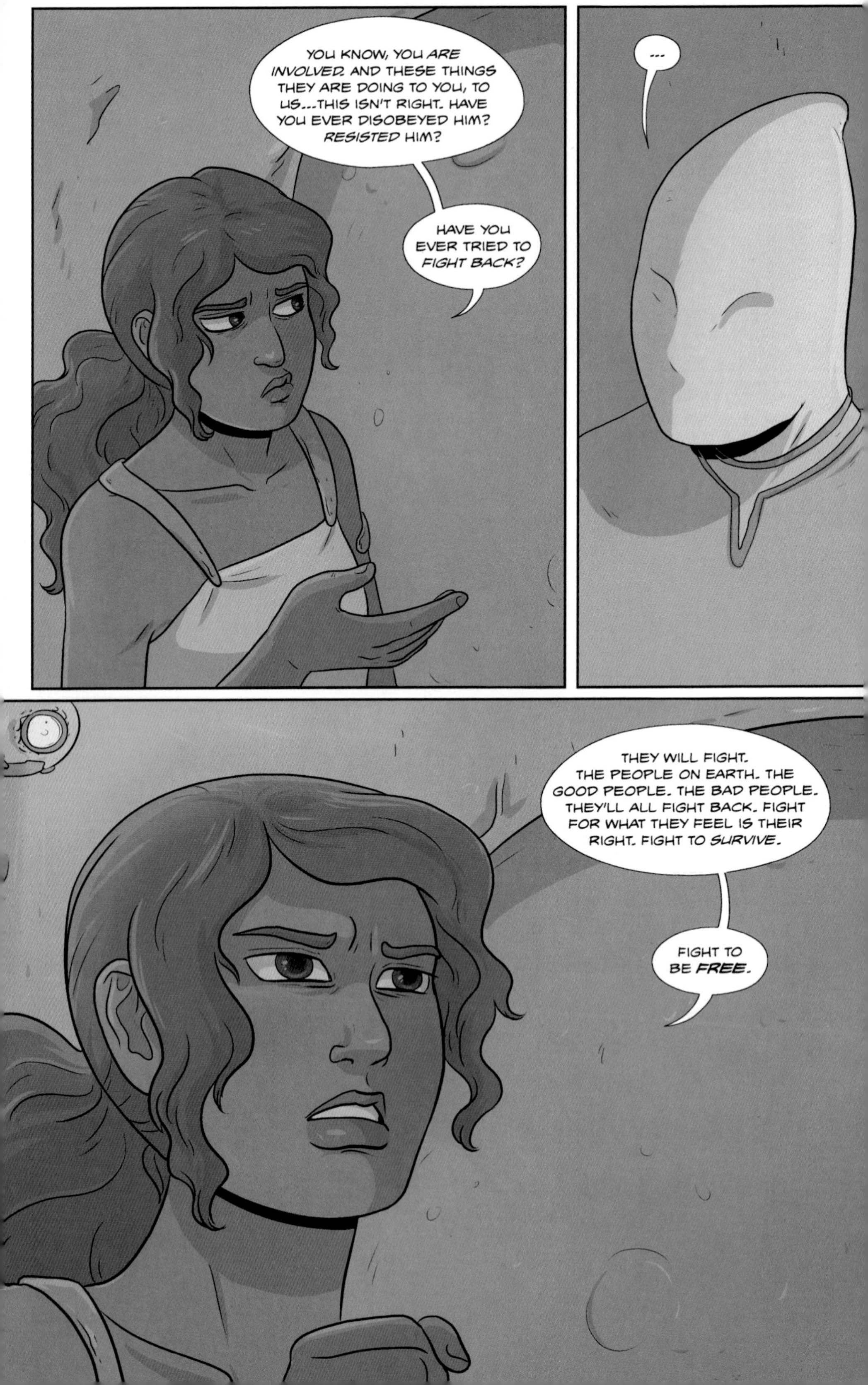
YOU KNOW, YOU *ARE INVOLVED.* AND THESE THINGS THEY ARE DOING TO YOU, TO US...THIS ISN'T RIGHT. HAVE YOU EVER DISOBEYED HIM? *RESISTED* HIM?
HAVE YOU EVER TRIED TO *FIGHT BACK?*
...
THEY WILL FIGHT. THE PEOPLE ON EARTH. THE GOOD PEOPLE. THE BAD PEOPLE. THEY'LL ALL FIGHT BACK. FIGHT FOR WHAT THEY FEEL IS THEIR RIGHT. FIGHT TO *SURVIVE.*
FIGHT TO BE ***FREE.***

FOUR

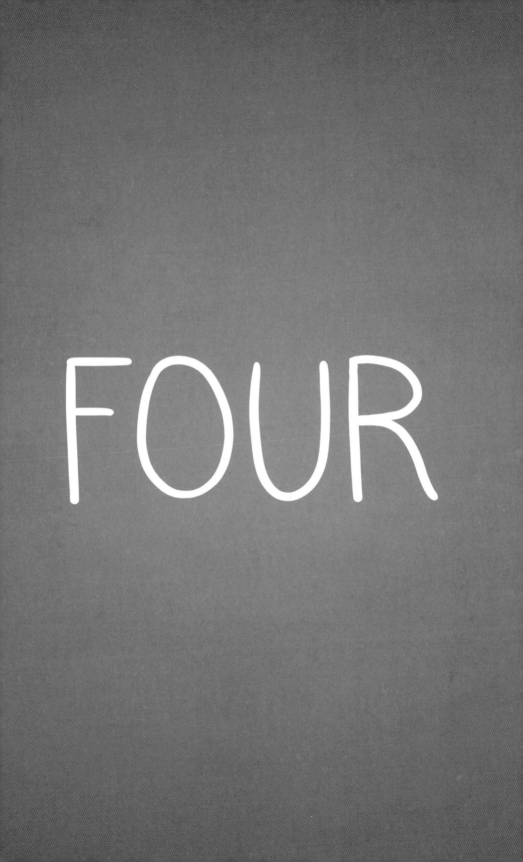

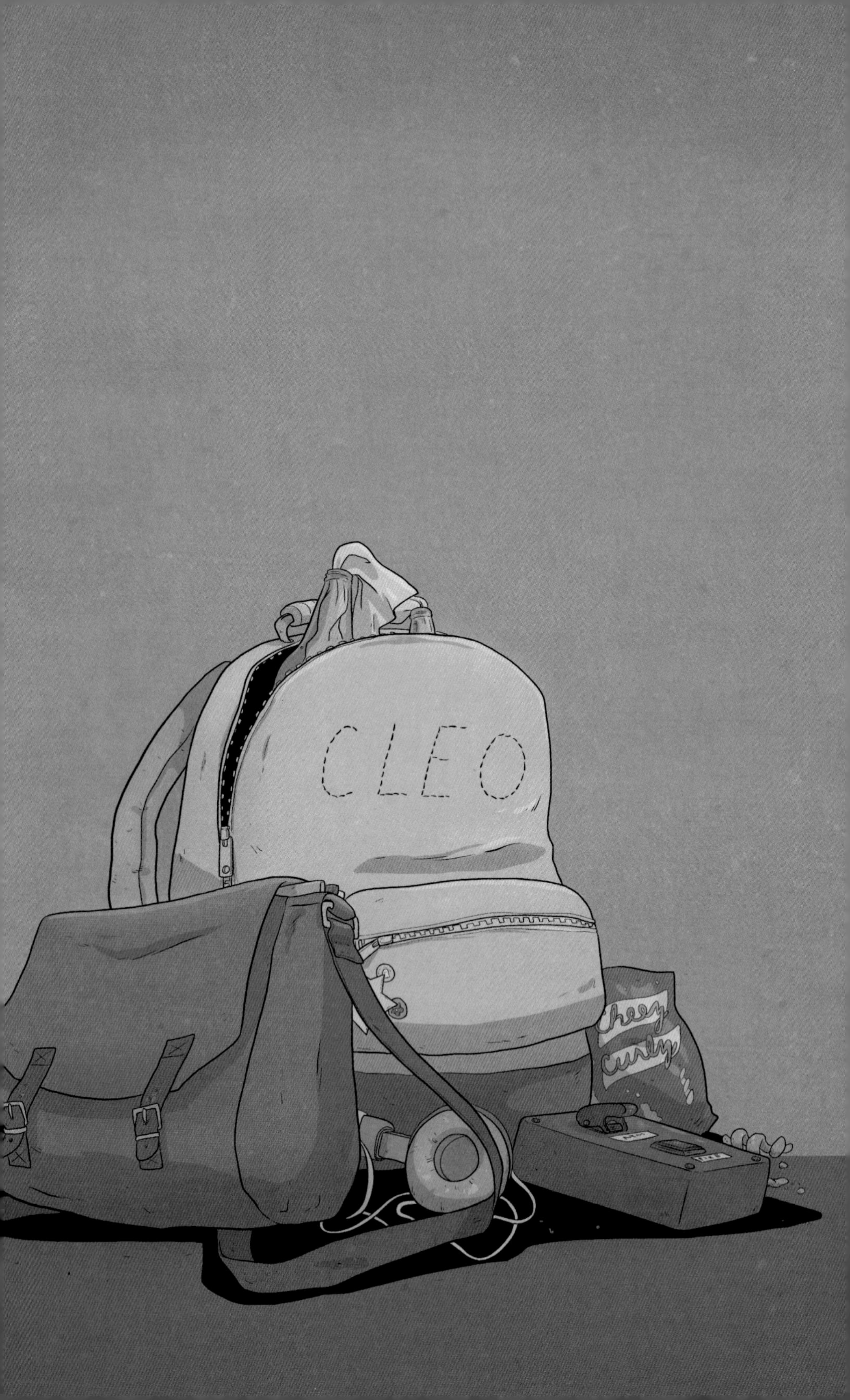
CLEO
curly

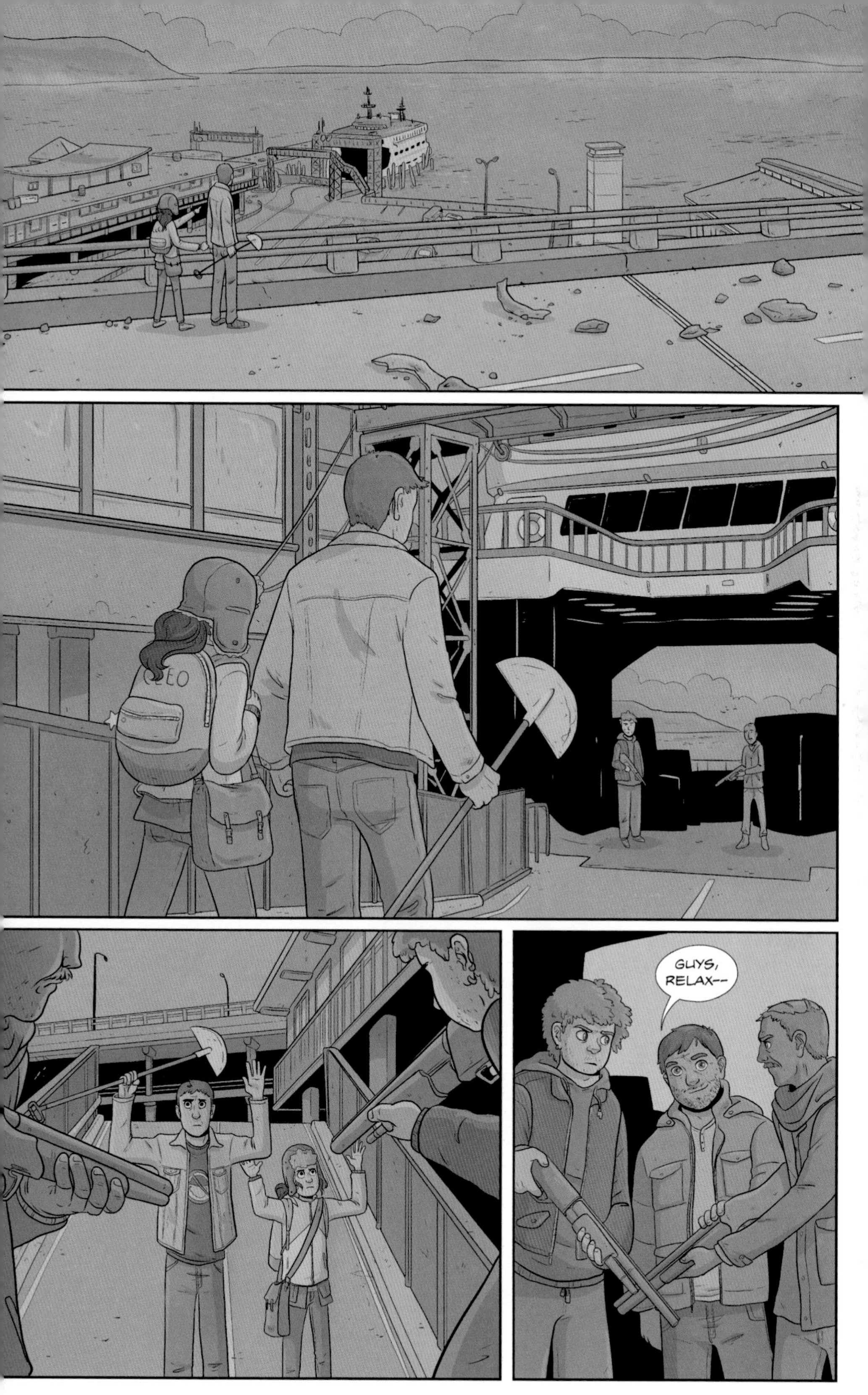
GUYS, RELAX--

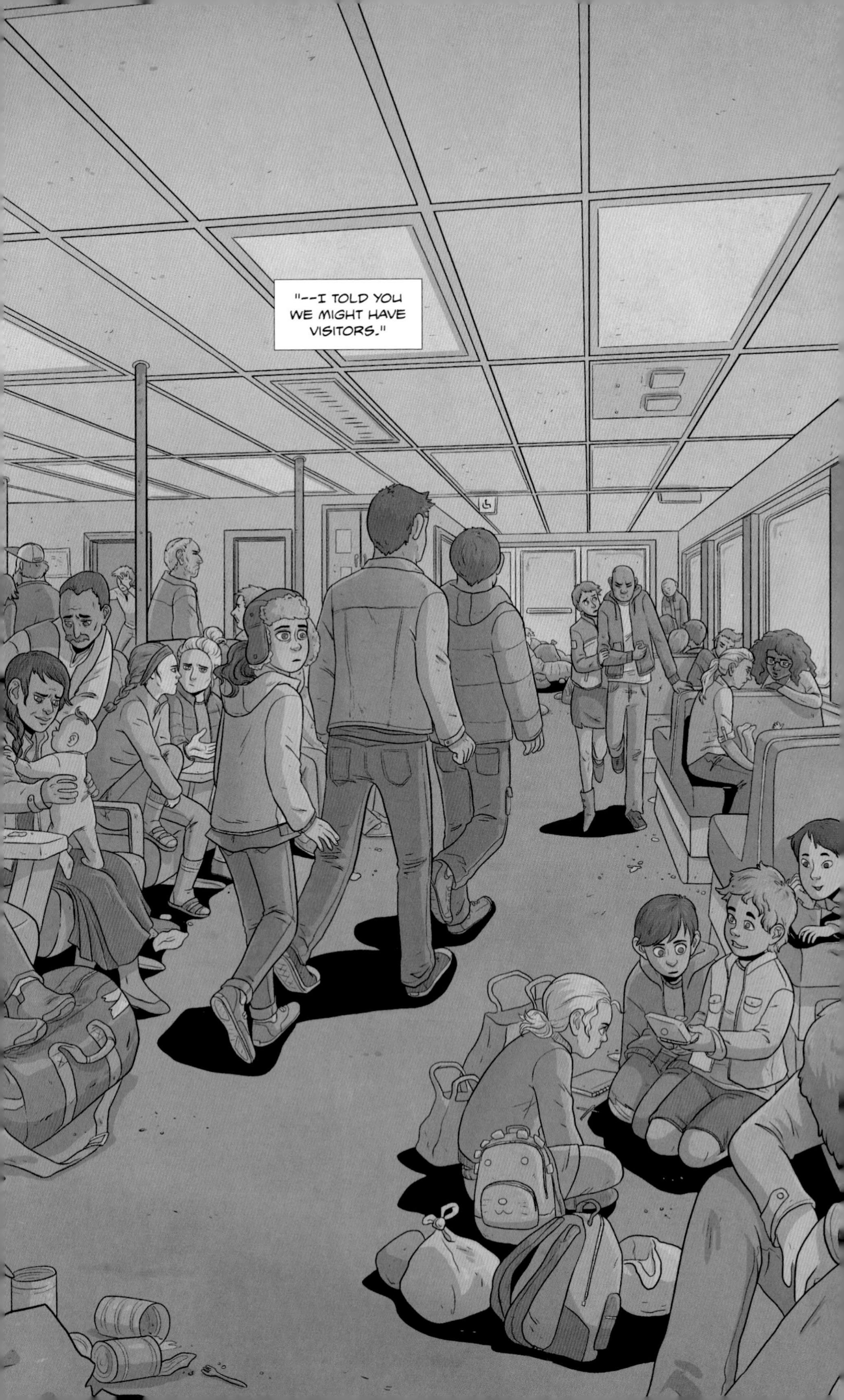
"--I TOLD YOU WE MIGHT HAVE VISITORS."

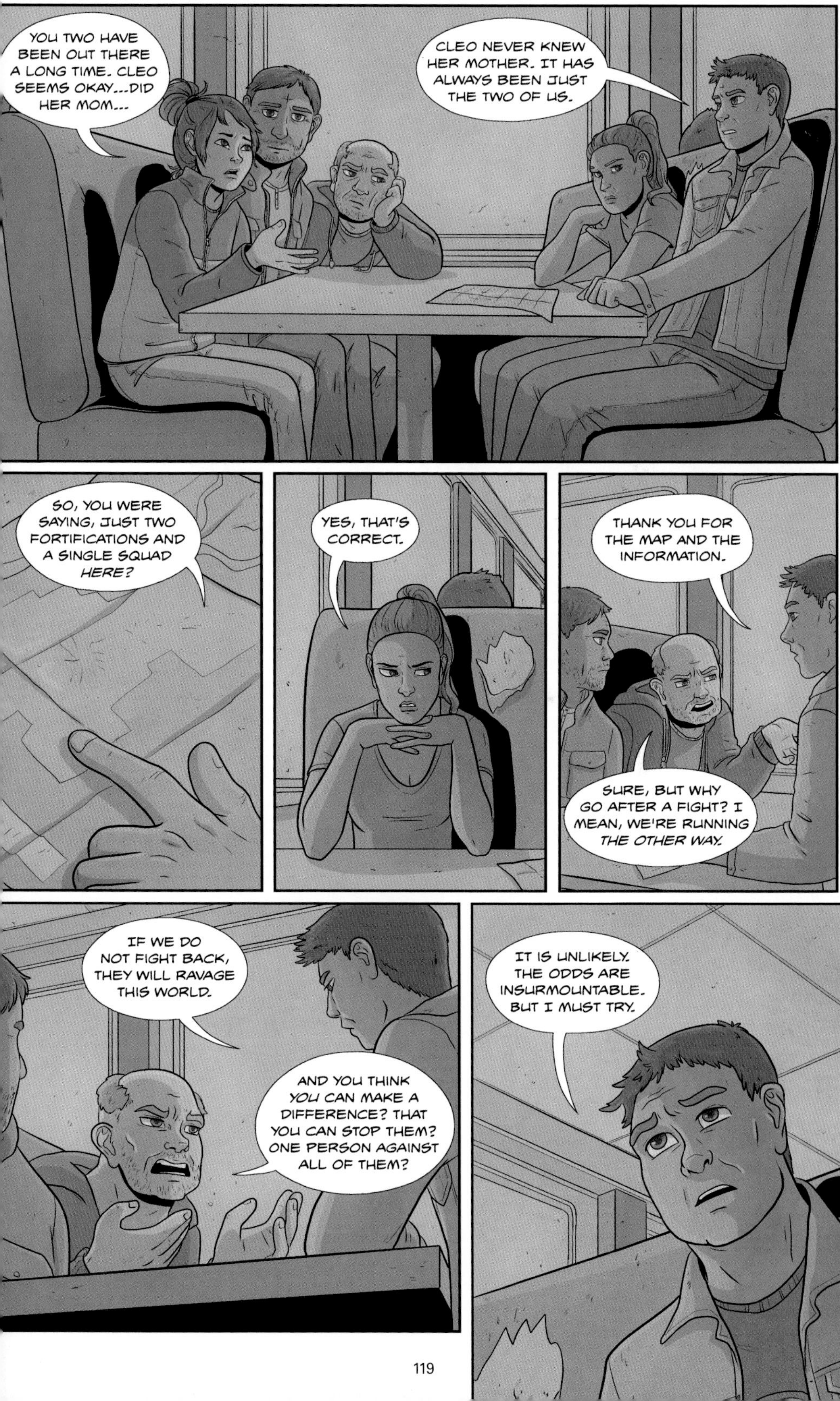

YOU TWO HAVE BEEN OUT THERE A LONG TIME. CLEO SEEMS OKAY...DID HER MOM...
CLEO NEVER KNEW HER MOTHER. IT HAS ALWAYS BEEN JUST THE TWO OF US.
SO, YOU WERE SAYING, JUST TWO FORTIFICATIONS AND A SINGLE SQUAD *HERE*?
YES, THAT'S CORRECT.
THANK YOU FOR THE MAP AND THE INFORMATION.
SURE, BUT WHY GO AFTER A FIGHT? I MEAN, WE'RE RUNNING *THE OTHER WAY.*
IF WE DO NOT FIGHT BACK, THEY WILL RAVAGE THIS WORLD.
AND YOU THINK *YOU* CAN MAKE A DIFFERENCE? THAT YOU CAN STOP THEM? ONE PERSON AGAINST ALL OF THEM?
IT IS UNLIKELY. THE ODDS ARE INSURMOUNTABLE. BUT I MUST TRY.

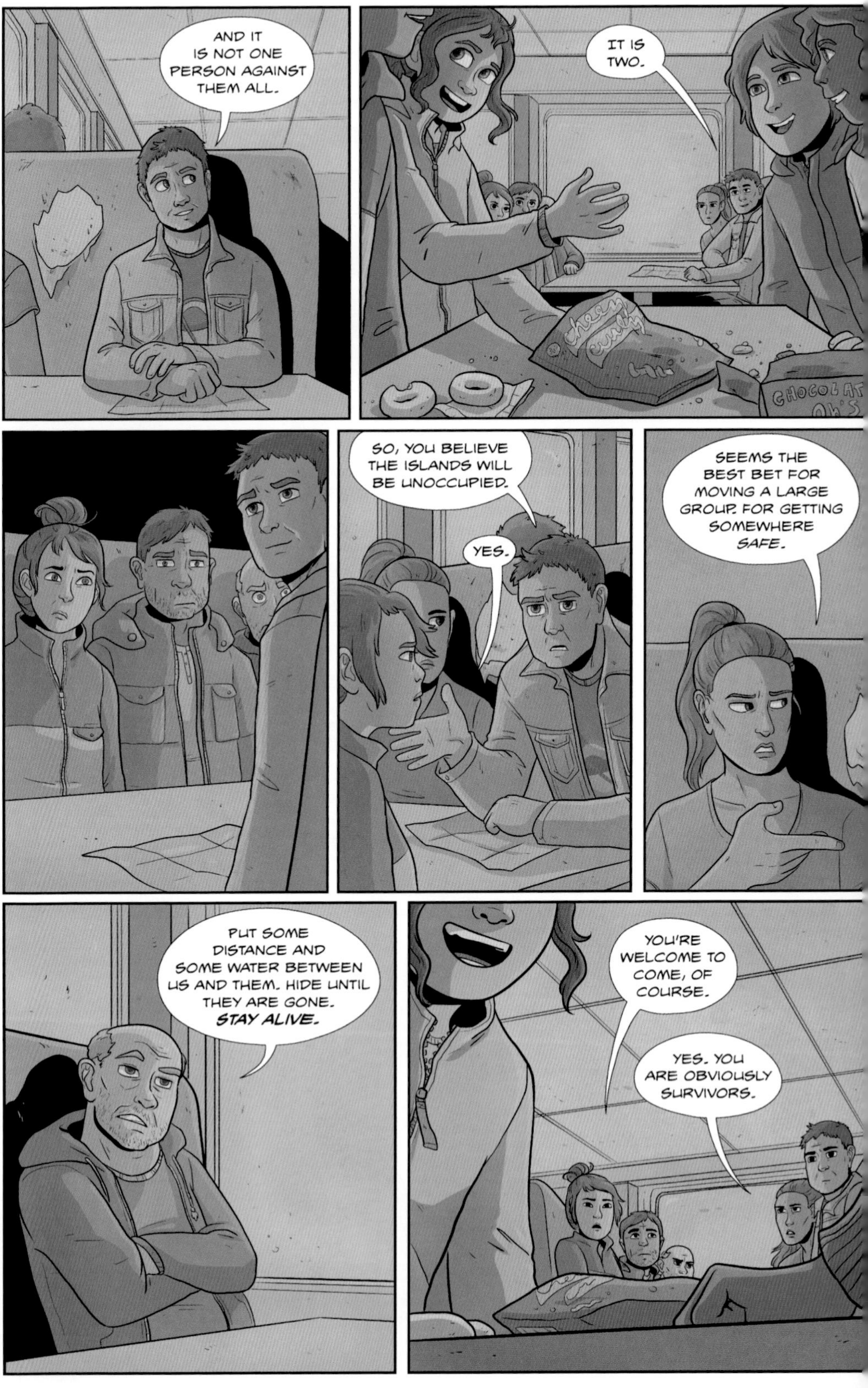
AND IT IS NOT ONE PERSON AGAINST THEM ALL.
IT IS TWO.
cheesy curly
CHOCOLAT Oh'S
SO, YOU BELIEVE THE ISLANDS WILL BE UNOCCUPIED.
YES.
SEEMS THE BEST BET FOR MOVING A LARGE GROUP. FOR GETTING SOMEWHERE *SAFE*.
PUT SOME DISTANCE AND SOME WATER BETWEEN US AND THEM. HIDE UNTIL THEY ARE GONE. ***STAY ALIVE.***
YOU'RE WELCOME TO COME, OF COURSE.
YES. YOU ARE OBVIOUSLY SURVIVORS.

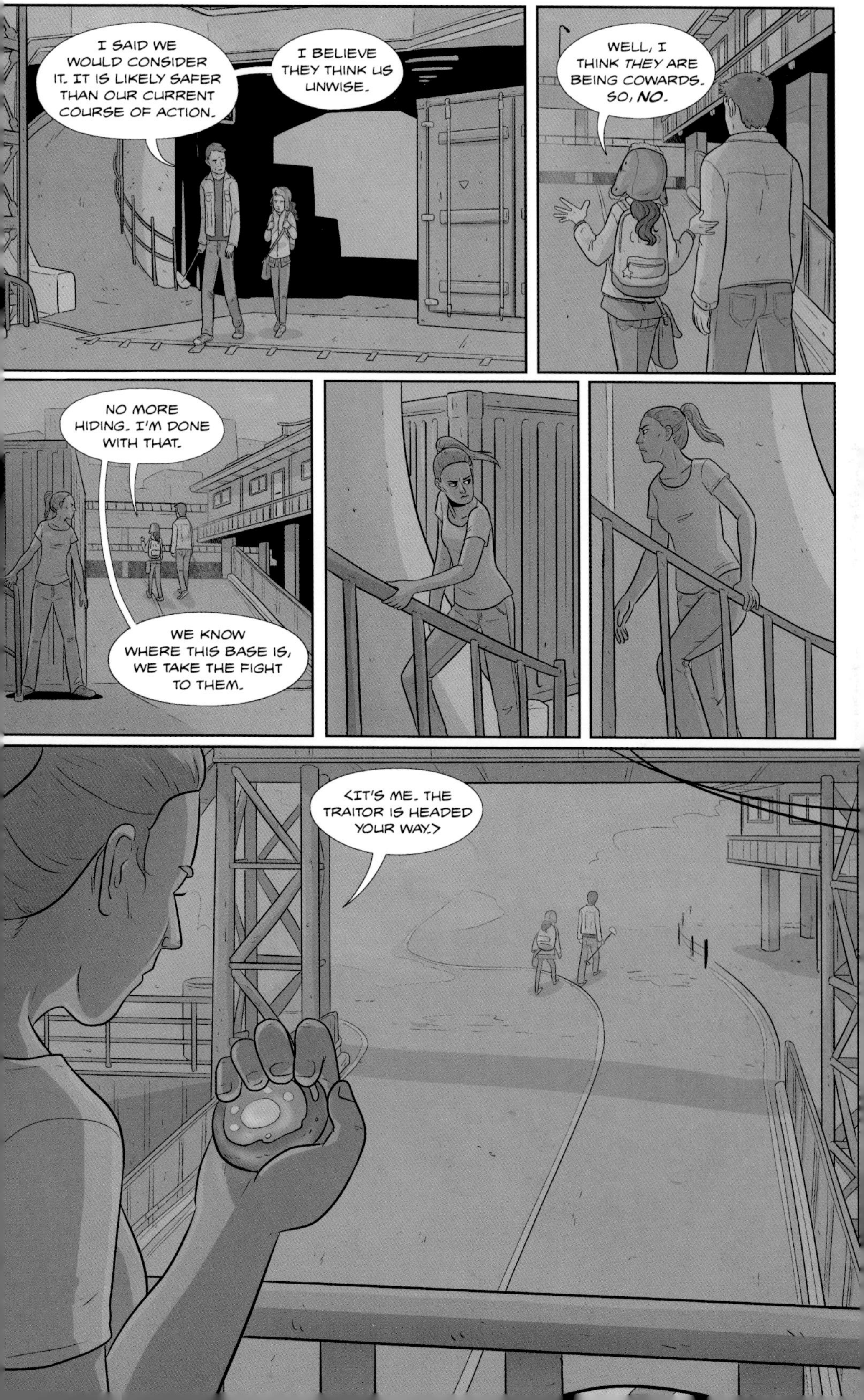
I SAID WE WOULD CONSIDER IT. IT IS LIKELY SAFER THAN OUR CURRENT COURSE OF ACTION.
I BELIEVE THEY THINK US UNWISE.
WELL, I THINK *THEY* ARE BEING COWARDS. SO, **NO**.
NO MORE HIDING. I'M DONE WITH THAT.
WE KNOW WHERE THIS BASE IS, WE TAKE THE FIGHT TO THEM.
<IT'S ME. THE TRAITOR IS HEADED YOUR WAY.>

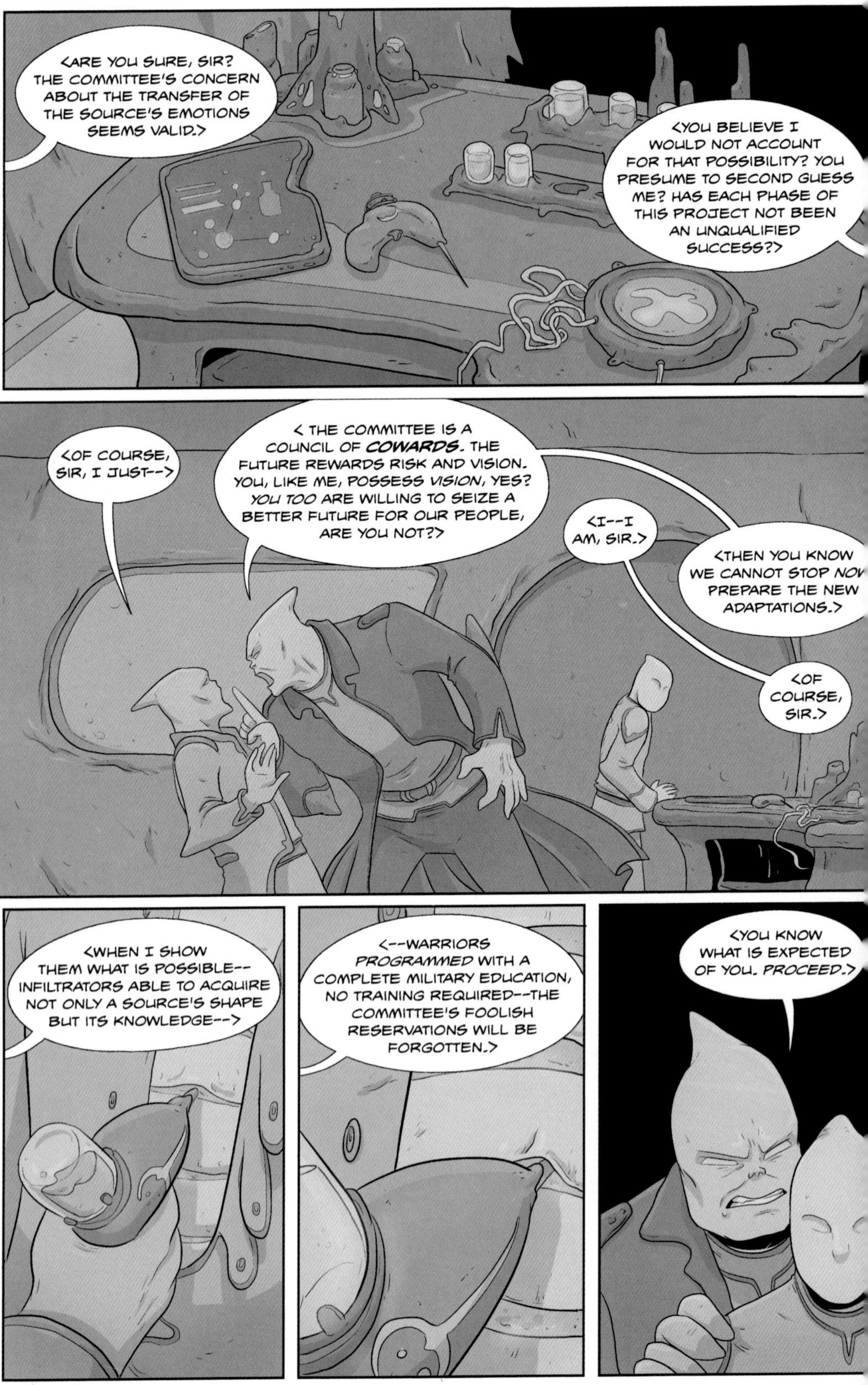
<ARE YOU SURE, SIR? THE COMMITTEE'S CONCERN ABOUT THE TRANSFER OF THE SOURCE'S EMOTIONS SEEMS VALID.>
<YOU BELIEVE I WOULD NOT ACCOUNT FOR THAT POSSIBILITY? YOU PRESUME TO SECOND GUESS ME? HAS EACH PHASE OF THIS PROJECT NOT BEEN AN UNQUALIFIED SUCCESS?>
<OF COURSE, SIR, I JUST-->
< THE COMMITTEE IS A COUNCIL OF **COWARDS**. THE FUTURE REWARDS RISK AND VISION. YOU, LIKE ME, POSSESS *VISION*, YES? *YOU TOO* ARE WILLING TO SEIZE A BETTER FUTURE FOR OUR PEOPLE, ARE YOU NOT?>
<I--I AM, SIR.>
<THEN YOU KNOW WE CANNOT STOP *NOW*. PREPARE THE NEW ADAPTATIONS.>
<OF COURSE, SIR.>
<WHEN I SHOW THEM WHAT IS POSSIBLE-- INFILTRATORS ABLE TO ACQUIRE NOT ONLY A SOURCE'S SHAPE BUT ITS KNOWLEDGE-->
<--WARRIORS *PROGRAMMED* WITH A COMPLETE MILITARY EDUCATION, NO TRAINING REQUIRED--THE COMMITTEE'S FOOLISH RESERVATIONS WILL BE FORGOTTEN.>
<YOU KNOW WHAT IS EXPECTED OF YOU. *PROCEED.*>

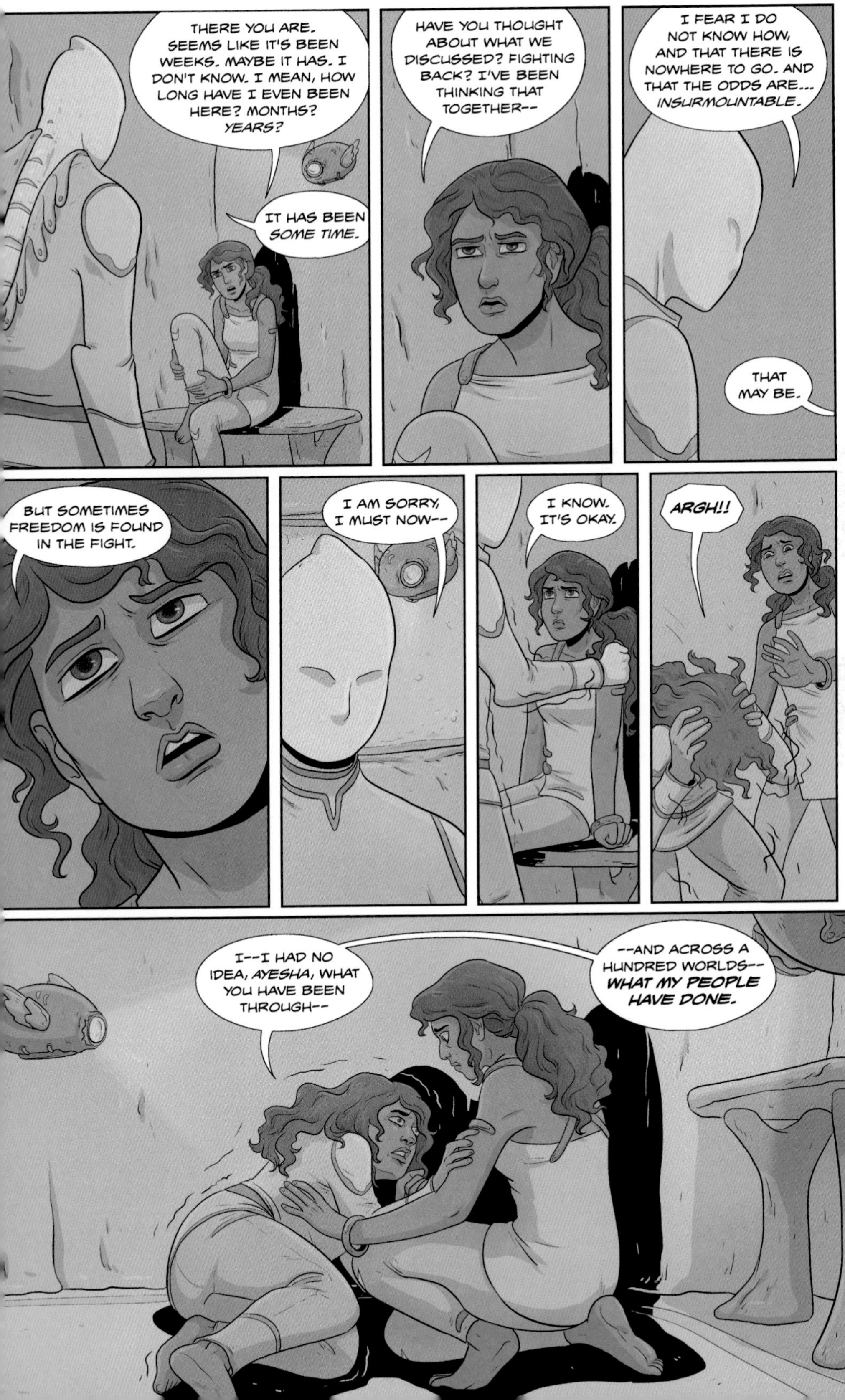
THERE YOU ARE. SEEMS LIKE IT'S BEEN WEEKS. MAYBE IT HAS. I DON'T KNOW. I MEAN, HOW LONG HAVE I EVEN BEEN HERE? MONTHS? *YEARS?*
IT HAS BEEN *SOME TIME.*
HAVE YOU THOUGHT ABOUT WHAT WE DISCUSSED? FIGHTING BACK? I'VE BEEN THINKING THAT TOGETHER--
I FEAR I DO NOT KNOW HOW, AND THAT THERE IS NOWHERE TO GO. AND THAT THE ODDS ARE... *INSURMOUNTABLE.*
THAT MAY BE.
BUT SOMETIMES FREEDOM IS FOUND IN THE FIGHT.
I AM SORRY, I MUST NOW--
I KNOW. IT'S OKAY.
ARGH!!
I--I HAD NO IDEA, *AYESHA,* WHAT YOU HAVE BEEN THROUGH--
--AND ACROSS A HUNDRED WORLDS-- ***WHAT MY PEOPLE HAVE DONE.***

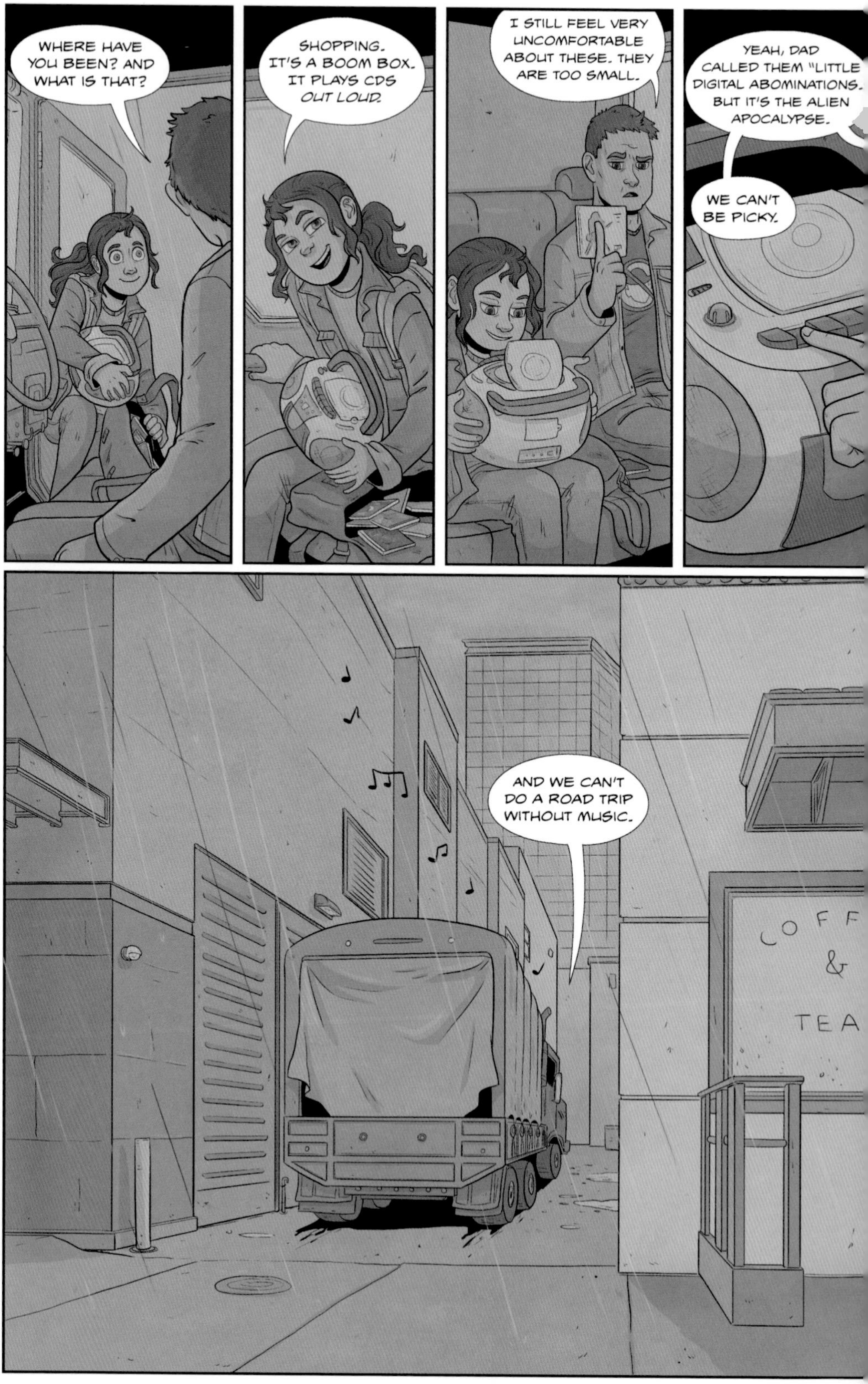
WHERE HAVE YOU BEEN? AND WHAT IS THAT?
SHOPPING. IT'S A BOOM BOX. IT PLAYS CDS OUT LOUD.
I STILL FEEL VERY UNCOMFORTABLE ABOUT THESE. THEY ARE TOO SMALL.
YEAH, DAD CALLED THEM "LITTLE DIGITAL ABOMINATIONS. BUT IT'S THE ALIEN APOCALYPSE.
WE CAN'T BE PICKY.
AND WE CAN'T DO A ROAD TRIP WITHOUT MUSIC.
COFF
&
TEA

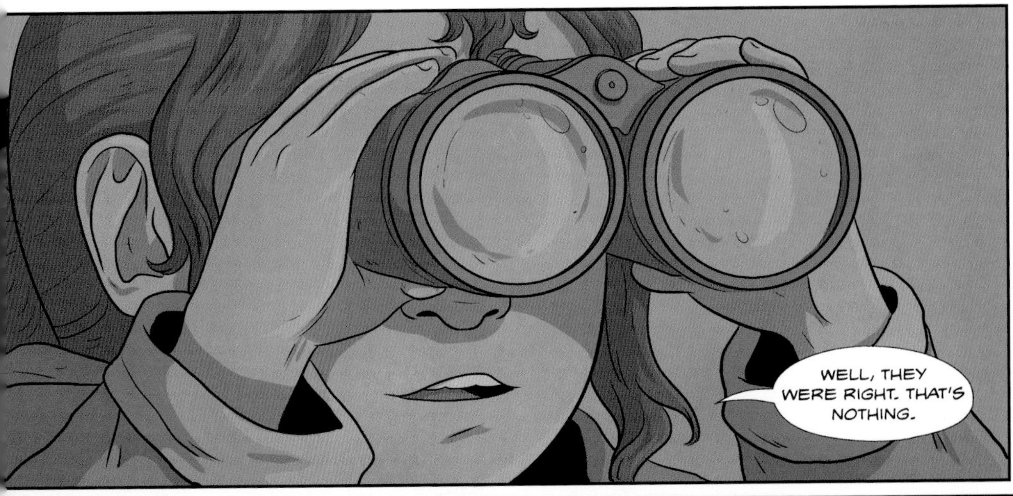
WELL, THEY WERE RIGHT. THAT'S NOTHING.

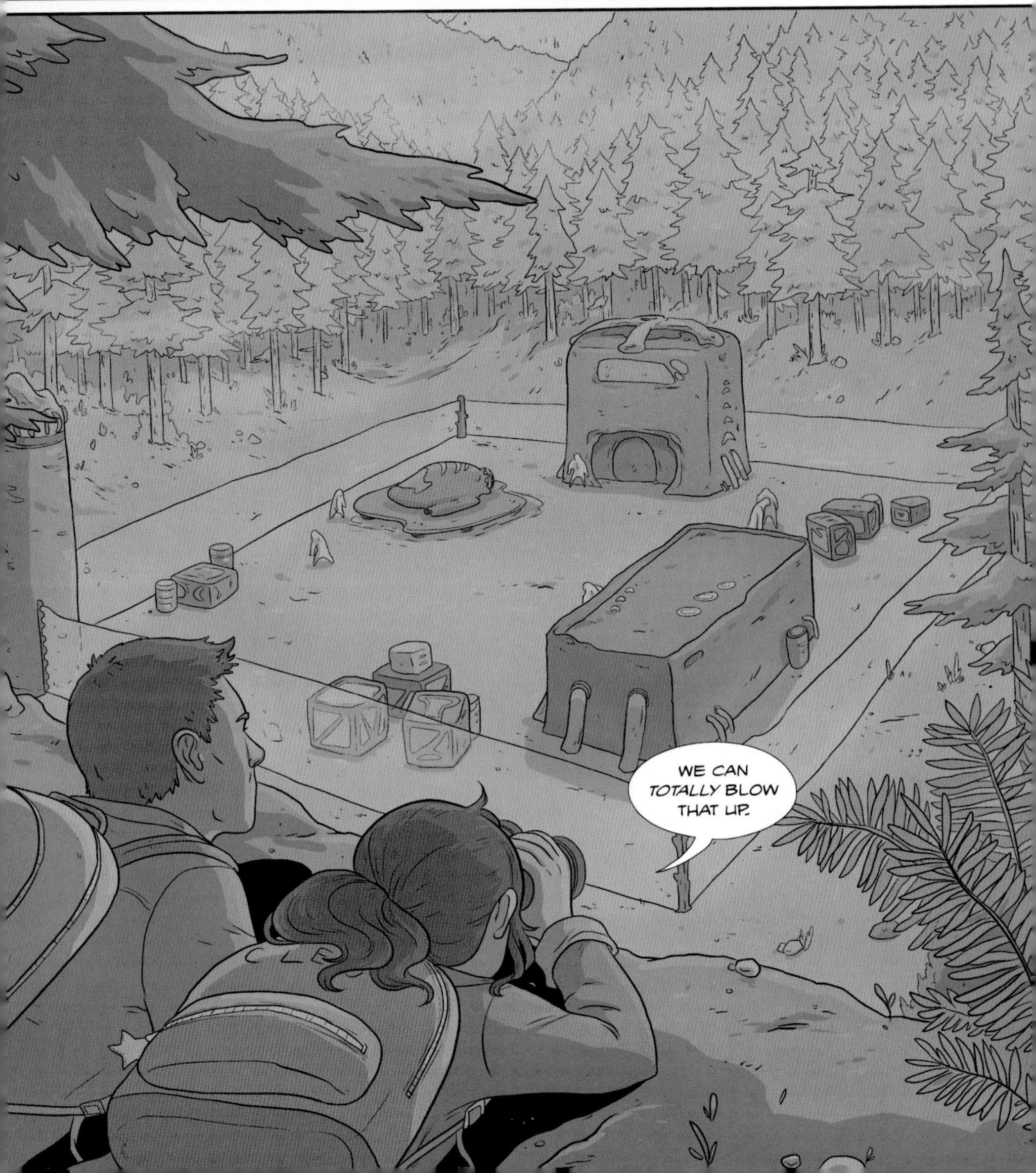
WE CAN *TOTALLY* BLOW THAT UP.

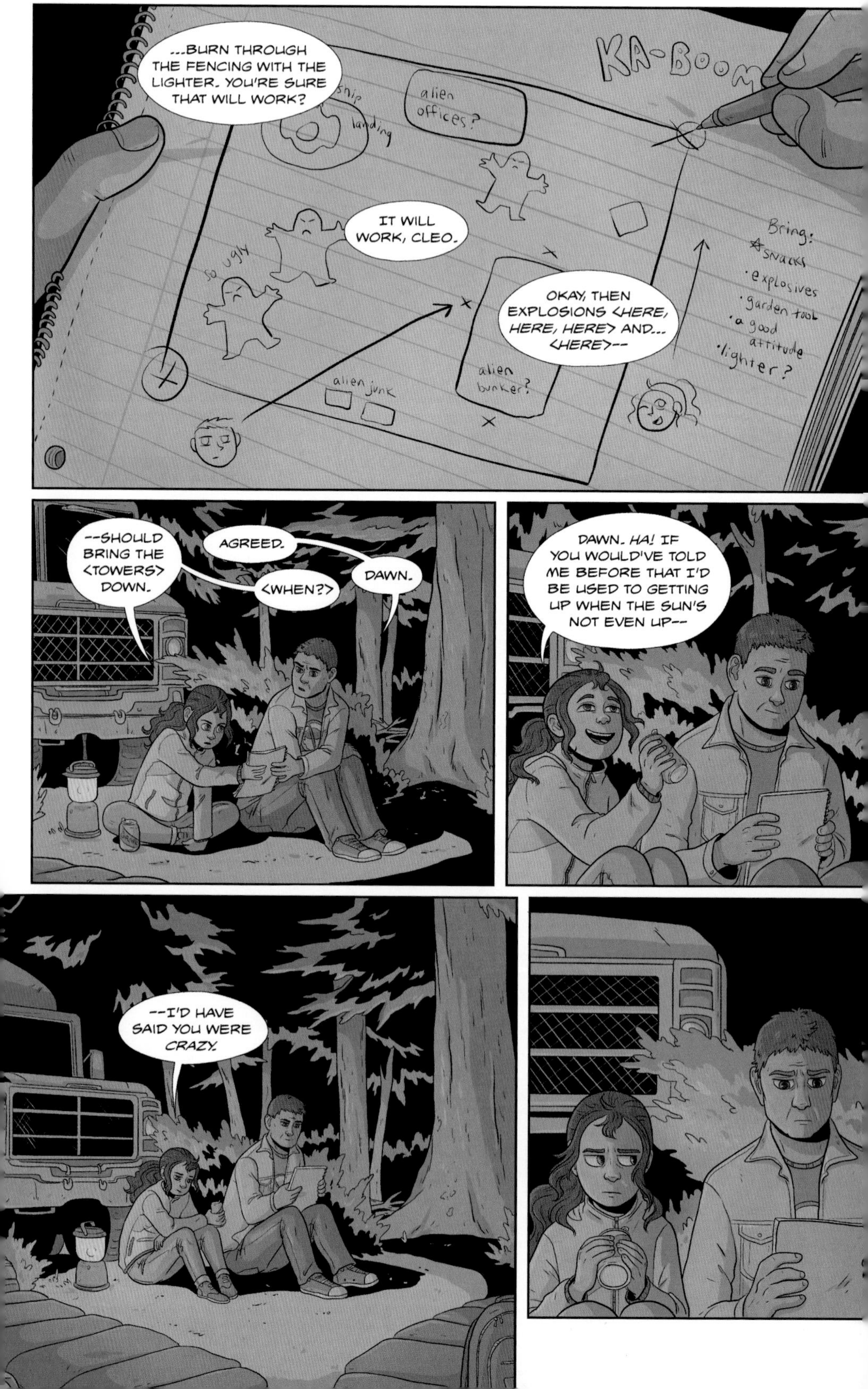
...BURN THROUGH THE FENCING WITH THE LIGHTER. YOU'RE SURE THAT WILL WORK?
KA-BOOM
ship landing
alien offices?
IT WILL WORK, CLEO.
so ugly
OKAY, THEN EXPLOSIONS <HERE, HERE, HERE> AND... <HERE>--
Bring:
snacks
explosives
garden tool
a good attitude
lighter?
alien junk
alien bunker?
--SHOULD BRING THE <TOWERS> DOWN.
AGREED.
<WHEN?>
DAWN.
DAWN. HA! IF YOU WOULD'VE TOLD ME BEFORE THAT I'D BE USED TO GETTING UP WHEN THE SUN'S NOT EVEN UP--
--I'D HAVE SAID YOU WERE CRAZY.

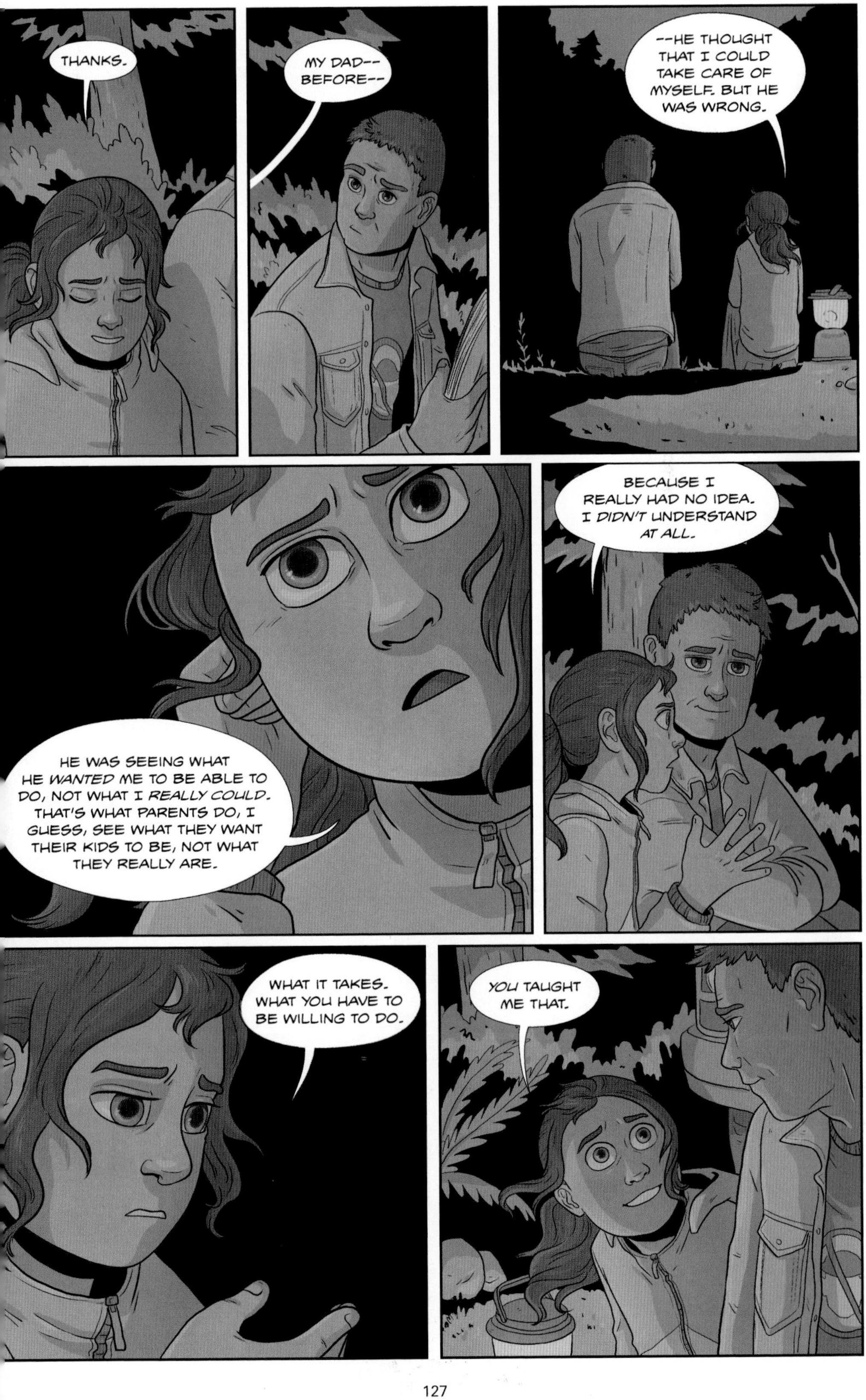
THANKS.
MY DAD-- BEFORE--
--HE THOUGHT THAT I COULD TAKE CARE OF MYSELF. BUT HE WAS WRONG.
BECAUSE I REALLY HAD NO IDEA. I *DIDN'T* UNDERSTAND *AT ALL.*
HE WAS SEEING WHAT HE *WANTED* ME TO BE ABLE TO DO, NOT WHAT I *REALLY COULD.* THAT'S WHAT PARENTS DO, I GUESS, SEE WHAT THEY WANT THEIR KIDS TO BE, NOT WHAT THEY REALLY ARE.
WHAT IT TAKES. WHAT YOU HAVE TO BE WILLING TO DO.
YOU TAUGHT ME THAT.

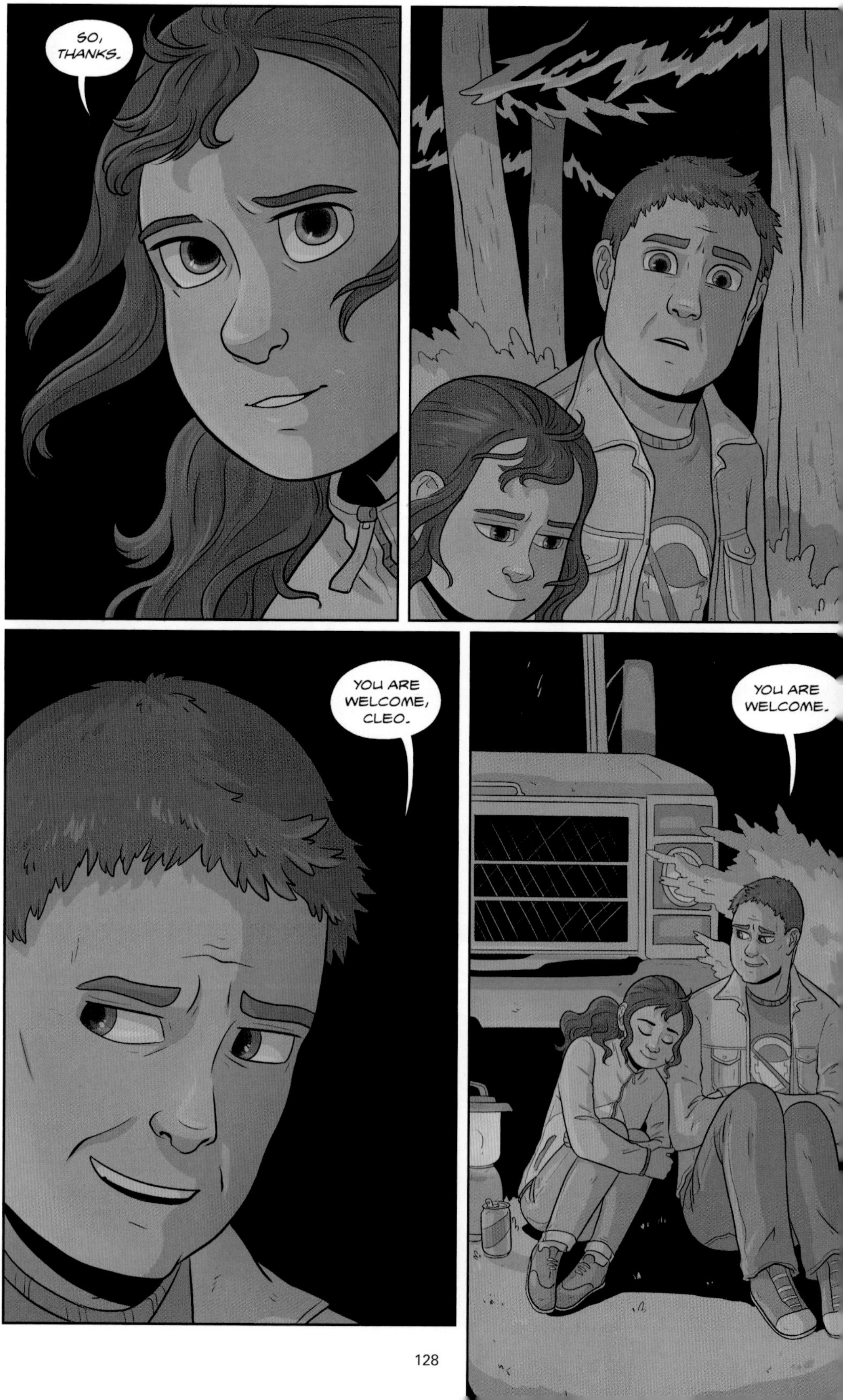
SO, THANKS.
YOU ARE WELCOME, CLEO.
YOU ARE WELCOME.

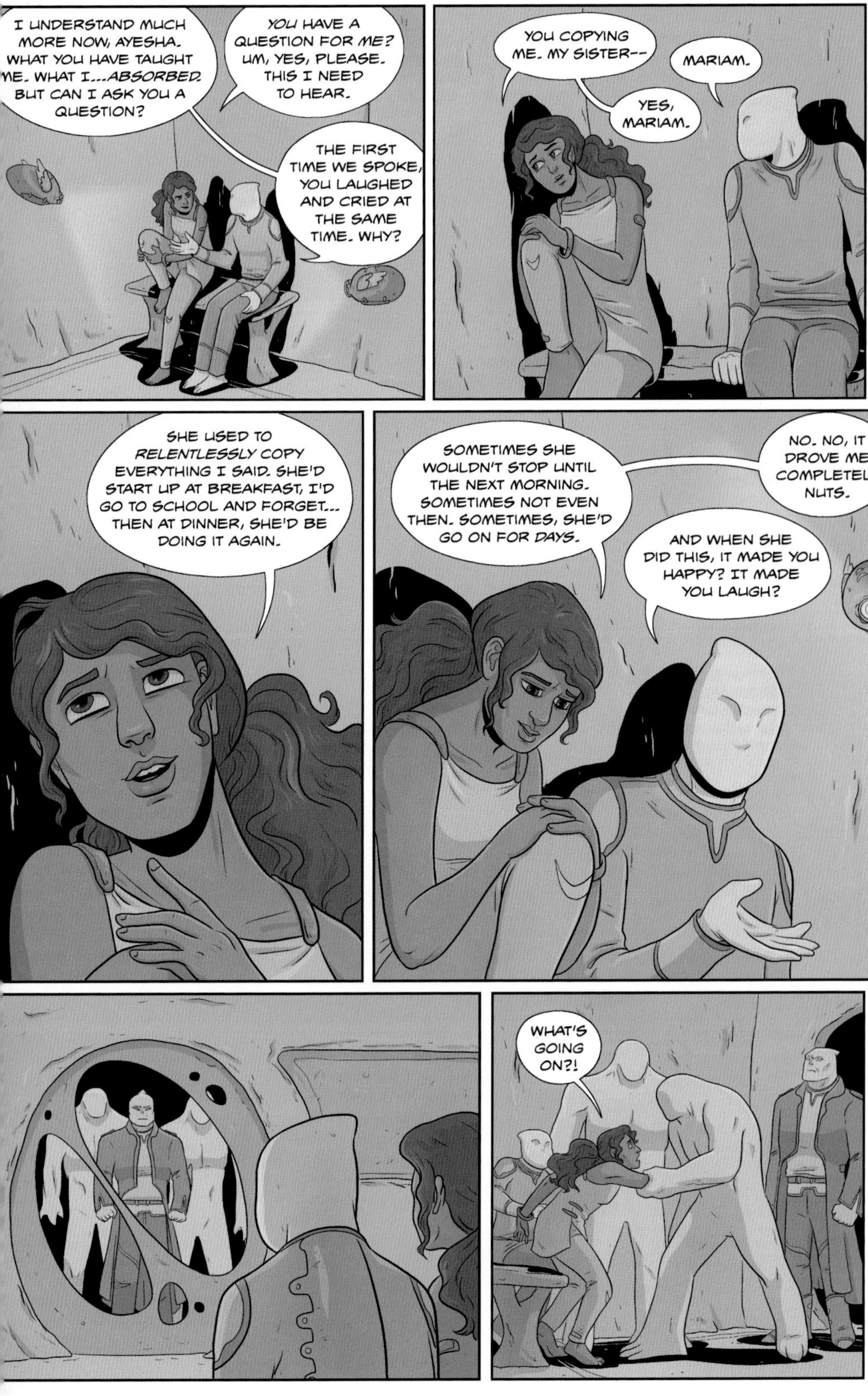

I UNDERSTAND MUCH MORE NOW, AYESHA. WHAT YOU HAVE TAUGHT ME. WHAT I...*ABSORBED.* BUT CAN I ASK YOU A QUESTION?
YOU HAVE A QUESTION FOR *ME?* UM, YES, PLEASE. THIS I NEED TO HEAR.
THE FIRST TIME WE SPOKE, YOU LAUGHED AND CRIED AT THE SAME TIME. WHY?
YOU COPYING ME. MY SISTER--
YES, MARIAM.
MARIAM.
SHE USED TO *RELENTLESSLY* COPY EVERYTHING I SAID. SHE'D START UP AT BREAKFAST, I'D GO TO SCHOOL AND FORGET... THEN AT DINNER, SHE'D BE DOING IT AGAIN.
SOMETIMES SHE WOULDN'T STOP UNTIL THE NEXT MORNING. SOMETIMES NOT EVEN THEN. SOMETIMES, SHE'D GO ON FOR *DAYS.*
AND WHEN SHE DID THIS, IT MADE YOU HAPPY? IT MADE YOU LAUGH?
NO. NO, IT DROVE ME COMPLETELY NUTS.
WHAT'S GOING ON?!

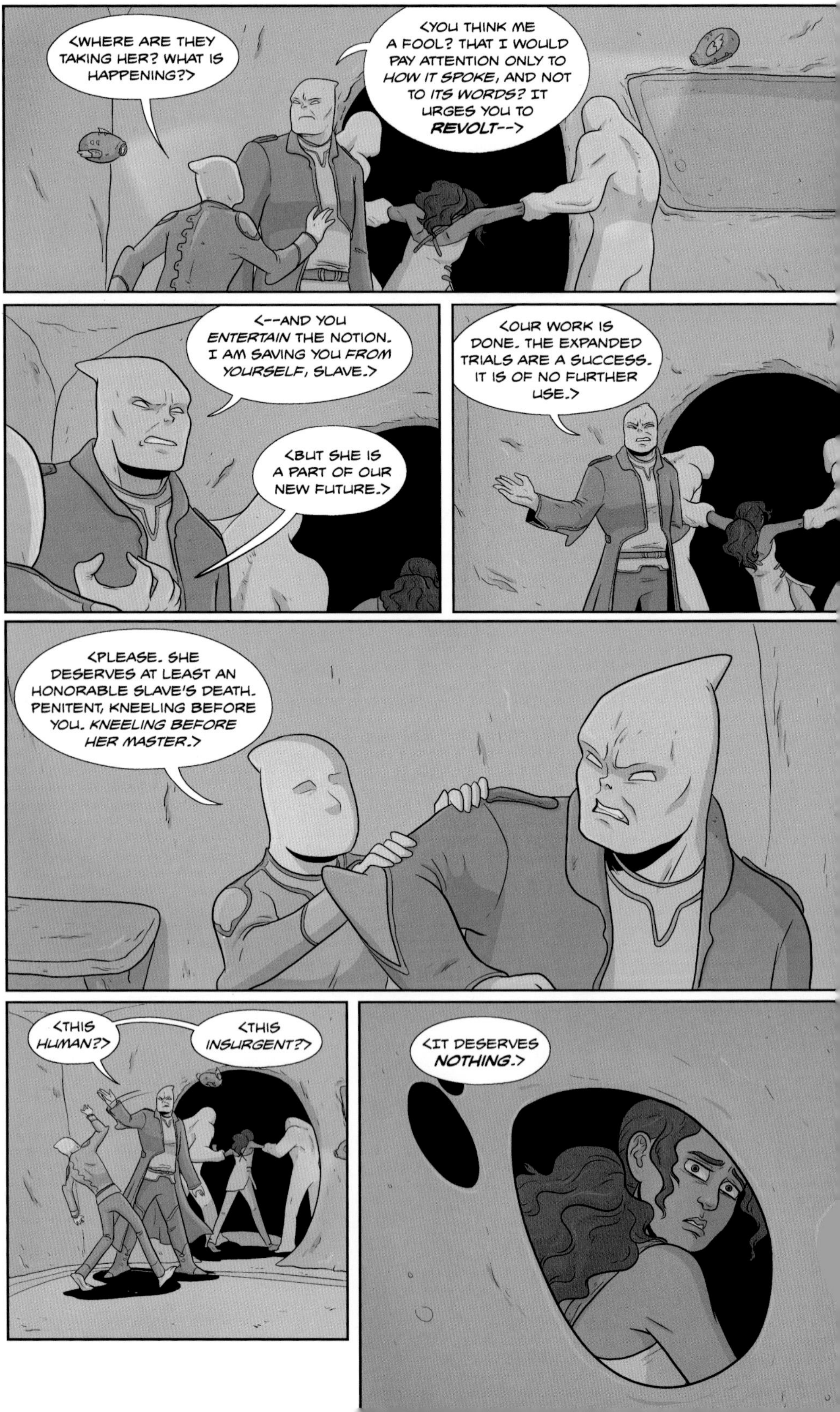
<WHERE ARE THEY TAKING HER? WHAT IS HAPPENING?>
<YOU THINK ME A FOOL? THAT I WOULD PAY ATTENTION ONLY TO *HOW IT SPOKE*, AND NOT TO ITS *WORDS*? IT URGES YOU TO ***REVOLT***-->
<--AND YOU *ENTERTAIN* THE NOTION. I AM SAVING YOU *FROM YOURSELF*, SLAVE.>
<BUT SHE IS A PART OF OUR NEW FUTURE.>
<OUR WORK IS DONE. THE EXPANDED TRIALS ARE A SUCCESS. IT IS OF NO FURTHER USE.>
<PLEASE. SHE DESERVES AT LEAST AN HONORABLE SLAVE'S DEATH. PENITENT, KNEELING BEFORE YOU. *KNEELING BEFORE HER MASTER.*>
<THIS *HUMAN?*>
<THIS *INSURGENT?*>
<IT DESERVES ***NOTHING.***>

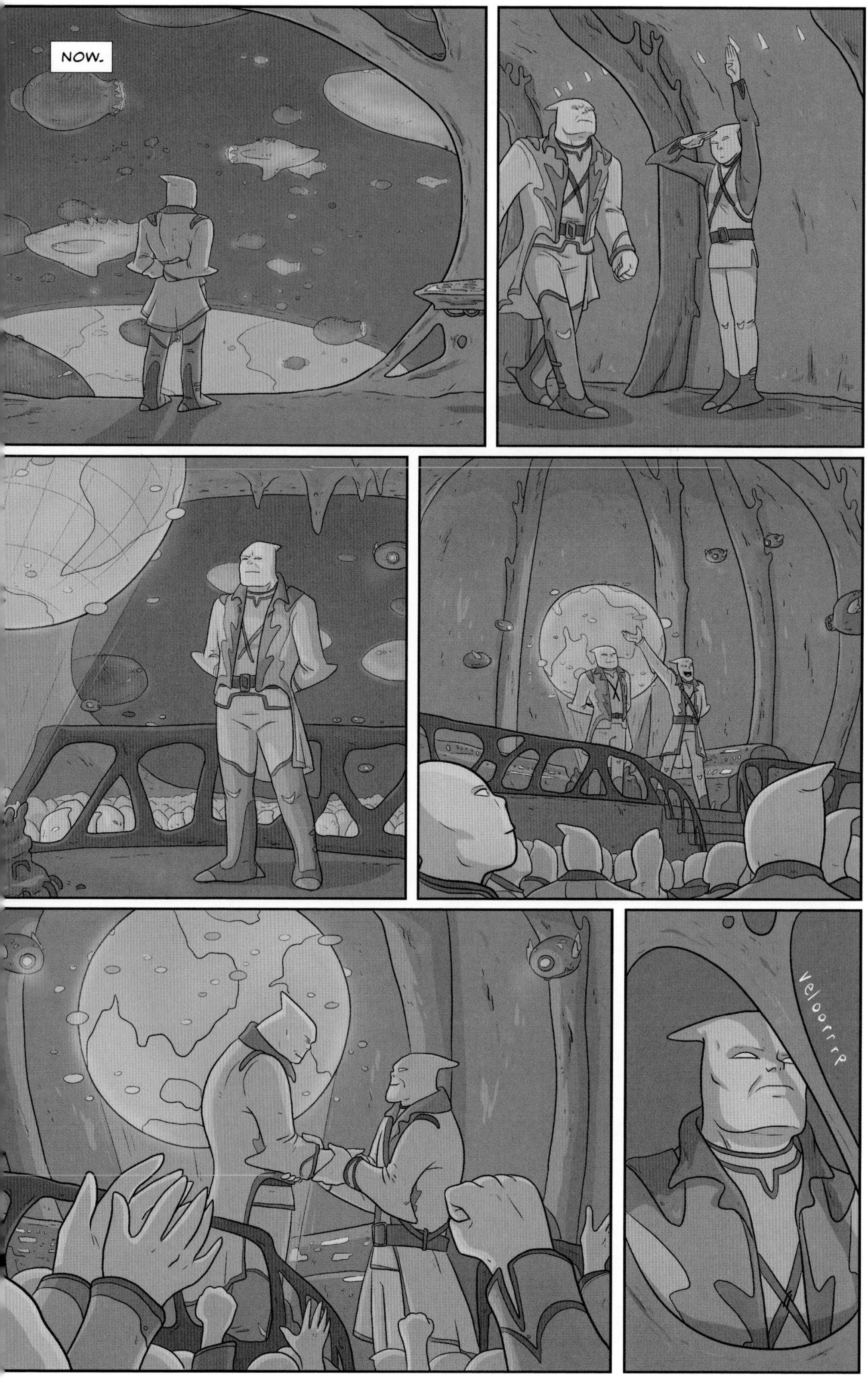
NOW.
Veloorrre

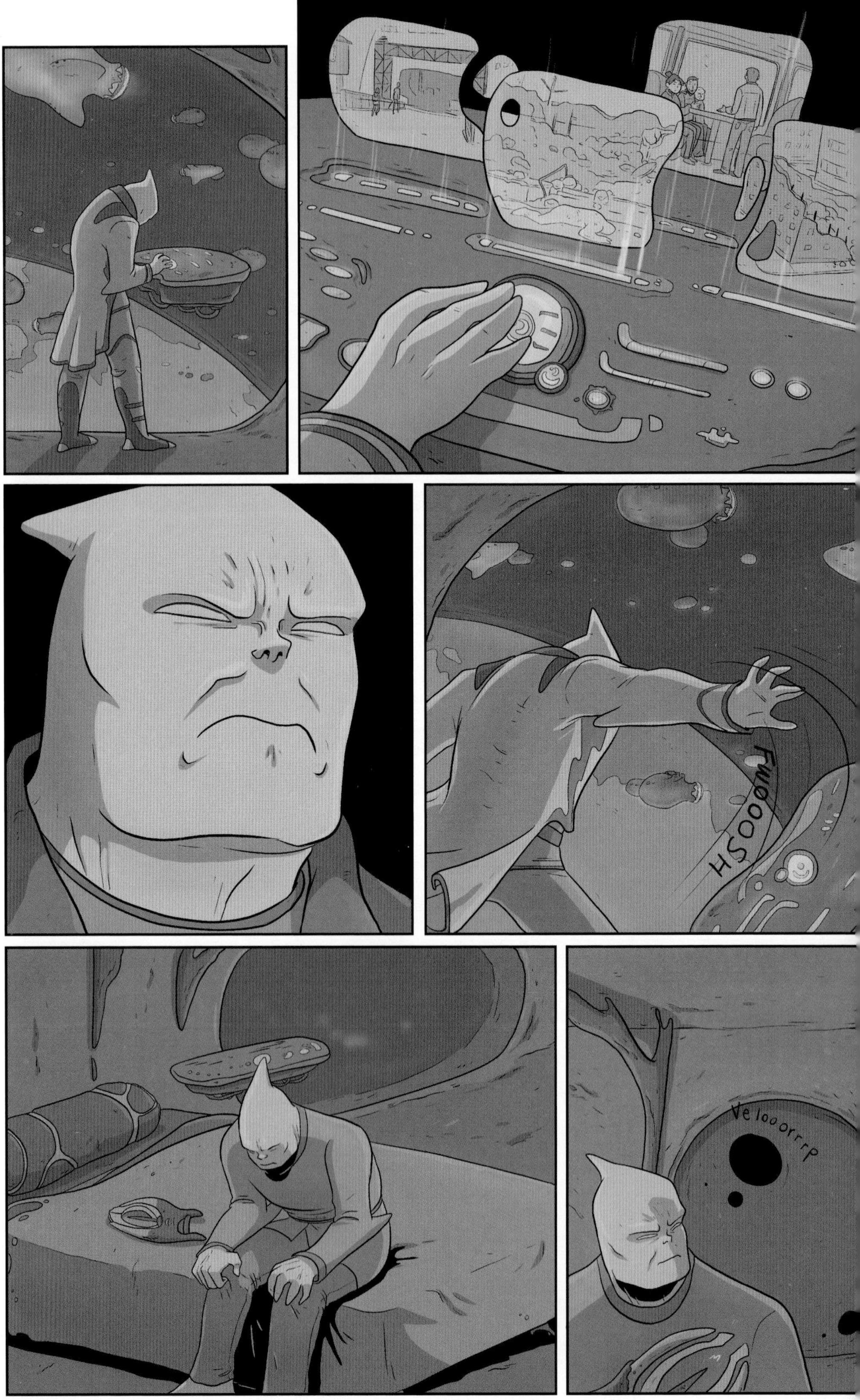
FWOOOSH
Velooorrrp

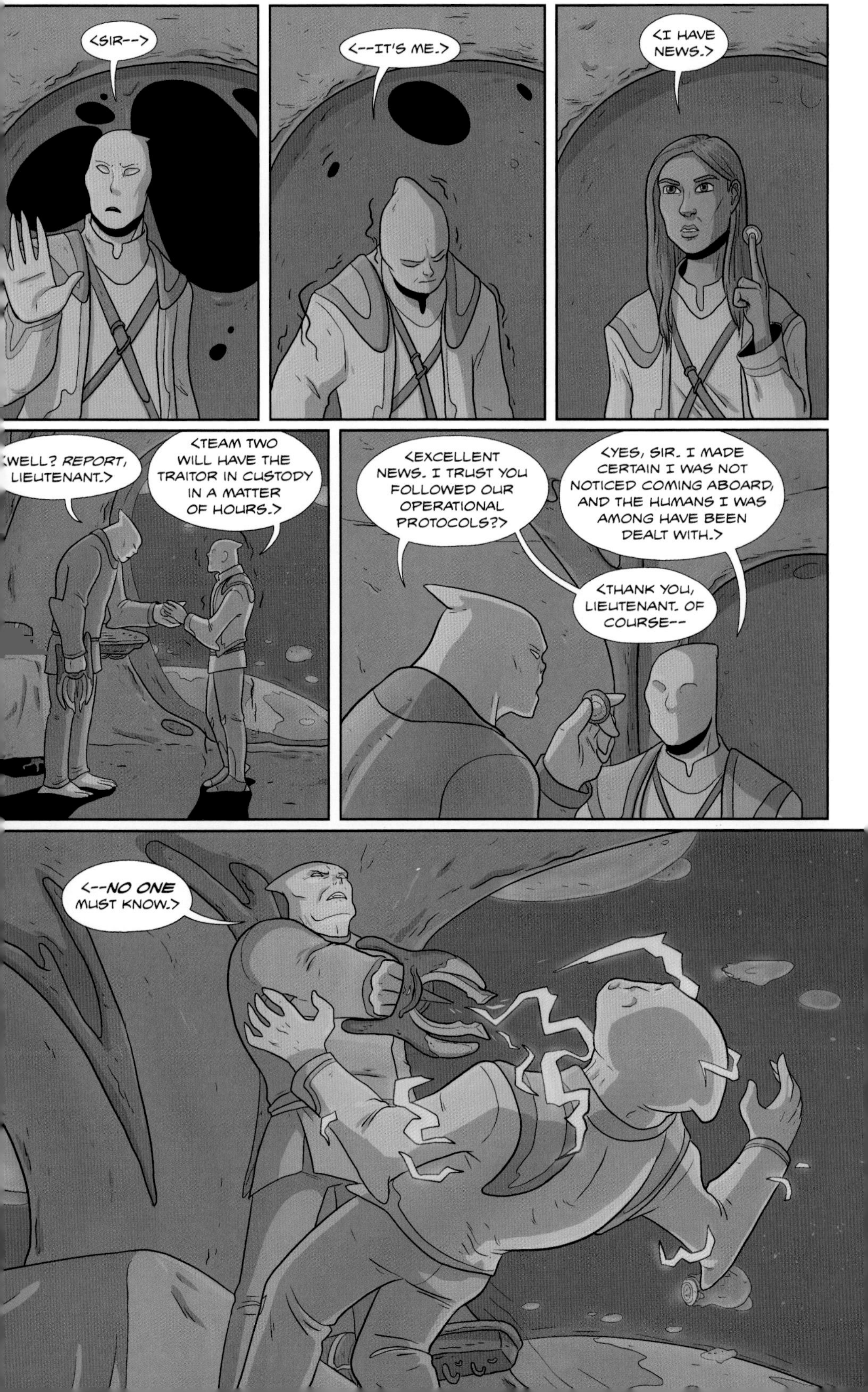
<SIR-->
<--IT'S ME.>
<I HAVE NEWS.>
<WELL? *REPORT,* LIEUTENANT.>
<TEAM TWO WILL HAVE THE TRAITOR IN CUSTODY IN A MATTER OF HOURS.>
<EXCELLENT NEWS. I TRUST YOU FOLLOWED OUR OPERATIONAL PROTOCOLS?>
<YES, SIR. I MADE CERTAIN I WAS NOT NOTICED COMING ABOARD, AND THE HUMANS I WAS AMONG HAVE BEEN DEALT WITH.>
<THANK YOU, LIEUTENANT. OF COURSE--
<--*NO ONE* MUST KNOW.>

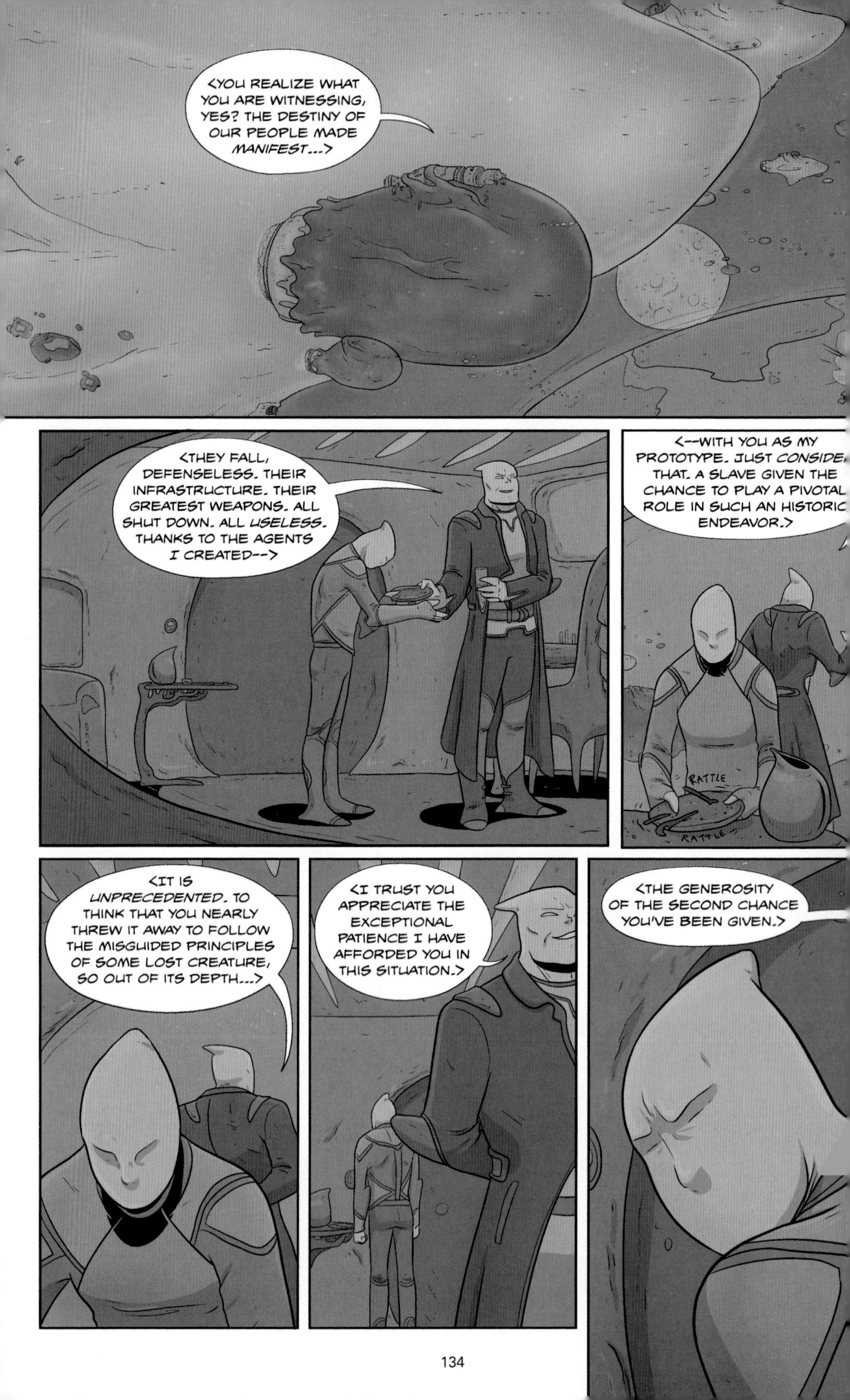
<YOU REALIZE WHAT YOU ARE WITNESSING, YES? THE DESTINY OF OUR PEOPLE MADE *MANIFEST*...>
<THEY FALL, DEFENSELESS. THEIR INFRASTRUCTURE. THEIR GREATEST WEAPONS. ALL SHUT DOWN. ALL *USELESS*. THANKS TO THE AGENTS *I* CREATED-->
<--WITH YOU AS MY PROTOTYPE. JUST *CONSIDE* THAT. A SLAVE GIVEN THE CHANCE TO PLAY A PIVOTAL ROLE IN SUCH AN HISTORIC ENDEAVOR.>
RATTLE
RATTLE
<IT IS *UNPRECEDENTED*. TO THINK THAT YOU NEARLY THREW IT AWAY TO FOLLOW THE MISGUIDED PRINCIPLES OF SOME LOST CREATURE, SO OUT OF ITS DEPTH...>
<I TRUST YOU APPRECIATE THE EXCEPTIONAL PATIENCE I HAVE AFFORDED YOU IN THIS SITUATION.>
<THE GENEROSITY OF THE SECOND CHANCE YOU'VE BEEN GIVEN.>

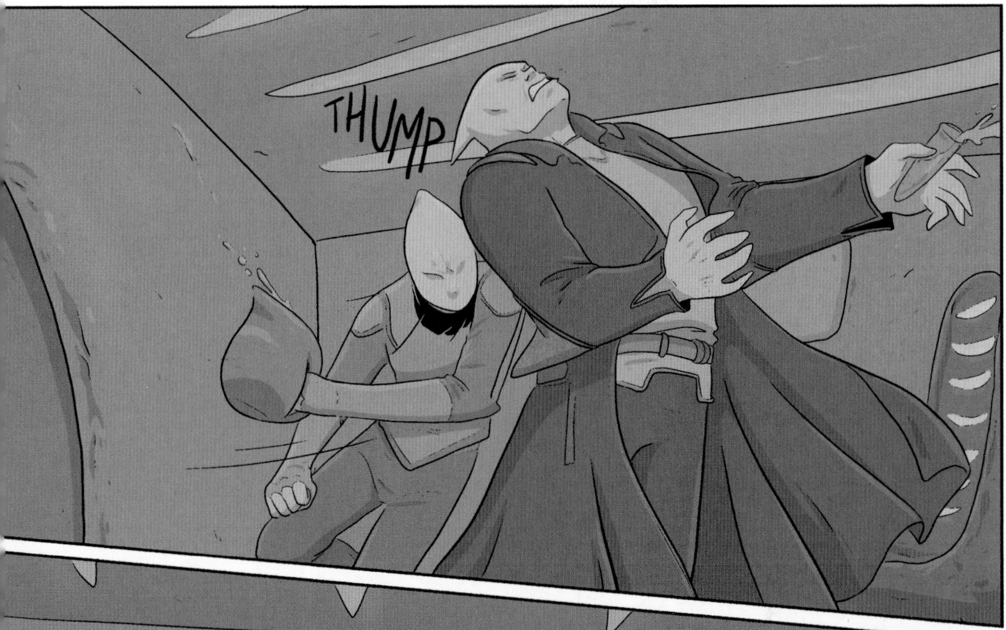
THUMP

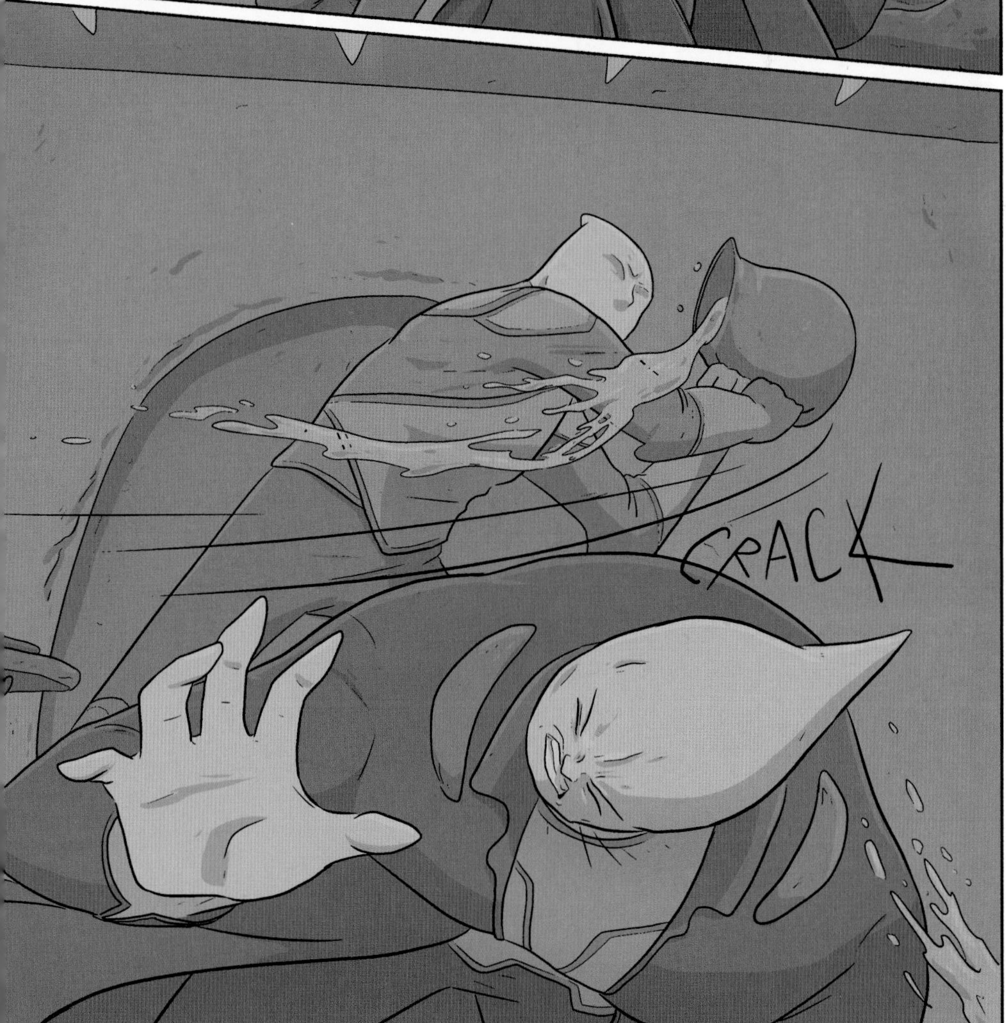
CRACK

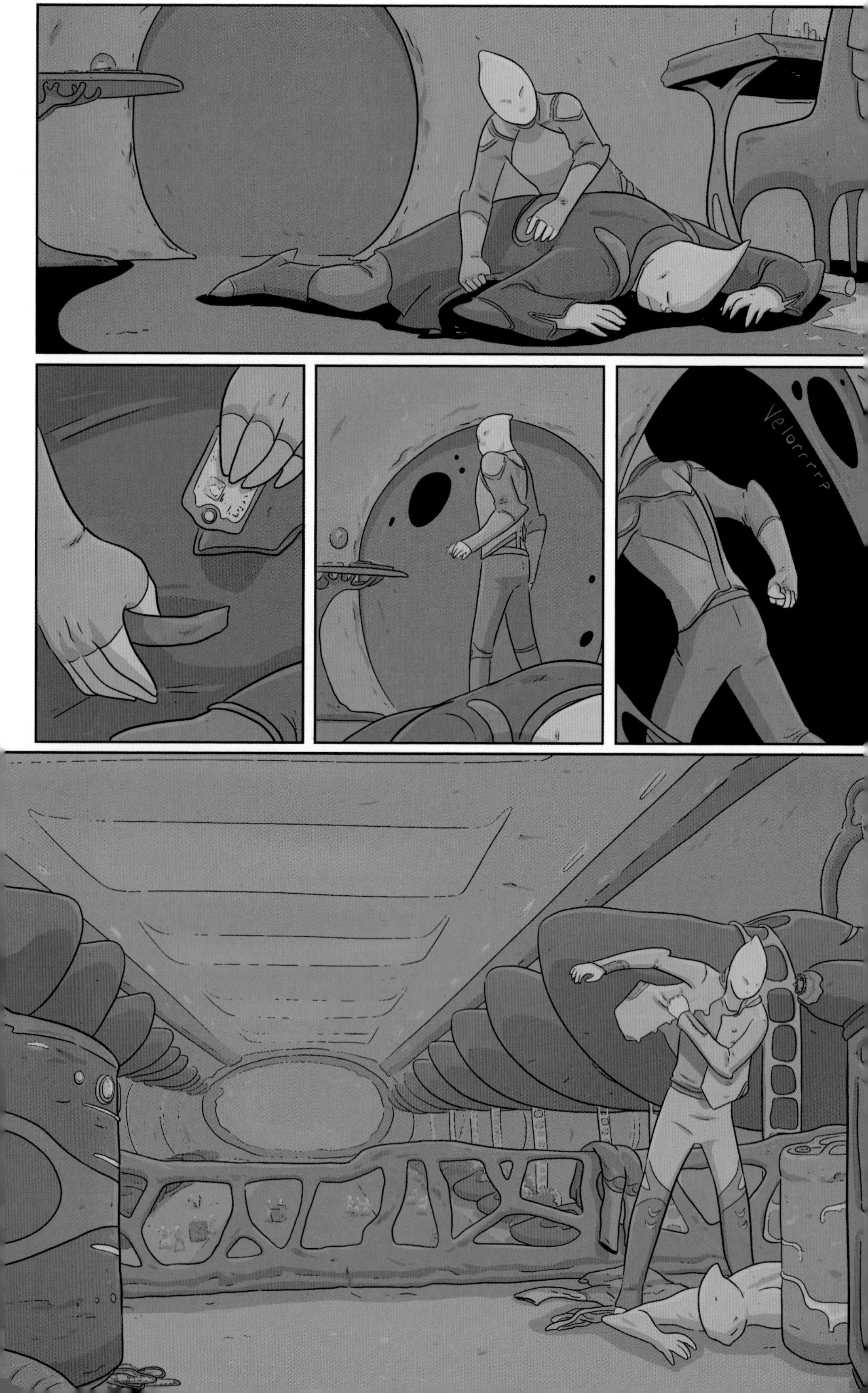
Velorrrrrp

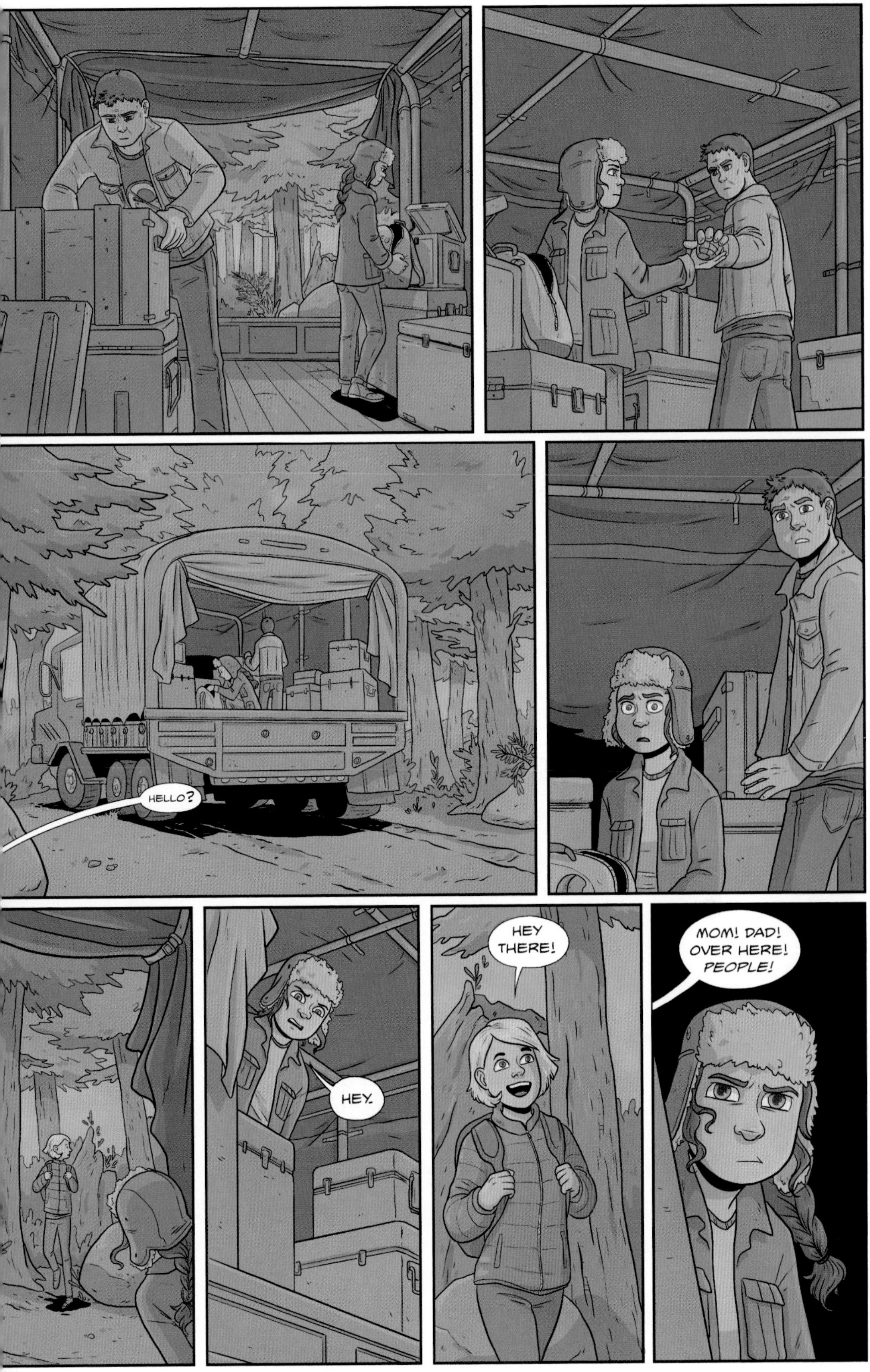

HELLO?
HEY.
HEY THERE!
MOM! DAD! OVER HERE! PEOPLE!

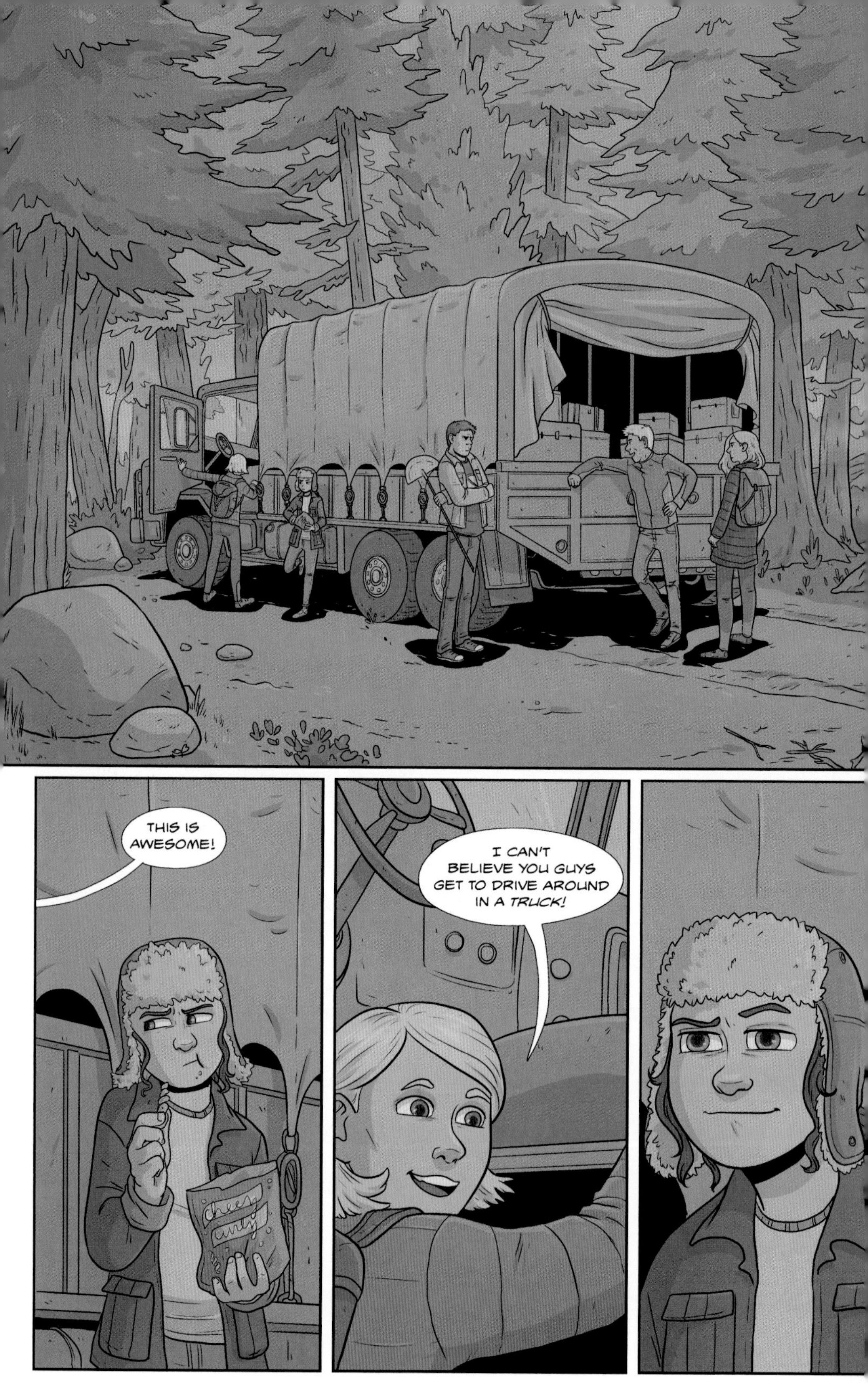
THIS IS AWESOME!
I CAN'T BELIEVE YOU GUYS GET TO DRIVE AROUND IN A *TRUCK!*

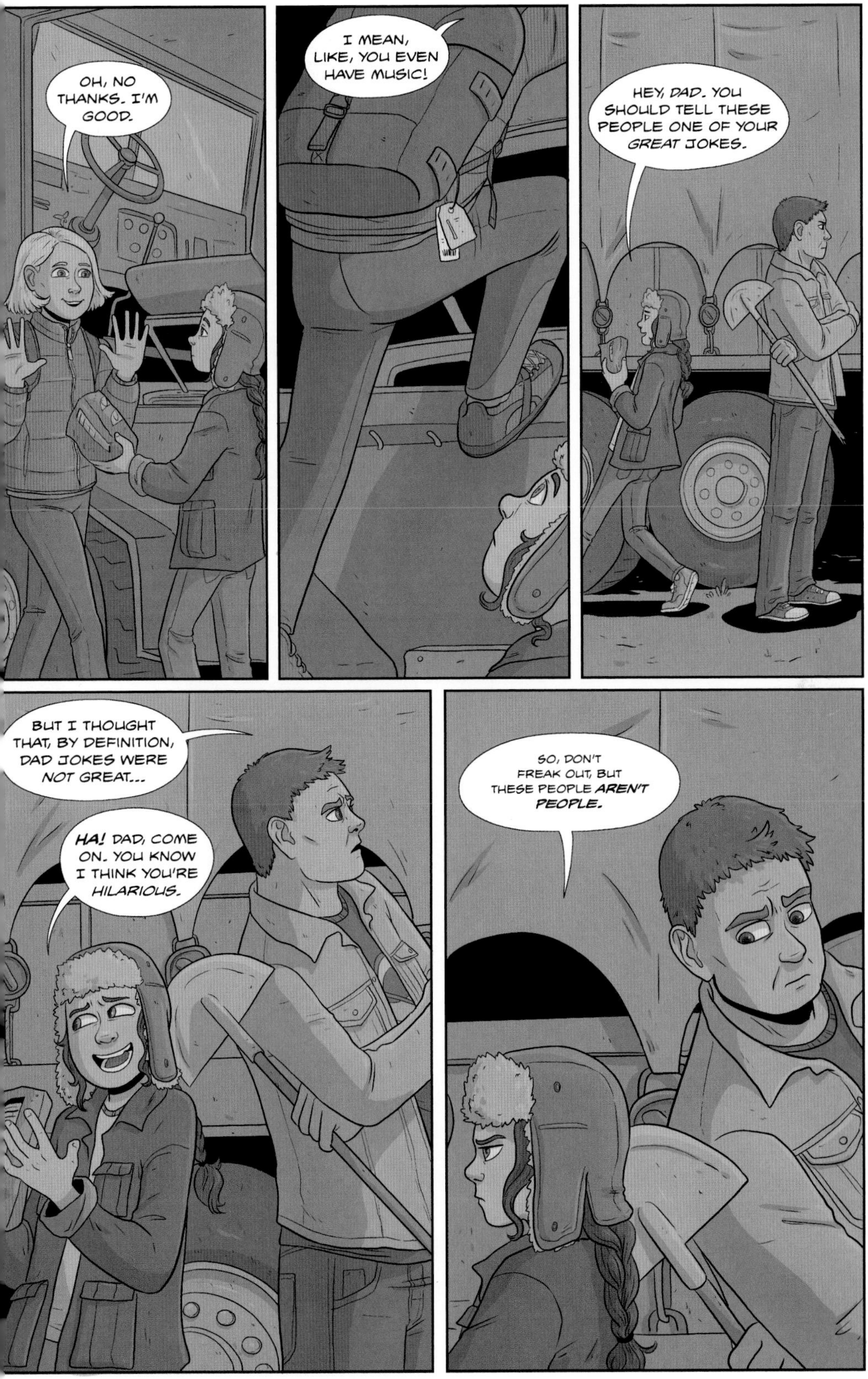
OH, NO THANKS. I'M GOOD.
I MEAN, LIKE, YOU EVEN HAVE MUSIC!
HEY, *DAD*. YOU SHOULD TELL THESE PEOPLE ONE OF YOUR *GREAT* JOKES.
BUT I THOUGHT THAT, BY DEFINITION, DAD JOKES WERE *NOT* GREAT...
HA! DAD, COME ON. YOU KNOW I THINK YOU'RE *HILARIOUS*.
SO, DON'T FREAK OUT, BUT THESE PEOPLE ***AREN'T PEOPLE.***

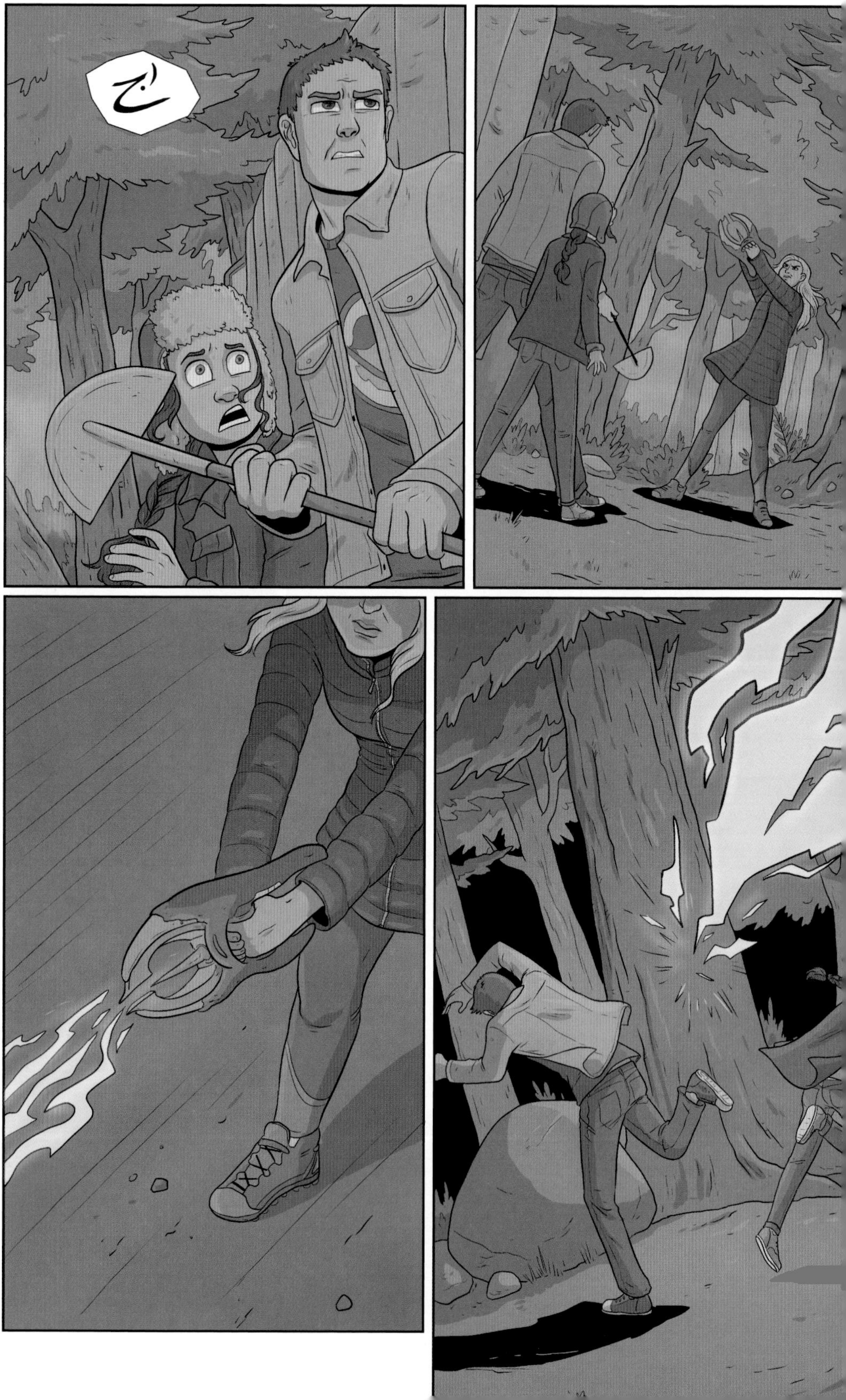

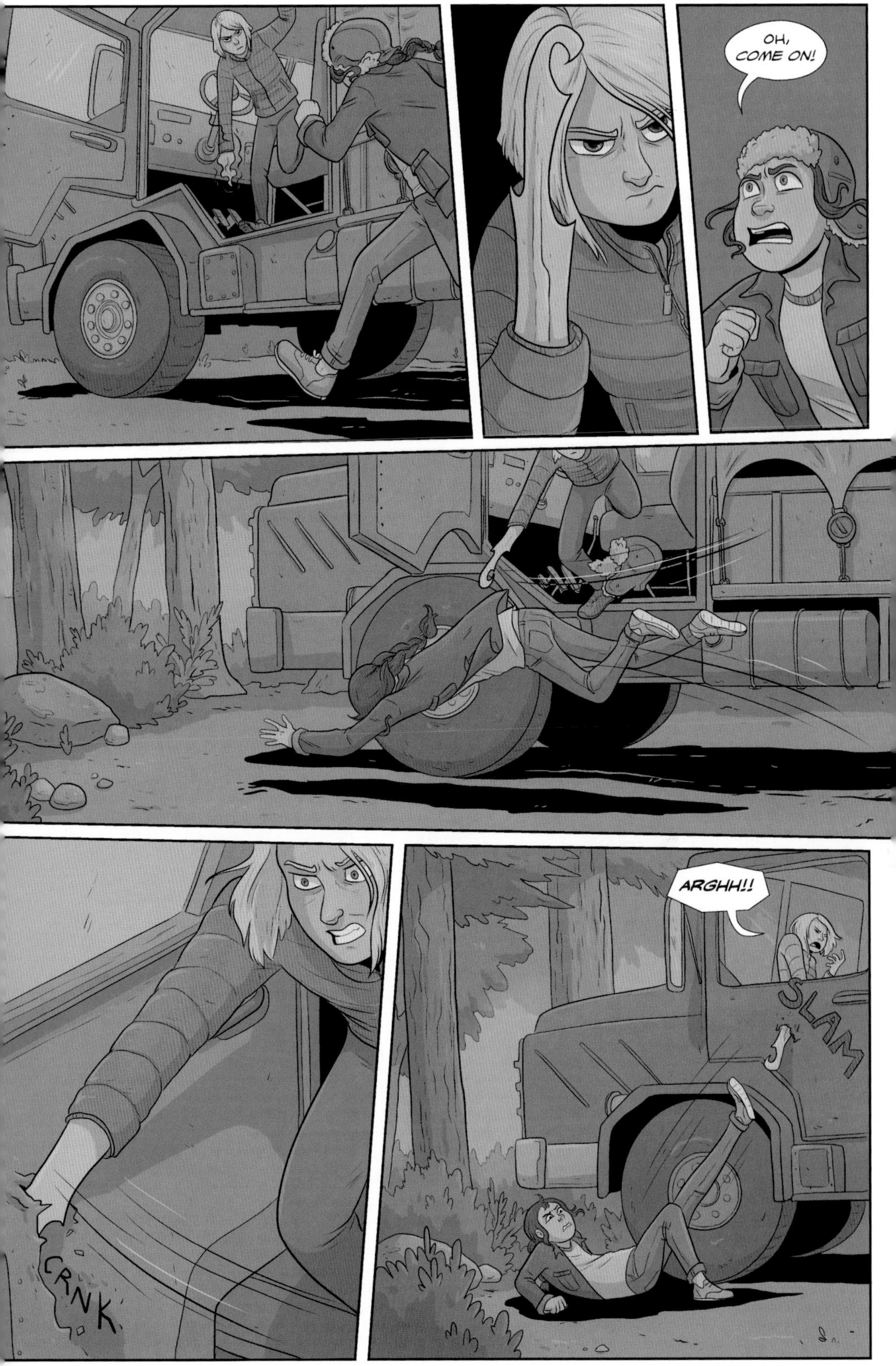
OH, COME ON!
CRNK
ARGHH!!
SLAM

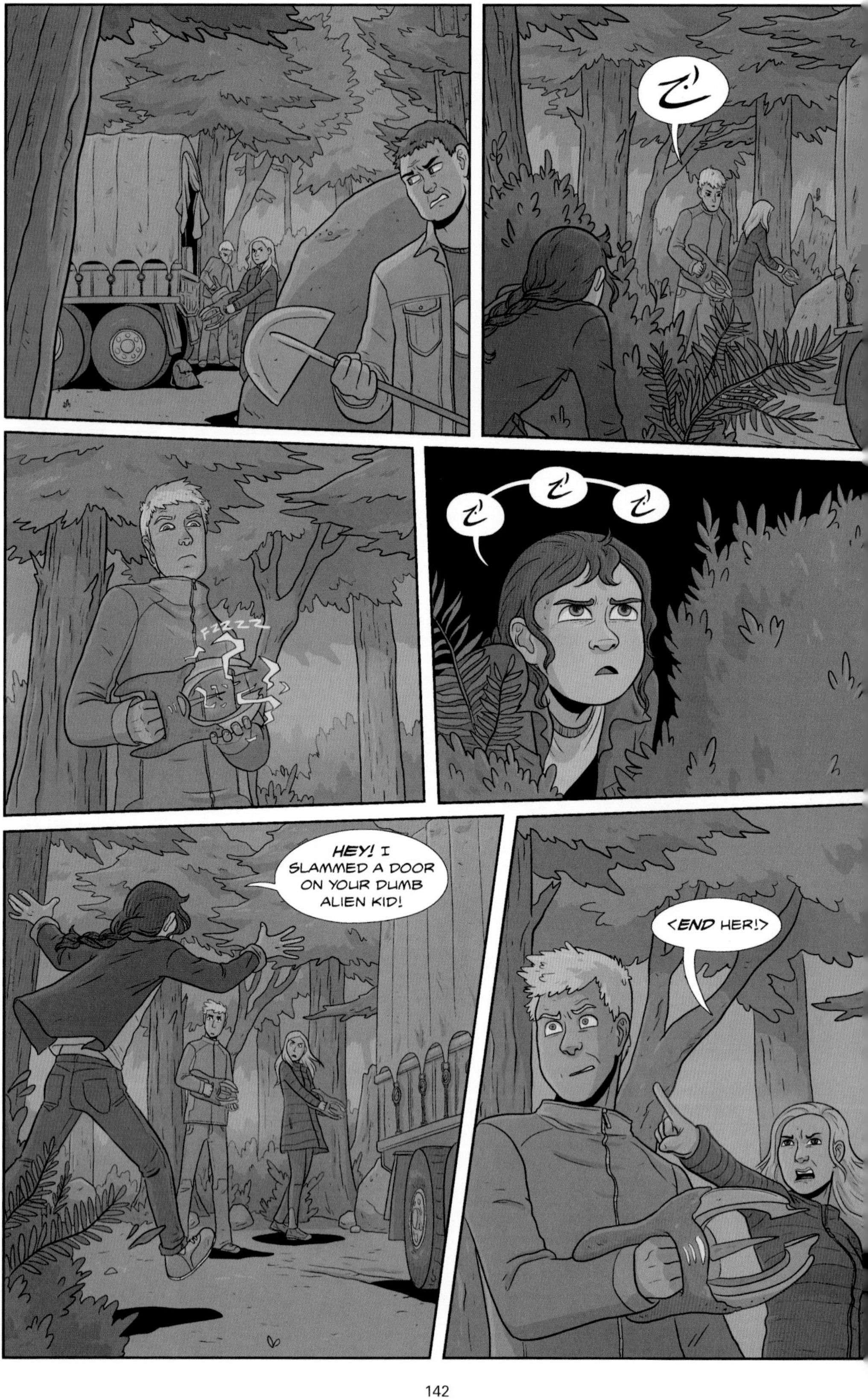
FZZZZ
HEY! I SLAMMED A DOOR ON YOUR DUMB ALIEN KID!
<END HER!>

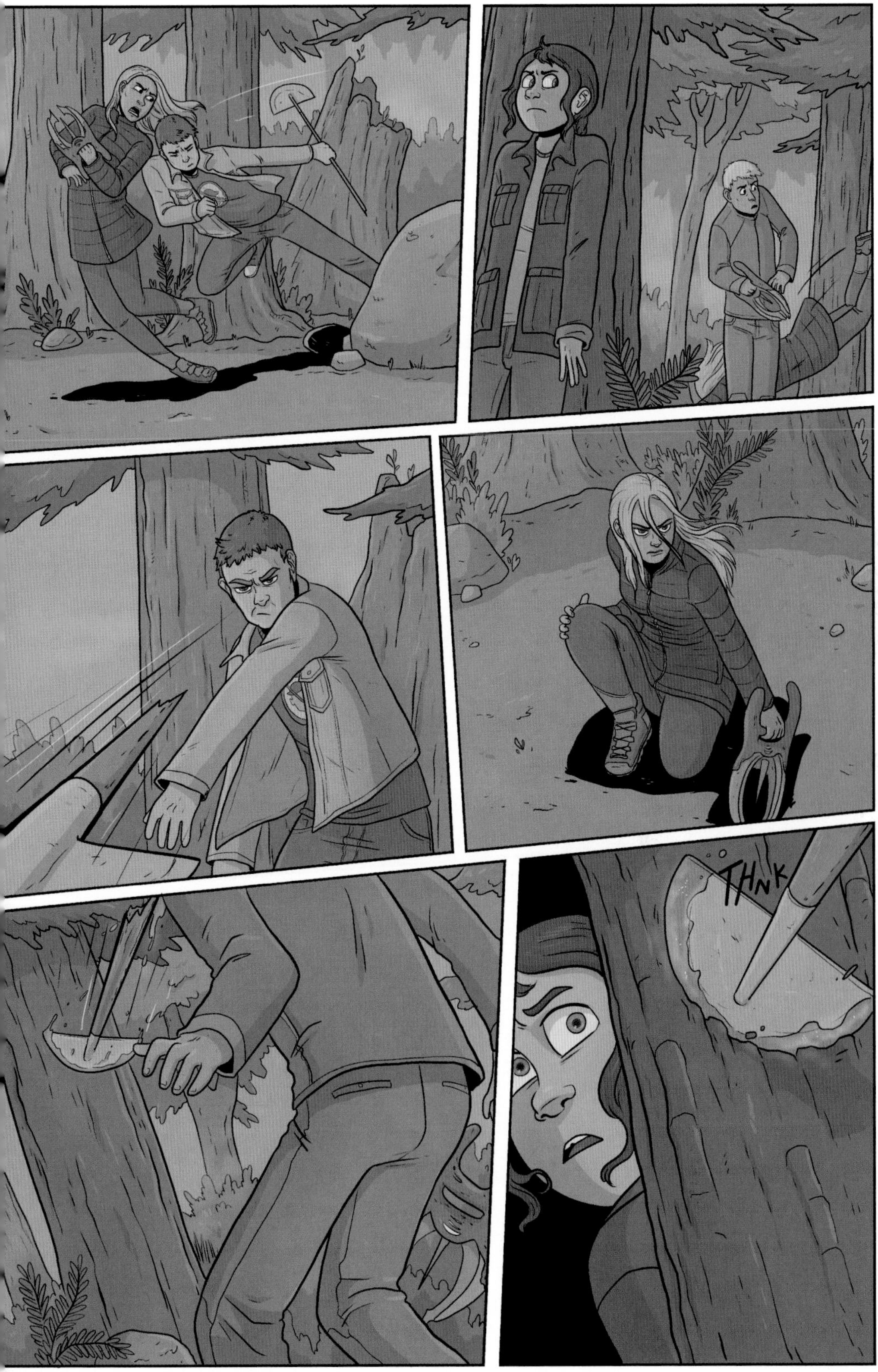
THNK

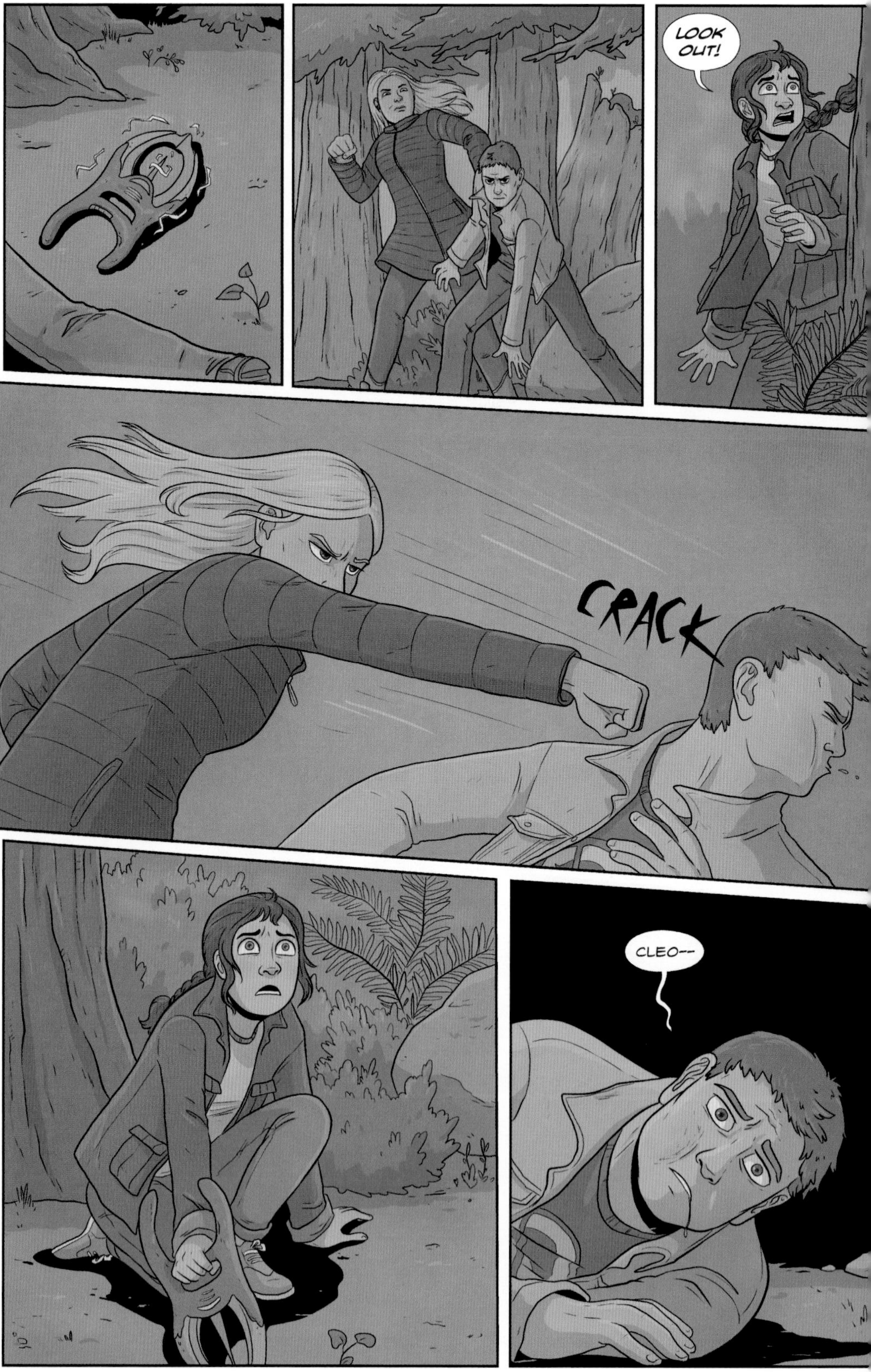
LOOK OUT!
CRACK
CLEO--

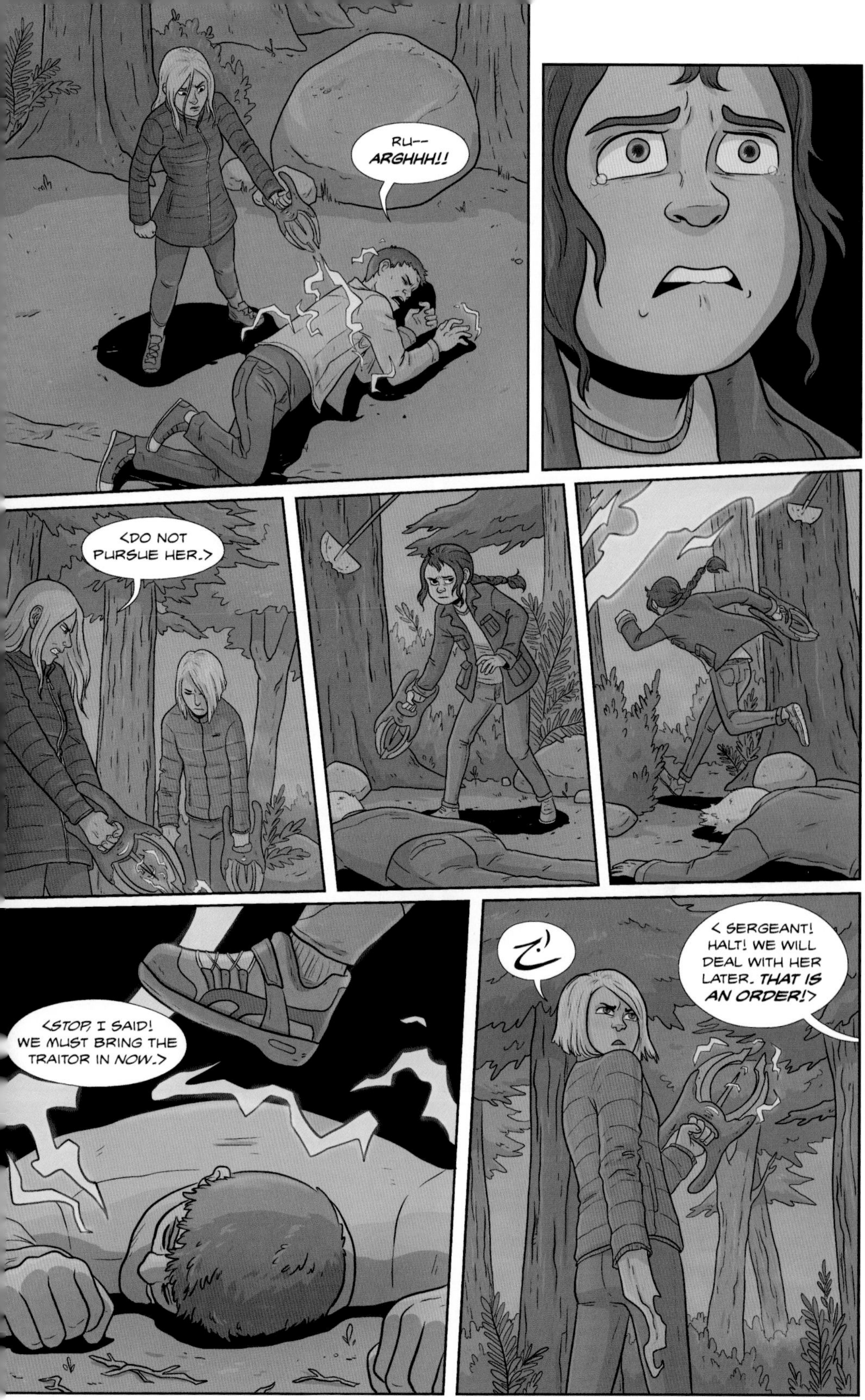
RU--
ARGHHH!!
<DO NOT PURSUE HER.>
<STOP, I SAID! WE MUST BRING THE TRAITOR IN NOW.>
< SERGEANT! HALT! WE WILL DEAL WITH HER LATER. THAT IS AN ORDER!>

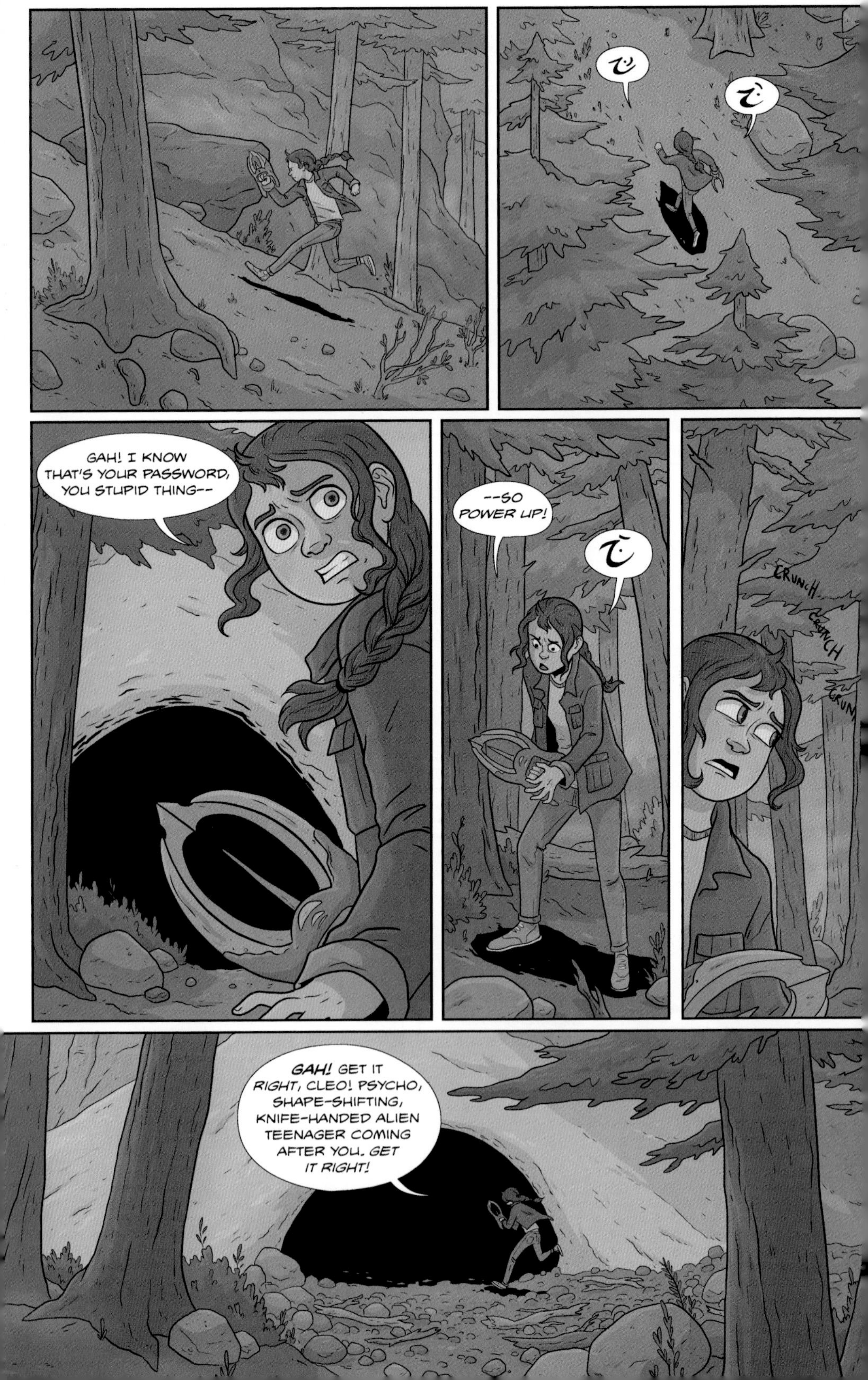
GAH! I KNOW THAT'S YOUR PASSWORD, YOU STUPID THING--
--SO POWER UP!
CRUNCH
CRUNCH
GAH! GET IT RIGHT, CLEO! PSYCHO, SHAPE-SHIFTING, KNIFE-HANDED ALIEN TEENAGER COMING AFTER YOU. GET IT RIGHT!

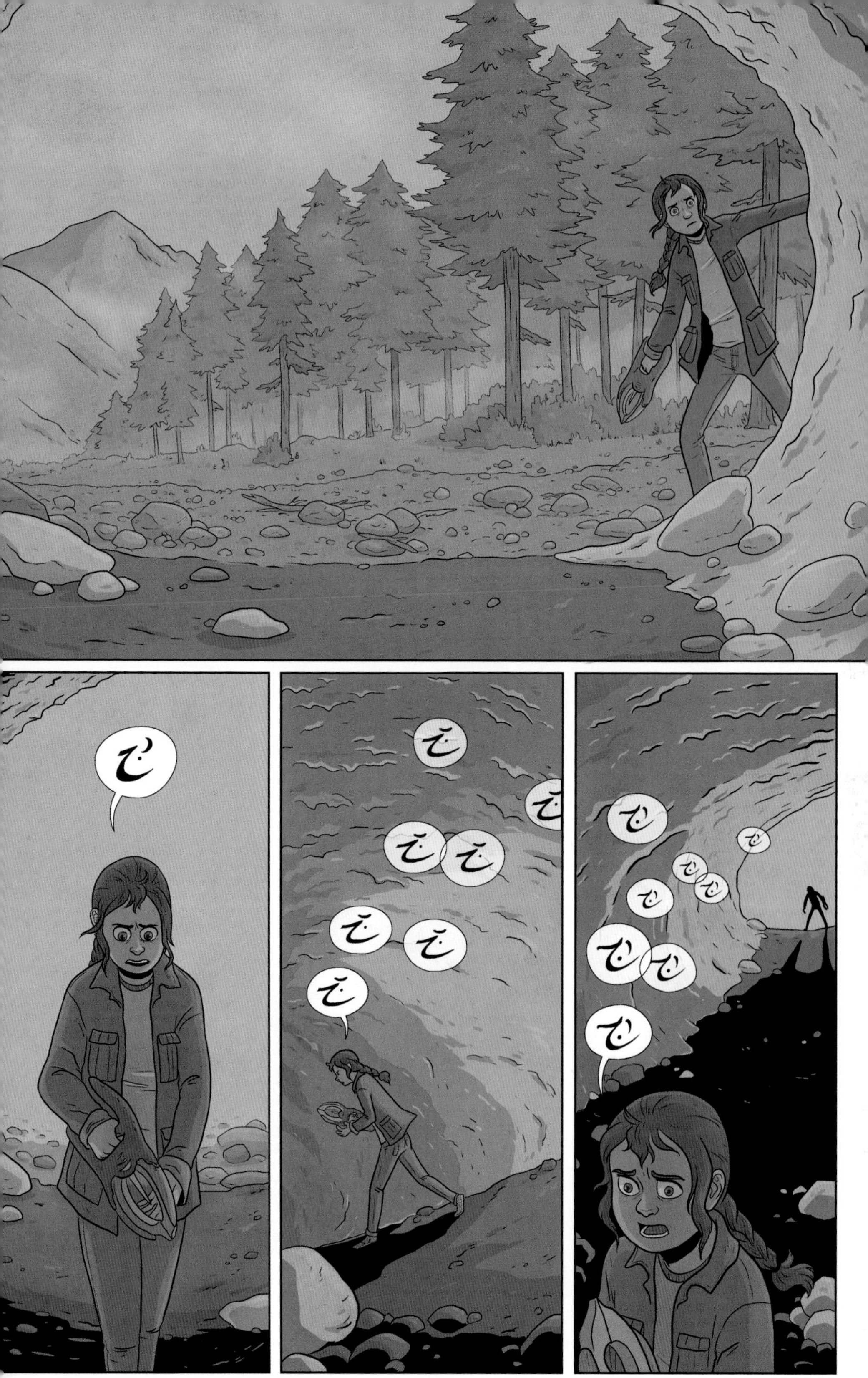

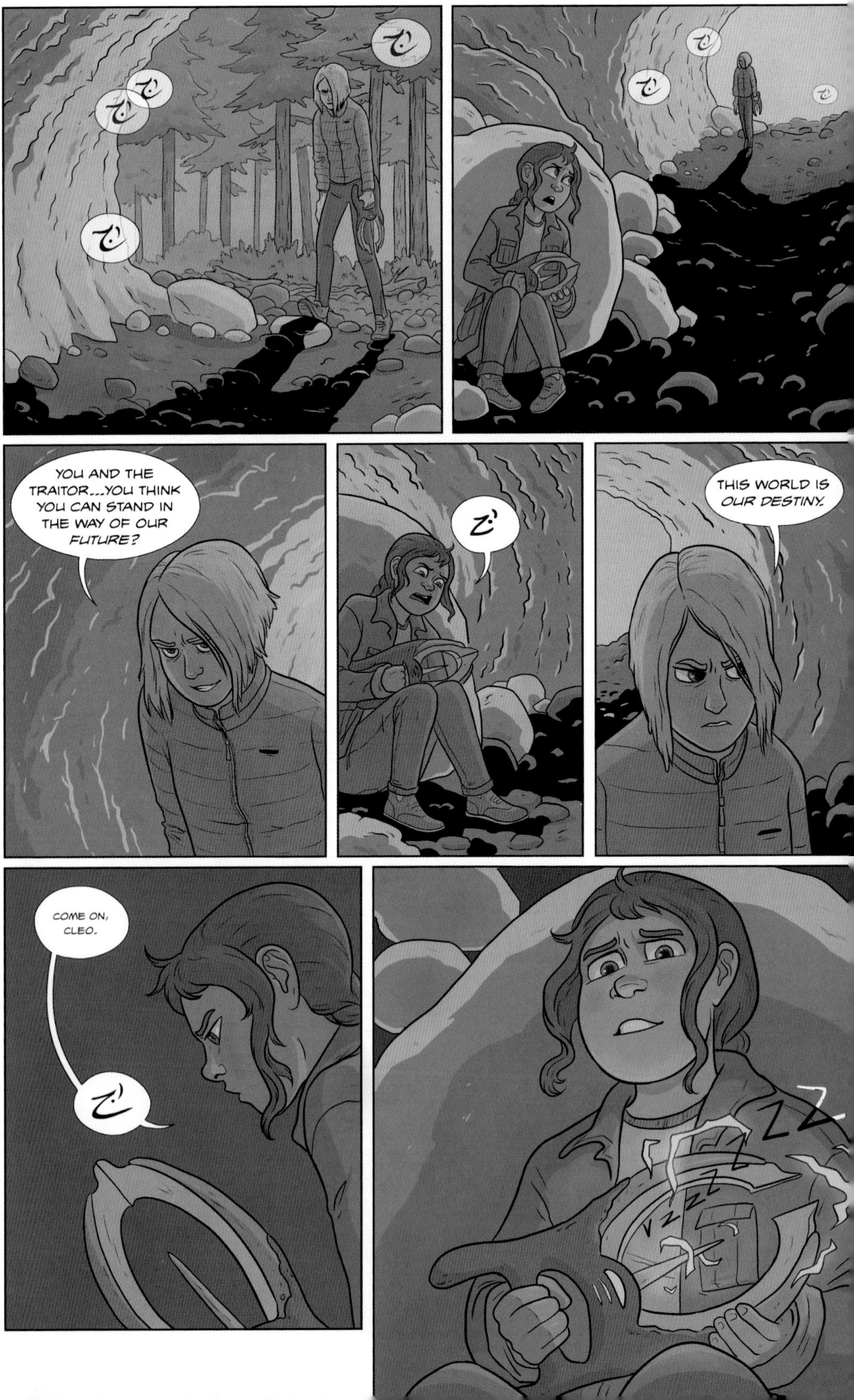
YOU AND THE TRAITOR...YOU THINK YOU CAN STAND IN THE WAY OF OUR FUTURE?
THIS WORLD IS OUR DESTINY.
COME ON, CLEO.

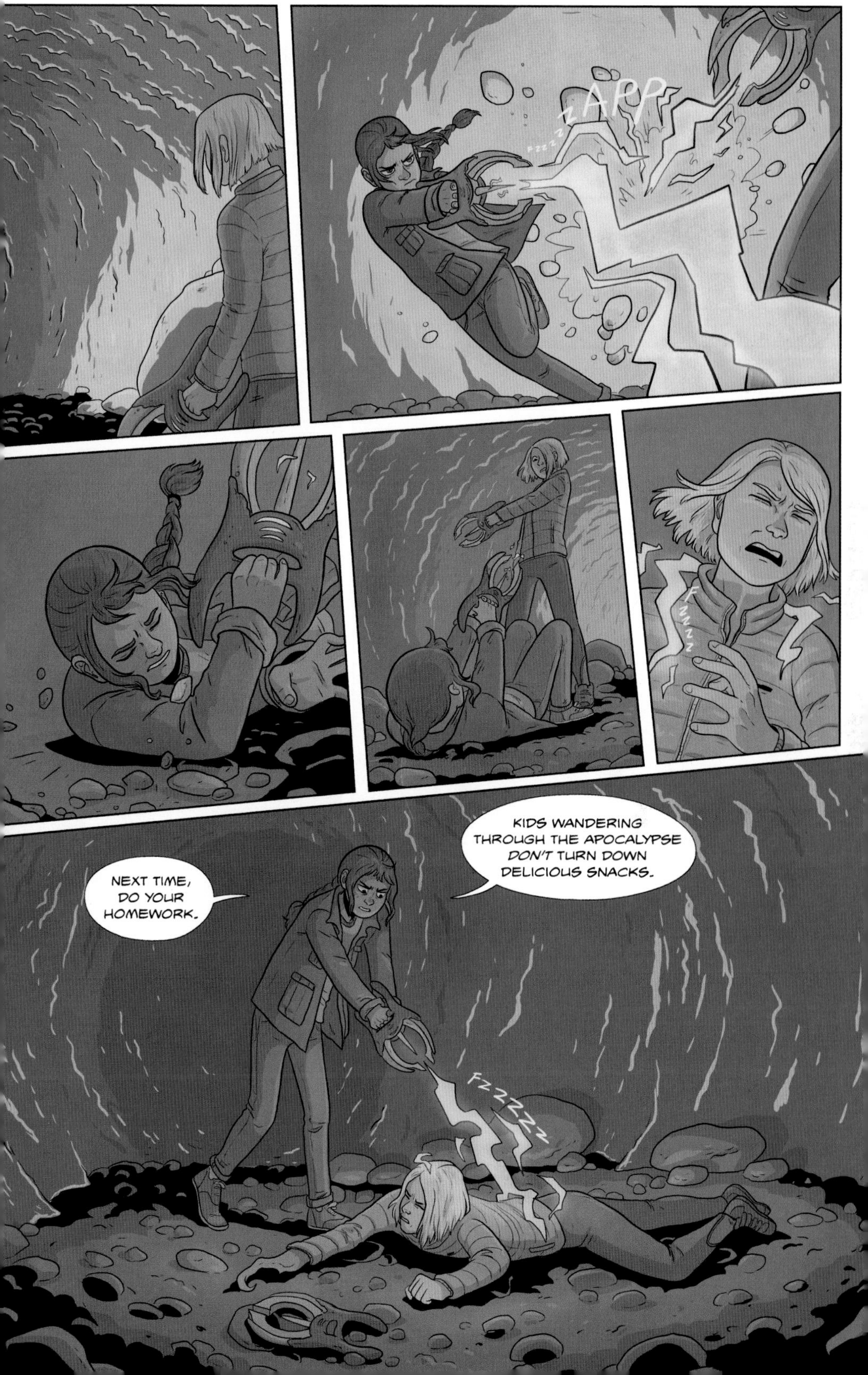
FZZZZ ZAPP
FZZZZ
NEXT TIME, DO YOUR HOMEWORK.
KIDS WANDERING THROUGH THE APOCALYPSE DON'T TURN DOWN DELICIOUS SNACKS.
FZZZZZ

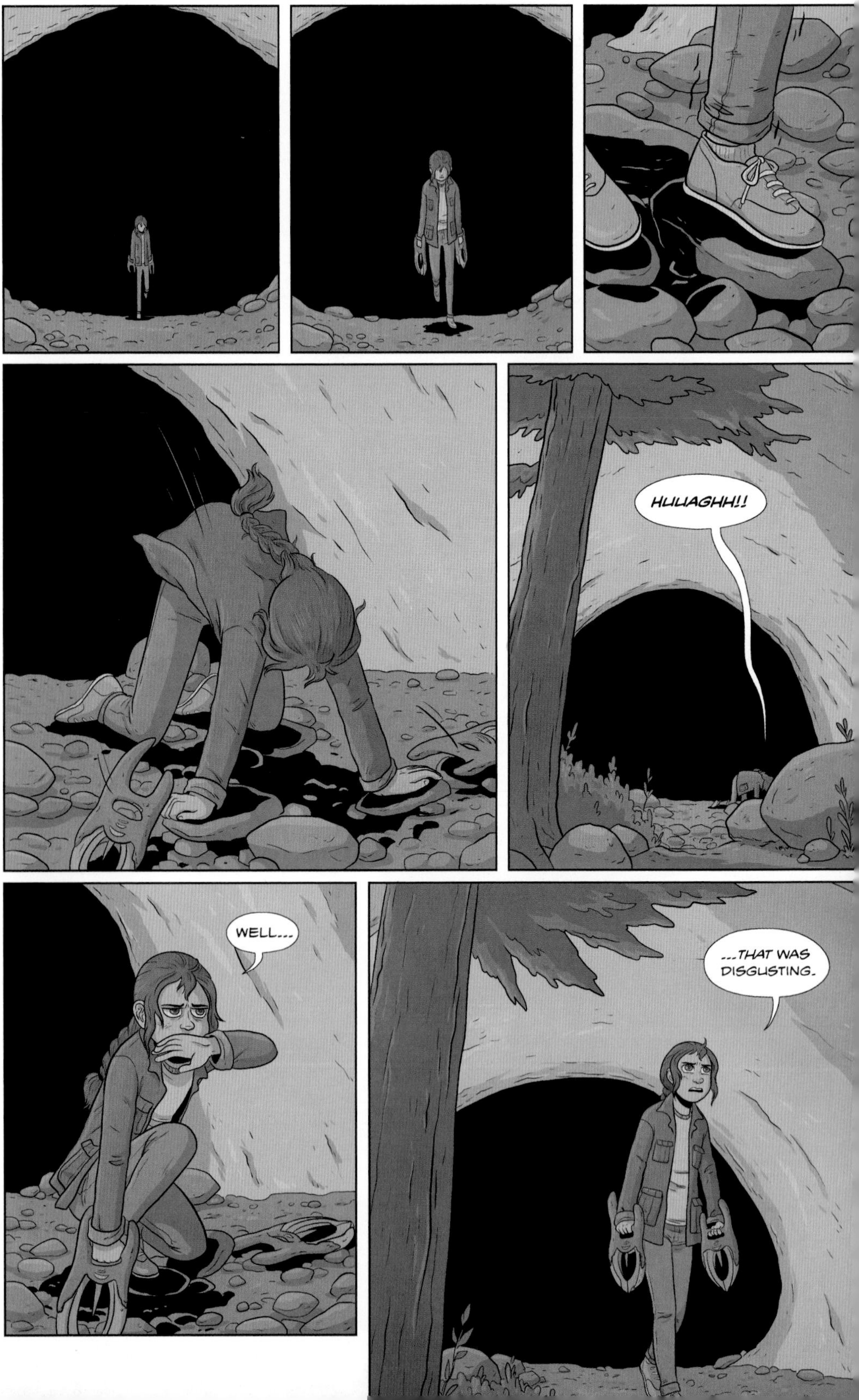
HUUAGHH!!
WELL...
...THAT WAS DISGUSTING.

FIVE

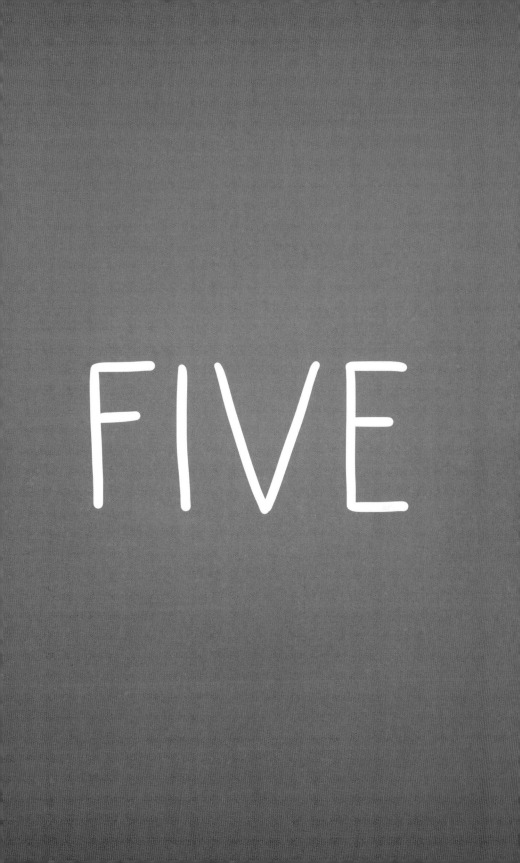

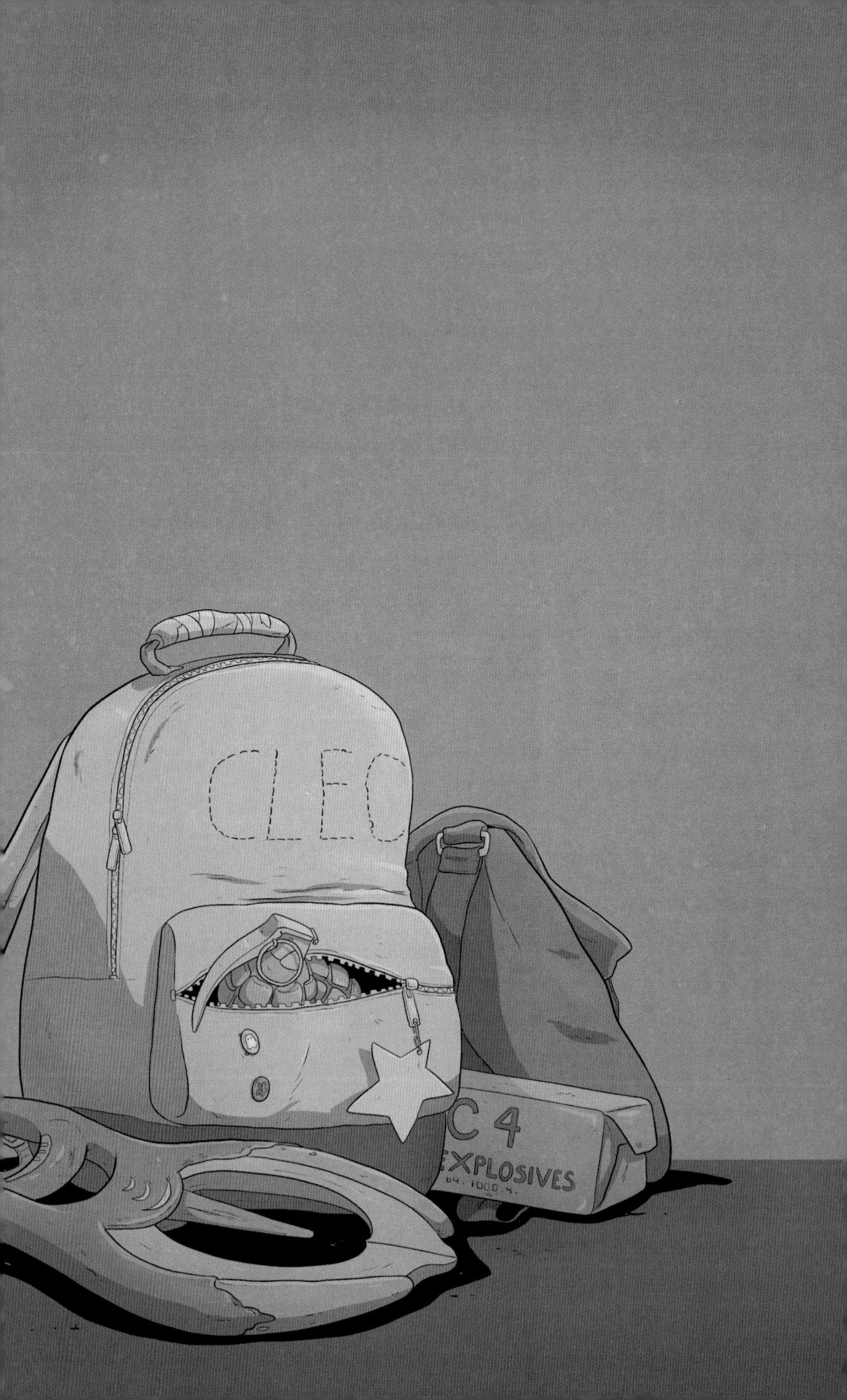
CLEO
C 4
EXPLOSIVES

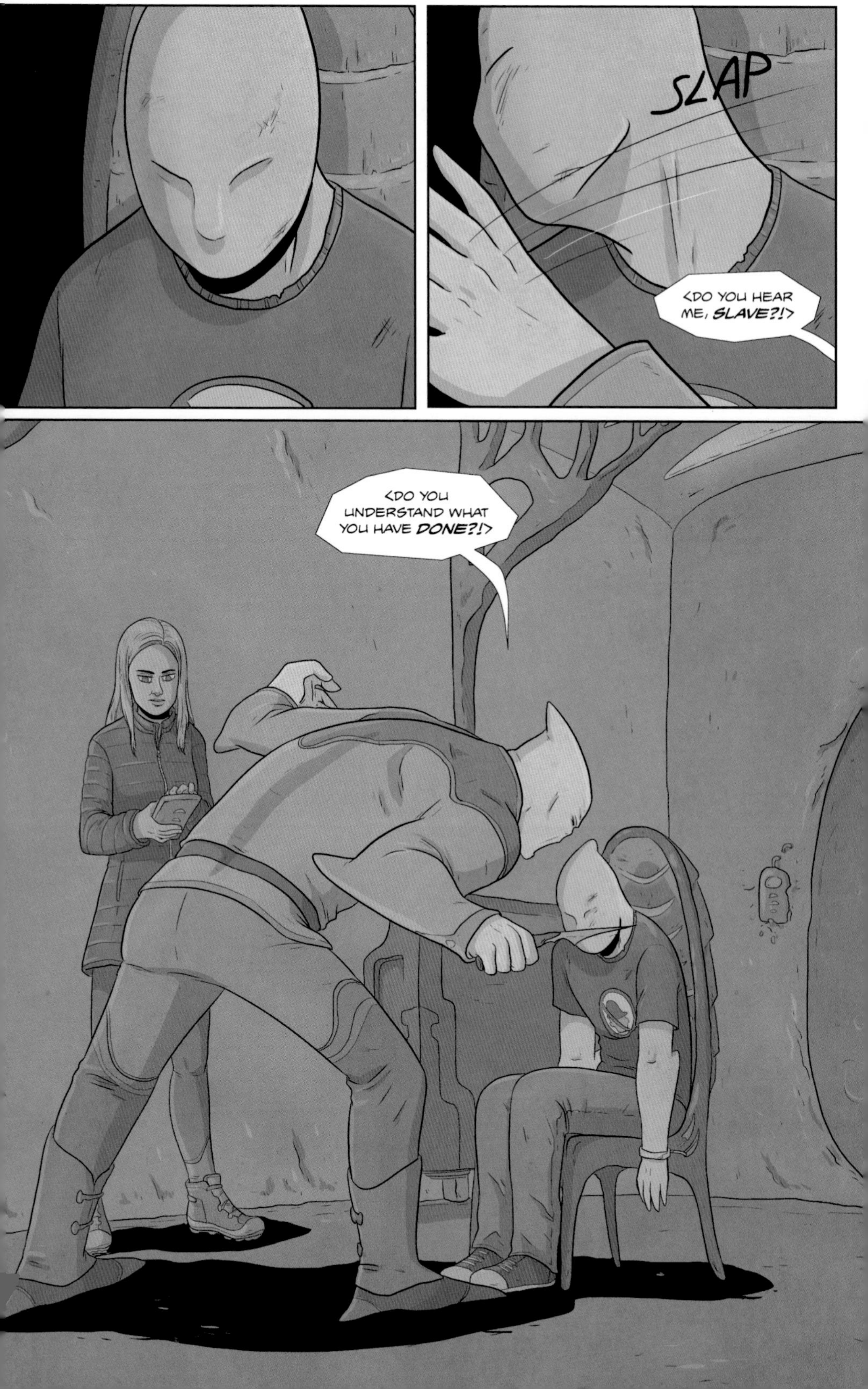
SLAP
<DO YOU HEAR ME, SLAVE?!>
<DO YOU UNDERSTAND WHAT YOU HAVE DONE?!>

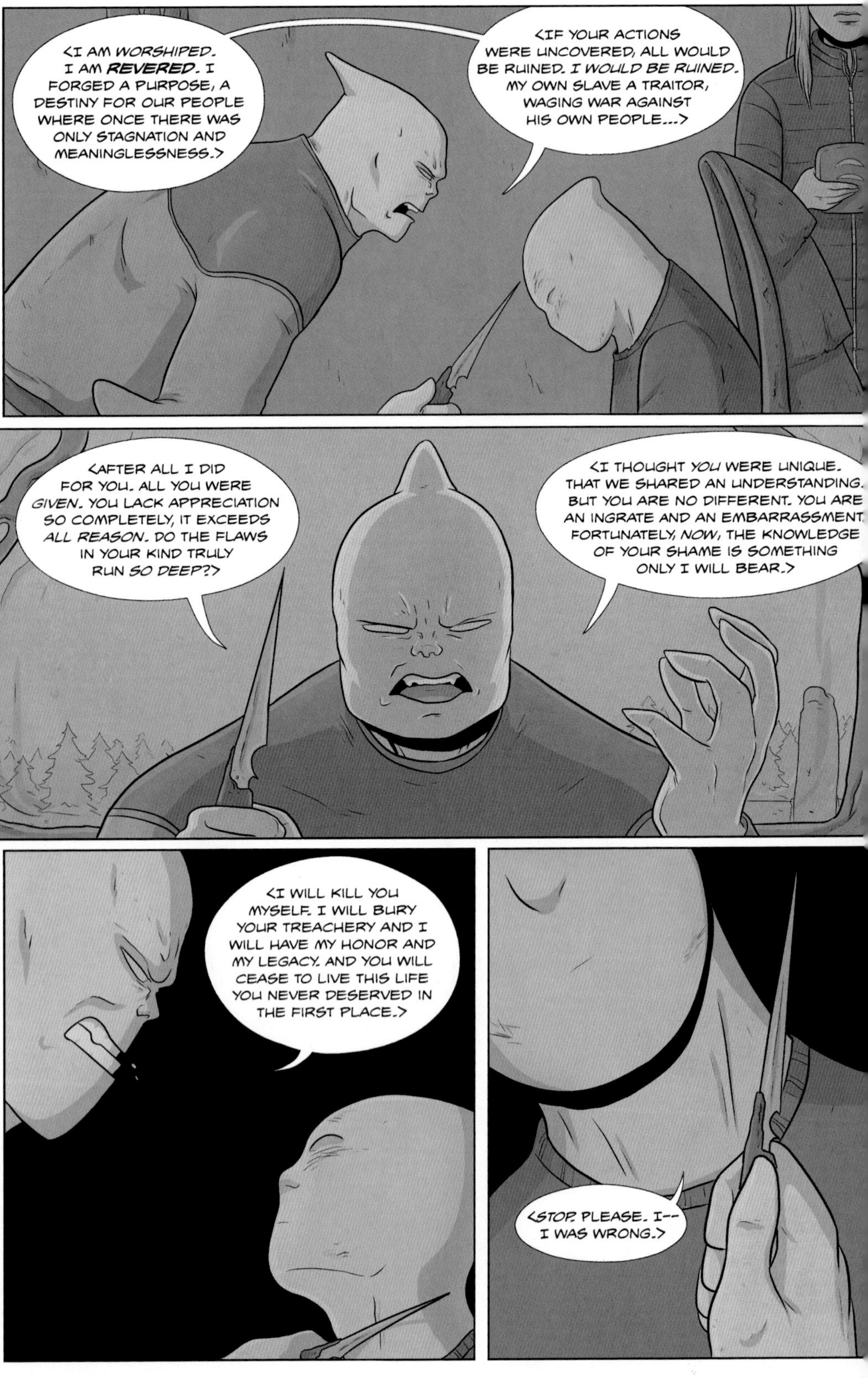

<I AM WORSHIPED. I AM REVERED. I FORGED A PURPOSE, A DESTINY FOR OUR PEOPLE WHERE ONCE THERE WAS ONLY STAGNATION AND MEANINGLESSNESS.>
<IF YOUR ACTIONS WERE UNCOVERED, ALL WOULD BE RUINED. I WOULD BE RUINED. MY OWN SLAVE A TRAITOR, WAGING WAR AGAINST HIS OWN PEOPLE...>
<AFTER ALL I DID FOR YOU. ALL YOU WERE GIVEN. YOU LACK APPRECIATION SO COMPLETELY, IT EXCEEDS ALL REASON. DO THE FLAWS IN YOUR KIND TRULY RUN SO DEEP?>
<I THOUGHT YOU WERE UNIQUE. THAT WE SHARED AN UNDERSTANDING. BUT YOU ARE NO DIFFERENT. YOU ARE AN INGRATE AND AN EMBARRASSMENT. FORTUNATELY, NOW, THE KNOWLEDGE OF YOUR SHAME IS SOMETHING ONLY I WILL BEAR.>
<I WILL KILL YOU MYSELF. I WILL BURY YOUR TREACHERY AND I WILL HAVE MY HONOR AND MY LEGACY. AND YOU WILL CEASE TO LIVE THIS LIFE YOU NEVER DESERVED IN THE FIRST PLACE.>
<STOP. PLEASE. I-- I WAS WRONG.>

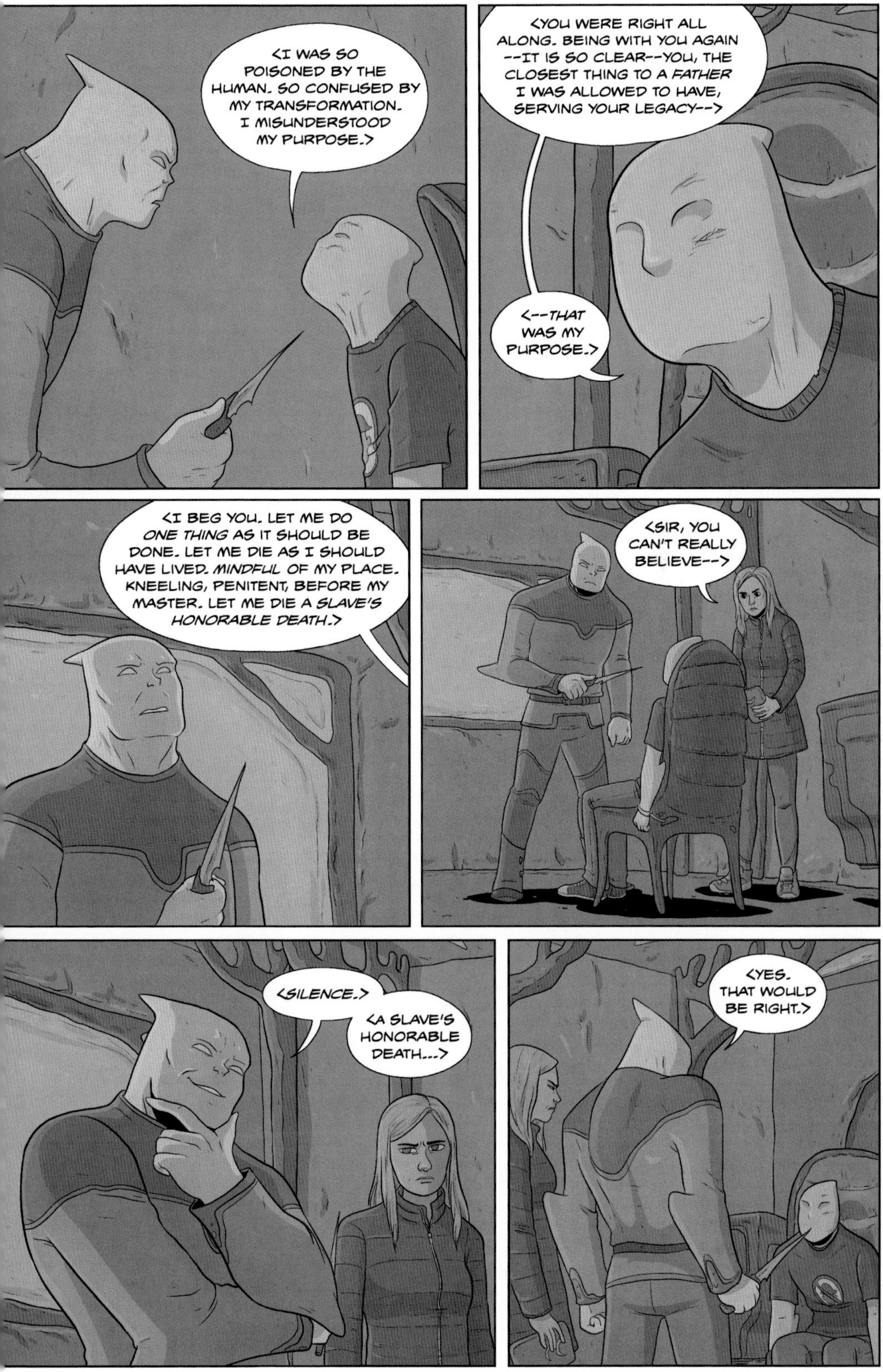
<I WAS SO POISONED BY THE HUMAN. SO CONFUSED BY MY TRANSFORMATION. I MISUNDERSTOOD MY PURPOSE.>
<YOU WERE RIGHT ALL ALONG. BEING WITH YOU AGAIN --IT IS SO CLEAR--YOU, THE CLOSEST THING TO A *FATHER* I WAS ALLOWED TO HAVE, SERVING YOUR LEGACY-->
<--THAT WAS MY PURPOSE.>
<I BEG YOU. LET ME DO *ONE THING* AS IT SHOULD BE DONE. LET ME DIE AS I SHOULD HAVE LIVED. *MINDFUL* OF MY PLACE. KNEELING, PENITENT, BEFORE MY MASTER. LET ME DIE A *SLAVE'S HONORABLE DEATH.*>
<SIR, YOU CAN'T REALLY BELIEVE-->
<*SILENCE.*>
<A SLAVE'S HONORABLE DEATH...>
<YES. THAT WOULD BE RIGHT.>

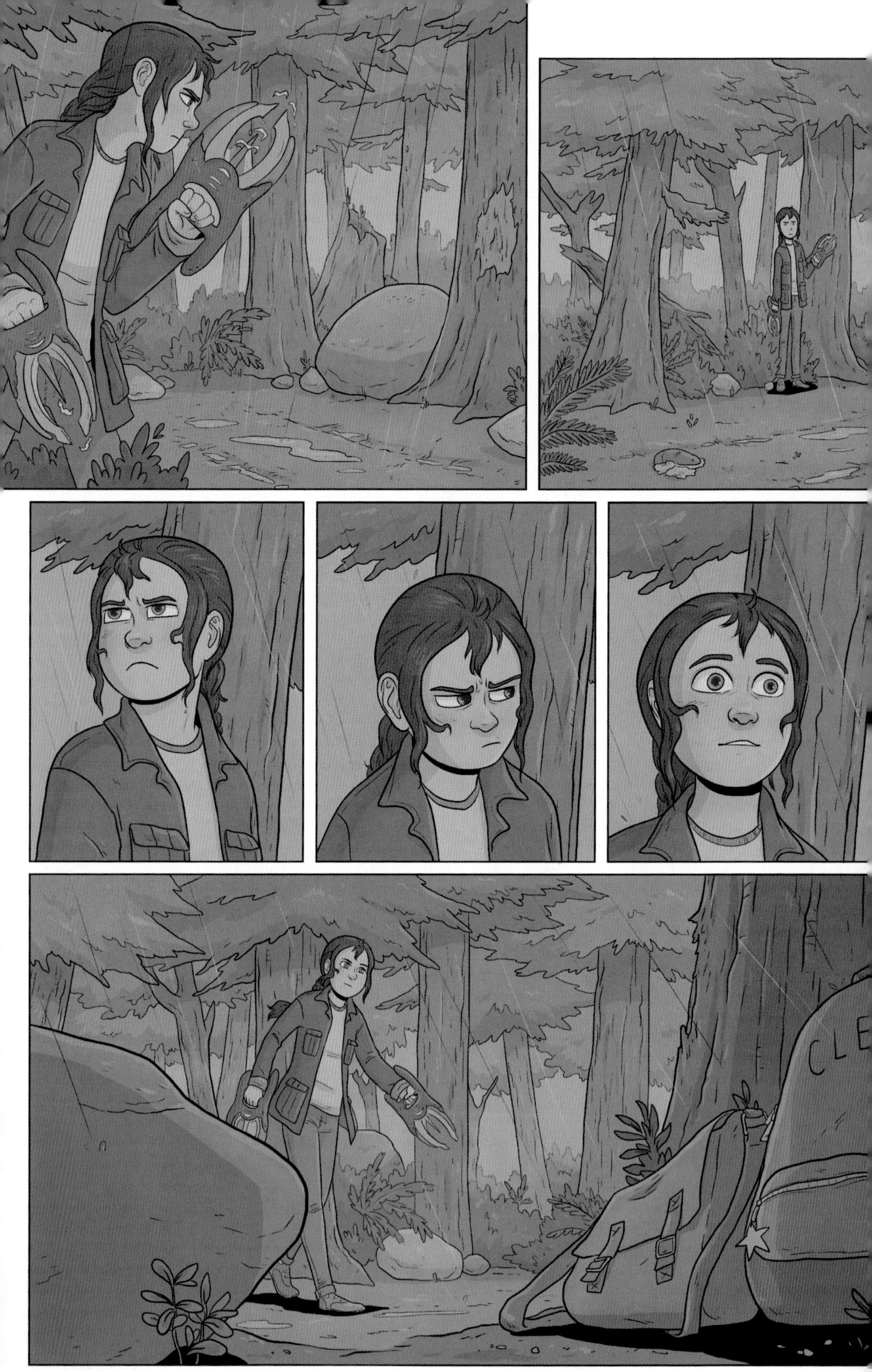
CLE

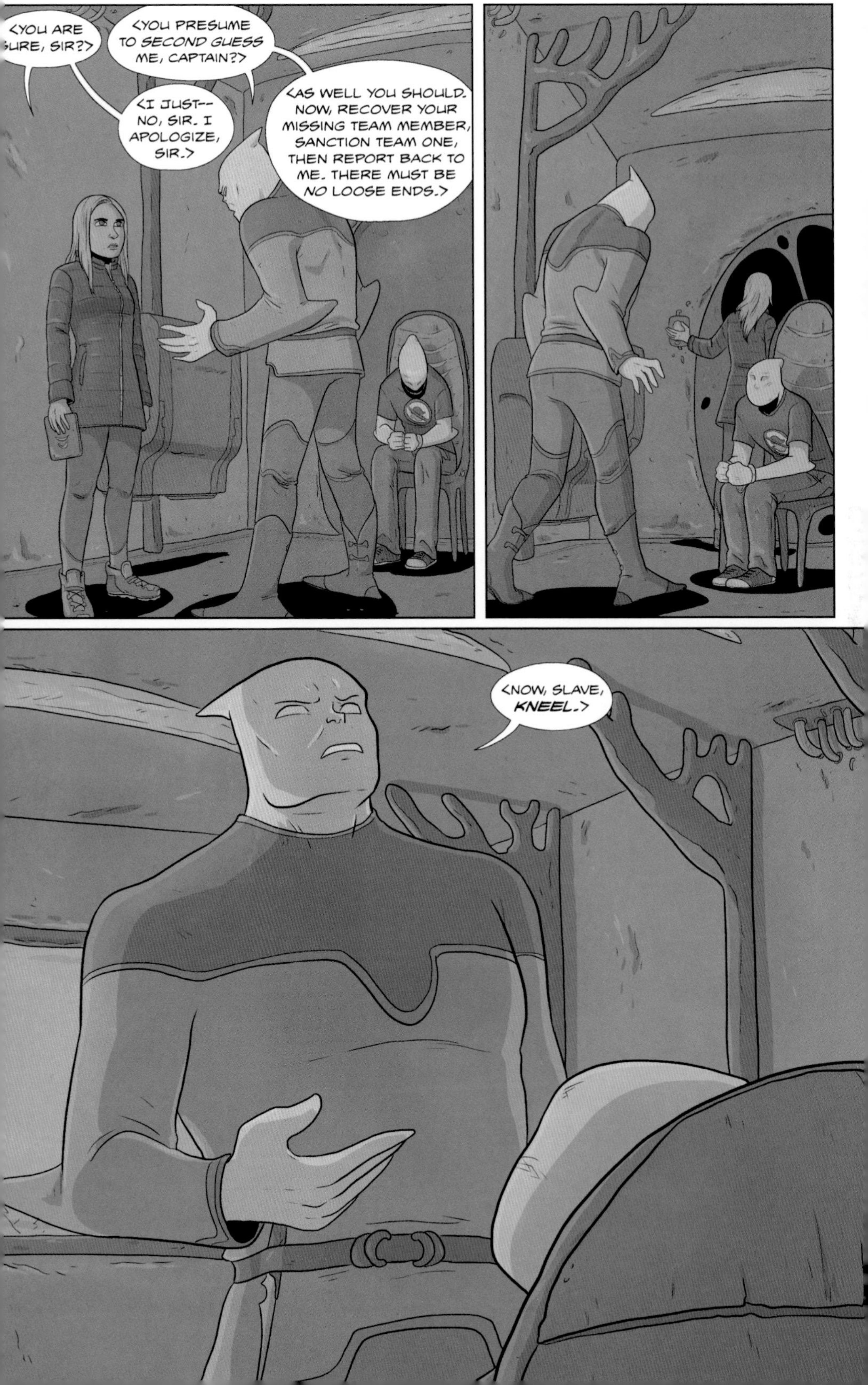

<YOU ARE SURE, SIR?>
<YOU PRESUME TO *SECOND GUESS* ME, CAPTAIN?>
<I JUST-- NO, SIR. I APOLOGIZE, SIR.>
<AS WELL YOU SHOULD. NOW, RECOVER YOUR MISSING TEAM MEMBER, SANCTION TEAM ONE, THEN REPORT BACK TO ME. THERE MUST BE *NO* LOOSE ENDS.>
<NOW, SLAVE, **KNEEL.**>

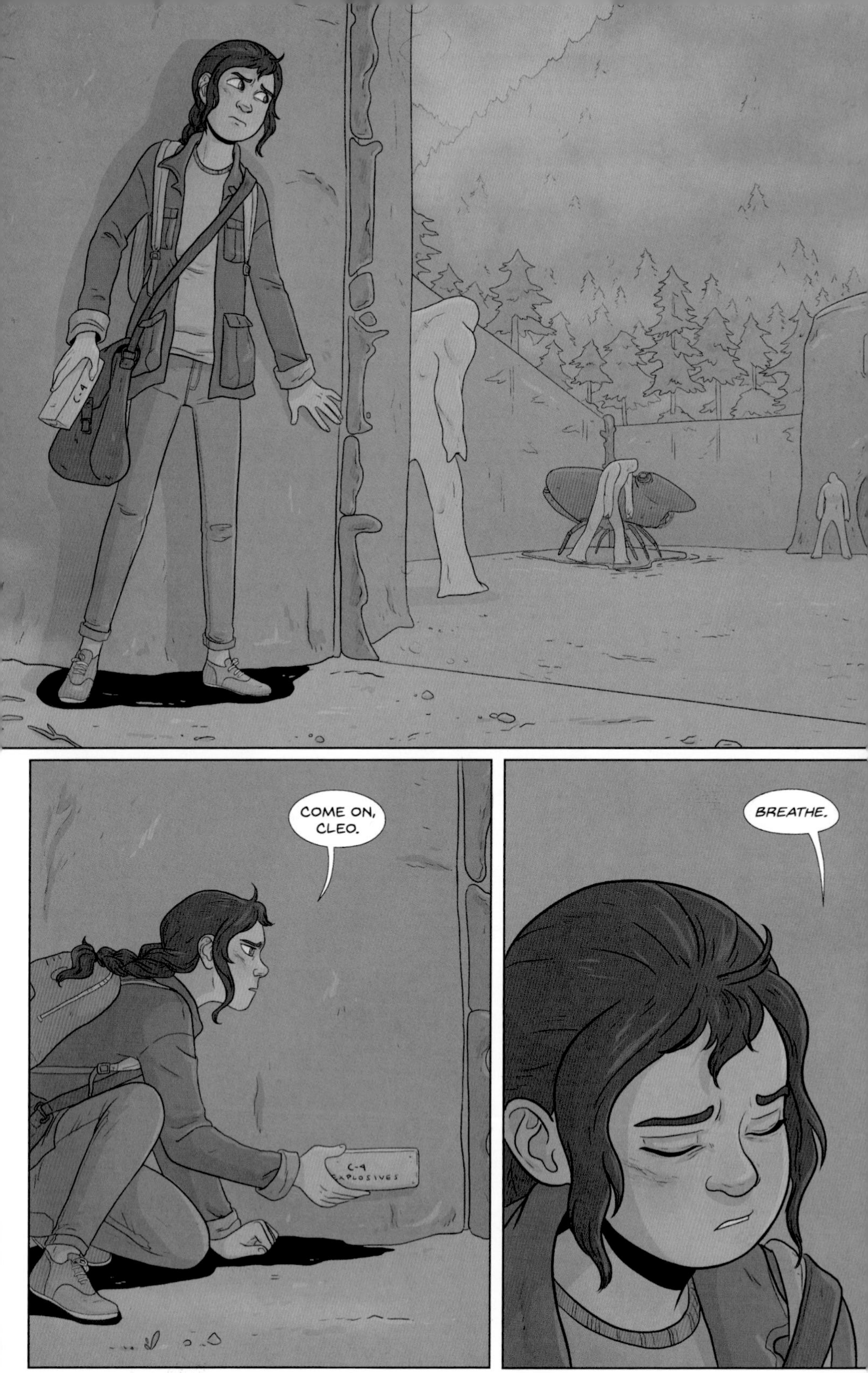
C-4
COME ON, CLEO.
C-4 EXPLOSIVES
BREATHE.

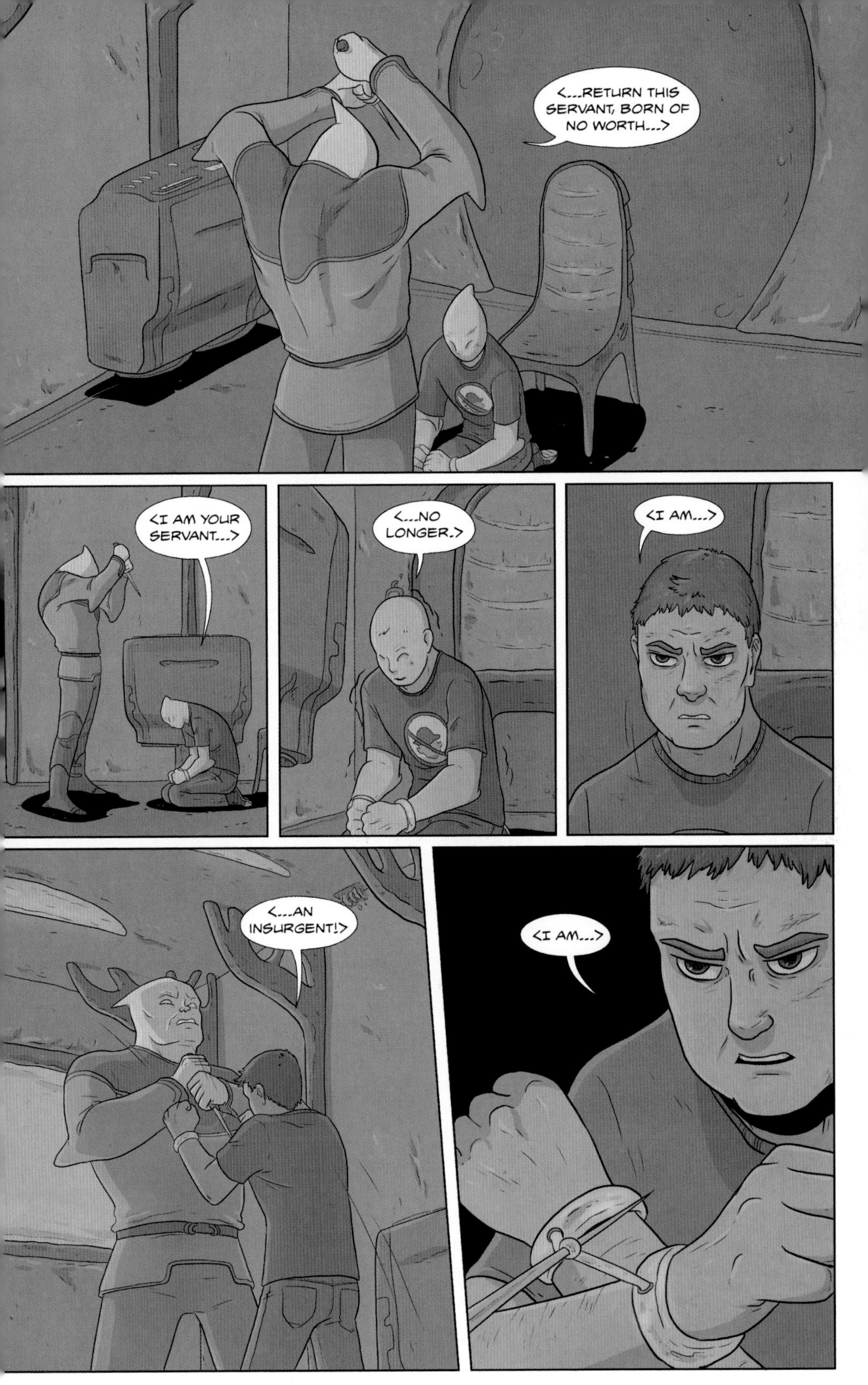
<...RETURN THIS SERVANT, BORN OF NO WORTH...>
<I AM YOUR SERVANT...>
<...NO LONGER.>
<I AM...>
<...AN INSURGENT!>
<I AM...>

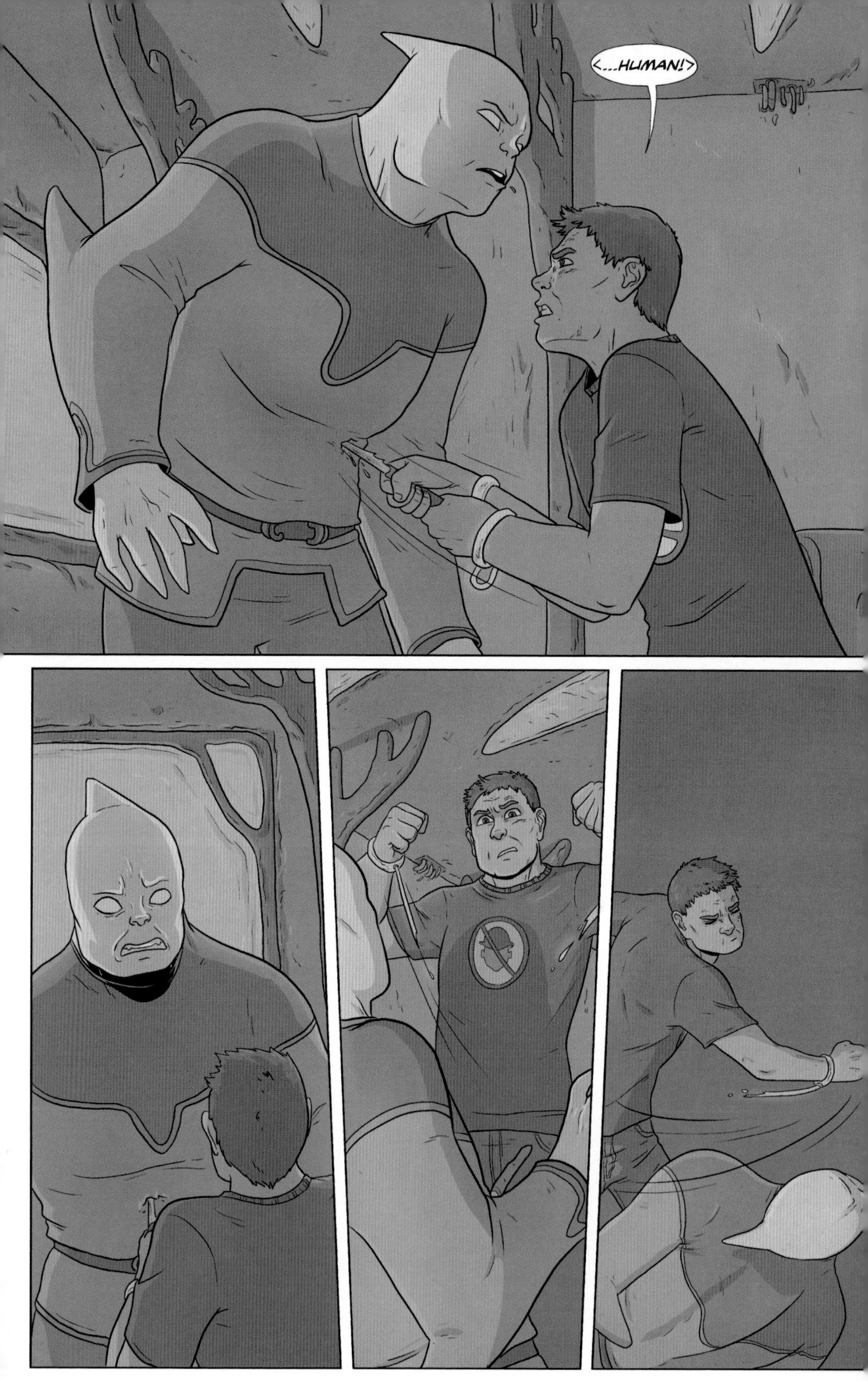
<...HUMAN!>

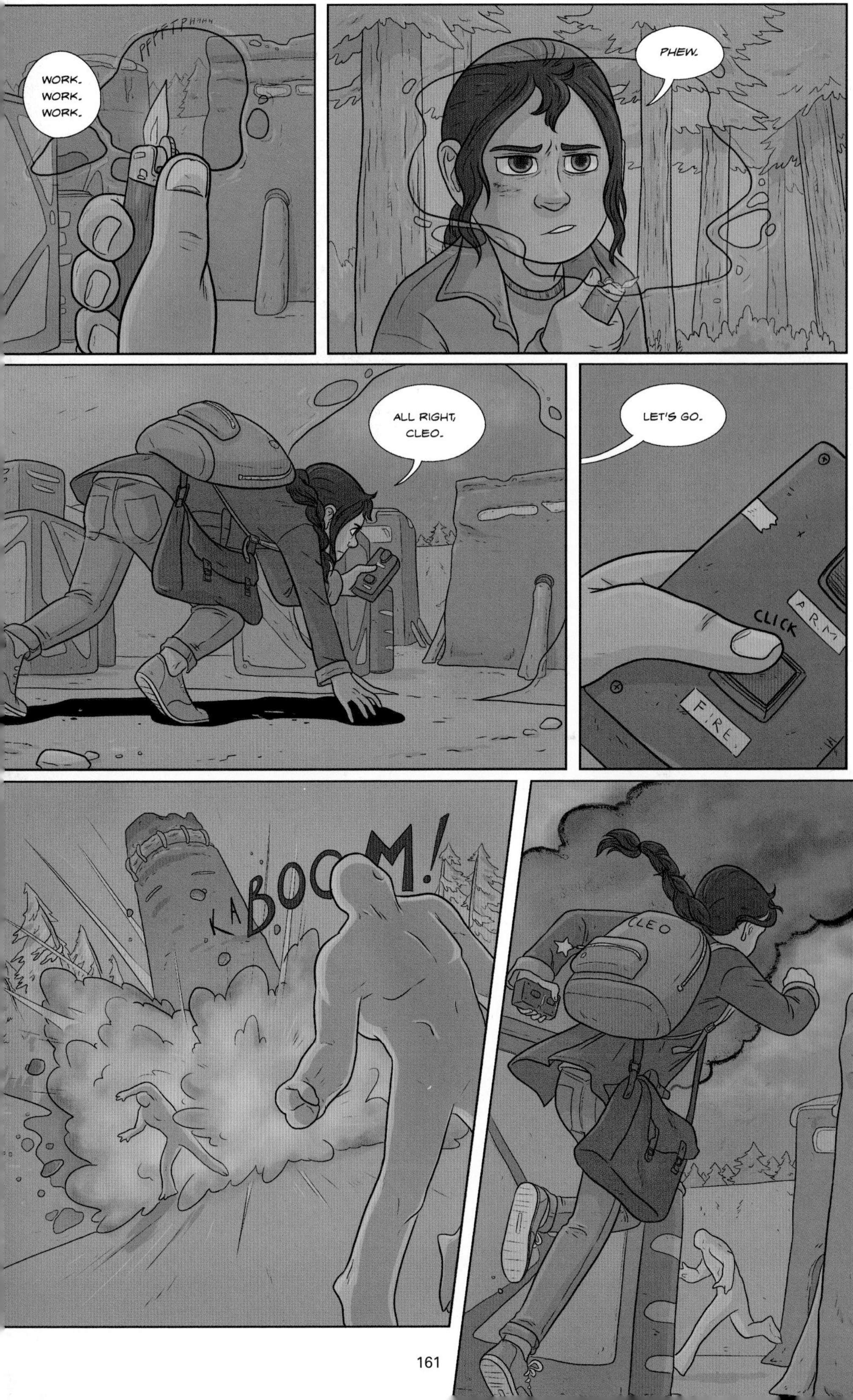
PFFFTPHHHH
WORK. WORK. WORK.
PHEW.
ALL RIGHT, CLEO.
LET'S GO.
A.R.M.
CLICK
FIRE.
KABOOM!
CLEO

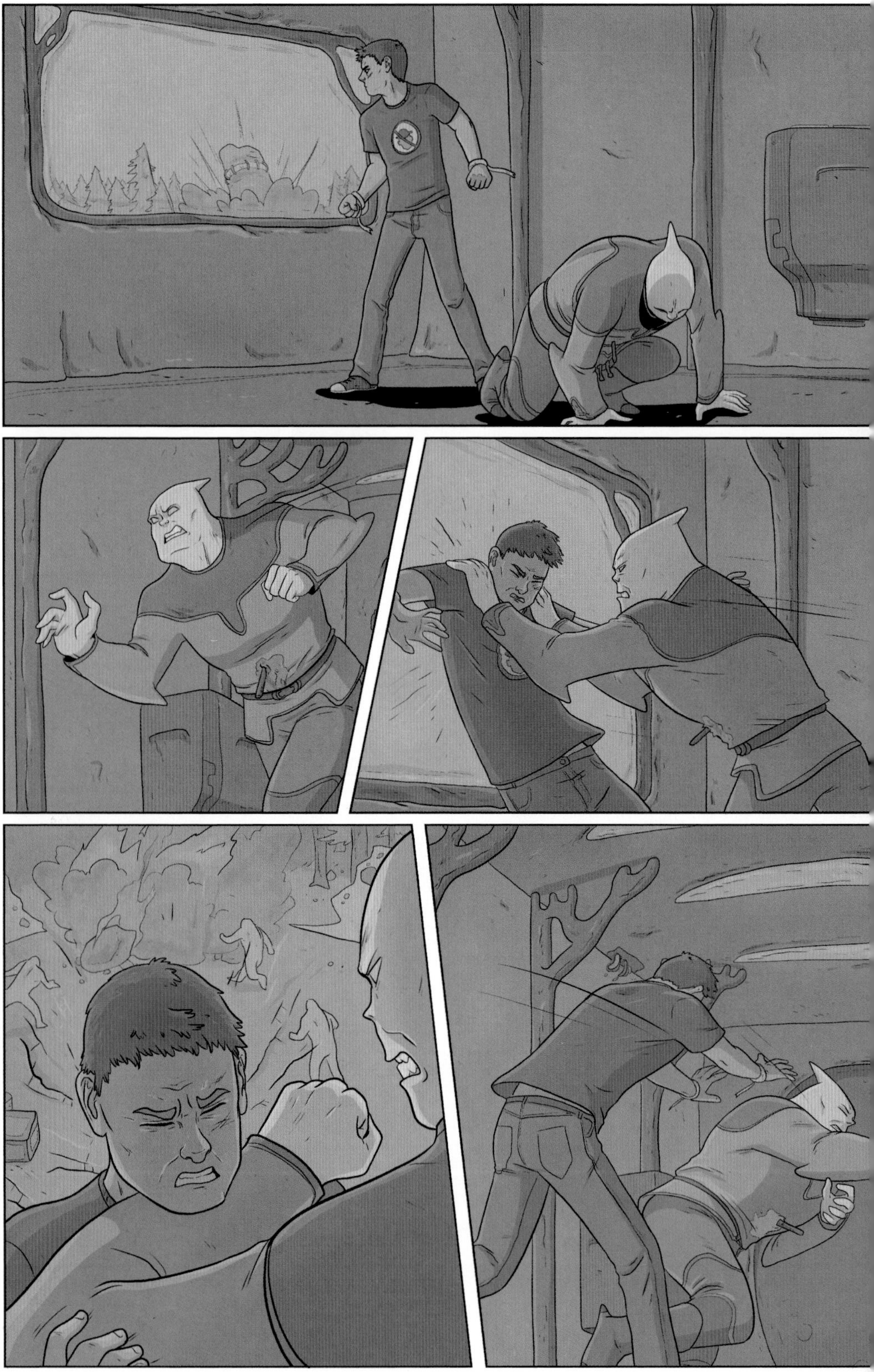

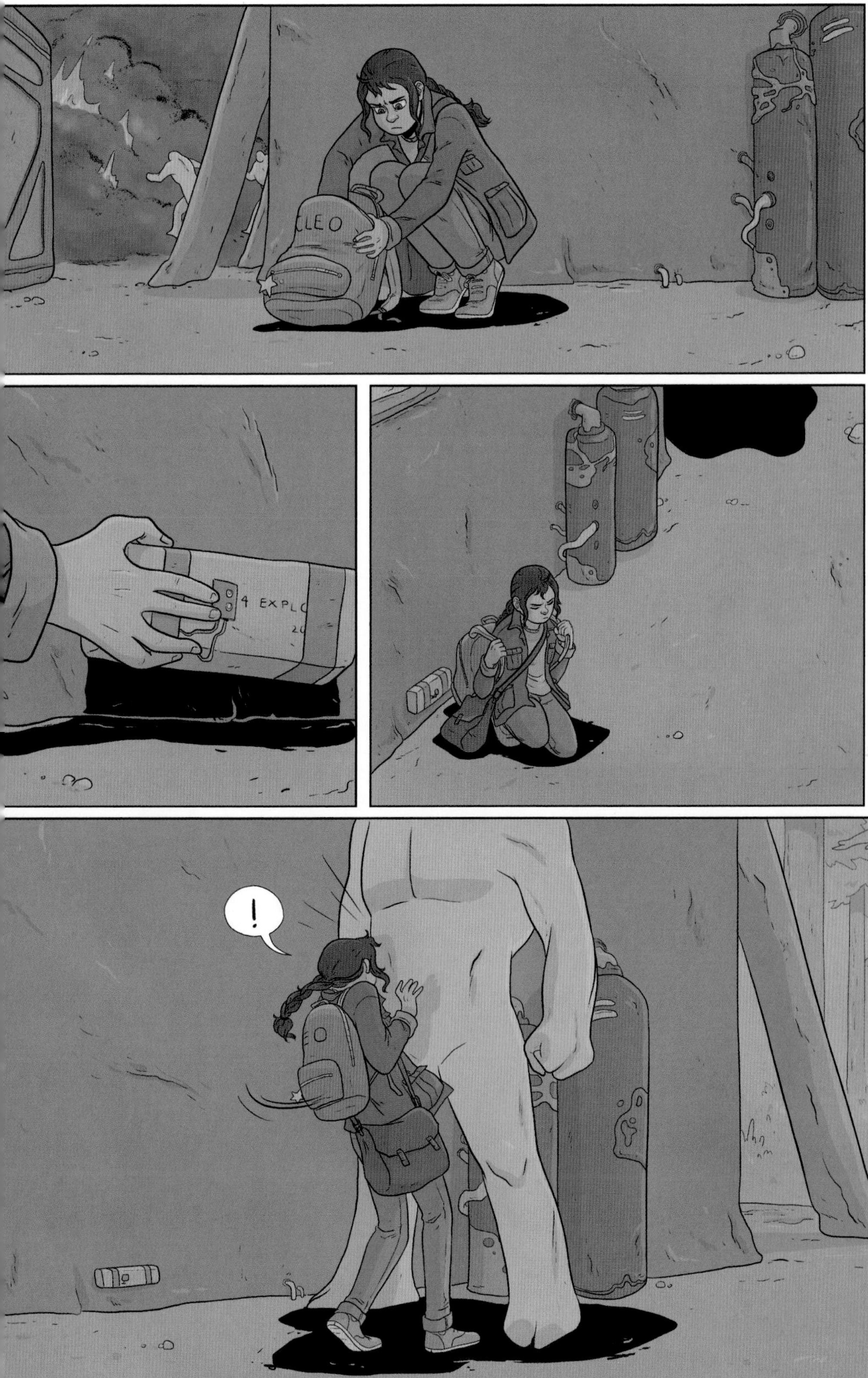
CLEO
4 EXPLO
20
!

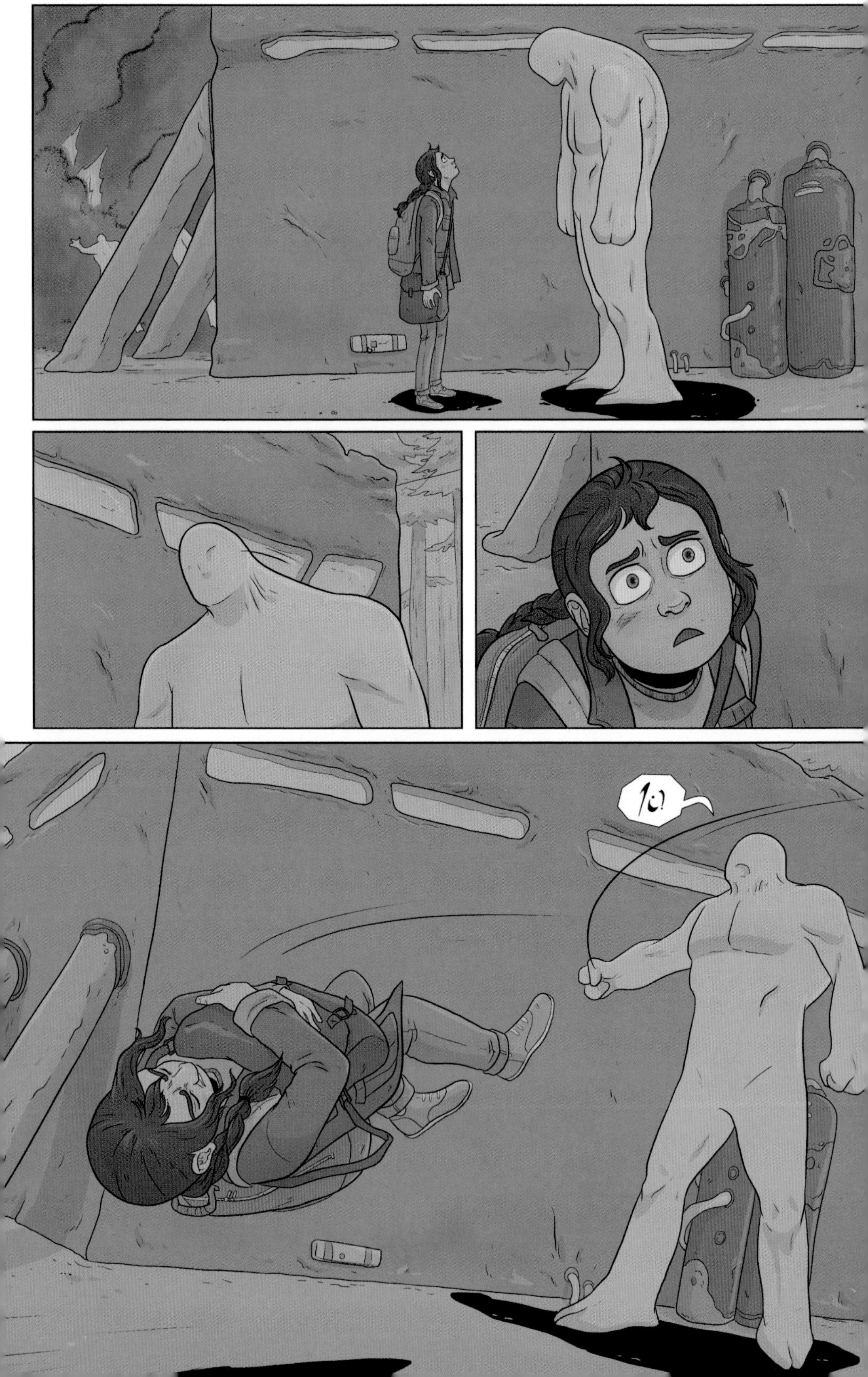

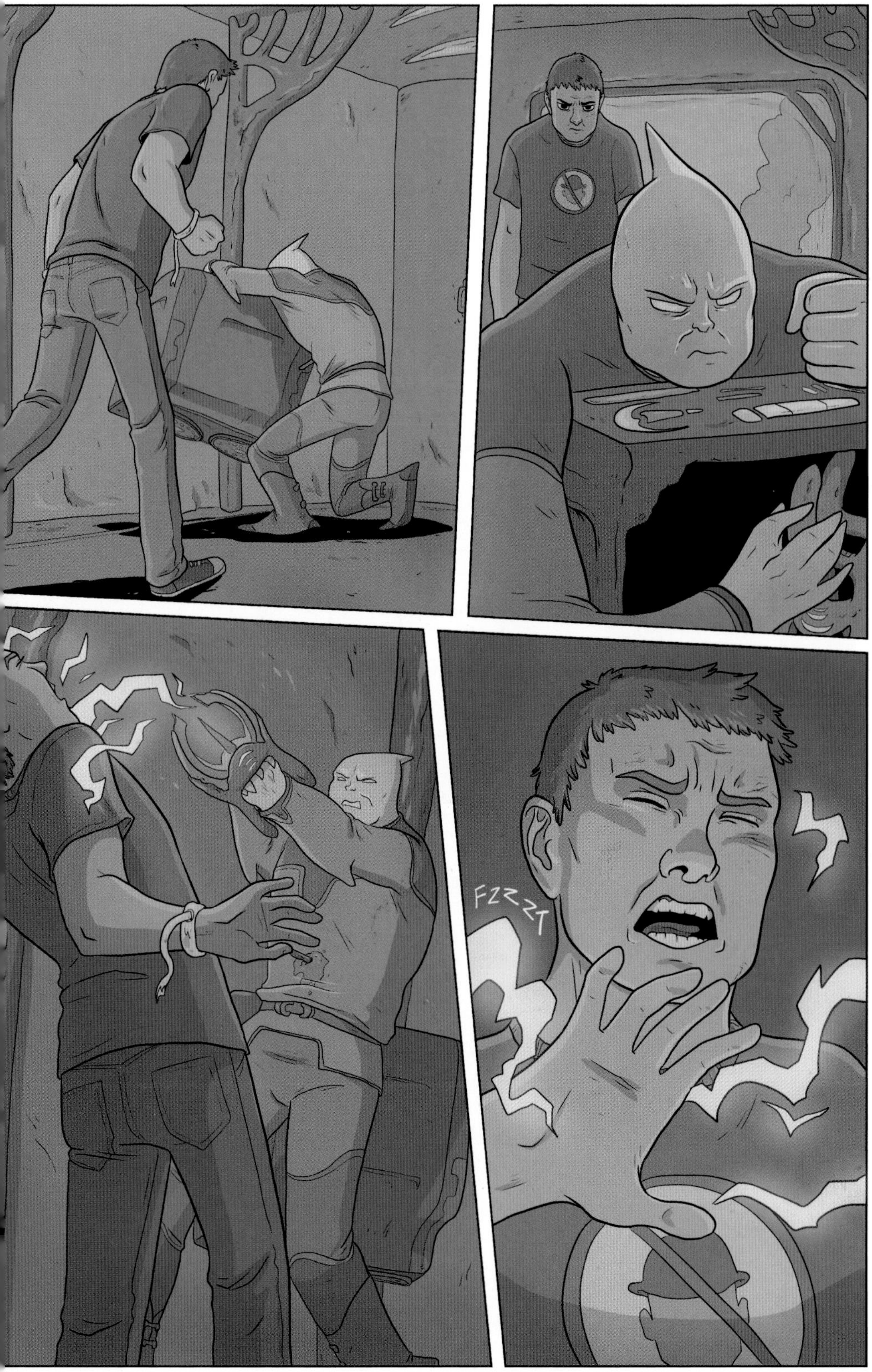
FZZZT

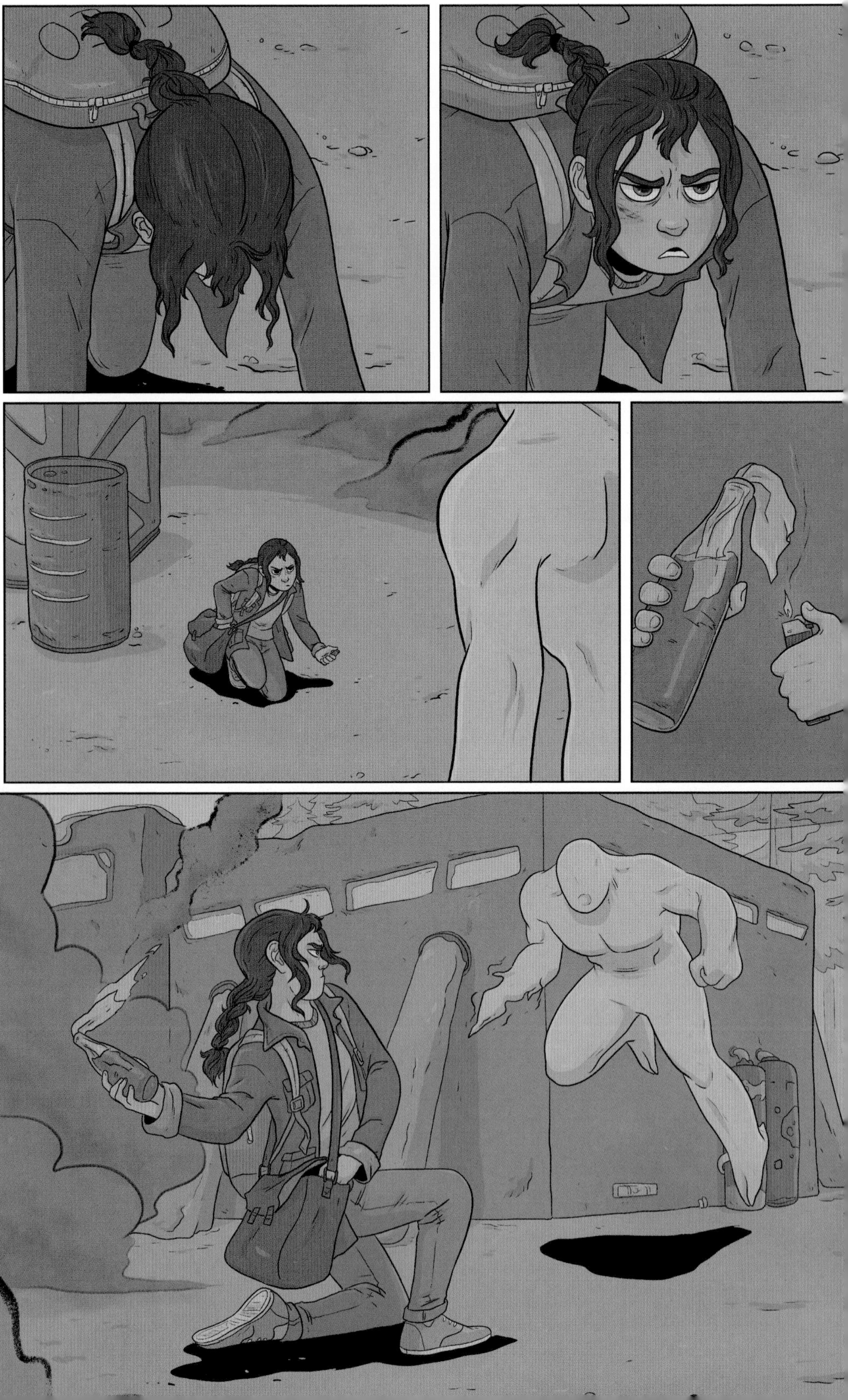

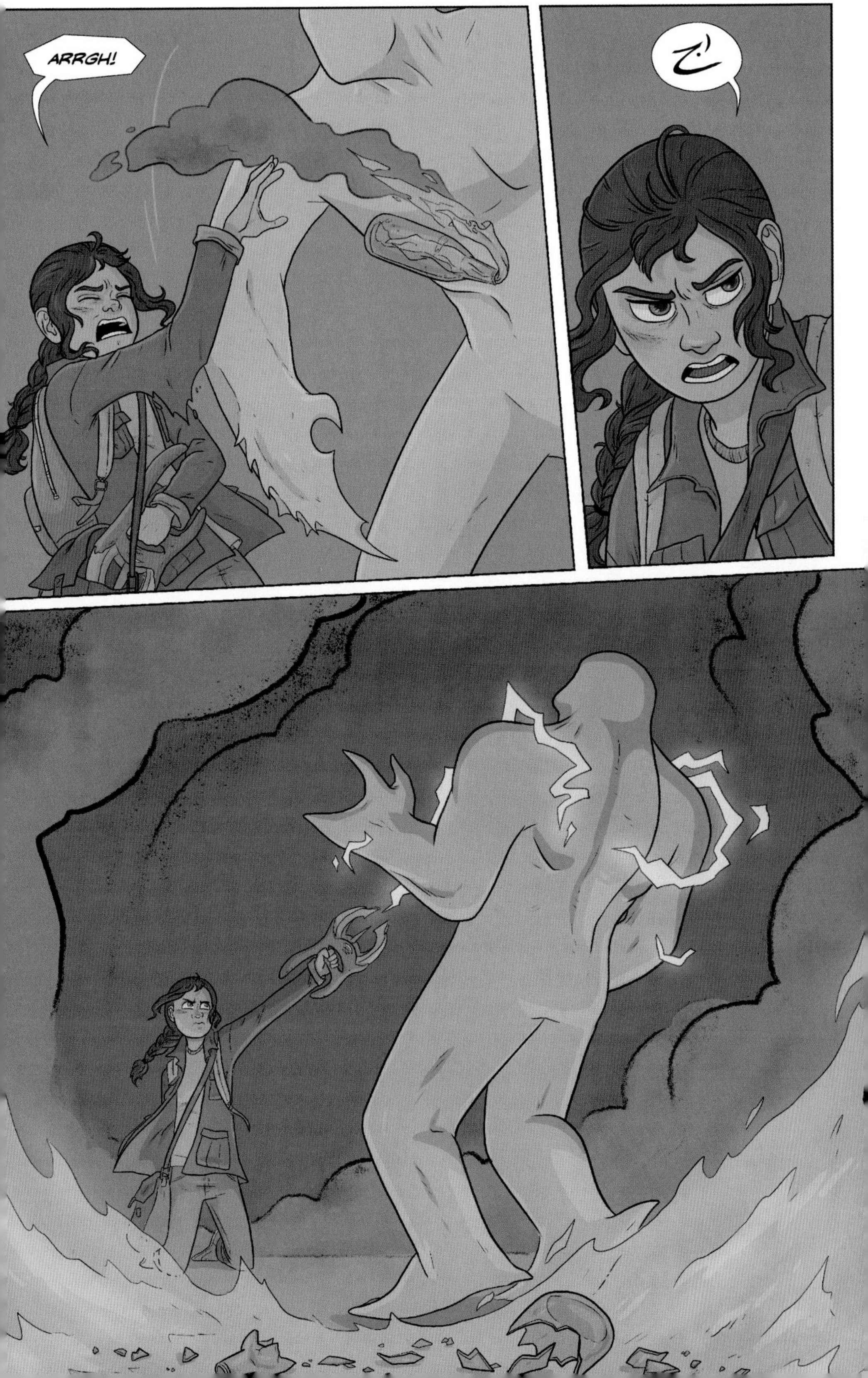
ARRGH!

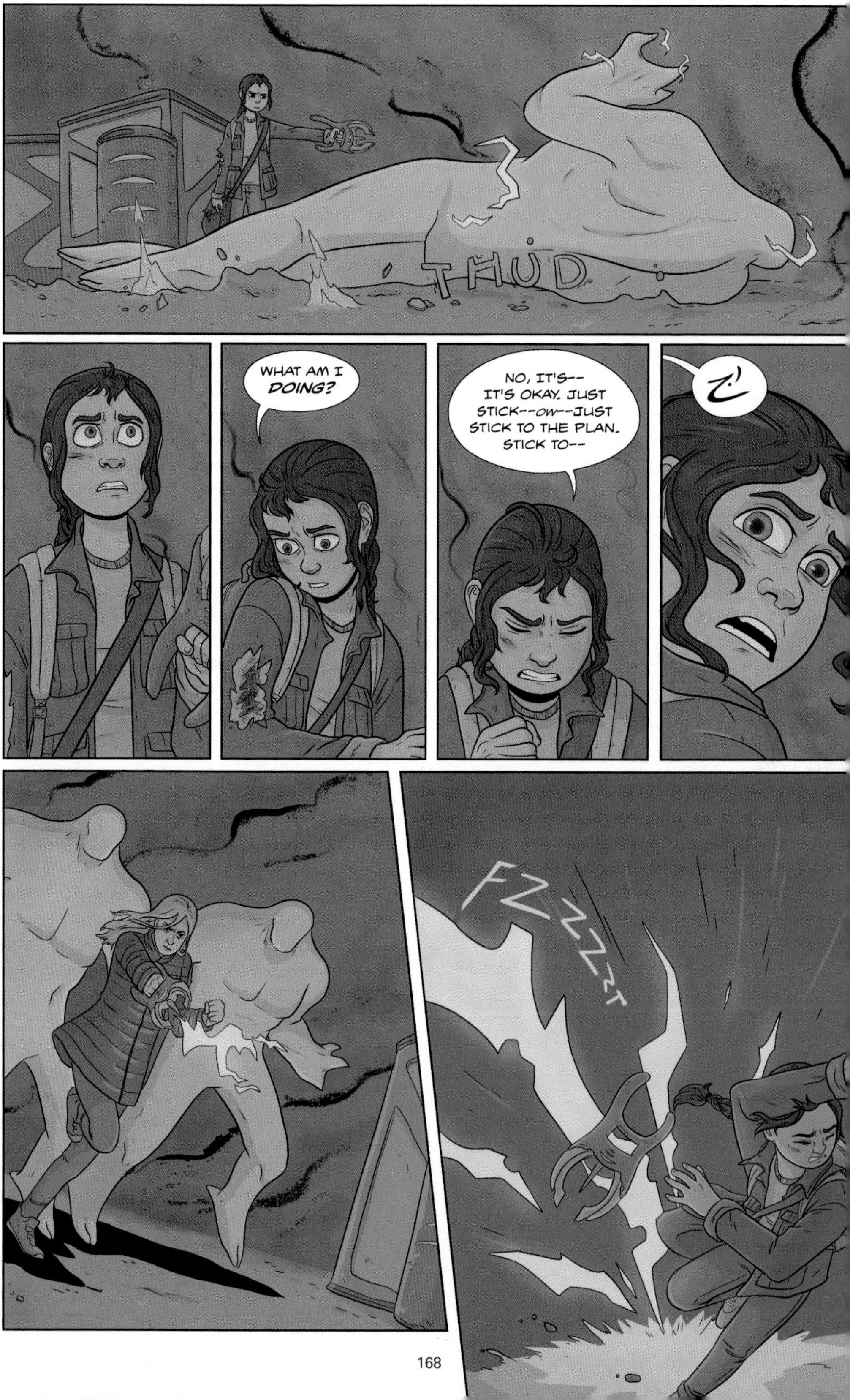
THUD
WHAT AM I DOING?
NO, IT'S-- IT'S OKAY. JUST STICK--OW--JUST STICK TO THE PLAN. STICK TO--
FZZZZT

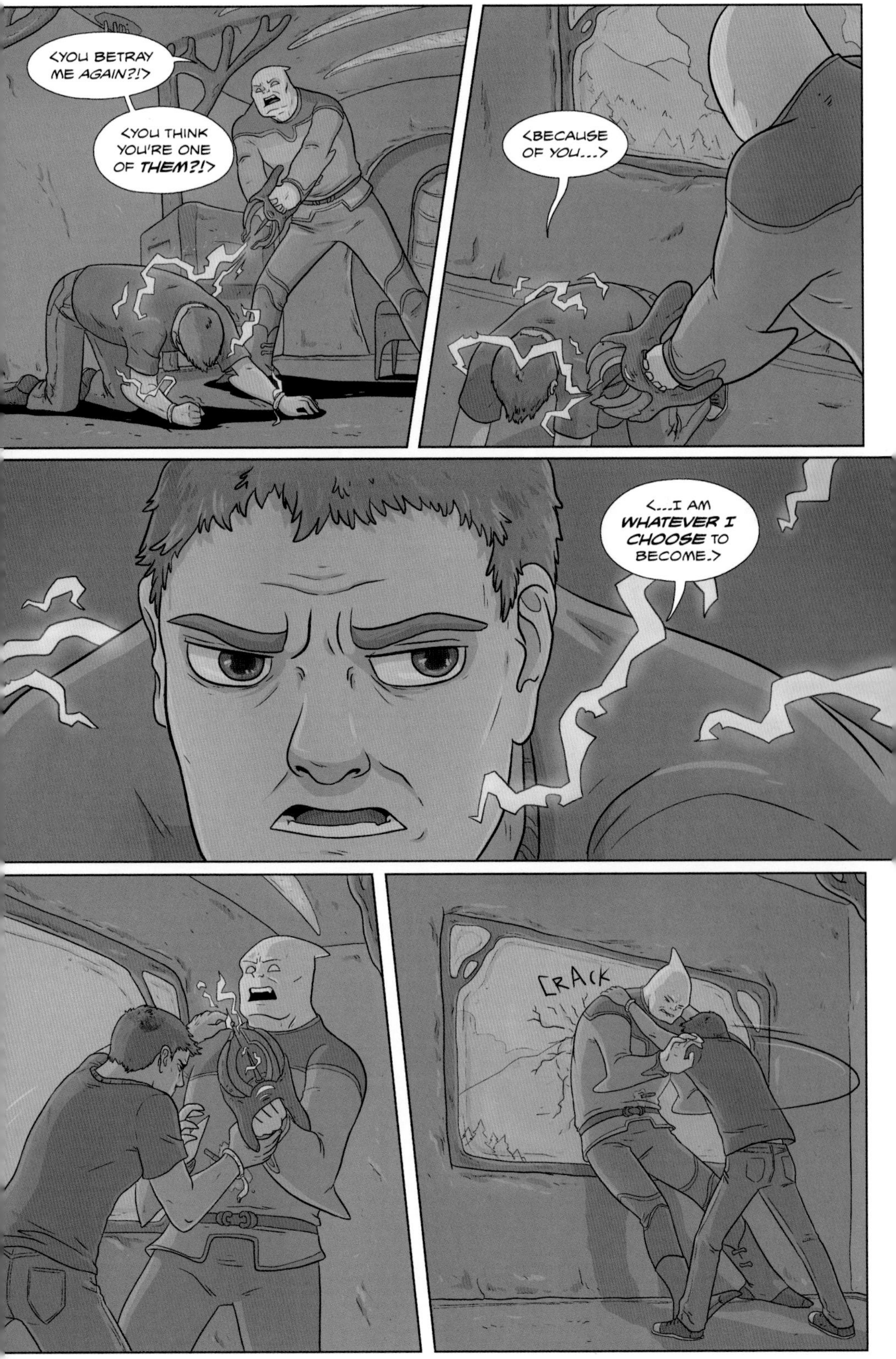

<YOU BETRAY ME AGAIN?!>
<YOU THINK YOU'RE ONE OF THEM?!>
<BECAUSE OF YOU...>
<...I AM WHATEVER I CHOOSE TO BECOME.>
CRACK

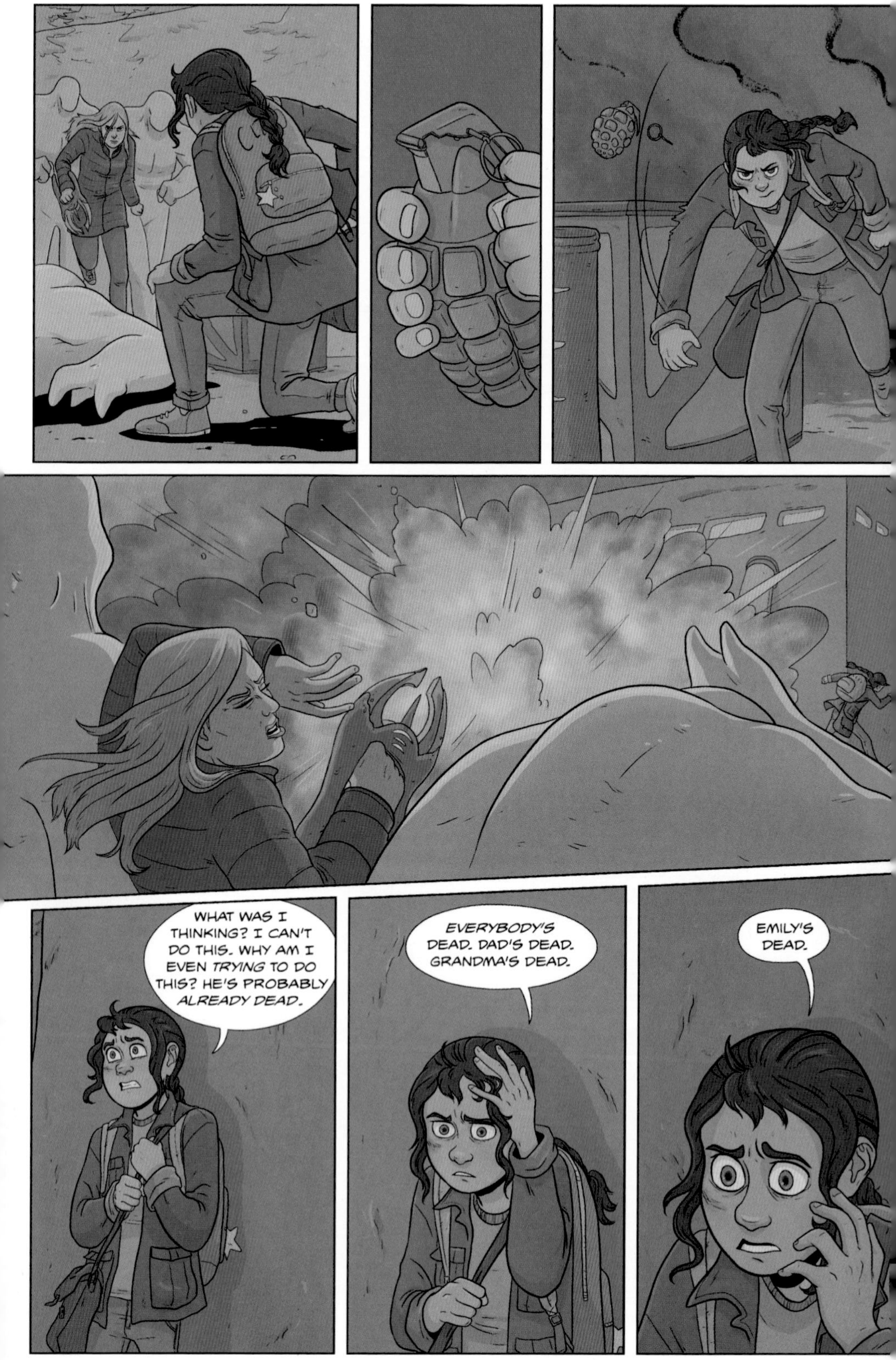
WHAT WAS I THINKING? I CAN'T DO THIS. WHY AM I EVEN *TRYING* TO DO THIS? HE'S PROBABLY *ALREADY DEAD*.
EVERYBODY'S DEAD. DAD'S DEAD. GRANDMA'S DEAD.
EMILY'S DEAD.

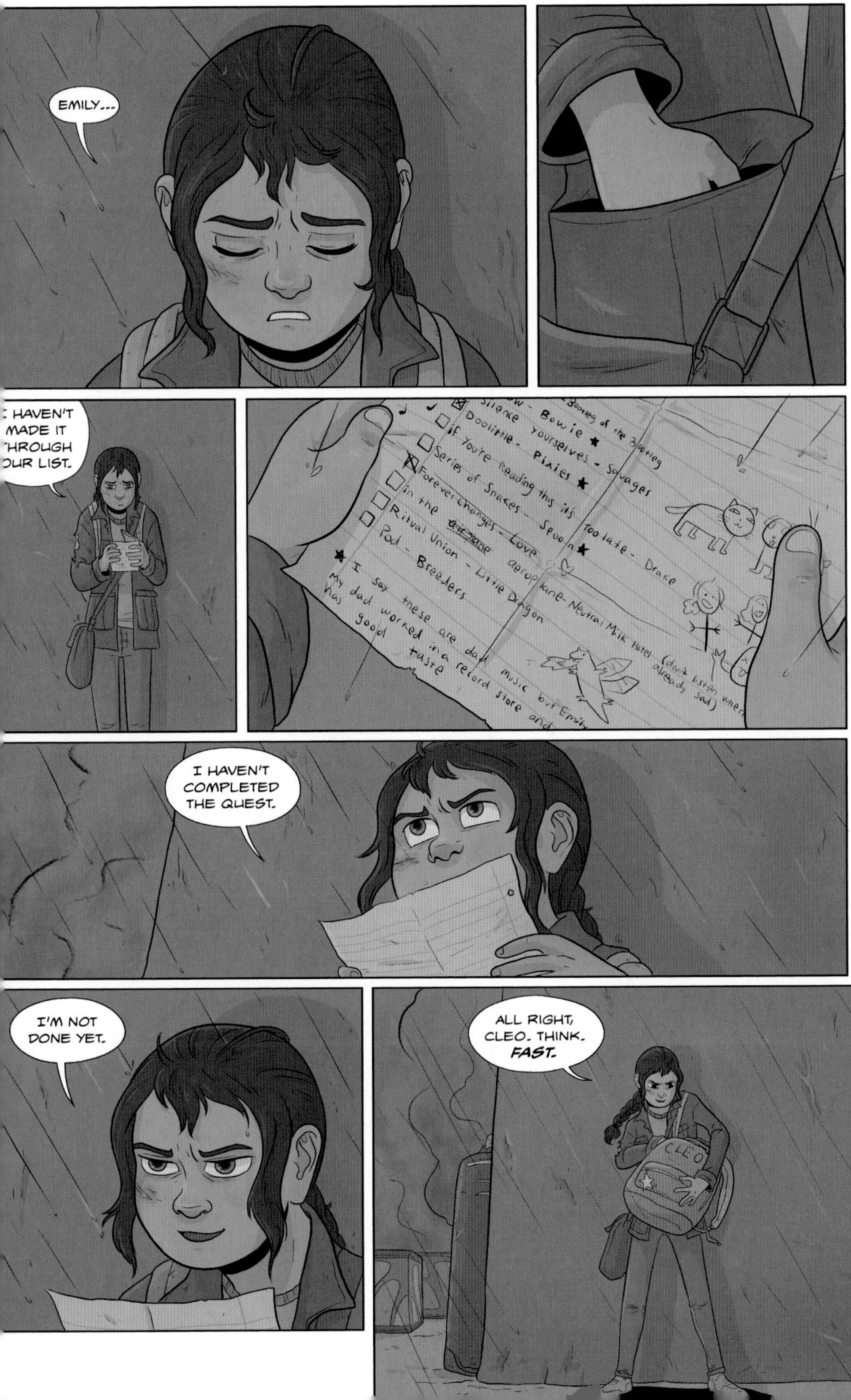
EMILY...
HAVEN'T MADE IT THROUGH OUR LIST.
Silence Yourselves - Savages
Bowie
Bootleg of the Bootleg
Doolittle - Pixies
If You're Reading this it's Too late - Drake
Series of Snakes - Spoon
Forever changes - Love
in the aeroplane - Neutral Milk Hotel (don't listen when already sad)
Ritual Union - Little Dragon
Pod - Breeders
I say these are dad music but Emily
My dad worked in a record store and has good taste
I HAVEN'T COMPLETED THE QUEST.
I'M NOT DONE YET.
ALL RIGHT, CLEO. THINK. FAST.
CLEO

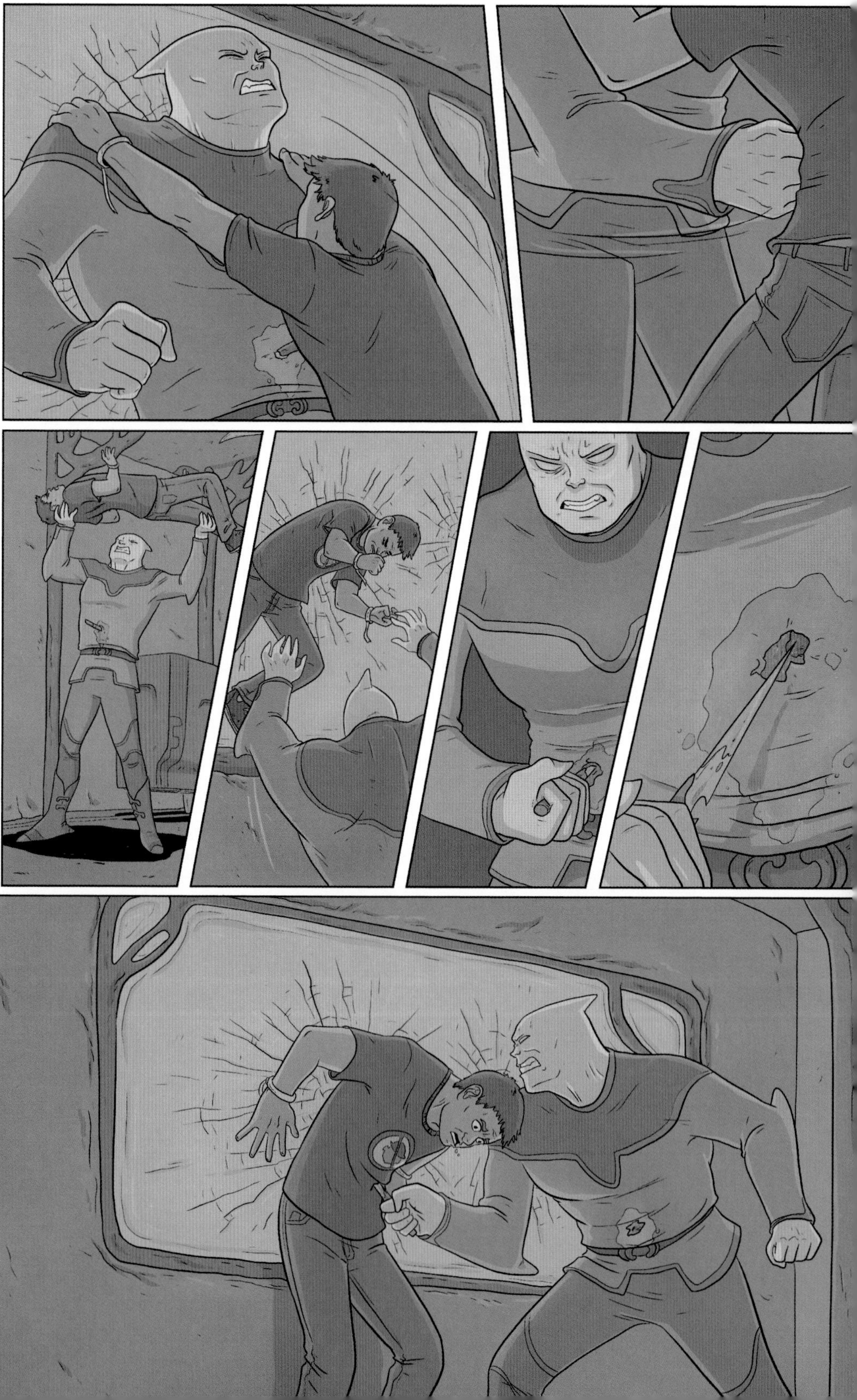

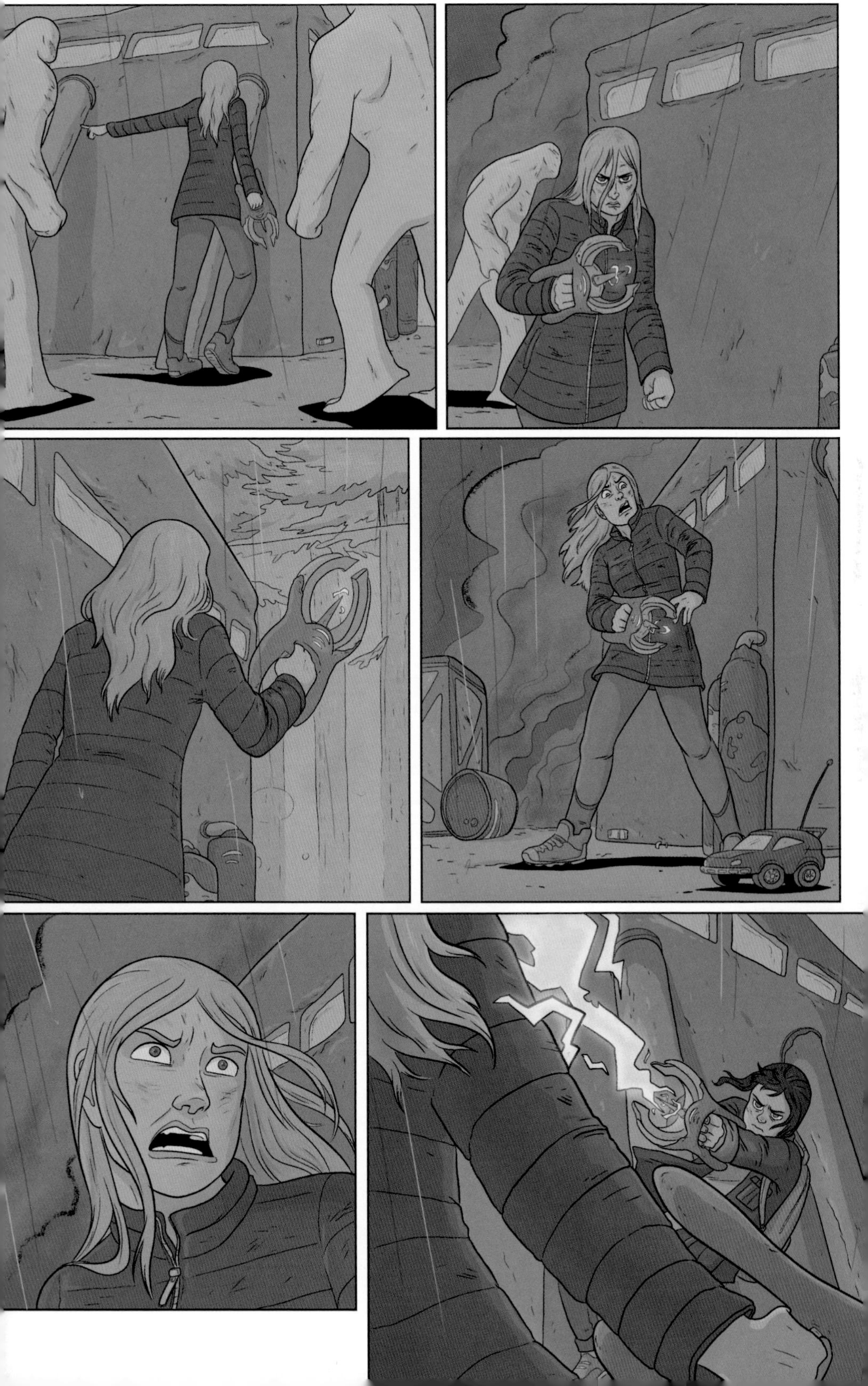

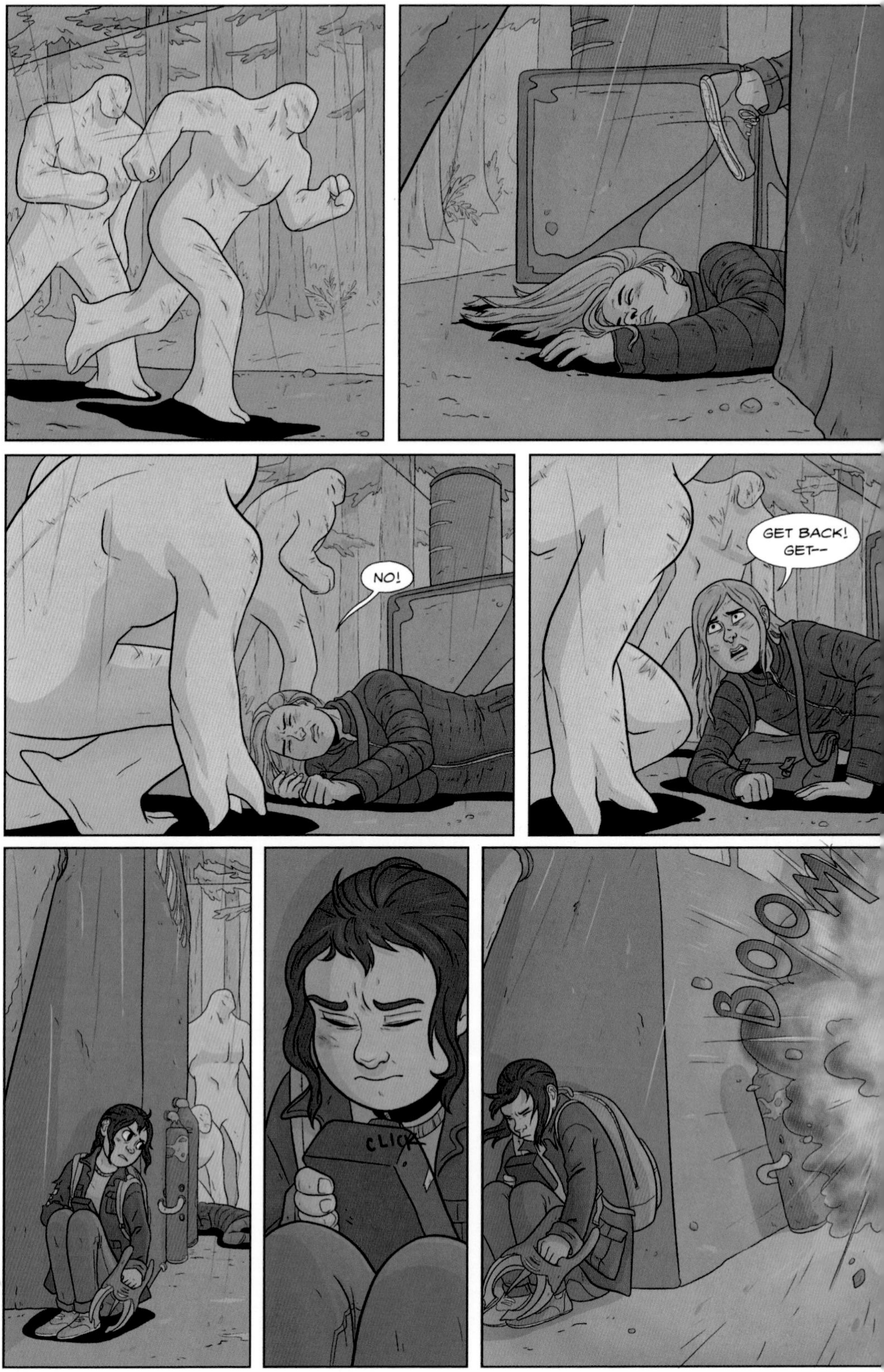
NO!
GET BACK! GET--
CLICK
BOOM

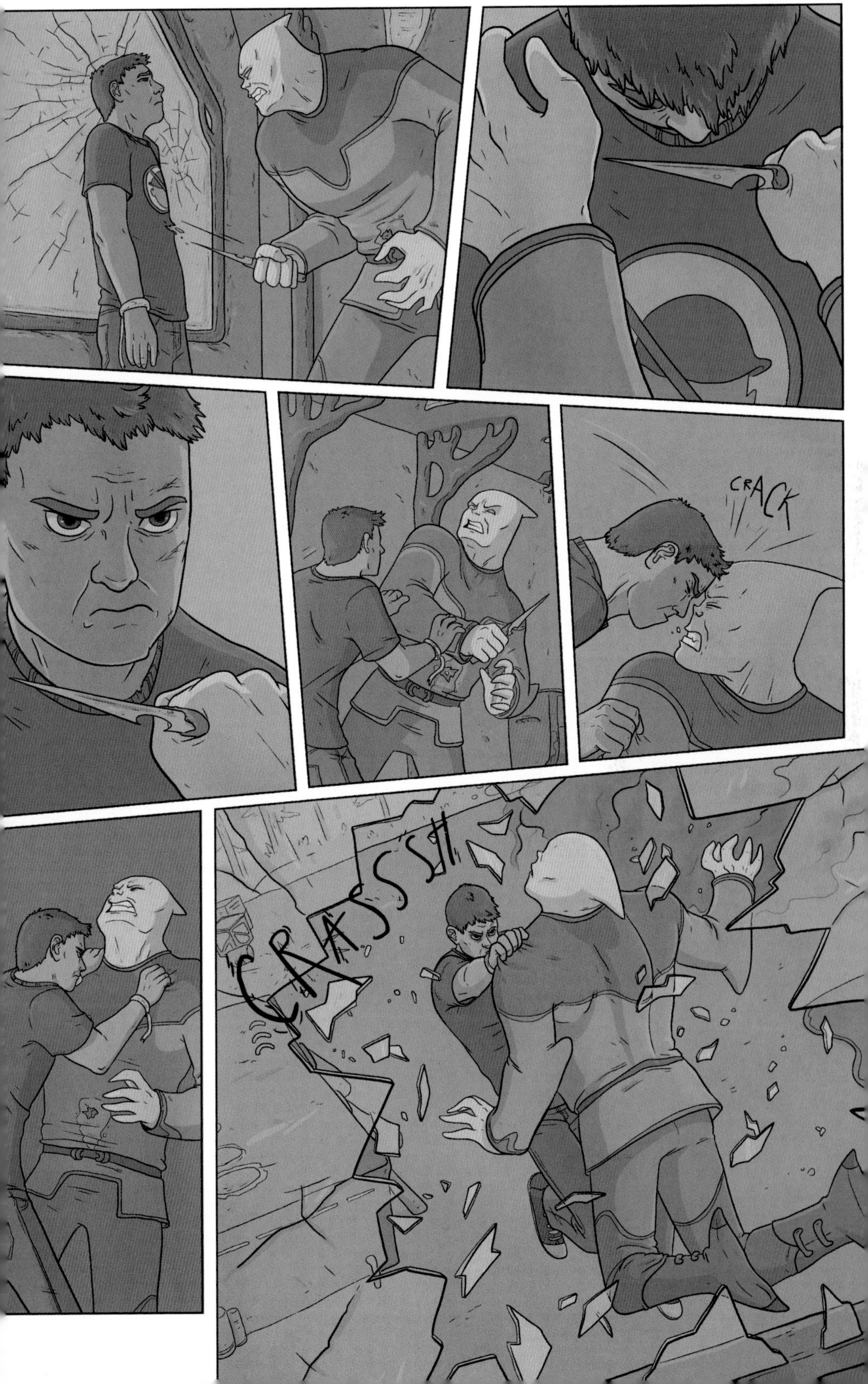
CRACK
CRASSH

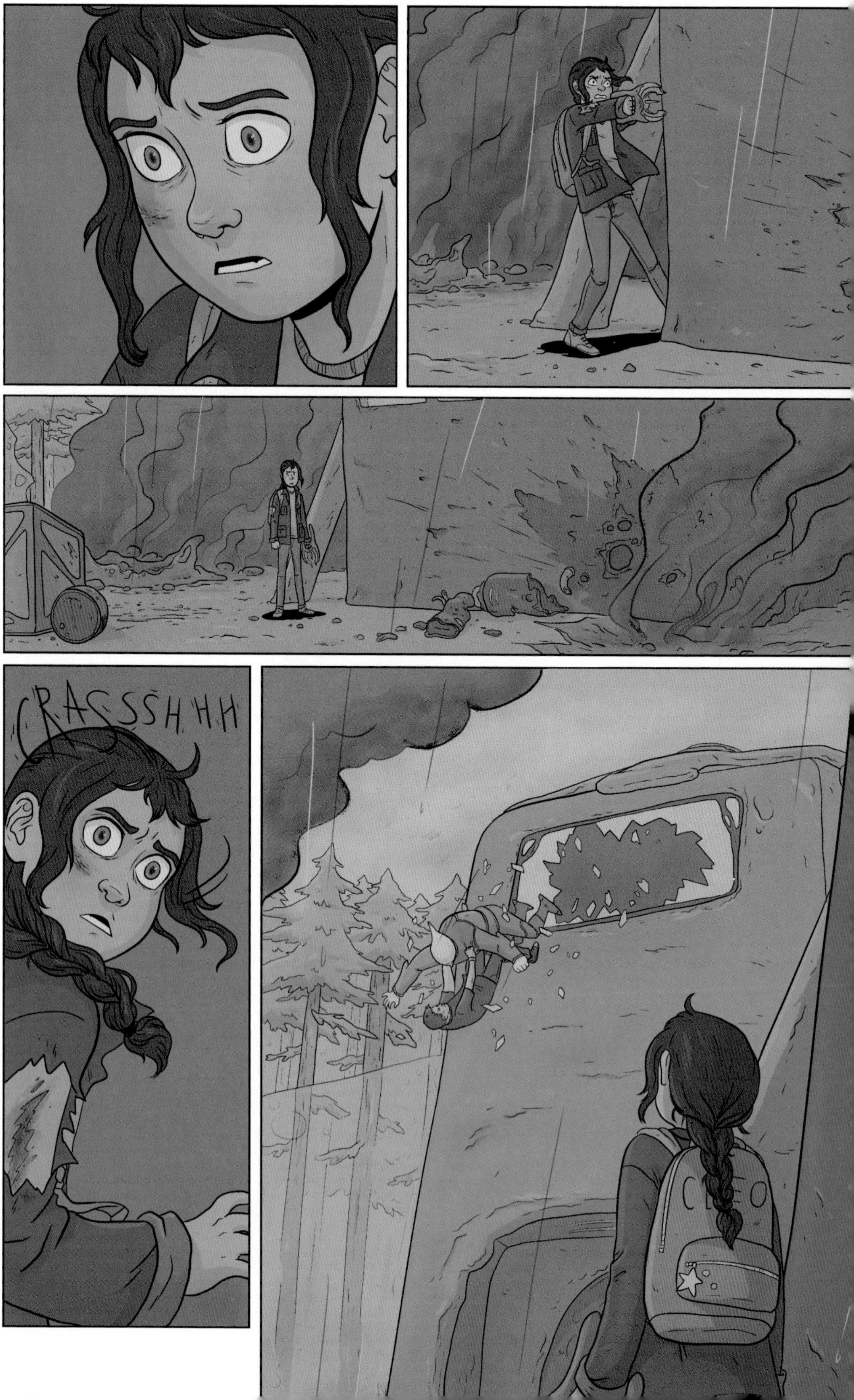
CRASSSHHH
CLEO

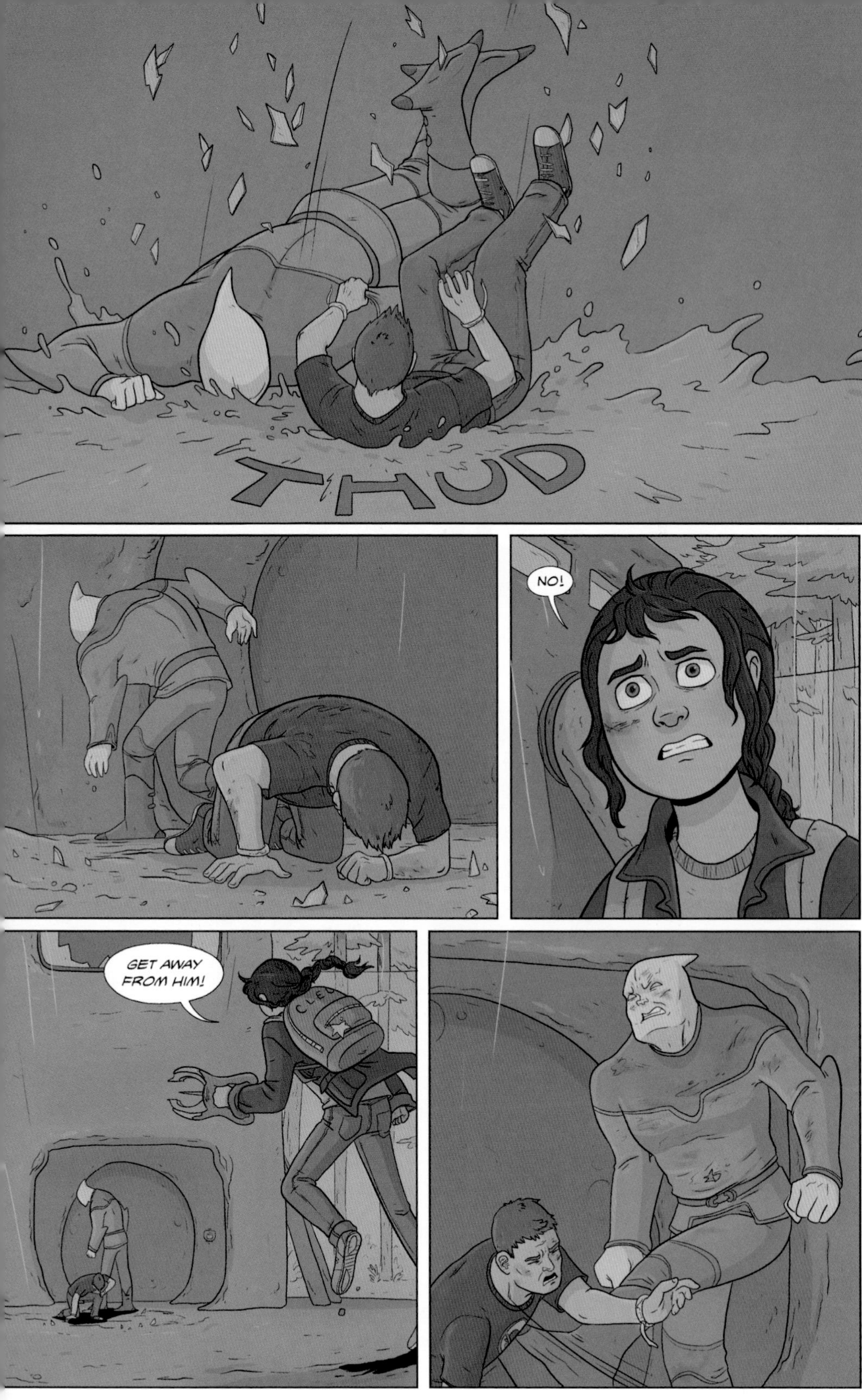
THUD
NO!
GET AWAY FROM HIM!

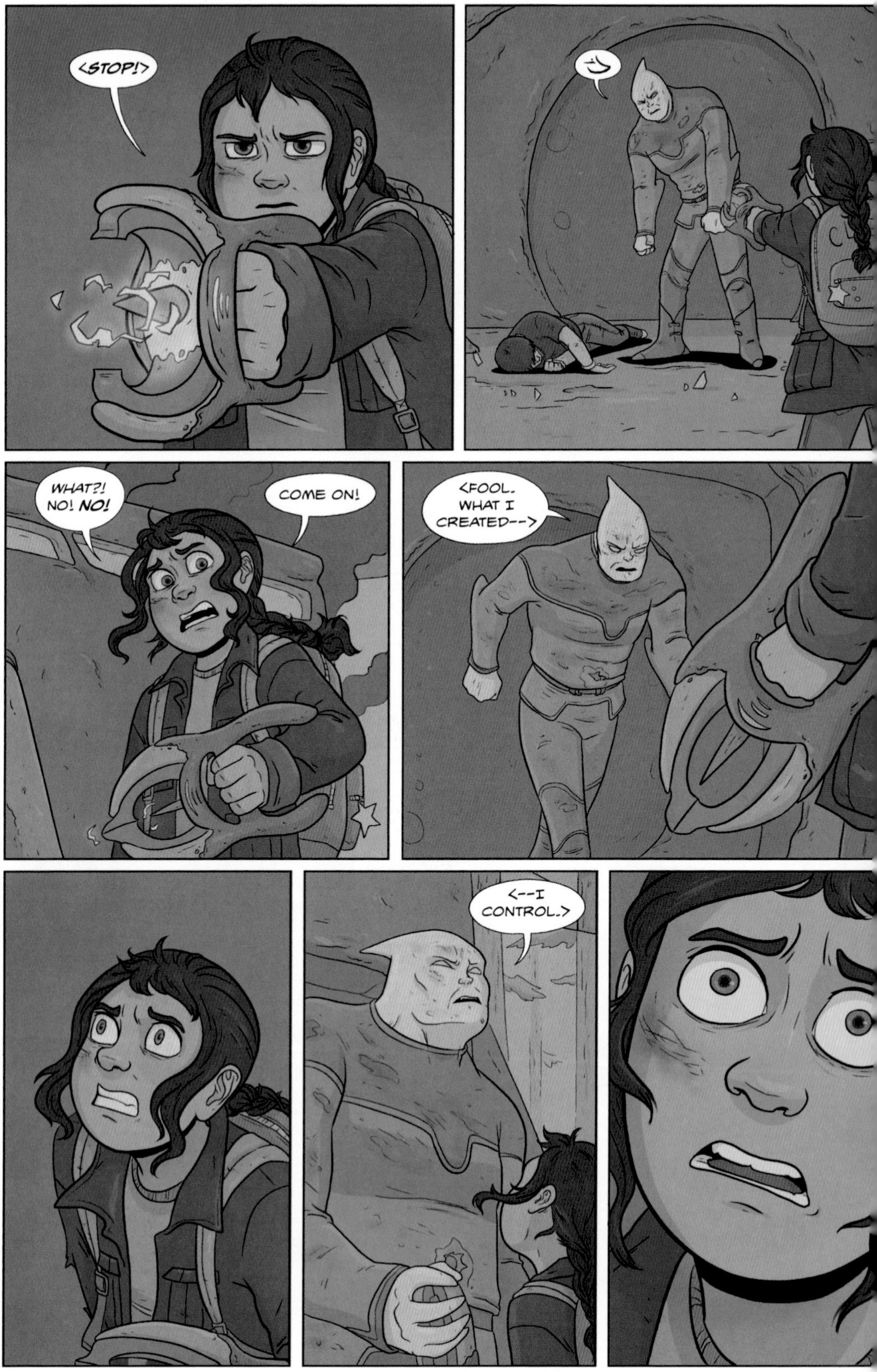
<STOP!>
WHAT?! NO! NO!
COME ON!
<FOOL. WHAT I CREATED-->
<--I CONTROL.>

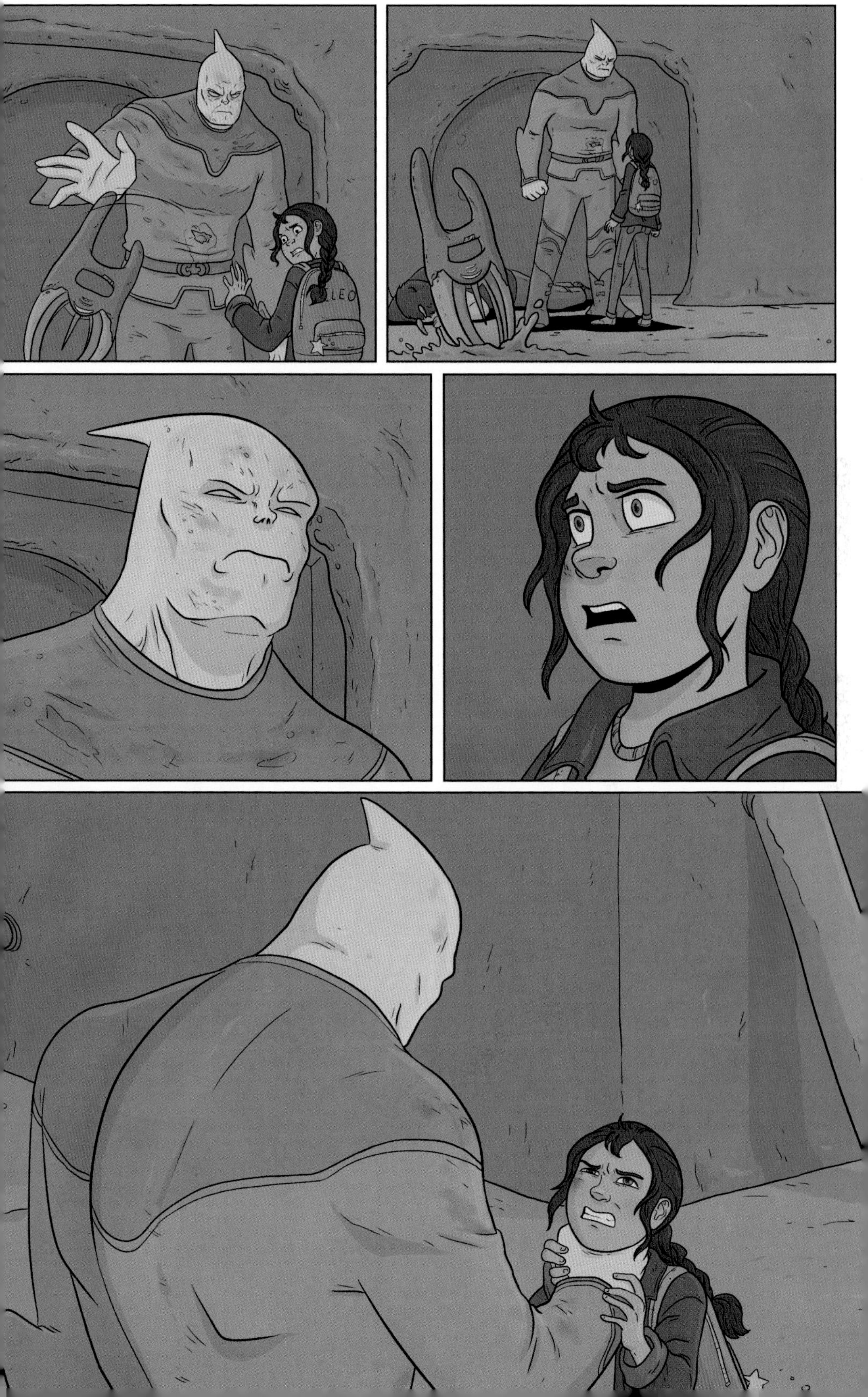

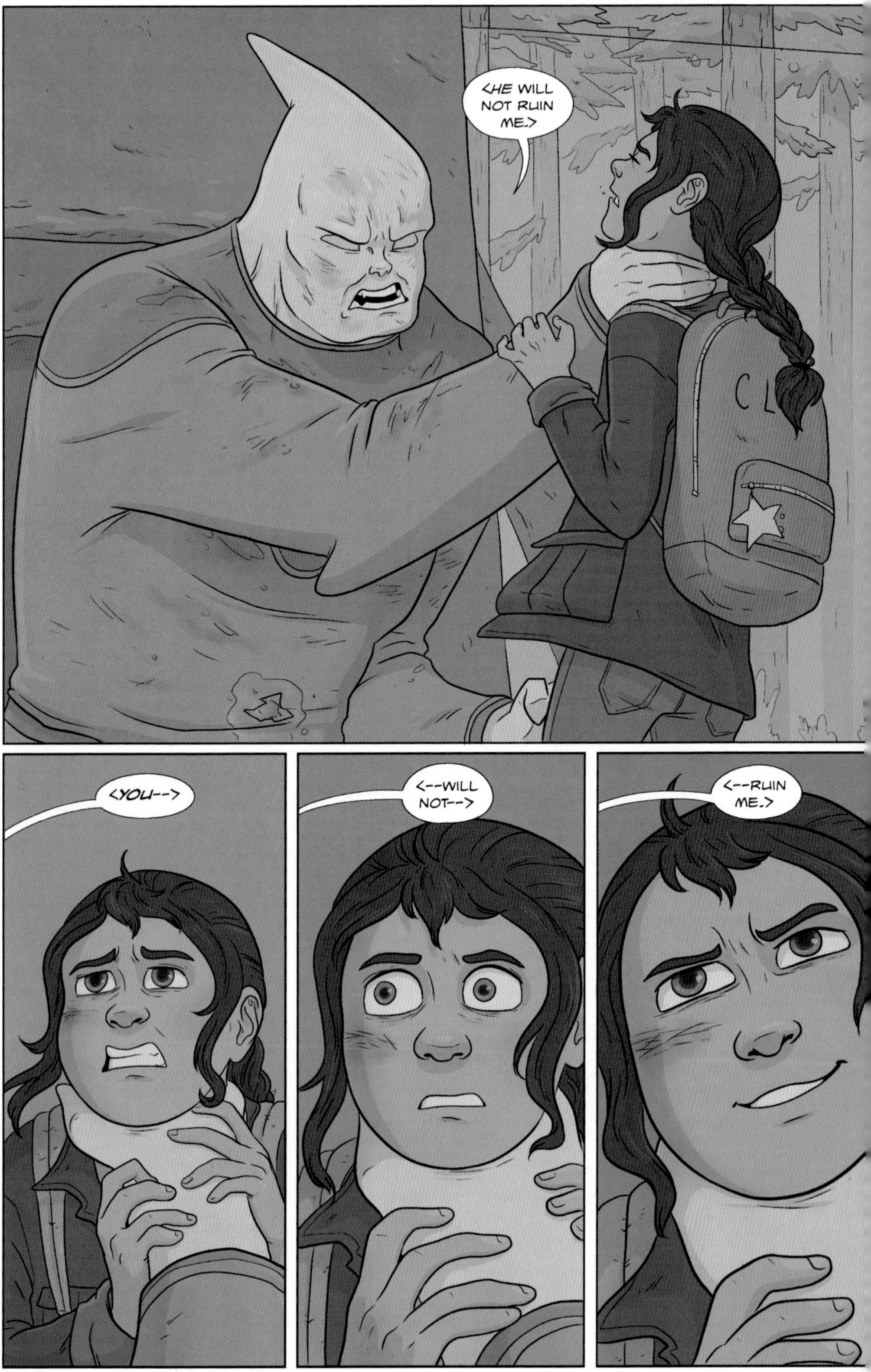

<HE WILL NOT RUIN ME.>
<YOU-->
<--WILL NOT-->
<--RUIN ME.>

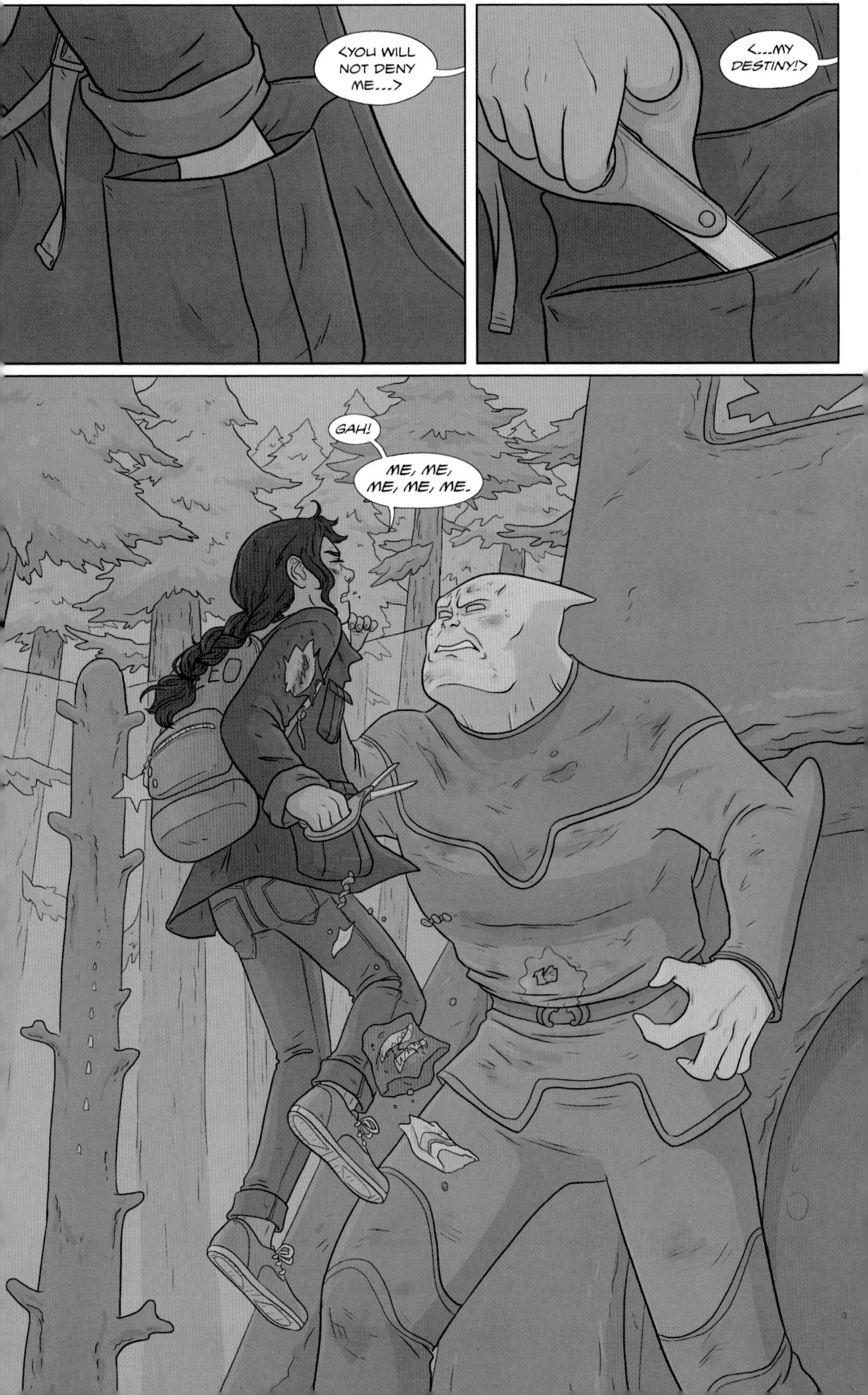
<YOU WILL NOT DENY ME...>
<...MY DESTINY!>
GAH!
ME, ME, ME, ME, ME.

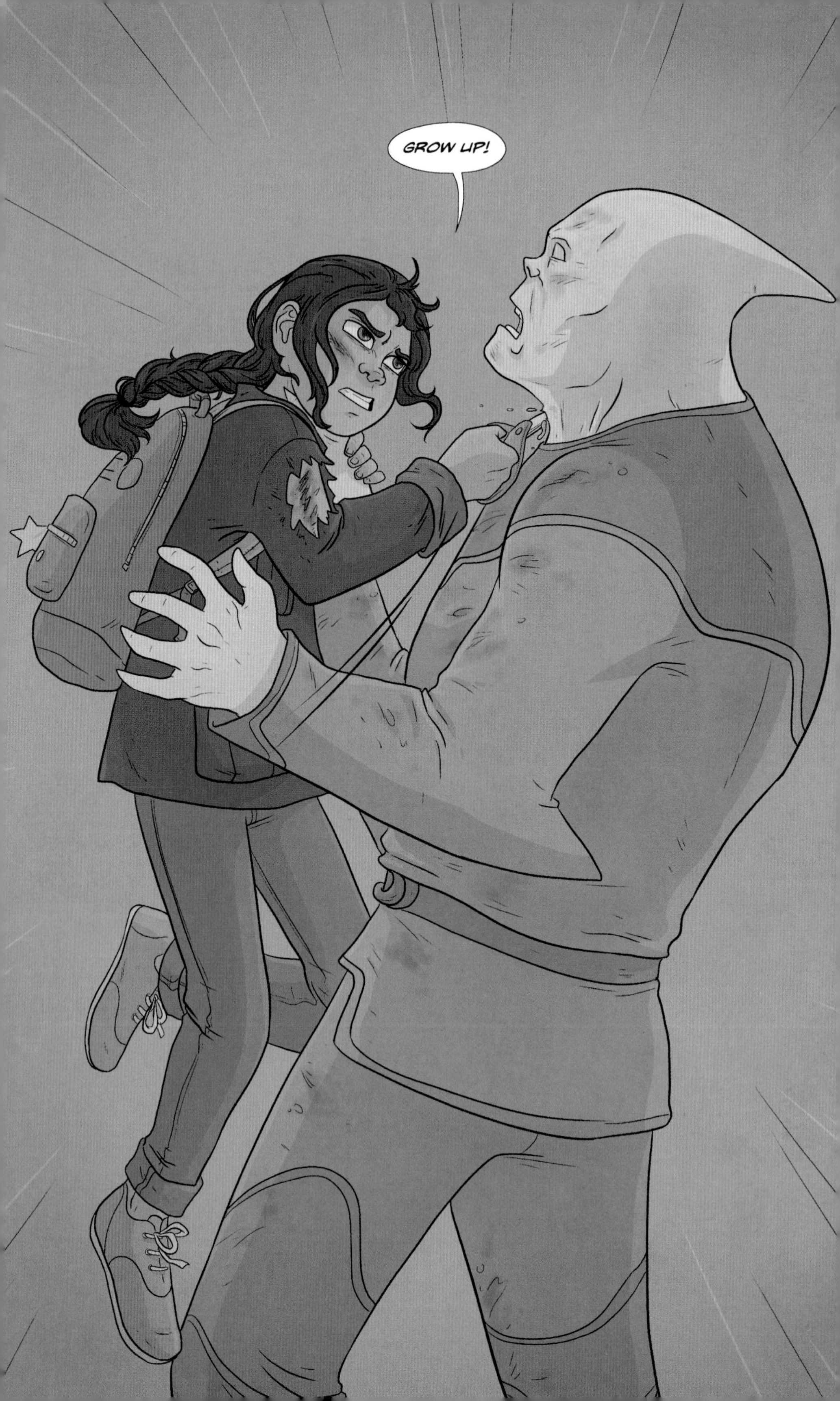
GROW UP!

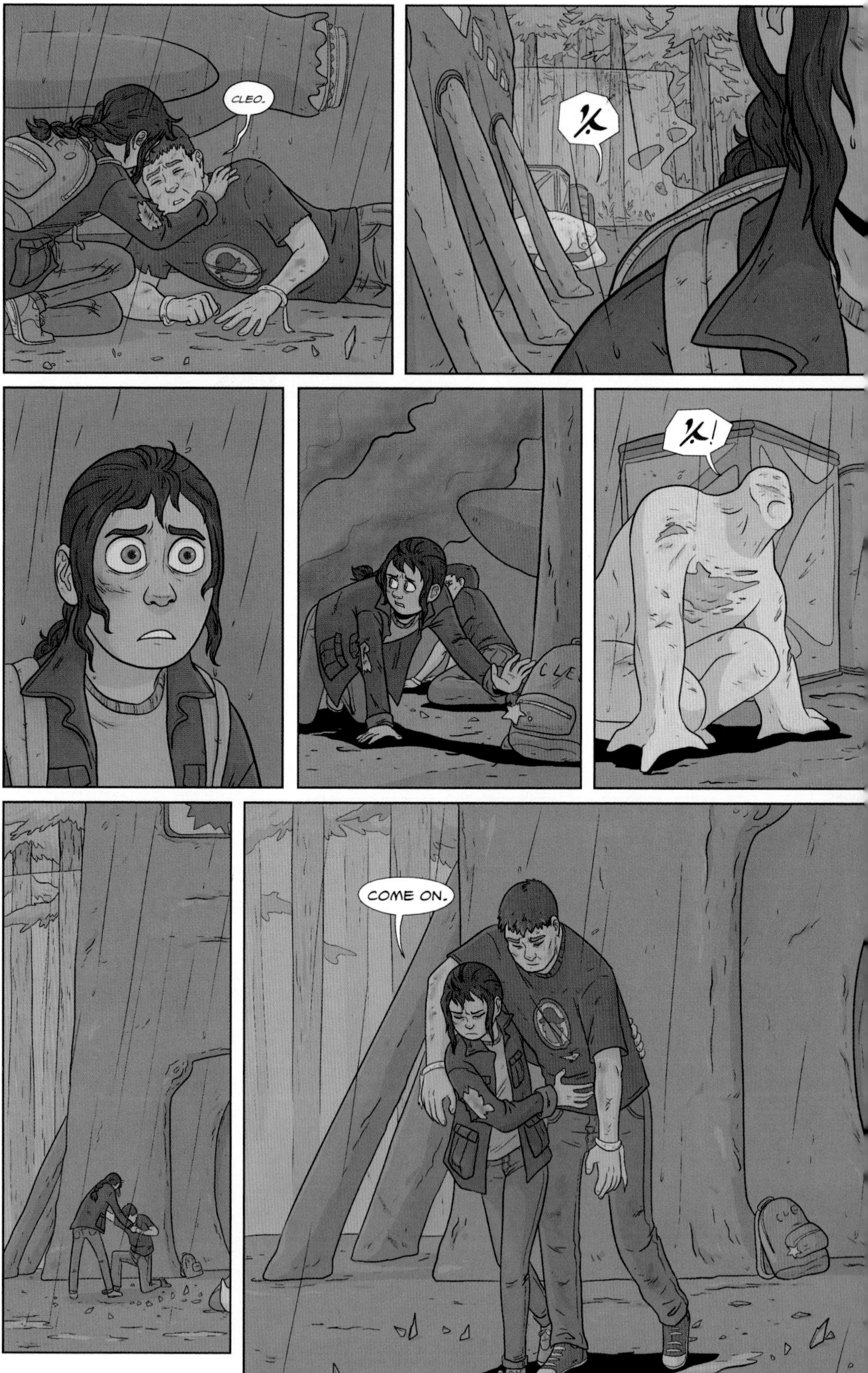
CLEO.
COME ON.

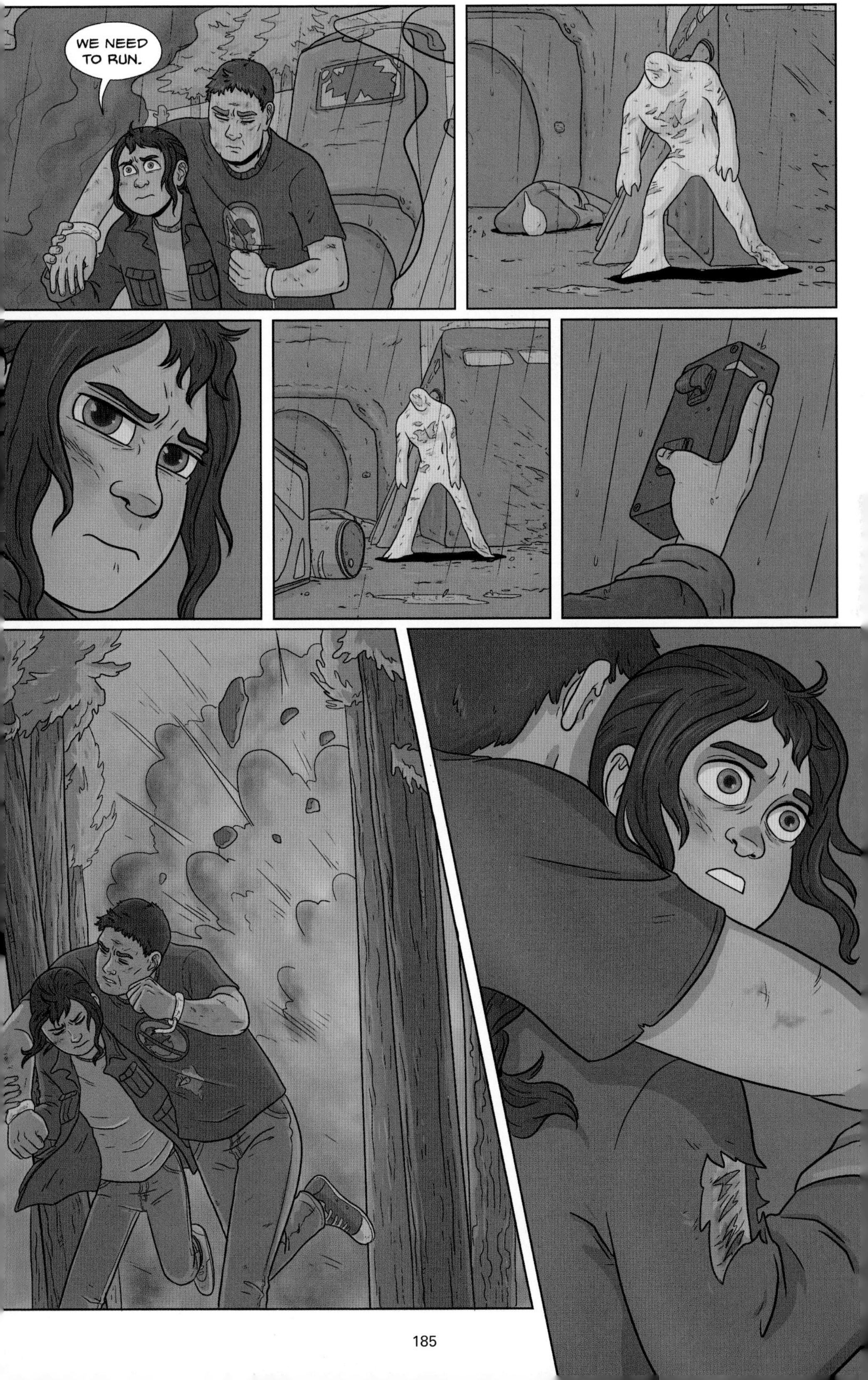
WE NEED TO RUN.

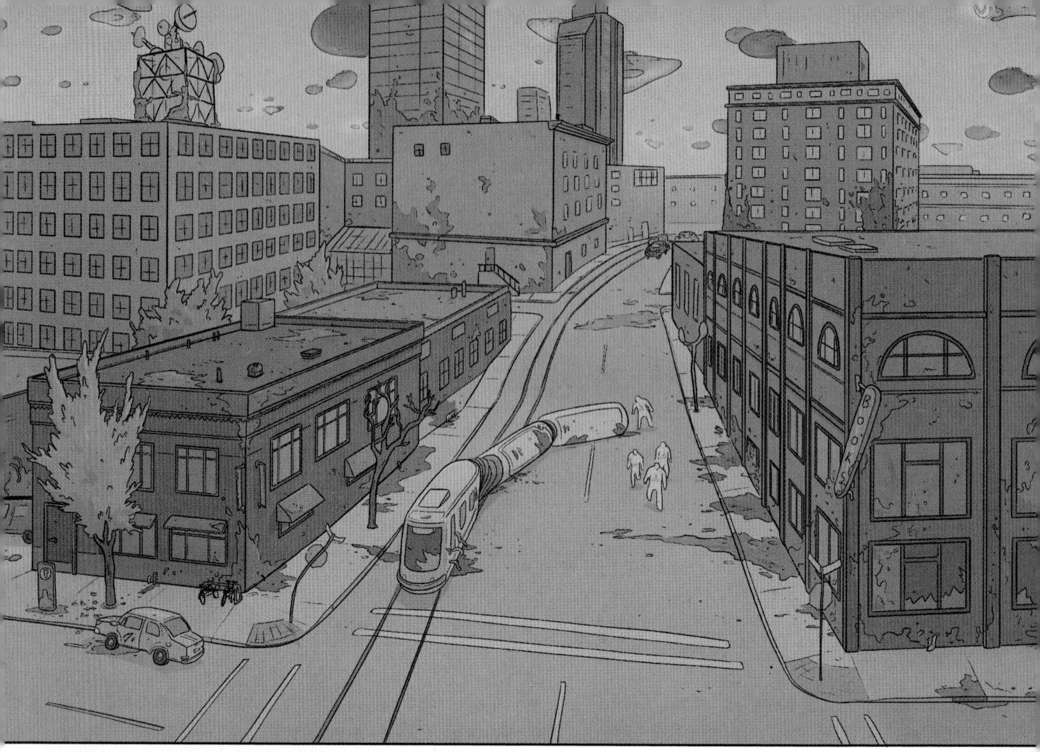
BOOKS

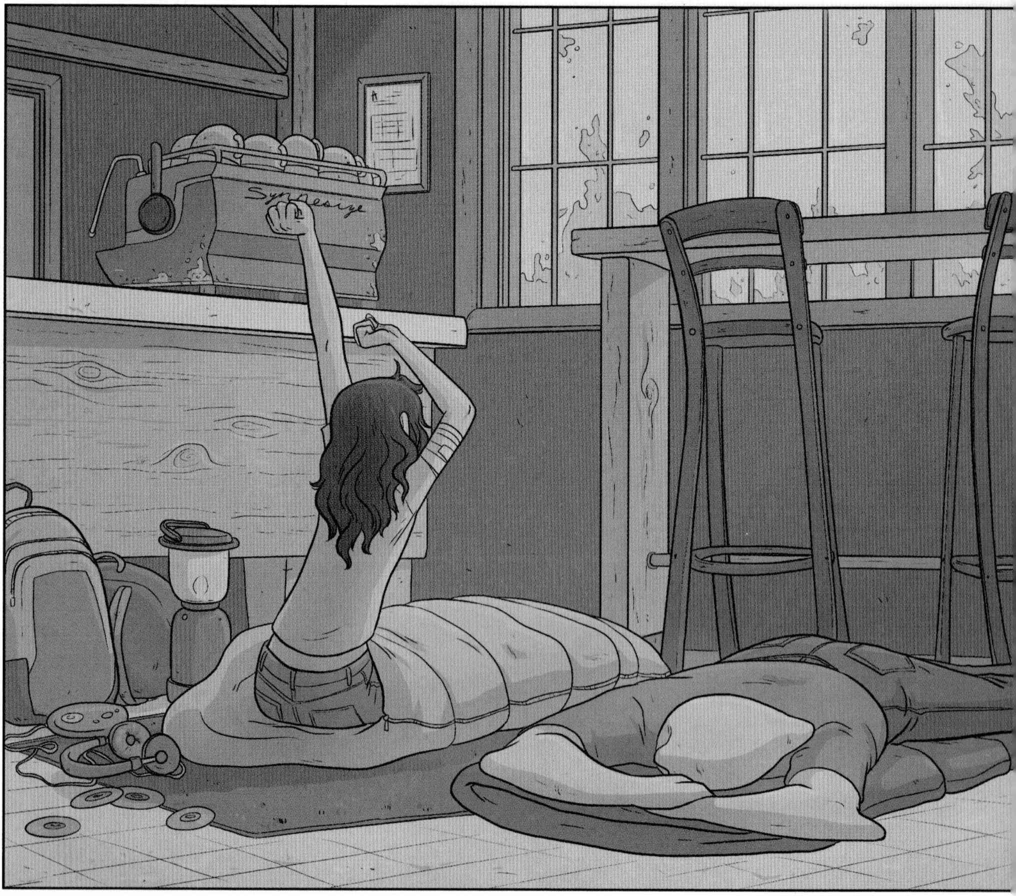

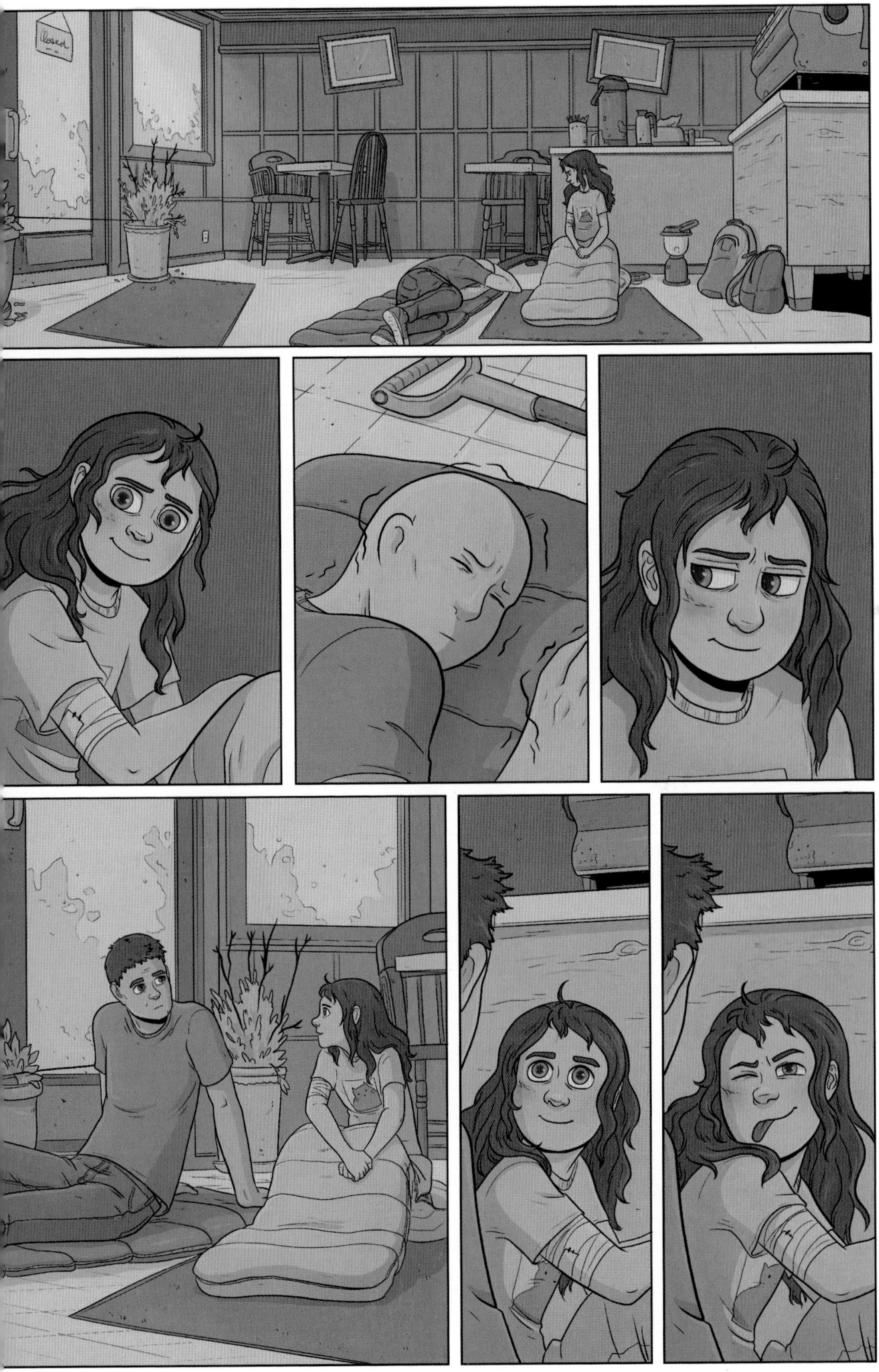
Closed

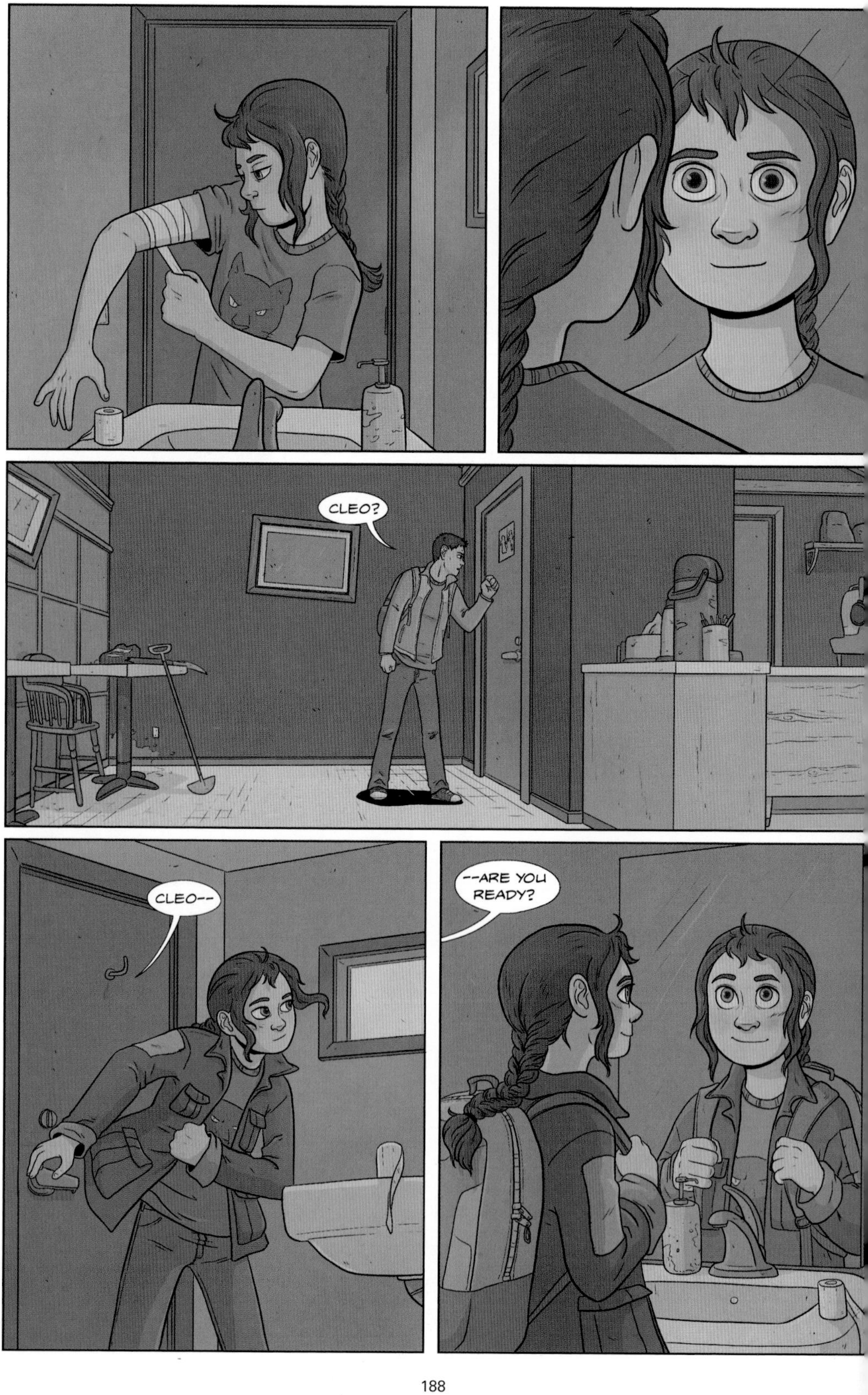
CLEO?
CLEO--
--ARE YOU READY?

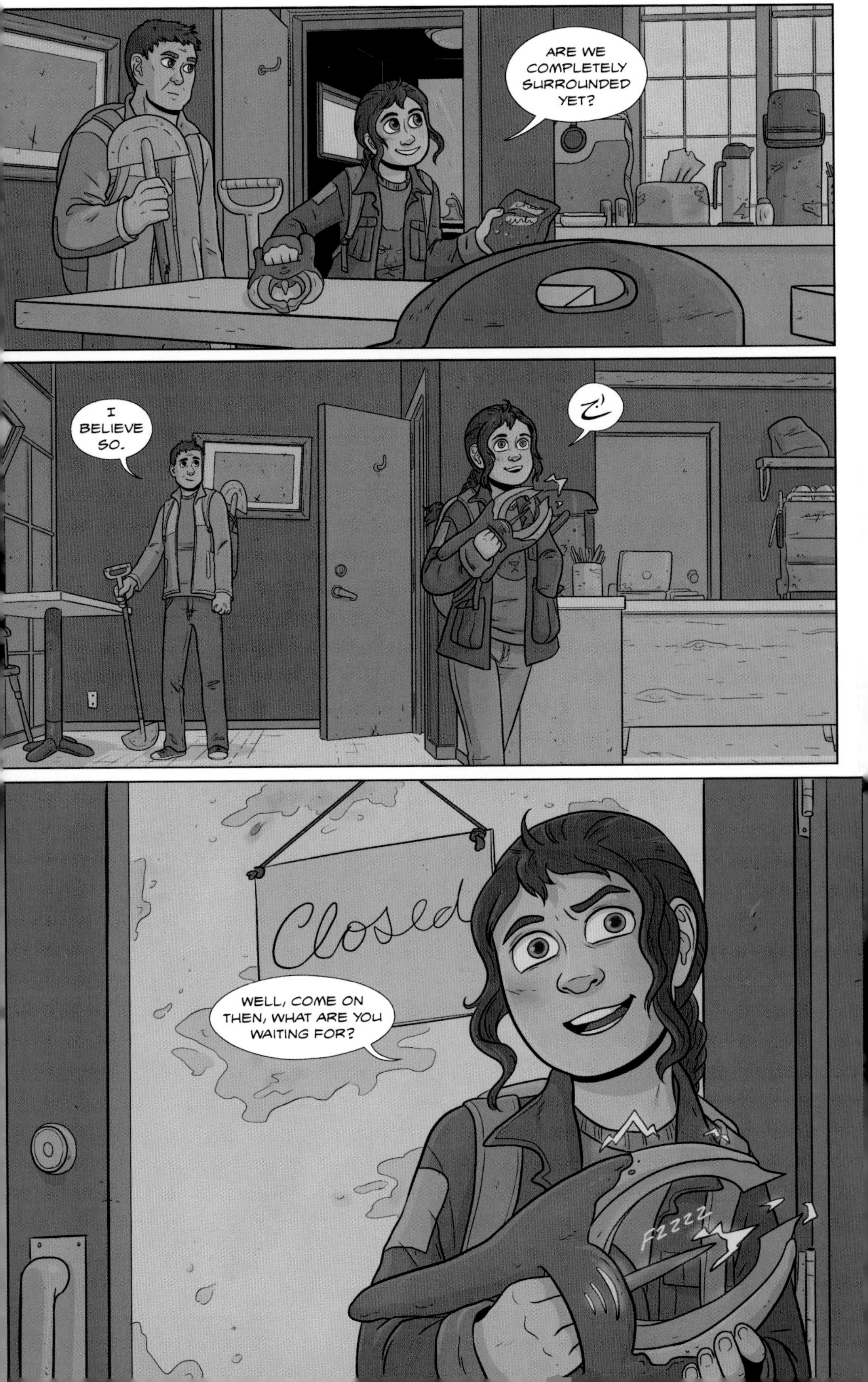
ARE WE COMPLETELY SURROUNDED YET?
I BELIEVE SO.
Closed
WELL, COME ON THEN, WHAT ARE YOU WAITING FOR?
FZZZZ

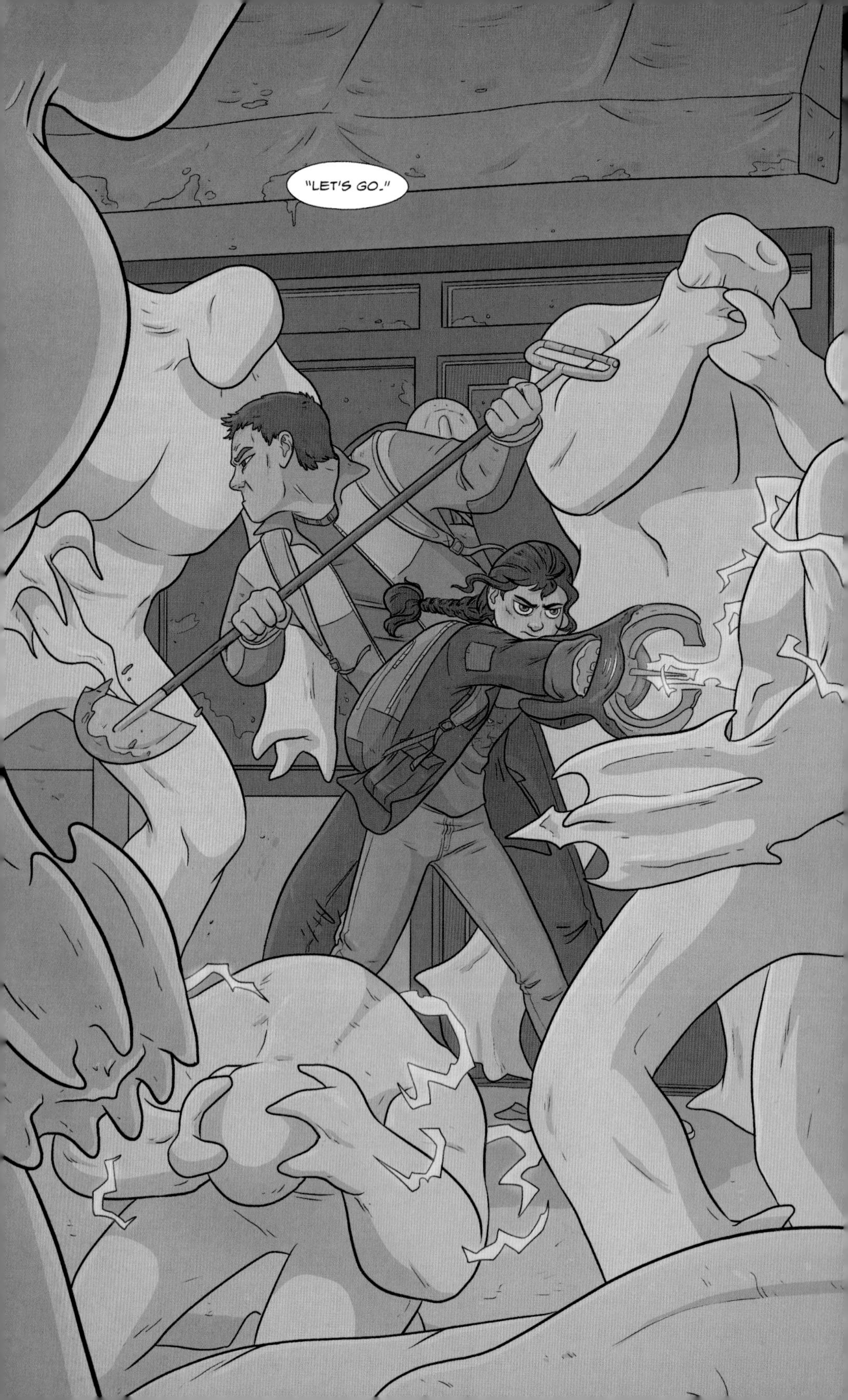
"LET'S GO."

ACKNOWLEDGMENTS

Wow, I can't believe this book is finally in print! Thank you to everyone who has come alongside me in this project. Thank you to all the editors—Dave Marshall, Aaron Walker, and Rachel Roberts—who worked on this book and helped it become the best it could be. Thanks to my friends and family for being my cheerleaders, getting me through the tough parts of the process, and celebrating with me at all the milestones. Thank you, Lisa, for commiserating with me. Thank you, Grace and Laura, for putting up with my crazy comic life. Thank you, Naomi, Joe, Henry, and Lola, for your constant enthusiasm. Thank you, Mom, Dad, Bryan, and Reesa, for just being you. I love you all. And thanks to everyone else who encouraged me in my work. You know who you are.

—CASSIE

Thanks to Dark Horse, especially Dave Marshall, for the opportunity to put our story into the world, and to him, Aaron Walker and Rachel Roberts for helping Cassie and I shape the journeys of Cleo and Alex. To Michael Winston, Merrick Monroe and Michael Ring at Bridge City Comics: your support and counsel has been invaluable and visiting the store each week is a joy and inspiration. Thanks to Mike Russell, provider of sage wisdom in this endeavor and in careers past, and to my beta reader friends, especially Julie Vakoc, Ben Vakoc, Paul DeVe and Kyle Walters Sheaffer, for their time and thoughtful feedback. Thanks to my wife, Rebecca, for her support and for always being ready to discuss and dissect stories, and, of course, to my daughters, Adeline and Eliza, who provide inspiration and enthusiasm whenever mine flags. Finally, a big thanks to Ivan Doroschuk and Men Without Hats for permission to use their logo (which was designed by Ivan). It was a fun to be able to include a prominent nod to one of my favorite bands.

—MATT

ABOUT THE WRITER

Matt Mair Lowery, a Portland native, studied journalism and creative writing at the University of Oregon. He maintains (and sometimes tests) his sanity by nerding out with his two daughters, running through North Portland's industrial landscapes, and overanalyzing everything with his wife.

ABOUT THE ARTIST

Cassie Anderson is a freelance artist and the creator behind the web comic *An Ordinary Princess*. After earning a degree in sequential art (read: comics) from the Savannah College of Art and Design, she moved to Portland, OR, where she currently lives. When she's not drawing comics, she can be found baking tasty treats or exploring the great outdoors.

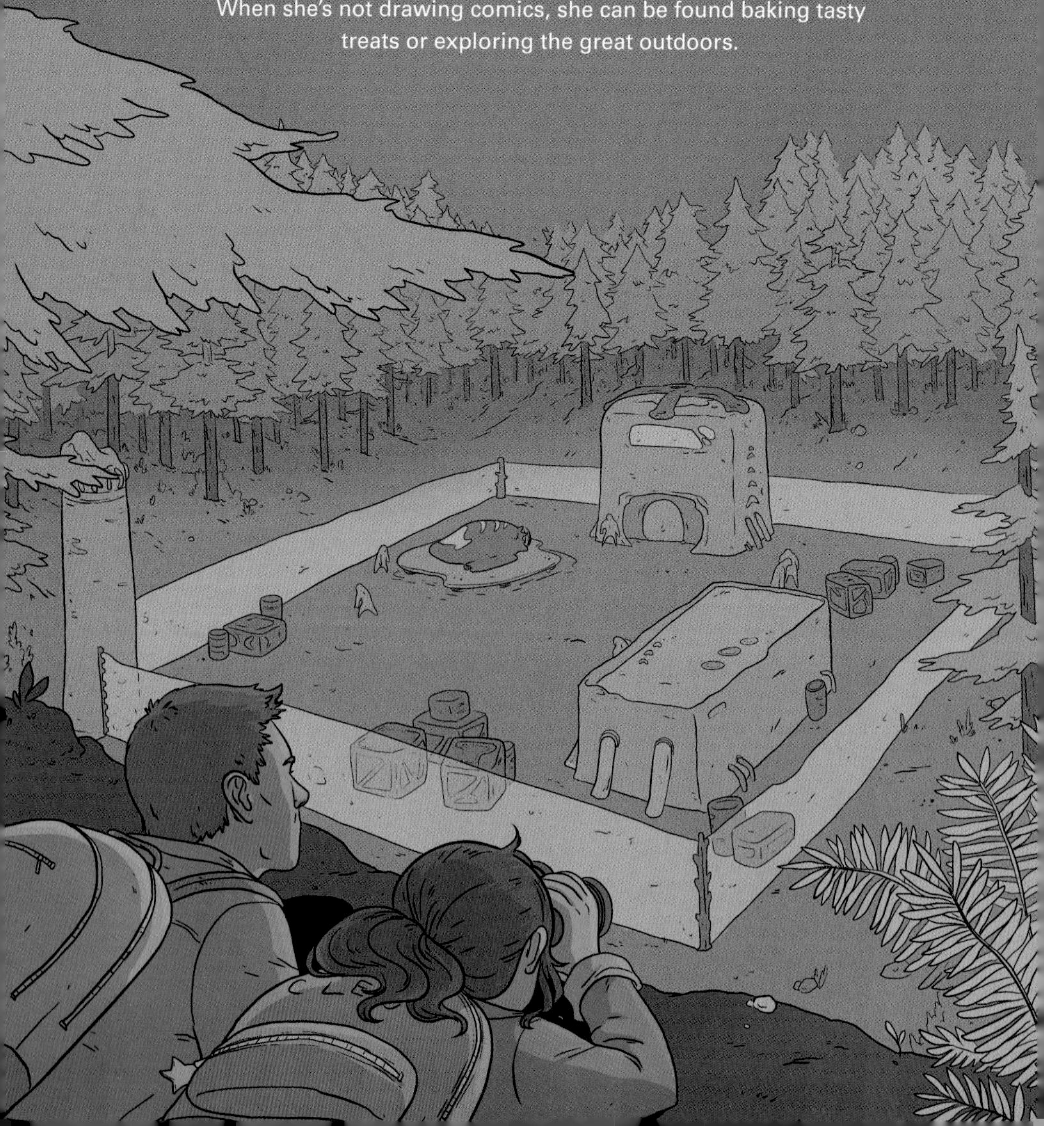